OPERATION POPPY

by
***Capt. Edward M. Brittingham,
USN (Ret.)***

ASW Press
Richmond, Virginia

TABLE OF CONTENTS

INTRODUCTION

THE COLD WAR WAS A MODERN DAY application of the principles laid down by the ancient Chinese philosopher, Sun Tzu, in his book, "The Art of War." Whether it was the silent hunt of submarines deep under the surface of the ocean or the subtle game of spies, it was a war fought in shadow.

Sun Tzu said that all warfare is based on deception. A skilled general must be master of the complementary arts of simulation and dissimulation. While creating shapes to confuse and delude the enemy, he conceals his true dispositions and ultimate intent. When capable, he feigns incapacity; when near, he makes it appear that he is far away; when far away, that he is near. Moving as intangibly as a ghost in the starlight, he is obscure, inaudible. His primary target is the mind of the opposing commander: The victorious situation, a product of his creative imagination. To gain a hundred victories in a hundred battles is not the highest excellence; to subjugate the enemy's army without doing battle is the highest of excellence. Therefore, the best warfare strategy is to attack the enemy's plans, next is to attack alliances, next is to attack the enemy; one who is skilled in warfare subdues the enemy without ever doing battle.

Foreknowledge is required for this extraordinary success. It cannot be elicited from ghosts and spirits, it cannot be inferred from comparison of previous events, or from the calculations of the heavens, but must be obtained from people who have knowledge of the enemy's situation.

It requires spies.

The primary purpose of a spy is to gather information from the enemy. Over the years, the Soviet Union created a new type of spy, one that also had a combat role. This transformation began back in World War II with the use of partisans. It eventually culminated in the Special Operations Forces.

A formal bond was established between partisans and the Soviet intelligence-gathering mechanism during World War II. Partisans were indigenous to the local environment and were particularly effective. They knew the customs, surface features of the land and local culture. A formal bond was established between the two and, in 1943, the Soviet Intelligence developed a successful method of operations to integrate partisans into combat operations.

The partisan functions were doled out as follows: 1) gather intelligence; 2) collect political intelligence for the Soviet agencies; 3) maintain security of the partisan group. The Soviet Union provided special schools in the USSR to train the partisan leadership. The graduates would return to their hometowns to recruit new members into their small cell.

The partisans were trained to gather intelligence, and some even provided misinformation to the German occupying troops by becoming double agents. They were trained to spread lies. At critical stages, the partisans were even tasked with sabotage missions.

The Manchurian Operation in August 1945 showed the effectiveness of Special Operations Forces. The operation plan called for 20 airborne assaults using groups of 35 to 40 men for the Soviet attack against the Japanese. The groups were dropped close to Central Manchuria where they infiltrated into the local population. When the offensive began, the Special Operations Forces attacked key infrastructure and critical facilities. The teams were small, but their damage threw the Japanese into a panic. The destruction was strategically minimal, yet it occurred deep behind the enemy lines. This exaggerated the effectiveness of the attacks by increasing confusion across the depth of the battlefield.

The partisans and early Special Operations Forces were the forerunners of the Special Operations Forces like the Soviet Navy's reydoviki—meaning "raid"—that became known to military forces around the world as Spetznaz, an acronym from the Russian spetsialnoe naznachenie, meaning special purpose.

The Spetznaz troops took a brisk part in the devastation of Prague, Czechoslovakia. In May 1968, a group attached to the 103rd Guards Airborne Division seized Prague Airport after they deceived the airport control tower. They claimed to have engine trouble and received permission to land. When the plane touched down, the Spetz group jumped out and seized control of the airport.

Other groups seized checkpoints within Prague, holding them until the rest of the division landed at the airport and moved to secure the city. The confusion and shock was overwhelming; the Czech military and government couldn't react quickly enough to offer more than a modest defense. The victory went to the Soviets.

The Soviets again used Spetznaz units in 1979. The special units surrounded President Hafizullah Amin's palace in Kabul, Afghanistan. Using weapons with silencers, they systematically moved through the palace, assassinating the president and almost everyone inside. They then seized the airport, allowing Soviet airborne troops to land safely. As a nation, Afghanistan fell after the Soviets seized the capital of Kabul. The only losses that Soviet troops faced were against the Mujahadeen—Afghan freedom fighters—who fought to regain Afghani independence. The war in Afghanistan quickly descended into a guerilla war, where over the next 10 years even the Spetznaz units weren't immune to the Mujahadeen's hit-and-run ambush tactics.

Spetznaz were trained to be soldiers, assassins and spies. Some served in uniform, others gathered intelligence while wearing corporate attire or participating in the Olympic Games. Still others were sleeper agents hidden under deep cover across the world.

During the height of the Cold War, these specialized killers were kept on a tight leash. Then the Soviet Union began to disintegrate in early 1990. Opposing factions within the Communist party, KGB and military vied for power over what they thought would remain of the once-great superpower. The leashes on the Spetznaz units exchanged hands numerous times. The most publicized story was the KGB and Spetznaz attempted coup attempt when they seized Mikhail Gorbachev in August, 1991.

This is the little-known story of an event that took place at the time the Union of Soviet Socialist Republics disintegrated. It was a time when chaos ruled. The Spetz were the Soviet's most dangerous dogs of war, and the leash of one group fell to a pair of Soviet admirals. Both men knew that their nation was falling apart, and both had their own reasons for their actions. They set into motion a plan with only one goal.

Revenge.

A STORM BREWING

0800 hours Local, 13 November 1990,
Outside Moscow, Russia (USSR)

DEEP DOWN INSIDE OF THE SOVIET NAVY there lived an ultra top-secret organization. Similar to the American's legendary "Skunk Works," this organization was responsible for developing cutting-edge technology for a favored combat arm. The Americans were an air power, and their research organization developed the next generation of combat aircraft. The Union of Soviet Socialist Republics had traditionally been a sea power, and so this secret organization focused on developing the next generation of naval vessels…specifically, ballistic missile and attack submarines.

This was a world that shunned outsiders. Only loyal party members of sensitive thought, marked by a dialect of discretion, were allowed into the hallowed laboratories and research sites. Analyst, chemist, physicist and above all, genius worked behind closed doors. They congregated in various labs, talking in low voices as they made incessant tests. Even the atmosphere reeked of excessive security.

It was odd, then—almost offensive to some of the scientists—to see a stranger standing beside the podium of the briefing room. The man's clothing marked him as an outsider. His white dishdasha, the full-length dress-like traditional attire of an Arab, was out of place in a room full of pants and white lab coats.

Asadollah Shazi was uncomfortable under the open stares from his audience. The geologist/physics professor was Iranian. Born in Tehran during the reign of the Shah, he had been a child prodigy who raced through the educational system by the age of 14. America's Massachusetts Institute of Technology accepted him, and his pro-Western dream of becoming a renowned physicist seemed attainable. Then, in November 1979, his 15-year-old world changed. Islamic radicals seized the American Embassy in Tehran, and he became the focus of his MIT classmate's wrath. He was allowed to stay in the

10

States to finish his doctorate in chemistry and physics, and then the American government denied his request for political asylum in 1986.

Shazi returned to Tehran, where he suffered under a different kind of animosity. His time in America made him an outcast among the Islamic fundamentalist faithful. The government, distrusting his pro-Western background, assigned him to the submarine division of the Navy. It was a sign of ridicule, as Iran had no submarines.

That changed in 1990. The government watched the buildup of forces in the Arabian Gulf as the U.S. prepared to remove Iraqi occupation forces from Kuwait. American submarines patrolled silently in Iranian waters, and American aircraft flew arrogantly through Iranian airspace. The government in Tehran feared they would be the next target after the Americans destroyed Baghdad. Suddenly there was an interest in increasing Iran's naval power, and the government decided to purchase three Kilo-class attack submarines from the Soviet Union. The submarine division was no longer a place of exile.

The Arabian Gulf is shallow compared to the world's oceans, averaging 50 meters in depth. Hiding a submarine, even a diesel boat like the Kilo-class, would be difficult in shallow waters. Every submarine gives off noise, and the Americans were very skilled at using sonar to detect subs. At first the purchase seemed foolish to the Soviets.

That's when Asadollah Shazi stepped into the spotlight. His theory was revolutionary, and it captured the attention of the Soviet admiral in charge of the secret submarine research division. Vice Admiral Steustal gave the task of bringing the Iranian scientist to Moscow to a person he had no reason to trust, but who was the perfect man to fulfill the assignment.

Rear Admiral Klos Sloreigh didn't know what had blown his cover, but he wasn't surprised that his superior knew of his secondary assignment. After a few delicate inquiries through his other superior at the Komitet Gosudarstvennoi Bezopasnosti—known throughout the world as the KGB—the admiral managed to obtain the Iranian governing Islamic Revolutionary Council's permission to bring Asadollah Shazi to Moscow.

Admiral Sloreigh was a thin man, almost anorexic. His chalky pallor matched the Iranian's clothing, making his long nose and hard cheekbones cadaver-like under the harsh fluorescent lights. The ribbons for valor on his chest were poor recompense for too many years working near experimental nuclear reactors. Cancer slowly ate away at him. Only harsh chemicals flowing in his bloodstream kept the cancer from running rampant. The life-saving drugs carried a price of their own, though. His once-thick brown hair was now a wispy white.

He glanced around the room. His gaze passed over Vice Admiral Lawrence Latvia and he clamped down his emotions. The last thing he needed was to show hatred for the man and his renegade brother, Rear Admiral Alexei Latvia, sitting beside him. They were the last of their kind, "Heroes of the Great War," and he would be glad for the opportunity to finally dispose of them.

Klos hated everything they stood for; especially the respect they held for Americans. The two admirals weren't afraid to discuss openly how the United States had thrown the logistical lifeline that kept Mother Russia from falling to the Nazis in the Great War. They also placed family above party. If it wasn't for their remarkable abilities and unwavering loyalty to their country, Klos was certain the two admirals would have been purged long ago. They were relics, but that didn't make disposing of the two elderly officers any easier. Like all roaches, they were extremely difficult to kill. Klos was looking forward to his next opportunity.

Part of the problem sat beside the rear admiral. Vice Admiral Steustal, for some unfathomable reason, had placed the two admirals under his protection. The man was a formidable opponent with many comrades in high positions of power within the party. Klos knew the man's reputation. Few men who opposed him had survived. It made the situation a challenge.

Vice Admiral Steustal rose from his chair and glanced around the small auditorium. He nodded to the armed guards, waiting until they had stepped from the room and closed the soundproof doors behind them before speaking. "Comrades, let us begin. Two months ago, I gave the department heads a synopsis of a revolutionary theory in submarine design. Your responses were that this was an impossible feat, and you demanded to speak with the Soviet scientist who developed the theory. I give you the scientist, although he is not a Soviet. Gentlemen, give your attention to Doctor Asadollah Shazi of the Iranian Submarine Division."

The burly gray-haired admiral settled into his chair and adjusted his heavy uniform tunic. Then he nodded to the Iranian standing beside the podium. "You may begin, Comrade Shazi."

"Thank you, Vice Admiral Steustal." Shazi cleared his throat, uncomfortable under the numerous glares focused on him. "Please forgive my Russian. I speak it poorly, please interrupt if I am unclear."

Shazi motioned for the lights, then faced the projection screen at the front of the auditorium. "My country buys three Kilo submarines from you soon, but we have a problem. The Arabian Gulf is too shallow, and even the Kilo radiates too much noise there. Keeping the submarine as quiet as it can is something we had to wonder about."

The slide changed to an American Los Angeles class attack submarine. "United States submarines have the edge in open ocean, but even they have the same problem. Nuclear and diesel submarines have noisy engines when running at 12 knots. In theory, the nuclear power device is technically correct, but there is no way to tone it down. Numerous iron minerals have been tried to promote elimination of sounds, however a new light has been shed on the chemical element scale. The number one subject is how can we find a chemical element, a mineral or a substance that will calm down the amount of radiated noise of the submarine as it makes its way across the high seas.

"The answer is magnetite." Shazi waited for the slide to change, then pointed toward the map shown on the screen. "Magnetite is a strong ore mineral that is located in these areas in the world. It is used as iron ore, but magnetite offers a blend of iron ore and that of an oxide. Magnetite, the mineral, is a member of the spinel structure group with composition of iron in both valences converting with oxygen. Within this substance it possesses the spinel construction which the ferric iron is tetrahedrally half of this mineral and the remaining half as well as all ferrous iron are octahedrally organized by the cubic closely-packed oxygen molecules. Iron-black and streak black, the hardness is six Mohs scale and the habit is octahedral. Granular to massive and sometimes of enormous structure, it possesses no cleavage but has octahedral parting."

The next slide wasn't one that Shazi had placed in the presentation. It showed the ore in its natural form and several graphs. Shazi squinted at the information, taking several moments to determine its relevance before continuing.

"Magnetite is a natural ferrimagnet which becomes para-magnetic when heated above 578 degrees Celcius. The substance can be further heated in a reducing atmosphere whereby the oxidation of the magnetite gradually inverts to hematite. Major magnetic ore of iron, including magnetite, often occurs in sufficient quantities around the world. Magnetite segregation in basic rocks as in gravity settling is a principal source of iron. It may be a contact metamorphic product coming with limestones and lepidolite. Detrital sands tell another story of this mineral that is moderately resistant.

"When discussing magnetism the iron-like magnetite has two poles. A magnetic field can be shown as imaginary lines that flow out of the North and into the South Pole of the magnetic. The magnetic within the substance magnetite is the strongest near the magnet's poles where lines lie closest to each other."

The Iranian's voice gradually changed during his speech. He turned to face his audience, forgetting for the moment that they were brilliant scientists and naval officers of a major superpower. His voice became the confident speech of a professor lecturing students.

"Magnetism and electricity are closely related. Electromagnetism, one of the basic forces in the universe, reacts to a moving magnet near a coil of copper wire. Thusly, it can induce electrical current in the wire that creates a magnetic field about the wire. The right-hand rule is the given rule. If the thumb of the right hand points along the flow of current, the fingers curl around the wire depicting the direction of the magnetic field. A coil or solenoid is another right-hand rule, in that it shows that the right also shows the direction of the magnetic field lines.

"Finally, the magnetism of atoms plays a vital part in this discussion. Atoms have a small dense center that is called a nucleus surrounded by a body of negatively charged electrons. Nuclei include protons that have a positive charge and neutrons that have no charge. The relationship to magnetism and electricity equals the negatively charged electrons that make an electric field, in other words, a magnetic field. In addition to circling the nucleus, an electron spins on its axis like a top. The orbiting motion of paired electrons changes slightly when an atom is placed in a magnetic field. When such an occurrence is felt, it is diamagnetism or opposite magnetism. In iron, the pins of some electrons are not paired. As a result, each atom has a magnetic field and acts as a tiny magnet. Such atoms are called an atomic dipole. These materials have particular properties because the arrangement of atomic dipoles creates their ferromagnetic ordering. Magnetite is a case whereby the dipoles align in the same direction as neighboring dipoles."

Shazi paused to wait for questions. Some members of his audience, including two elderly admirals, were nodding as if they understood. He cleared his throat, and then continued. "The primary system for the generation of electrical power through the interaction of flowing fluid is defined as a magnetohydrodymanic or MHD power generator. Solid conductors are replaced by electrically conducting gases or plasmas that are established from associated relationships of plasma physics. The MHD generator works with five segments, which gives a boost to the flow entering the Faraway induction. The cathode and the anode consolidation—power electronics—provide a thermal energy to a working fluid. The incorporation of magnetic field direction, the power is translated into quantum production."

A thin man interrupted. "Excuse me, Doctor Shazi."

"Yes, Admiral...?"

"Sloreigh. Klos Sloreigh." The admiral pointed to the new slide displayed on the projection screen. "I'm beginning to feel like my time is being wasted. What you have discussed so far is known to most of us here. A MHD power generator is something that several sections have been working on for the past five years. It would increase the time our diesel submarines can remain underwater without snorkeling or surfacing to recharge their batteries. There is another system under development as well, a propeller-less caterpillar drive using MHD propulsion. If you would, please explain your conclusion about what makes your MHD power generator different."

"Bit harsh, even for you, Klos," spoke a voice from across the room. Shazi turned to face the new speaker, an elderly admiral.

The man beside the admiral grinned and said, "At least he didn't call him a fraud."

"That's enough, gentlemen," barked Admiral Steustal. His voice left no doubt who controlled the room. "Continue, doctor."

"Yes, thank you, admiral." Shazi blinked in surprise at the sudden tension that filled the room. "Yes, I continue. The difference is that I propose a hybrid system. Please, five slides forward, please."

The Iranian physicist waited until the new slide appeared. "We know that moving water creates electricity, yes? That is hydrodynamic power generation. We also know that submarines are very noisy because they require moving metal parts. A diesel submarine spends its time underwater using battery power to move its propeller, and a nuclear submarine uses steam. We know this, yes?"

Shazi stepped toward the projection screen and tapped his finger against the diagram. "The efficiency is very low. For the diesel engine, it is at most 40 percent in converting mechanical to electrical energy. More loss of energy happens with storing the electrical energy in batteries. We have an average of 30 percent or less. That means more time on surface running the diesel engines to recharge the batteries. Even when snorkeling—using a snorkel to vent the combustion gases— just below the surface, the submarine is vulnerable to detection. The engines are noisy and can be heard by sonar very far away. The propeller blades create low-pressure bubbles in the water that collapse quickly. This is called cavitation. Sound travels well through water, and the propeller cavitation can be heard far away using sonar. That is unacceptable in shallow waters like the Arabian Gulf. Americans would quickly find and destroy the submarine."

The doctor motioned for lights, then retracted the projection screen to use the blackboard behind it. With sure fingers holding the chalk, he quickly sketched several diagrams and equations on the blackboard.

"The admiral is correct, I offer nothing new about the MHD theory. I talk application here, not theory. Sound travels in relatively straight lines from the source in water. We must disguise the sound of the propellers. That is problem one.

"Problem two, we must decrease the time a submarine must spend on the surface recharging its batteries—or for nuclear submarines, the time that noisy steam generators must operate. Call this problem Two A and Two B.

"Look now at this diagram. It shows a modification to the Kilo submarines we buy from Soviet Union. On starboard and port sides of submarine, we attach two scoops the length of the vessel. Each is a large tube, like a venturi with a large opening and small exit. Water moves through as the submarine is pushed by the propeller, and it comes out here to provide a directed stream. Since the exit is a narrow line parallel with the propeller shaft, the cavitation of the venturi itself creates a different noise...and it also redirects and disguises the sound of the propeller. In essence, the water will disguise 30 to 40 percent of the propeller's cavitation noises. That is just one benefit.

"Charged particles experience a sideways force when they pass through a magnetic field, causing voltage to develop. Water contains many ions, or charged particles. The scoops are made of highly refined magnetite and coils. When water passes through them, it creates electricity. That is free energy to recharge diesel submarine batteries while it is still underwater. It also works when sub is snorkeling or on the surface to recharge its batteries using diesel power."

Shazi had been wildly adding equations to the chalkboard. He stopped, dropped the chalk into its tray and turned to face his audience. "The final part is the MHD power generator itself. The exhaust of the diesel turbine itself creates charged particles. We simply pass that exhaust through a MHD and generate more power. The final result of this combination of systems allows the diesel submarine to generate more power in a shorter period of time. If my calculations are correct, it will take two minutes using a hybrid MHD system for every 15 minutes of the current diesel-recharging rate. Also, the MHD venturi will add another 12 hours duration for submerged operations using batteries. That is my theory, gentlemen. What are your questions?"

The skeletal admiral spoke first, his voice containing barely concealed sarcasm. "What benefit does it have for nuclear submarines?"

The Iranian doctor decided that he truly didn't like the man. He replied coldly, "That is your problem to answer, admiral. The Kilo class submarine is not nuclear, so does not concern me or my country. Next question?"

"If I may use the blackboard for a moment, doctor?" asked one of the pair of elderly admirals across the room. "It would be easier to show my question and calculations, to see if you agree with my conclusion."

"Of course, Admiral…"

"Latvia, doctor. Lawrence Latvia." The vice admiral stepped to the chalkboard and spent several minutes writing equations on the board. He paused for a moment and looked the Iranian physicist in the eye. "Am I correct with your theory so far, Doctor Shazi?"

A chill had crept up Asadollah's spine as he watched the admiral. The calculations were flawless, and they revealed an understanding of physics principles that few in the world could match. He steeled himself for the inevitable, then nodded. "Yes, Admiral Latvia, you are correct."

"Then the next calculations would appear like this, I presume." Lawrence erased the previous equations and added a new set. When he finished, he turned and nodded to the doctor. "If you wouldn't mind taking a few moments to confirm them, doctor?"

"Of course." Shazi didn't understand what had happened. He inhaled deeply, then stepped toward the blackboard and closely examined the equations. They were brilliant.

They were also as mistaken as his had been.

"Are they correct, doctor?

Shazi nodded slowly. "Yes, admiral. You have touched on something that I hadn't even considered."

"I know." Lawrence Latvia turned toward the other scientists sitting in the auditorium, confident that none there would be able to reach anything else but his conclusion. He waited for the first few nods of understanding, and then spelled it out for the rest.

"I agree with Doctor Shazi's theory, Admiral Steustal. There is only one problem." Lawrence pointed toward the final equation. "The tolerances for the MHD power generator and venturi hybrid system are very rigid. Magnetite is readily available, but in its common form it will not suffice for our requirements."

Admiral Steustal leaned back in his chair, frowning as he laced his fingers together. "You are telling me that it will not work."

"No, admiral, I'm not saying that." Lawrence dusted the chalk off his hands, then faced his superior. "The critical element to make the MHD generator work is magnetite. The problem is that we need a specific type of magnetite. It is extremely rare, and there is only one place in the world where it can be found."

"Don't tell me," interrupted Admiral Sloreigh. "America, right?"

"No, Comrade Admiral Klos, but close. Projectionist, place the world map slide on the screen." Lawrence pulled the screen down, and then pointed to the location on the slide. "The magnetite we need can only be found in Canada. Specifically, near the U.S. Navy base at Argentia, Newfoundland."

Admiral Steustal nodded slowly, thinking. He seemed to be weighing options. Then his head snapped up and focused on Lawrence Latvia. "You have a plan, then."

"No, Comrade admiral. I simply state the requirement." Lawrence shifted his gaze and challenged Klos Sloreigh with his eyes. "This is beyond the capability of the Navy. It requires the hand of the KGB."

The senior officer faced the KGB spy beside him. With his next words, he announced to everyone in the room the double hats that

Sloreigh wore. "Admiral Sloreigh, you will coordinate it. Develop a plan and present it to me in three days."

Klos looked at his superior, stunned. "Admiral, I…"

"That is not a request, Rear Admiral Sloreigh." Steustal stood, signaling that the briefing was over. "Three days. Coordinate with Doctor Shazi and Vice Admiral Latvia on their requirements. Then brief me on how the KGB will assist the Navy in obtaining the magnetite we require."

"Yes, admiral." Klos rose and stood at attention. "It will be done."

"Dismissed, admiral." Steustal turned his back on the rear admiral and motioned toward the other senior admiral in the room. "Lawrence, once again you have aided Mother Russia with your brilliance. Come, let us talk in my office."

Doctor Asadollah Shazi waited in silence as the room emptied around him. An armed guard stepped forward to escort him from the facility. He didn't argue as the junior officer blindfolded him. It would be several hours before the blindfold would be removed, and then he would find himself back at his Moscow hotel room.

The dark trip gave him time to think. He didn't understand what the admiral—what was his name, Latvia?—was doing. The Iranian physicist's calculations had been sufficient to get him this far, yet the Soviet admiral had seen through his mathematical deception. Then the elderly officer took it one step further, proving scientifically that there was only one place in world where such a substance could be found.

It was all a lie. Magnetite would not provide the power-generating benefits that either of them had ascribed to it. Shazi knew his reasons for the deception. He had thought himself too brilliant to be discovered until billions of Iranian rials had been wasted in the fruitless research.

It was his way at striking back at the Islamic Revolutionary Council and its backward anti-progress treatment of its citizens. Unknown to his employers and government, Shazi was a member of the Mujahedin-e Khalq Organization, a rebel group that advocated the return of secular power to Iran.

The Mujahedin-e Khalq was formed in 1960 by college-educated children of Iranian merchants. The MEK sought to counter excessive Western influence in the shah's regime and supported the seizure of to power and began enforcing Islamic fundamentalism, the MEK turned against its own government. It planted bombs in the Islamic

Republic Party and premier's offices in 1981, killing 70 high-ranking Iranian officials including the premier, president and a chief justice.

Shazi had been very discrete about his participation in the rebellion. He attended the required military training in Yemen and Syria in order to prove his loyalty to the cause, disguising his absence to his Navy employers as a haj to the Holy Cities of Mecca and Medina. At the camps, Shazi learned the fine arts of terrorism, sabotage, guerilla warfare and espionage. Later, he went to a follow-on camp near Quiddafi, Libya. His brilliance soon developed into natural leadership ability. He even spent a year in Moscow learning Russian in order to make him a vital asset to his Navy bosses.

The training had placed him here, where he was set to implement the greatest and most expensive deception ever run on the Iranian government. He knew that the American CIA would learn of Iran's interest in purchasing Russian Kilo-class attack submarines. It would only be a matter of time before his name became associated with the clandestine magnetite program. When he offered to defect to the United States, the CIA would bend over backwards to grant him citizenship and protection. After almost seven years, Asadollah Shazi would be able to return to the only country he had truly considered his home.

A bright light stabbed his eyes as the blindfold was suddenly removed. Shazi blinked and tried to focus. He was in his hotel room. Then two hard hands grabbed his face and twisted his head.

The Russian officer stared with cold-blooded killer eyes into the Iranian doctor's face, then spoke in broken Arabic. "You stay inside hotel, yes? It would be bad for you to go outside. Russian winter can be fatal."

Shazi tried to nod in the soldier's grip. He had no illusions that the winter would have nothing to do with his sudden demise. "I understand."

The man in front of him released the doctor and stepped back. "Speak to no one. If someone approaches you or you have problems, you say my name. Sasha Ivanov. I will be there immediately."

"Yes," Shazi replied. "Sasha Ivanov, I will remember. Thank you."

The officer nodded again, then walked from the palatial hotel suite.

The Iranian physicist slowly released a long breath. He rubbed his cheek with a trembling hand, and then lowered himself into a nearby chair. Barely a second passed before he jumped up and dashed to the bathroom. The remnants of his lunch splattered into the toilet.

He knelt beside the cold porcelain until his stomach finally settled. All of the Mujahedin-e Khalq training seemed worthless. He had been trained to deal death, but it had always been a hypothetical mental exercise for him. In his 27 years, he had never seen death....until he had looked into Sasha Ivanov's steel-gray eyes.

Asadollah Shazi breathed a silent prayer to Allah for protection and guidance. In just a few hours, it seemed like all of his plans had gone wrong. Admiral Latvia had seen his deception and then added to it...why? Sasha Ivanov was definitely a trained killer, most likely KGB or one of the dreaded Spetznaz soldiers. The man seemed to expect trouble. Was he guarding Shazi? If so, from what? All of a sudden, the Iranian's detailed plans seemed minor compared to the game being played around him.

He felt like a small fish swimming in a pool of sharks.

LAWRENCE LATVIA

1930 hours Local, 13 November 1990,
Zhodochi, Russia (USSR)

VICE ADMIRAL LAWRENCE LATVIA SETTLED BACK INTO the comfort of his favorite chair. He didn't even bother to remove his uniform jacket. The heavy weight of medals and ribbons didn't matter to him anymore. They were trinkets, nothing more. Like many others in the Party, he knew that soon none of it would matter. The Union of Soviet Socialist Republics was falling apart, and his beloved Mother Russia was unlikely to survive the impending turmoil.

A fire crackled and popped before him, warming his feet. Like the political atmosphere in the Kremlin, the Russian winter outside was bitterly cold. It settled into his 66-year-old bones like a parasite, igniting his arthritis. Even the third glass of vodka in his hand would do little to remove the pain.

Unlike his inner turmoil, his country home—a dacha located in the woods outside Zhodochi near Moscow—was meticulous. After 15 years, he no longer came home and tossed his clothes haphazardly throughout the house. It was the least he could do for his beloved Tosarina.

Fifteen years. Lawrence took another gulp of the harsh vodka and swallowed hard. Tosarina would always gently scold him about his poor housekeeping skills. Lovingly she would pat him on the head as she walked by; his clothes bundled up in her arms. She'd reminded him again that, "You must learn to pick up after yourself, my love. I won't always be here to do it for you."

It was this exact night 15 years ago when she'd said it. Then he had been called away to meet with his youngest brother, Alexei. Tosarina wasn't home when he returned in the early hours the next morning. From the conversation with Alexei, Lawrence knew what had happened.

Her body was found in the woods outside Moscow two days later. The single bullet in the back of her head, KGB execution style, required a closed casket. His love and life had been taken from him. Lawrence wasn't even given the opportunity to kiss her goodbye.

The last memory Lawrence had of her was that gentle chiding and pat on the head. Since then, he ensured everything was in its place at the dacha, exactly as she had left it. "You see, my love," he whispered to the empty air around him. "Even I can be trained."

He knew that this wasn't a wise time to drift into memory and melancholy. That didn't matter to him. Others used words like "brilliance" and "genius" to describe him. "Wisdom" wasn't what anyone expected of him.

He had thrown the dice of fate today. Only time would tell how they landed. What he did on this night would make no difference. It was his life. How he spent the moments he had remaining was his to decide.

Lawrence Latvia refilled his glass from the bottle beside his chair. The day had gone very well, considering. Even Klos Sloreigh, the KGB agent, failed to notice the Arab physicist's shocked expression when Lawrence manipulated his calculations.

The aged admiral debated again whether to include the Iranian in the plot. Another gulp of vodka, then he answered his own question. "Not yet, Latvia. No, not yet."

The loyal Navy Spetznaz captain-lieutenant would keep even the KGB away from the physicist. Lawrence had no doubt of that. Sasha Ivanov knew his instructions and would follow them to the letter. Unless the KGB killed him first, of course.

No need to borrow trouble, Lawrence reassured himself. Sloreigh and his traitorous gang didn't suspect anything. Although they were true Party members and Soviets, they weren't Russian. Only a Russian would be paranoid enough to track 15 years worth of subtle clues.

Lawrence was Russian. Like the old Czars, political deception and intrigue was in his blood. He knew its value and portrayed exactly what the KGB expected to see. To any observer watching through his window, he was simply an old man whose life had been shattered by the death of his wife. He was an obedient servant of the party, too broken to step out of line again. His flashes of brilliance, so common early in his career, had become sporadic. He was no threat, not anymore.

Another gulp of vodka to help with the illusion and then Lawrence settled back into his chair. It wasn't wise to think about his life, but it was expected. He picked up a picture of his beloved wife from the table beside him.

"Ah, Tosarina," he said, staring forlornly at the aged photo, "remember where it first began?"

For Lawrence Latvia, it began in the spring of 1924. He was brought into the world with the assistance of a midwife. The old woman assisted in the birth of the boy just as she had years before with his mother, Oblisha. The infant Lawrence Latvia was covered with mucus and a layer of mass, but the midwife scrubbed him until he was clean. Then she gave him to his mother while she cut the umbilical cord. He was a cute baby and immediately began to look for his supply of mother's milk.

Lawrence was the name his parents had settled on during the cold, blistering winter before his birth. He was born into the Latvia household near the town of Leningrad, far away and north from Moscow.

The baby made the sixth child of the family. The Latvia children ranged from the ages of 15 on down. There were three boys and three girls. The father was an industrial worker, a manager in a farm implement factory. He wasn't there to greet his new son, of course; he had to work.

Leningrad is located on the Baltic Sea, which has access to the open sea. It was a city with a confused identity; for hundreds of years it had been known as St. Petersburg. In 1914, in response to patriotic anti-German fervor, the city's name was changed to the more Russian sounding "Petrograd." Then in 1924, the year Lawrence was born, another patriotic renaming occurred by Stalin in honor of the death of Vladimir Lenin. The city was renamed Leningrad. It was a bustling city, an organized blend of ancient history and new industry. The train system for the harbor continued to grow as new tracks fed in from other cities throughout Russia. It was a busy city, too busy to notice even the loud cry of its newest citizen.

The Latvia family home was quite large and very comfortable even though there were only four rooms. The largest room was the living room/kitchen space, and the other three rooms were designed as bedrooms. These bedrooms were loaded with children including the four boys sleeping in one room. The living room/ kitchen had a gigantic fireplace that provided the heat and cooking fire for the family. Each child had a certain list of chores to be done daily. If one did not accomplish this, he or she would be punished by staying in the house for one day to help with Oblisha's weekly chores.

Lawrence was brought up in a loving family environment, confident that his parents and siblings would look out for him. He tried to bypass crawling and struggled directly into walking, then running. It was the first challenge for him, and led to many failures. He was undaunted, though. After falling, he would simply regroup and try again.

At three years old, he was helping with the chores, carrying the plates and silverware to be washed after meals. He also helped his closest friend—Ilya, his seven-year-old brother—with bringing in wood or coal to keep the family warm at night.

Another addition arrived in 1926, a boy child named Alexei. Lawrence became very fond and protective of the child. They were close enough in age to be twins. Several years passed and the bond grew closer. The two boys became inseparable. Alexei went everywhere with him.

Lawrence turned five and began his formal education in bagcha, or kindergarten. It was the first stage of a formal system of indoctrination. The first thing he was to learn was anti-patriotism. It wasn't a difficult task for a child of St. Petersburg, or Petrograd, or Leningrad. Changing attitudes was easy for someone whose hometown changed names on the whims of politics.

In an age grown skeptical of diluted or unbiased loyalty, true Russians were a minority. They were perhaps the most passionate of patriots with a tenacious and deep love of country. That was unacceptable to the tenets of communism. Loyalty to party was paramount; it was supposed to be the common voice of loyalty that cemented Soviet society. Russians were a stubborn people, though. Ardent patriotism for Mother Russia was carefully concealed from the party, but never forgotten.

The paradox lies in the fact that other Revolutionary leaders like Lenin—only a minority of them were ethnic Russians—set out to revise the patriotic tradition. Lenin professed anti-patriotism in 1915. The Bolshevik creed condemned national loyalties as heresy. By 1928, the First Five-Year Plan, bit by bit, had been instilled in the hearts of the anti-czarist heroes.

Stalin took anti-nationalism even further when he gained power in 1929. He instituted mass migrations of people under the guise of fighting nationalism. This had a definite factor on Lawrence Latvia. Even though he was only five, he soon learned to separate his loyalty for Mother Russia from the teachings of the Communist party.

Lawrence went to school with his brothers and sisters. He learned quickly and read everything he could. His oldest brother helped by tutoring him in elementary math using a second-hand textbook. With a deep sense of ability, Lawrence conquered all facets of this book and pleaded for more textbooks. Soon he had more books than was considered acceptable for a loyal Communist family. History, poetry, Russian language, and basic geography were among the books Lawrence collected.

By the time he was 10 years old, Lawrence was working on an adjacent farm. He planted corn, broke up gravel and mixed it with dirt containing the dung matte that beetles loved. From all of the available vegetables, Lawrence tried string beans, which did not grow very well in the environment.

Lawrence watched the crops grow and soon he returned and hoed the aspiring crops. He seemed to blossom like his crops, growing six inches during the summer. At last the corn ripened and was ready for harvest. The collective farmer gathered the crop and mowed down the stalks for livestock fodder. Nothing was wasted on the collective farm. The corn provided meal to the families; corn stalks provided feed for the cattle, which provided dung for heating when the coal ran low.

By 1938, the fascist revolution in Germany was widely reported in the Russian newspapers. Hitler was in his prime and had successfully built an elite superpower. Unlike Stalin's call for anti-nationalism, Hitler manipulated the emotional appeal of German nationality. He called on his people to believe the Teutonic ubermenschen "natural superiority" over other races and nations.

It was a foregone conclusion that Germany would eventually attack Russia. The Russian estimate of its enemy's intentions and capabilities suggested that it would attack Russia before 1942. Stalin and his generals knew that they needed the time. After years of economic crises and harsh governance, the Soviet Union was ill-prepared for war.

Lawrence celebrated his 14th birthday in 1938. It was the last time that he would ever see his family together. His two older brothers, Ilya and Marshal, had heard about the possibility of war and enlisted in the army.

The young Latvia also faced a crisis of his own. He started the eighth grade where he would face a mandatory test for higher schooling. If he failed, the communist system expected him to immediately report for work at a farm or factory. A passing score meant that he could continue school for another year. Then he would either enter college preparation classes or transfer to a technical school to learn a trade.

The test came and went. The results were announced before the end of the school year. Many of his classmates' faces would become dim memories; they wouldn't return for the fall semester. Lawrence's results weren't a surprise to anyone who knew him, though. His score was the highest in the region.

Lawrence volunteered to work on the collective farm over the summer. He spent many a day weeding, hoeing, and caring for the plants. Finally the crops were ready for harvest. The local collective farm manager gave him money, a substantial increase over the last summer's crop.

Classes began again in the fall as the drums of war began sounding. The school began plastering patriotic posters in the classrooms. The pictures showed men on warships, marching or standing beside tanks. They made Lawrence wonder how his brothers were doing in training. He wanted to join up, but he knew he wasn't old enough.

On August 24, 1939, Germany and the Russians signed a non-aggression treaty. The Soviet Union would supply Germany with raw materials in exchange for German goods. The Russians accepted this in order to buy time to build their army for the inevitable attack. Meanwhile, the German units crossed over the Polish border. The Polish government ceased to exist and almost five million Poles were reported dead, more than any other country lost in any previous war.

Between 1939 and 1941, a vast program of military spending put the Russian military back into shape. The opening of mills, plants and factories produced munitions, tanks, rifles and the materiel for war. The army grew from 4.1 million to 5 million men, adding 125 new Red Army divisions. It was still too small when compared to Hitler's force of 8.5 million, even if it included the one million other troops drawn from "outback lands."

The magnificent German force considered Soviet forces as untermenschen: subhuman. The illiterate Russian peasants weren't expected to be capable of fighting in a modern war. It was the first step in the propaganda campaign leading up to war.

The communist army ignored the insults. Systematically, they began equipping their divisions with two types of tanks, the KV-1 and the T-34. Both were believed to be superior to anything the German army possessed. German aircraft were also considered similar to Russian standards. Essentially the Red army was producing new rifles, new special types of artillery, and new, fearsome weapons such as the Katyusha rocket.

The German aircraft production averaged well above 9,000 planes a year, while the Fuhrer maintained his superiority over the eastern front. His armor and mechanized forces were capable of overwhelming the hopelessly ill-equipped Soviet troops. It was simply a matter of time before he used them.

The brothers came home for Christmas that year of 1939, a delight for Lawrence. The oldest brother, Ilya, had completed officer training and been promoted to lieutenant. He belonged to a brigade of the new T-34 tanks, which trained south of Moscow. His other brother, Marshal, graduated infantry training. Both were going to be in units stationed at Kaharkov Army Base about 400 miles south of Moscow.

The Soviet Union invaded Latvia, Lithuania and Estonia in June of 1940. The war that everyone expected had finally arrived, but it didn't make sense to Lawrence. After hearing years of warning about the Nazi threat, it seemed odd that the Red Army was used to attack other nations.

Lawrence went to work at the munitions factory that summer. Now 16, he had grown to almost six feet tall and weighed a slim 165 pounds. The plant supervisor put him in the shipping department. Machine gun and antiaircraft cartridges were run at different times of the week. His department packed the shells for shipment to all facilities. Trucks lined up to take the shells to the bases where the men were training.

It didn't take long for the young Latvia to learn the routine. Then he made two mistakes for a factory worker. The first was that he thought about inefficiencies in the loading system. The second was that he took the initiative; he made changes within his section.

After two weeks on the job, his supervisor called him over. The older man had noticed how Lawrence's group of workers was far ahead of the others. Five minutes of lecture about the proper attitude and place of a worker had no effect on the young Lawrence Latvia. The supervisor had no other choice: He made a note in Latvia's work file. Then he transferred the insolent boy to the production line where tank rounds were made. Perhaps a minor explosive mishandling incident could be arranged to teach the arrogant boy.

Of course, the supervisor also reported the new system to his superior and claimed credit for himself. That was the party way.

Lawrence saw the transfer as a promotion. He knew the tank rounds were volatile. Simply dropping one could result in an explosion. To his 16-year-old mind, that placed his brother Ilya at risk. He was determined to resolve the design flaw. War was dangerous enough without the hazard of getting blown up by one's own ammunition.

He happily took his place in line where the tank rounds were banded together and loaded on pallets. The line leader, a girl of 25 with pretty long brown hair, showed him the procedures. Lawrence fit right in and was up to speed in an hour.

Within a week he was arguing with the ammunition designers. They grudgingly acknowledged to each other that the boy was right in his engineering calculations. It was intolerable. Once again, negative marks were recorded on his work record. The engineers also followed the Party tradition: They took the credit for the new tank round design. Lawrence was sent back to the line.

School began again that fall, and Lawrence was the happiest he had ever been. He was in the college preparatory class, which meant a new set of textbooks. Two months later the instructor gave him books reserved for the next semester. By Christmas, Lawrence Latvia had diligently worked through all of the pre-college texts.

Another reason for his happiness was that Lawrence had met a new classmate. Her name was Tosarina, and she was remarkable. It didn't concern him that her future was already determined. She was 16, beautiful, and of more importance, she loved him. By Christmas they had declared their personal vows to the other. New Year's Eve was a joyous occasion as they consummated their love. The only barrier to marriage was the career that the party had selected for Tosarina.

She had been hand-selected for Nejvyssi Kontrolni Vladce Davu-the NKVD-training upon graduation in the spring. The NKVD, or People's Commissariat for Internal Affairs, was Stalin's domestic and international intelligence and assassination service. Tosarina was excited about her future with the agency. The NKVD's reputation for torture and mass murder was lost on the 16-year-old girl. To her, it was simply an opportunity to see Mother Russia. Perhaps someday she might even be given an assignment to Europe.

The two young lovers talked about this and many other possible dreams. Unlike Tosarina, Lawrence wasn't certain what the future held for him. His grades were outstanding, but it was doubtful that he would be offered one of the coveted quotas to attend college. He was the third son of a loyal Communist Party propagandist; his father was active within the district committee but had no political ambitions. In Lawrence's mind, there was only one avenue open to him. The war was coming. He would enlist and see what the army could offer.

He took his final exams shortly before his 17th birthday in March, 1941. Leningrad was filled with rumors of war. Three dates were given for the impending German invasion…April 6, April 20 and June 22. The Soviet government added to the fear with its visible signs of increased troop movements. The Defense Commissariat ordered the Transbiakal and Farm Eastern military districts to prepare two airborne units, three motorized and six infantry divisions for transfer to the western front.

Lawrence's examination results arrived several weeks later. They were exactly as he feared. Although he placed in the highest percentile, there were no vacancies in the allotted university allotments. It was party language that his family didn't have the proper connections.

Ignoring his parents' protests, Lawrence Latvia walked into the enlistment station on the morning of his 17th birthday. After 15 minutes of paperwork and a brief physical examination, he was pronounced fit for service in the army. He was given a week to place his affairs in order.

Tosarina was supportive of his decision. Their last night together was brief and intense. The dark-haired girl laid her head on his chest after their lovemaking and wept. "It is so unfair, my love."

"Shh, now. It is life, simply that. Fair has nothing to do with it."

She ran smooth fingernails across his chest. "You deserve better."

"It will suffice." He captured her hand with his, then gently forced her lips up to his. "My service is for a year, and then I will return to what I deserve. You, my love. Then we will marry, yes?"

Tosarina raised her head and smiled. "A year, then, and no longer. But for now, would you like to, again?"

Her fingernails moved, slowly drawing a line down his chest to a more sensitive place. Lawrence smiled and rose to the occasion.

The next morning found him waving goodbye to his parents and Tosarina as he boarded the train for Moscow. He was sadly excited. There was no other way he could describe his feelings. Sad that he left behind his family and love, yet excited to step into his adult life.

There were other enlistees on the train with him. He met several in the dining car. It didn't take long after exchanging names and several bottles of vodka that the young men became best of friends. They stumbled off the train many hours later, exhausted from the trip and alcohol.

The army sergeant waiting for them had no sympathy. With a bellowing voice, he soon had the large group of enlistees in a semblance of order. The young men crowded into the back of several trucks. Lawrence slept through the 45-mile trip to the army base.

Training at the Topima Army base north of Moscow was rapid, no questions asked and these lads were trained in eight weeks. The Soviet army wasn't interested in finding the exact position of these men in the army. Basically, they were trained to fight and not give one step of ground to the enemy.

Intense instruction in proper political behavior, weapons training, leadership and tactics brought various men to the forefront. Lawrence excelled in tactics and leadership. His sergeants were amazed at his skill and development. As a result, he was quickly promoted to private first class.

Lawrence was still in training when Germany invaded on the twenty-second of June 1941. The attack, called Operation Barbarossa, required an Eastern army of 121 divisions, most of which were Panzer segments. The points of entry of the Nazi regime spread across the Polish-Russia border. The Pripet Marches was number one, as many of the battles were being waged along the corridor of the 200-mile gap in front. The second was to venture into the south and capture the Donets coal basin, and thusly to gain rapid control to reach Moscow, thereby winning the chokehold of its adversary.

German Army Group North, composed of two armies, stretched from Prussia to Lithuania and would settle with its destruction of Kronstadt and Leningrad. Army Group South waded through the marshes taking Gabcia and the Ukraine, and was to take the Sniper crossing and seize Kiev. Lastly, Army Group Centre, the most prolific of all three elements, was to encircle Bezelorrissia to destroy the Soviet Air Fleet and lead the force to Moscow. Colossal strikes by the armies were to smash open the Russian front before grinding down the lackluster Soviet troops with sustained attacks in the enemy rear area. Finally, the Nazi forces would come to rest at the Volga. From there the long range bombing raids would pound all remaining resistance to submission.

The Germans on the other hand, found that the Russian army had moved up along the western Dunia and the Dniepr. The 16th Army was sent from Transbaukal to the Kiev military district. Nearly a million troops were called up out of the reserve.

The army activity at the base was catastrophic. Great holes were the result of huge bombardments over the past week. This was the result of picking up the perils of all commands and strategically placing them around the outskirts of Moscow. The German forces incessantly piled over the best Russian Army with motorized means and the so-called Panzer operations. The women for example, found their way into the Red Army by volunteering and placing women into the bomb requirements. Many women worked for the Red Army and medical corps that maintained the sick and wounded. Many situations occurred where they thought of how epidemics and diseases would affect Moscow's hospital systems. Nurses were quickly replaced by the Army Red Cross who were also internists, pediatricians and the like to perform operations as necessary.

Lawrence was expecting a change to his command, but the stakes were getting grayer. En masse, approximately 2,000 men were lined up in formation outside the commandant's building. The commander stepped outside and he looked over the group assembled. He spoke with a guarded voice as he explained the reason for leaving this camp. "The German bombers found our position and destroyed numerous equipment. They will likely be back tomorrow to bomb the remaining communications site. Starting tomorrow, we will take trucks and head toward Moscow. I have not been told where we will be, but the order has not been rescinded as of yet." He then excused himself and went back into the administration building.

Lawrence and his group of corporals went to their barracks. The bombs had missed their home. They discussed how to evacuate the building if the camp came under attack while they were still there.

The conversation turned and each man talked about different tragedies that had been going on at home. Reges, who was from outside of Moscow, related that many had been establishing secret bases to fight the enemy. He stated that the population of the city had had banded together a force of women, men and children to deal "death to the invaders" from every street, rooftop and sewer. He also said that the advancing murderous force was already quite impressed with the Soviet courage. The people were prepared to sacrifice more in their country's defense.

Another gentleman spoke up, explaining that the word "Tievoga" was a code word warning all the citizens that a bombing attack was underway. The people were to immediately seek the shelters or underground stations.

Reges reported that the Home Guard was digging ditches around the outlying district of Moscow. The guard worked around the clock digging shelters and bomb container devices. Tank control was the purpose of these high ridge embankments, which would keep the Germany tanks from backing off the high trees. Additionally, the rattle of the enemy machine guns was a constant threat to the capitol city.

Many industrial plants that manufactured rifles, pistols and machine gun bullets critical to the war effort were suddenly aware of the Nazis blitzkrieg throughout Russia. It was dangerous to have them all in one location. The matter was solved and the plants began to dismantle their equipment. As little as a month earlier, they received orders to establish their plants in the Urals. This included industrial plants, which were to be moved there also.

Many of the workers refused to budge, but the younger worked until the 450 or so factories were disassembled. Seven hundred railway vans contained these parts that were covered with brick and shipped to sites in the east. Packed separately, the flywheels, machine parts, cogs, greased and wrapped, were packed in the van. Over 200,000 workers with their families followed these miracle vans. Also, tons of art objects and museums followed with trucks bogged down with their treasures.

The next morning, Tomina Army base was no more. A series of blasts had destroyed the buildings of the camp, leaving nothing but the barbed wire fence standing. The men loaded up in trucks and headed north. Lawrence and the others were outfitted in military attire with the appropriate rifle.

They were in the back of a truck, which had seats for 16 men and towed a small cannon. The commandant was headed in the general direction of Moscow. There they were cheered several times as they passed several small towns. Most of the civilian people were moving away from this part of Russia.

The trucks stopped every three hours to let the men go to the bathroom and smoke a cigarette. During one of those stops, a flight of German Stuka single-engine fighter aircraft came over the horizon. The Russian troops jumped out of the trucks and ran under the trees and branches. The Stukas made only one pass before Russian fighters arrived to chase the German Wolfgang. Cheers of gladness and joy sounded, and the sergeant ordered all trucks manned.

The trucks plunged on until the convoy encountered a snowstorm. The lieutenant in charge stopped the detachment and told the men to set up tents in the adjacent field. One truck had tents and food supplies. Cooks prepared the meager dinner of soup and loaves of bread, with coffee as a topper. Lawrence fixed his tent in a field recently covered with snow. He stood in line to get his supper along with the rest. That night was bitterly cold. There was nobody else in his tiny pup tent. He only had memories of his last night with Tosarina to keep him warm.

The next morning a motorman arrived with an urgent message for the battalion. The lieutenant told them that they were going to Vologodamsk where the German militia had broken through. After breakfast they loaded up the trucks and headed out for the besieged city.

Within ten miles of Vologodamsk, the soldiers could hear the loud rumbles of long-range guns belching. They watched the battered remnants of supply vehicles head toward the battle; there were little or no replacements to be seen. Next came the division aid camps where the numerous wounded were being cared for.

The truck stopped and the men were mustered. With a loud cry, the sergeant motivated the men by yelling, "Each one of us is going into combat! Check your rifles and load them."

Lawrence snagged three grenades from the full ammunition box. Nobody else wanted the grenades. He didn't understand why. It didn't matter that their army training never covered grenades. They were simple in principle to use, and he thought they might come in handy.

His squad began marching single file with three meters spacing between them. They traversed a half-mile past the base before they had their first glimpse of how the Germans waged war. Hundreds of Russian soldiers lay dead, left to decay on the ground or in tanks and trucks. The sergeant, a veteran of the first war, refused to look at the decay of common men but looked beyond. He was a true Russian soldier. The dead were dead; the battle was ahead where he could repay the Germans for their brutality.

Finally they reached the front line. The squad was ordered into trenches, their only protection against the German tanks. The German armor had regrouped on the horizon and was once more going to try to break the defensive line. The Panzers moved forward. Cries went up as the Russian soldiers suffered hits. The German tanks fired continuously, blowing through the berms blocking them from penetrating Russian lines.

A Nazi tank punched through into Lawrence's perimeter. It opened fire, killing at least four of his comrades. He fired at the German infantry moving forward. Four fell. Others moved forward to take their place.

Lawrence assessed the situation. The tank and its mobile gun was the greatest threat. There was no other choice. As his comrades fell around him, he sneaked out of the trench and crawled toward the tank. A moment later he saw a German who was doing the same thing. Lawrence shot him when he wasn't looking.

He crawled until he could hear the rumbling tank engine. The normal soldier would've given a loud war cry as he leaped up; Lawrence was silent as he rolled sideways toward the tank. He could feel the burning exhaust in his face as he scrambled up the back of the tank. One bullet from his rifle took care of the tank commander. His grenade, dropped down the open hatch, took care of the rest.

Lawrence jumped to the ground, enemy bullets tracing his escape. A loud thunderous explosion sounded behind him as the tank and its ammunition burned. He zigzagged across the battlefield. When he reached his trench, he found his comrades dead. The sergeant yelled from another trench 30 meters away. The enemy had penetrated the line and the Russians were falling back. The young Latvia scrambled to the new position.

"Well done, young man," praised the sergeant. "You will make junior sergeant for your bravery, if we get out of this. Let's pull back." He, following Stalin's orders, took the rifles and ammunition belts off the dead men. Nothing was to be left behind for the Germans.

The war in 1941 went poorly for the Russians. Lawrence gained a squad of his own as the battalion fell back to defend Moscow. He heard that Leningrad had held the initial June attack, but the Germans had laid siege to the city a siege that would last over 400 days. Half a million people would die of starvation until the city was finally relieved. Lawrence could only hope that his family and Tosarina weren't among the dead. All he could do for them was kill as many Nazis as possible, forcing the German High Command to send reinforcements toward the Moscow front instead of Leningrad.

The city of Moscow was being hammered. In a one hundred mile radius around the city, 800,000 soldiers fought on three fronts. The city was evacuated in October. Two million people headed east as the army made fanatic efforts to save Moscow. Hedgehogs were emplaced, barbed wire entanglements laid, and reinforced concrete pillboxes created for anti-tank guns. "Molotov cocktails," half-liter bottles of inflammable liquid, were stockpiled to be thrown at the tanks.

The German offensive in November failed, and Stalin called for an immediate counter-offensive. On December 4, the Red Army counterattacked, catching the Germans by surprise. The enemy was pushed back 200 miles by January.

Lawrence continued to show his brilliance in tactics. He received a battlefield commission to junior lieutenant in recognition of his valor and heroism. It was also for practical reasons; the casualty rates left too many officer positions vacant.

The Germans assembled large land and air forces for the offensive against Stalingrad. The assault began in August 1942 with a terror raid of bombs. This raid killed 35,000 people, leaving thousands to crawl into the safety of caves across the Volga River. The Germans, over the next three months, pulverized the city with 24-hour raids. The predator had the advantage over numerous roads, and the Soviets were limited to only one road across the Volga.

By September 4, the Nazis reached the river on the south side of Stalingrad and the all-out attack commenced. The town sustained fierce fighting until finally the battle began to turn towards the Soviets. By mid-November the Red Army counter-offensive had started. On November 19, the offensive had encircled 300,000 Germans.

The Germans tried to break through the entrapping Russian force to let General Paulus' Sixth Army retreat from Stalingrad. The rescue attempt failed on December 12. By the 24h the Nazis were thrown back to the Aksair River. They were in full retreat by the 29th.

Stalin decreed that new units would be used for the new offensive. In this way, he allowed combat-weary units to withdraw to the rear while the Soviet army still maintained its offensive tempo. Lawrence found himself with extra time on his hands as he trained new recruits to replace fallen comrades. By chance or fortune, that was when he received the first letter from Tosarina.

Her words were a comfort to him. Thankfully, she was not trapped in the siege of Leningrad. She had left the city for NKVD training in Moscow before the Germans invaded the previous June. Her training completed, she had been assigned as the political officer for submarine forces operating from the Kola Peninsula.

The Kola Peninsula was a critical resupply system for the Soviets. Allied war materiel and equipment sustained the Soviets until they could increase their own industrial base to manufacture tanks and aircraft. The allied assistance had to cross the Atlantic, elude German U-boat wolf packs and safely reach the Kola harbors.

The letters became regular during 1943. Lawrence could read between the lines to see Tosarina's frustration. In one letter, she mentioned that the submarines were doing poorly against the superior German fleet and U-boats. Over the next few months they developed their own code words and language to discuss what was technically classified material.

He queried her over the next few months about specifications, confident that the letters would seem innocent if captured by German forces. The problem soon became obvious to him. The Russian M-class submarine had batteries that limited its subsurface maneuvering time. It also had a design flaw that would shatter the spine of the submarine if it tried to submerge below 50 meters. There was no way to repair it; a new class would have to be designed and constructed. He wrote his conclusions in code and sent them, along with heartwarming words of love and affection, to Tosarina.

The Germans had regrouped. By August, they were again threatening Stalingrad. Lawrence's unit had received orders to join the counterattack force. He was in his tent, taking care of last-minute details, when his commander summoned him to the battalion command center.

Lawrence was surprised at the distinct and easily recognizable uniform of the man standing beside the commander. The other officers in the command tent bore expressions of fear on their faces. Having a NKVD officer in the area was never a good thing. The repressive intelligence organization was responsible for identifying and eliminating traitors within the Soviet populace.

"You are Lieutenant Lawrence Latvia?" asked the man bluntly.

"Yes, Comrade." Lawrence was puzzled. How did the regional NKVD know his name?

"You will come with me."

Those dreaded words were typically the last that one would hear. There was no arguing or bargaining with the NKVD. The trial had already been held and the suspect had already been found guilty. The next act of the harsh play would be to walk outside a short distance. Then there would be one gunshot.

Lawrence simply nodded. "Yes, Comrade."

He stepped through the tent door and to the outside. His mind was abuzz with confusing thoughts. Had his family done something that betrayed the people? Was there something he had done? He couldn't see how. The rows of medals for valor and heroism on his dress uniform jacket had been earned the hard way: In combat. There was no higher decorated soldier in his battalion. What was happening?

"Comrade, please. A question, if I may?" he said over his shoulder to the dark form behind him.

"Ask."

It was a single word, yet it meant the world to Lawrence. The NKVD officer was willing to converse with him. Perhaps there had been a mistake.

"Have I or my family done something to offend the party?"

The soft laugh behind him was surprising. "No, tovarisch. A mutual acquaintance has brought your brilliant mind to my attention. Your skills are required elsewhere."

"Elsewhere, Comrade?"

"Yes," the NKVD officer said, stepping beside the young Latvia. "You are to report to the Bureau of Ship Design Submarines in Murmansk."

PENTAGON

HALFWAY ACROSS THE WORLD FROM THE IRANIAN physicist's hotel was an odd-shaped concrete building. Its five-sided structure contains 17 1/2 miles of corridors and has three times the office space of the Empire State Building. From stem to stern, it is a 27-mile walk and yet Rear Admiral Joseph Allen Henry could reach any point in the five wedge-shaped sections in seven minutes.

The admiral wasn't happy. After 27 faithful years in the Navy, he was soon destined to "go with the wind." His personnel file was in front of the Navy promotion board. The recent high-level gossip racing through the halls of the Pentagon told him that there was little chance of him seeing his next star.

The location of his office in the Pentagon was part of the reason. There was a shooting war going on in the Persian Gulf—he refused to use the Middle East name of "Arabian" Gulf—and he wasn't part of it. To the victor go the spoils, and promotions would be given to the admirals on the other side of the Pentagon; the ones coordinating battle plans for the Gulf War.

The heels of his highly polished "low quarters" shoes clicked against the equally polished floor. The others in the hallway, enlisted and officers, moved briskly toward their destinations without looking at him. That was the way the Pentagon worked. Everyone went about their tasks with a sense of purpose. Rank didn't matter in the hallways.

Another reason that he would fail promotion was because of the rumors racing through the four million square feet of offices. Politicians and analysts both forecasted the imminent fall of the mighty Soviet empire. Talk already contained the new slogan of "peace dividend." It was slang for the downsizing of the American military. Without the Cold War foe, the United States would no longer need its massive military infrastructure. Thousands of careers would end, and his was one of them.

Admiral Henry wasn't bitter about it. He could sense the wind in the sails, and an old surface fleet officer like himself soon wouldn't be needed. The Navy that had been his only family and life would ask him to retire, and he would do so gracefully. That was the way of things.

He reached his destination and stepped into the briefing room. He announced his presence with a calm "as you were" before anyone could call the room to attention. Several of his staff still popped up from their chairs. He waved them down, then took his seat at the head of the long table.

The admiral automatically reached for his morning cup of java, confident that it would be there. A young female steward had quietly placed the coffee at his elbow as he took his chair. He was accustomed to the ritual and didn't even notice her presence.

Joe Henry scanned the faces of the young officers seated before him. They were all good sailors. Like him, they knew that their presence in the room was a sign of their forthcoming exile from the service. Morale was low, but he had to give them credit. They performed their duties professionally.

He once again made a mental note to see what he could do for them. There had to be some way to transfer them from this section to one of the Gulf War staffs. Of course there really wasn't any—but he had an obligation to try.

It was obvious to everyone in the Pentagon that his staff was superfluous. They were responsible for tracking Soviet submarine research activity. That was almost an oxymoron; the Russians could barely pay their soldiers, much less dedicate billions of dollars on developing a new submarine. It was like his staff was the winning team in a football game. Fourth quarter, ahead by four touchdowns, the victory guaranteed and the stands almost empty as the crowd left early.

The admiral sensed something new in the air today. A sense of life and purpose, absent for many months, seemed to radiate from his subordinates. He almost allowed a smile to cross his lips as he said, "Good morning, ladies and gentlemen. What do we have today?"

The liaison officer from Defense Intelligence Agency, Captain Bill Blast, replied. "Looks like we have a new player in town, admiral."

"Really? Who might that be?" Joe Henry sipped his coffee, granting his staff their fun.

Captain Blast grinned. "Iran."

"What? That's ludicrous!" Coffee splashed as Admiral Henry slammed the cup into its saucer. "They don't have a navy to speak of, and now they're making submarines?"

"Exactly what we thought, sir," laughed Commander Don Beltcavative.

Admiral Henry grabbed a napkin and wiped the spilled coffee off his hand. "This is all we need, gentlemen. If the higher-ups think we're a joke already, imagine what they'll say now."

The room fell into an awkward silence. It took a moment for Joe to recognize the uncomfortable looks on his subordinates' faces before he realized what he'd said. It was one thing for each officer to think that they were assigned to a useless section. Having their commander say it aloud was something else. Nobody at the table would meet his eyes.

"Hell." His voice was sharp enough to grab their attention. Joe tossed the napkin aside and leaned forward. "Let them think whatever they want. We know better. So the Iranians want to become a submarine navy, huh? Tell me about it, Bill."

"Seems that they're purchasing three Kilo-class diesel attack boats from the Soviets with a few homegrown modifications." Captain Blast extended a folder to the admiral. "The top is a photo of Vice Admiral Steustal greeting an Iranian physicist at Moscow Airport. Background check says he's Asadollah Shazi, MIT grad, brilliant mathematician and very under-appreciated by the Iranian Navy. Until now, that is."

Admiral Henry glanced through the photos. He didn't bother to read the numerous pages detailing sources and assessment. That's what he had staff for, to explain it concisely for him. A date caught his eye. He read the section briefly and shook his head. "This is impossible, Bill. The photos were taken three days ago in Moscow? How'd we get them so fast?"

"Trade secret, sir." Bill grinned and shrugged. "DIA's had a source in Moscow for close to 15 years now. He's a hundred percent reliable. Came up with some terrific stuff in the past, and all of it has been confirmed by other sources. Only difference is that this agent lets us in on things three to five years before anyone else in Moscow 'mentions' it to us."

"What kind of things?" The admiral raised his hand before the DIA liaison could become defensive. "You guys may trust this character, but I've never heard of him before. So introduce me to him. What kind of things has he passed on?"

Bill Blast looked down at the table, weighing his options. Then he raised his head. "The modified Delta IV, for one. The Joint Chiefs and admirals were briefed on it last year. You were there as well, if I remember it correctly."

"You're talking about the new SSGN, right? Yes, I was there for that brief."

The captain turned to the other officers at the table and explained. "It's an SSGN with four missile tubes removed. The Soviets added a Spetznaz diver excursion module in their place. They practiced insertions with it last year. North Korea provided the Special Operating Force teams and they raided the South Korean coastline."

"I heard about that," commented Commander Joe Turner. "The Russians are trying to sell an export model to North Korea, right? Except I thought they were going to use the old Yankee subs."

"That's right, for the export version." Bill looked at the admiral. "The point is, this agent told us about the SSGN modification plan five years ago."

Joe leaned back in his chair. He took his time sipping the refilled coffee—the steward was very efficient—before he spoke again. "Let me see if I'm reading this right. Your agent tells you about Soviet research plans when they're still in the design phase? If your example is any indication, we've got five years or more before we have to worry about the Iranians."

Bill shook his head slowly. "That's typically the case, sir, but not this time. The agent took some incredible risks to get those photos and documents to us. It has his handlers at DIA extremely worried. Something is going on in Moscow, and it all centers around this Iranian physicist."

"So what's all the fuss about?"

"According to our experts, this Dr. Shazi has developed a new theory toward submarine design. If it works, the Kilos will be up to 30 percent quieter than they are now—which is extremely quiet as it is."

"That's right," interrupted Commander Brian Engler. He was fresh from Patrol Wings Atlantic. "The Kilo is the quietest diesel attack sub in the world. Quite the pain to find when it's running silent."

The DIA liaison nodded. "That's not all. This won't require building a new class of submarine. The Russians will be able to modify all of their Kilos. Our ghost in Moscow is forecasting six months for trials and full modification in less than two years. He's also concerned that the new system could be applied to the boomers as well."

"Well, now." Admiral Henry sipped his coffee, taking his time to think through the ramifications of the news. Then he leaned forward, hands flat on the table and ready for action. "All right, ladies and gentlemen, looks like it's time to earn our pay. We're going to do an initial staff exercise on this. Commander Turner, you're the recorder. Don't miss anything, Joe."

The commander nodded as the admiral continued. "We'll work with the premise that the modification will make the Soviet missile subs are 30 percent quieter. They'll be harder to detect when submerged. Now tell me what we've got that'll let us find them. Keep in mind how the Russians have run their subs in the past as well. Since you're the expert on SURTASS, Joe, you won't need to keep notes on it. However, that means you're the first in the barrel to brief. Tell us about SURTASS."

The look of shock on the commander's face brought laughter to the room. Joe was very familiar with the system. He just hadn't expected the need to ever brief it. The slender officer stood and walked toward the white-board and picked up one of the dry erase markers. Then he grinned to himself. The past year's doom-and-gloom atmosphere was gone from the room. In its place was focused energy. It was like somebody rang general quarters. The staff was ready to face the new enemy.

He turned, facing the officers sitting at the table, and began a formal briefing. "Good morning. I'm Commander Turner, and my briefing will be on the Surveillance Towed Array Sensor System, or SURTASS. It is designed to replace the aging Sound Surveillance System (SOSUS) that been in place for years. I worked in SURTASS development in OP- 951.

"At the outset, the beginning of Sound Surveillance Systems markedly changed the supportable systems such as antisubmarine warfare systems; namely the VP or patrol squadron systems. SOSUS was started in the mid-1950s. It spans the globe with a network of over a thousand underwater microphones. These mikes are grouped in arrays tied to Navy shore stations. This offered detection of submarines and other phenomenon out to hundreds of miles from shore. The technology is outdated, but it was responsible for providing the background for developing new systems.

"Case in point, SURTASS was brought about by this same theory using sound detection or low-frequency radar. The experiment started on a long flat bottom boat. The towed array initially worked smoothly, but the rocking boat hampered the rolling human trying to run the device. The ship was to radio detection information to the land base. The navy was interested in the procedure and sent it to Commander Navy Electronic Command, where the project went through many tests.

"Out of this madness, came SURTASS. An Operation Test and Evaluation (OPTEVFOR) ship with some of the equipment was tested. The ship failed the first test. After replacing the old staff with a new one, the second ship—which was better configured—won the prize! Apparently the second ship had ballast that was used to stabilize the ship. This ship also used a new device, the satellite communication (SITCOM) system. The SITCOM system was placed on the highest part of the ship, the mast. It was rigged to communicate with a satellite and pass its data to Ocean Systems Atlantic. This system worked successfully during the test period.

"In July 1980, SURTASS began climbing up the procurement ladder. It made it to the Secretary of Navy and finally to the Department of Defense. Final approval was given to build 12 ships.

"USNS Stalwart, the first SURTASS ship, was a dashing wonder. She has an elongated beam with special stabilizers designed to be habitable. The array is mounted on a circular wheel on the back of the ship's stern. It is stowed when not in use, or when moving to or from the operational area. There is space available for 28 persons onboard.

"In January 1981, the Operational Test vehicle was slightly east of Bermuda when they gained contact on a Russian Yankee Class submarine. The range was validated by a P-3B aircraft, which revealed 500 miles. The second contact of this ship was 850 nautical miles; it was another typical Yankee submarine. Almost immediately, the officer who was responsible for SURTASS flew to Hawaii to tell the Chief of Pacific Fleet the news about the killer ship.

"Much controversy was allowed when the employment of ships was discussed. Essentially, the ships were delegated six to the West Coast and six to the East Coast. Naval Station Rota was designated a major port, with Honolulu the second port in the Pacific. It was finally worked out that three were in Norfolk and three were at

Rota on the East Coast. The SURTASS ships are deployed for 60 days. The operational commander has the authority to bounce ships to the North Atlantic or to the Mediterranean Sea if there are submarines in the area. That's SURTASS in a nutshell. Are there any questions I may answer?"

The first question was how many ships had been procured. Commander Turner replied that 18 ships were ordered. The next question was what was the greatest range reported during the Yankee prosecution; he said that the last reported range was 975 miles.

Admiral Henry thanked the commander and then turned to Commander Engler. "Alright, Brian, you're up. Tell us about the Patrol Wings."

Commander Brian Engler had been assigned to the Pentagon Command and Control Center for three months. His previous assignment had been commanding officer of Patrol Squadron Ten. He stepped toward the white-board and began his brief.

"Commander Patrol Wings Atlantic is located in Topsham, Maine, just north of Naval Air Station Brunswick, Maine. This is the focus of 12 East Coast antisubmarine warfare patrol squadrons. Rear Admiral Wallace is boss of these competing squadrons and has the appropriate staff to act on anything the Patrol Wings may find out of the ordinary.

"Patrol Wing Five is stationed at NAS—sorry, Naval Air Station—Brunswick, Maine which has a Tactical Support Center for operational use. It also has administrative, maintenance and operations staff. They use the P-3 Orion subchaser to locate and, if authorized, destroy enemy subs.

"Training and maintenance of these Lockheed aircraft is quite a task. In winter, snow must be plowed away from the runway so the P-3s launch on time. In order to keep up with the seasonal tons of snow, the base commander closes one of the dual runways to keep the other one open for 24 hours a day.

"The other half of the squadrons are shared by Patrol Wing Eleven in NAS Jacksonville, Florida. Wing Eleven has six squadrons and VP-30, the training squadron. All officers and enlisted report there for training before going to an active squadron. VP-30 provides the training for pilots, tactical coordinators and all other flight crew personnel that fly the airplane.

"Basically, deployments are a pain in the ass! A squadron deploys for five months and stands down for a month. Then they build up their proficiency again before deploying in about 10 months. For example, the Brunswick Wing satisfies Bermuda, Rota/Lajes and Naval Station Argentia by sending squadrons to these sites. I must be fair to Argentia, there are rumors that the base may be closed soon. Jacksonville will keep Iceland and Sigonella manned, but Wing Eleven takes NAS Argentia every other detachment, sending four P-3s to cover this commitment. Are there questions?"

The first subject to come up was the use of Argentia. Brian explained that the base was used as an EC-121 base to detect Soviet high flying bombers. In 1965 the mission changed when the EC-121 was decommissioned; the P-3A was sent there to support the emerging NAVFAC. The planes were subchasers, but recent events in the USSR had decreased their workload. It seemed as if the Russians had lost the ability to maintain their fleet, much less send it out to play cat-and-mouse with the U.S. Navy. Argentia flights were only being activated about once every two months now. The Pentagon feeling was that the Soviet ballistic and attack sub fleet was in such poor shape that they weren't even a serious problem anymore.

"Well, that may change shortly." The admiral thanked him and then announced the next speaker. "Your turn, Bill. Give us a brief background on how the Soviets have traditionally sneaked up on us."

Bill Blast reluctantly stood. He hated giving briefings. "Yes sir. I'll try to keep it brief."

He pulled the world map down from its storage space above the white-board, grabbed a pointer and slapped it against the map. "At the top of the earth is a storm-swept region locked in ice. Defying scientists for years and taking many sailors to their deaths, this ice cap borders all northern continents. It has been kind to some, but particularly brutal to others.

"The Arctic is characterized by distinctive polar conditions of climate. Arctic comes from the Greek term arctos or bear after the northern constellation of the bear. It is sometimes used to designate the area within the Arctic Circle—mathematical line drawn at 66-30' N marking the southern limit where there is a period of 24 hours during which the sun does not rise or set.

"The definitive line does not exist, however the regions of north of the tree line includes Greenland, Spitsbergen, Scabbard and other polar islands; the northern parts of Siberia, Canada and Alaska; the coasts of Labrador; Iceland; and the small strip of Arctic coast of Europe.

"The formation is centered about four types of ancient crystalline rock. The four types of protection or hidden with a shield are: 1) Canadian Shield which covers all of Canada East to Baffin Bay to include Greenland; 2) Baltic Shield which is centered in Finland and includes Scandinavia and northwest Soviet Union; 3) Angora Shield which is located in central Siberia; and 4) The Aldan Block which is comprised of eastern Siberia.

"Approximately one million years ago, the climate of these regions began to emote or begin the Pleistocene ice age. In North America the main ice sheet of glaciation began on Baffin Island and swept west and south through Canada forming the Laurentides ice sheet covering the North America continent as far south as the Ohio and the Missouri river valley.

"The Atlantic Arctic island was covered with ice except Iceland, where mountain peaks projected through the ice. When the Pleistocene sheets of ice melted, the seas flooded most of the Arctic lowlands throughout the Arctic. The winter cold is so frigid the ground remains permanently frozen except for a shallow upper zone that thaws during the summer. This permafrost, or permanently frozen ground, covers nearly one-quarter of the Earth's surface.

"Although the Arctic is thought to be frozen or ice covered, less than two-fifths of its land surface in fact supports permanent ice. The climate has received a cold temperature, for example, Yukon, Alaska a low of -81F degrees, while Greenland has a -80F degrees winter temperature. Both localities experience a remarkable 50F degrees during August.

"The constant move to explore the Arctic began in the late 1890s. A Norwegian explorer made the first move. The first thing that he made note of was the constant movement of the Arctic ice in 1893. When the Norwegian explorer Fridtjof Hansen drove his vessel in the ice pack, the ship froze. Driven by currents and the wind the icebound ship Farm, drifted some 2,200 miles in three years.

"Taking a page from the Hansen, the USSR mounted in 1937 the first of the 31 drift stations—vanguard of a program that gained intelligence, scientific data and military research. Paramount, this first Soviet station brought American Robert Peary aboard at the North Pole. Another scientist was Ivan Popanin which spent 274 days on the ice which, by the way, drifted about 2,500 kilometers. This massive campaign caused the Soviets to build up a hundred polar stations, at least 10 or one dozen ships, and vast airborne surveys. Primary in cultivating a massive technological and strategic event, the Moskva laid the background as the Soviet icebreaker left in August of 1966. Numbing cold and ice was part of the job for the sailor of this ship, but the world was not ready for the results and data they brought back.

"This and other scientific voyages nailed the Arctic as a place to occupy in the cold war. With almost 3,000 miles of coastline on the Arctic Ocean, Murmansk is the base for Soviet submarines. With the Yankee Class submarine and more variations on the drawing board, this is the avenue to project nuclear war from under the polar ice. Immediately the plan was set, with close attention by the Soviet Navy regarding the icy water at their doorstep. Scientists from the Arctic and the Arctic/Antarctic Research Institute (AARI) in Leningrad promulgated a search from top to the bottom depths of the Arctic.

"That concludes my brief. Are there any questions?"

A hand was raised. "What were the Soviet oceanographers contributing to the undersea water under the ice as far as Soviet Yankee's experimenting their role as missile shooters?"

Captain Blast explained that the study of the ocean has contributed immensely towards the flow and maneuvering of the Arctic submarines.

The briefing continued for the next several hours. It covered many topics about arctic exploration and U.S. efforts to conquer the ice. Admiral Henry remembered most of the information from his own studies. He let the other officers around the table brief the rest. Each of them had their own area of expertise; but it was important that everyone had at least a working knowledge in order to piece together the whole picture.

The age of excitement and exploration of the northern ice cap was started in 1893. Norwegian Fridtjof Hansen took his research vessel, the Farm, and went to the Arctic to begin to uncover the maze of ice. Hansen took this ship and drove it into the ice pack and, of course, the ship froze into the ice cap. Driven by the ferocious winds, the ship became icebound and drifted for about 2,300 miles in three years.

Hansen's expedition took a lot of data, which was plotted and reviewed. Food came at a premium, but the bear and seal meat kept the voyagers happy. They used the sun and the stars for celestial fixes and charted out the massive breakup. During summer, the dissipation of ice was due to the many glaciers and mountains perturbed to a case of avalanche.

Russia had a meeting in Leningrad in 1936 where the discussion centered on the Arctic. The Arctic and Antarctic Research Institute (AARI) promoted a meeting of which the spokesman went to Moscow to appeal for money to conduct this program. Leningrad hosted many oceanography proponents, weather experts and ice data. Expertise was at a minimum, but they set aside a plan to check all avenues of data and even the metric dimensions of a cake of ice that the scientists would experiment on. The second day, numerous committees were formed with different expertise to develop standard procedures for each activity that [we] are undertaking. Data was copied and the entire committee reviewed/voted on the appropriate procedure. The president of the AARI traveled to Moscow to present his proposal. There was a great deal of debate over this resolution. Numerous times he spoke of the cap lying just north of the USSR. Finally, the Soviet Academy of Sciences recommended that the proposal be accepted. Apparently the president was overjoyed and he caught the next train to tell his colleagues the splendid news.

Taking a page out of Russia's docket, a surge towards the Arctic was unveiled in May of 1937. Near the North Pole, the SP-1 was launched as a drift station manned by a radio operator, a hydrologist, a magnetic expert and the group leader Ivan Papanin. Papanin was a round, jovial man who was noted by his former Soviet secret police job.

Each of the team was outfitted in fur and lived in a tent. Keeping the draft out was quite a task, but their tent was soon insulated with eiderdown (insulation of several northern sea ducks). The four men contributed to the effort each day as they reported to the tents and wooden sheds where they did their work. A cable was lowered which routinely measured the water depth. Sediments from the sea bottom were obtained where judicious work was spent to determine the plants and plankton that were uncovered. Water temperatures were taken at various levels, including logged gravitational and magnetic readings. Continuous weather information was recorded, including how deep the snow, and the four men once again analyzed the ice. Field notebooks were packed full of observations since the notes were kept twice during the day. Incidentally, these log books would be stored at the AARI where they would be kept available to the military or the civilian Soviet scientists.

During the summer and fall of 1937, the floe went south in a zigzag pattern. With fall coming, the arctic winds announced the prevailing winds, which the currents responded to with gusto. By

December, the ice land had entered the Fram Strait centered east of Greenland. Pelted by storms and tossed by ferocious icy sea-like waters, the team headed south. Finally, a Soviet icebreaker picked them up just in time with the four scientists standing in seawater up to their ankles. The rescue caused a national celebration for the heroic team. Moscow granted and the team was given an outstanding ticker tape display through the streets of their favorite city.

The Soviets continued to hit the Arctic. In April of 1955, they began rolling out bulldozers for the drift stations. Blasting apart massive rocks of ice was tried with explosives in 1961 and eventually each ice station was supplied with plenty of dynamite. Almost every station had a runway built as the first order of business. Next they set up quarters mounted on sledges for flexibility and mobility. At last they would set up their oceanography lab where the weather monitor was designed to transmit readings to the AARI facility.

The final probing of the ice showed that under the ice deep brine seeps down from the ice. A Russian oceanographer in the water below the ice found the brine seeping, but the surrounding seawater was cool and formed stalactites. This discovery was astounding. Another tidbit is that when the outside temperature begins to get warm, algae begins to form on the thinning ice as the sun makes a light-green substance on the ice bottom. This green-like coloration grows and its thickness is dependent on how many types of fish eat this food. At the beginning of August and September, this algae as the sun loses its light and is gone in another month.

The Soviet mounted and built 31 drift stations covering all of the Arctic cap and prevailed in the collected of data. Their devotion to completing and carrying out this frozen and endless task is a tribute to all oceanographers.

The Arctic is a complex, circular system, which is difficult to put your hands on. Starting from the zero-degree longitude until it goes over the Pole where it is eventually at the 180 degrees longitude, this line is known as the cross section, which is the Arctic Basin. From the chart or from the south, this line transverses the Norwegian Basin, between Norway and Greenland, passing to the left of Scabbard and the Arctic Ocean (obviously the Farm Basin). The North Pole is here and the final landmark of the polar region is the tip of Wrangle Island and the coast of Africa. To the left of the Arctic Ocean is the Canada Basin, which snuggled up to North America and the outskirts of Canada. The outline of the chart shows that numerous routes are open during the summer months. Most of

Russia has open seaports extending to the Bering Strait. In fact, Alaska has open ports beyond Barrow, Alaska, which can help the coastline cities get supplies during the summer.

Whoever offers up this beautiful chart certainly speaks of great deal of testing, experimenting and analyzing of the Arctic problem. In essence, the section shows an area of vertical mixing in the Greenland gyre where the warmer water is pulled down, cooled and it's forming a deep mass of ocean water. This mass has been known to the institution for some time, yet it has not caused any peroration or any discovery as of yet.

Many men suffered pain and anguish as they weathered the Arctic. The many explorations and adventures are outlined on the depicted chart. All of the tracks by the both the Soviets and the United States are noted. Clearly, the Soviets with their meticulous investigations sure overturned the United States. The Americans had two submarine intrusions of the North Pole and did a vulgar job of refuting the Soviet indelible feat.

Complete knowledge of the methods of warfare in the technologies that underline the methods is essential for military operations. Ignorance concerning a particular method of warfare is a threat in itself. However, one that even recognized this seldom insights alarm or corrective actions. This body of water is quite unique. There are many currents, which are milling around this part of the northeastern United States and extending up to Canada. The Bermuda Current, which starts below Florida, comes up heading northeast and eventually flows toward Iceland, but turns toward the northeast where it winds down the coast of England. The second current, which is more prevalent along the coast of Canada, is called the Labrador Current. The Labrador Current is coming down from the heavy polar ice pack and it is very frigid water along the surface. Normally, it usually goes down to about 55 feet and drops off in a negative fashion to freezing temperatures of 100 feet. Very dense water, it does not carry characteristics of sound as we know from previous experience. Oceanographers proved this and another case, which causes concern in detecting submarines, is where the Labrador Current brushes and intermingles with the Bermuda Current. The depths differ between the two zones and the Labrador Current tries to mix with Bermuda, but it leaves a more undesirable equation, open for any imagination.

The Gulf Stream current is strategically important, in that the Gulf Stream is only about 20 to 33 miles wide. In it the waters are warmer, the depths of the sound, pressure and velocity are greater. It is quite a body in which to obtain contact with a Russian or United States nuclear or conventional submarine.

Shallow estuaries of large river are among the world's most difficult physical environments, where only relatively small and highly maneuverable and properly ballasted submarines can survive. Considering the sea ice covers the northern marginal sea ice (MIZ), this literally presents the most challenging environment of all. The northern MIZ is simply the arctic and sub arctic waters, which are covered in the winter and partially covered in the summer. Incidentally, the sub-arctic MIZ zone is below the arctic zone (66 North-33 West).

There are many noteworthy marginal zones in the Northern Hemisphere. Three strategically MIZ estuaries are of particular interest to the United States: The Gulf of St. Lawrence, the Beaufort Sea Shallows and the Kara Sea lead to many unrecognized submarines in World War II.

In September 1939, the German blitzkrieg stormed into Poland, and in May 1940 the Germans moved into France again with fighters and Stuka dive bombers. This presented significant problems for both countries, Poland and France, when Germany came in hell bent for leather. This brings to mind a case in point, that the Arctic Ocean lies beneath it a great sea. But which country has complete totalitarian rule of this water? A serious threat bordering on MIZ areas is the threat from Soviet hand- or land-launched missiles. Thanks to merchant shipping and fishing fleets in the Gulf of St. Lawrence and Kara Sea, it's self-evident because the Prudhoe Bay production and pipeline are strategic components of U.S. strategic, logistic reserves.

The Germans fought a successful literal campaign in the Canadian territorial waters during World War II. Canada suffered severe losses and shipping in the Gulf was paralyzed due to closure of the Gulf to traffic and a routine expectation to ice during the season. Germans compounded the problem by threatening traffic during the ice-free shipping period as well. During May 2-6 in 1943, the Germans entered the Gulf through the Cabo Strait and transited under ice to gain an open water approach to North Point, Prince Edward Island. U-262 was to pick up escaped German prisoners of war but that attempt was of an earlier unsuccessful escape attempt. Also, an additional extraordinary, unopposed intrusion took place in April 1943 when U-H37 planted an unmanned, automatic weather station in northern Labrador. The station was not discovered until Germany recognized it in July 1981.

In terms of human strategy, the most serious loss occurred in October 1942. There were 137 deaths including women and children, but the memory was painful because it had no long-term effect on national defense. Almost 40 years ago in April 1942, the ambassador to Canada stated, "Canada cannot defend the St. Lawrence River." The lessons not learned during World War II are still with us today. We are faced with a big problem in Canada with limited resources and small population. However, it wants the world to know it won't neglect the challenge, but solve it.

Environmental conditions in the approaches to Cabo Strait and inside the Gulf of St. Lawrence are nightmarish with packed ice, icebergs, drifters, density layers, fogs and upward reflecting submerged objects which would make it impossible for ASW forces to attack and detect interlopers. Temperature, wind and currents influence ice conditions in the Gulf of St. Lawrence. Most of the ice leaves the Gulf from between Anticosti Island and Cabot Strait. This region may continue to be ice-covered until March or early April.

The Gulf of St. Lawrence is relatively deep, with a wide stretch of water up to a depth of 100 fathoms or deeper stretches from the mouth of the river south and out to the Cabot Strait. One observer more or less stated: In general, nuclear submarines may be expected to operate in waters over 100 fathoms.

Case in point, an enemy nuclear powered submarine could easily enter the Gulf of St. Lawrence in March, for example, and launch a land attack missile with characteristics similar to a Tomahawk missile. A launch site in Labrador would be easier and more secure. So, in other words, a submarine could attack any city as far south as New York or even Philadelphia.

Confused sonar conditions, other vital essentials and icebergs could allow retreat towards the east to Denmark Strait and therefore, provide sanctuary there. The second area we must address is the Beaufort Sea. Robert McCourthy served as an executive officer on the USS Burton Island from 1949 through 1951. He carried out the first pioneer surveillance in the Beaufort during the summers of 1950 and 1951. The Barrow Island Valley was discovered and a highly accurate contour map was produced. Prudhoe Bay oil operations dominate the Alaskan slope. When oil was discovered on the North Slope, Navy Petroleum Reserve Number Four became a strategic asset. The rivers around Prudhoe Bay fed fresh water into the southern Beaufort shallows with substantial affect in the summer. As noted earlier, an enemy sub could use the ice cover, in other words the low salt water plus the shallow water in this sanctuary, could lob cruise missiles into areas known as Prudhoe Bay.

During World War II, the German U-boats caused havoc, by which they upset the apple cart with respect to the northern sea route. Being a mild ice year, the Nazis sent out two U-boats and rounded the northern tip of Novaya Zemlya. The summer of 1943 found the submarines supported by an alternate base in Kikenes, Norway, which made them available for arctic deployment. Numerous battles were fought, namely in 1943. A four-boat wolf pack sank four merchantmen, including a small antisubmarine ship. In addition, they laid mines and intercepted radio traffic, attacked shipping and bombarded shore installations. The Nazis basically operated in open sea, but on occasion they made dives under the ice to escape the surface ship attacks.

Soviet presence consisting of strategic subs was evident near Kara East Novaya Zemlya Trough. By and large, this created concern to main intelligence experts during that time. Attrition of northern sea traffic between Novaya Zemlya and Vaygach Island would be a prime target in a war with the Russians.

Looking at the Arctic from the other side of the globe, or the Pacific, a transit is required under the ice canopy over the Bering-Chukchi Shelf with water less than 150 feet for almost a thousand miles. Immediately, the U.S. Navy commanders knew the maneuverability was questionable. Transits in very shallow water requires extreme determination, particularly when 25 feet has to be trusted beneath the keel or when 25 feet gives you clearances above, while avoiding an ice ridge. When things get tough, we rally for a position every two minutes.

In 1946 the U.S. submarines began their first trial in figuring out what to do in the Arctic scenario. Numerous submarines made a sortie along the ice sheds in Western Chukchic. One submarine attempted to move under the ice and the USS Sennett struggled with sea ice and icebergs. These trails were partially successful and, as a result, the Navy initiated from 1947 until almost 1964 operating in the same area. The area was augmented with numerous subs, U.S. and Canadian icebreakers, and aircraft, including the P2V. Many things were completed, such as war shot torpedo firing in the ice, surface attack and detection and extensive sonar/oceanographic measurements, in or out of ice. Basically, the options thought that the sub had it easy, while the others thought special weapons, subs and ships could be designed.

The positive side generated six positions:

1. The cardinal rule, this was the plan as noted in the open sea and, therefore, the best evasion is moving into the sea/ice canopy.

2. Positioning the submarine in the canopy yielded a superior combat position, particularly invulnerable and without parallel in open sea warfare.

3. Encounters incurred—often unexpectedly—that meant imaging—space sensing, in other words, we need every optical, etc. was used to provide accuracy for close range weapons.

4. Silent operation is paramount! Detection was keen, but it occurs when the men are permitted to move about the submarine.

5. Both the aircraft and the surface force have little ASW capability in the ice

6. Detained knowledge and understanding was essential in order to plan and deliver an attack. Basic symmetry, density of water, bio-acoustics, sound information and the lack of ambient noise.

The tactical superiority gained by positioning a sub in the ice is best illustrated by a frustrated skipper during the trials. "Surface! Surface! Surface! Break out the pistols and swords. We shall march across the ice and board the bloody ship." That rule must include an evasion that had been neglected in the evolution of subs in the Arctic. Proponents envision that these vessels must be designed to live and quietly move through this cold mass. Ice is something that the sub must use to its advantage. Unlike freshwater, the underside of ice is composed of crystals; brine cells are a low class variable layer. In summary, all that has been reported unknown, we must get cracking in order to control the Arctic Basin.

In 1953, the USS Redfish (SS 395) became an experimental submarine for the study of Arctic warfare. The vessel had received considerable damage from the two summers spent on the Beaufort Sea. Most notably, her torpedo tubes were out of alignment. The Bureau of Ships designed a particular hull modification that would permit collision against the underside of the ice canopy at the cost that you would not believe! But, however, the Redfish returned to the fleet readiness at a much greater cost.

Also in 1953, in conjunction with the Redfish proposal, the Arctic undertook a construction of a sea/ice lab to grow, and therefore, study its principles and properties. Five years later, the laboratory was completed and the USS Nautilus (SSN 571) had sailed into the ice during September 1957. Consequently, the lab was used to solve the snorkeling of the snorkel head values and the periscope windows, but additionally, to test the cold suits and the Arctic specialty sonars. The Nautilus was given sonar equipment to make the Arctic Ocean crossing in 1958. This was strange, but this was a technology throwback because Russia launched Sputnik the previous fall.

The Arctic exertion and surveillance went to the USS Skate (SSN 578) class by making improvements for this submarine to be designed for the open sea. A hardened sail, forward/scanning sonar, inertial navigation to avoid ice at transit depth, position sonars to measure both the deep and shallow topography, measure ice draft and to measure a rate of assent buoyancy control mechanism were added. She was assigned to develop a routine surfacing through the sea/ice in 1959. A routine surfacing was designed as a stationary vertical ascent at a specified rate of x-feet per minute that was to obliterate a vertical impact on ice. Submarines did not break through the ice; however later routine surfacing for the Sturgeon Class was similarly designated. The thickness of ice that a sub can break varies from 10 to 60 inches, depending upon the conditions such as lateral compression, temperature and the amount of brine content. If unable to break through, another area is tried to attempt another ascent. Non-vertical ascent can damage the torpedo tubes, the sail, the sail windows or bell, and thus, abort the surveillance. By 1959 the under-the-ice capability had been established and the Skate began exploring the Arctic Ocean. In 1963, undersea navigation ability was applied to the builders of the Sturgeon Class SSN. These submarines joined on a systematic exploration of the Arctic and other adjoining peripheral areas.

The exploratory operations averaged one per year extending between the Atlantic and Pacific fleets and usually occurred with joint operation with acoustic camps or icebreakers already positioned on ice. Rotations occurred all year, with moving sonar, navigation and the like. Open sea techniques, for example, towed arrays, were adapted to under ice-reconnaissance. Sonar systems were developed for mounting in the ice canopy, as were various types of under-ice sonobuoys and an under-ice bathythermograph. Extensive use of all sciences known to mankind was indeed a stark contrast to the paucity of data available to the submarines starting in the Pacific.

From 1946 through 1970, the submarine force bit off a large piece of ice. The combat part of the problem is the offensive play in the ice canopy to be ready to evade an attack. If he becomes the hunted, what must he do to evade, escape, or blend-in with the environment? So, in other words, the attack sub picks up the aggressor at long range. The friendly submarine realizes this only after a torpedo in the water has detected him. So, let's review the bidding. The (red) sub is not moving, yet the moving target—he is dead meat upon hearing the torpedo. Now old navy commander, which cluster of ice is hiding the red sub? Which crystal of ice is the bad guy firing from? In a nutshell, a stationary target (zero Doppler) voids many attributes that one may concern. The particular target losses the effectiveness of active sonar weapon, a passive sonar weapon, and must rely on warhead influence sensors which effect target localization, for example, ice, noise and acoustic countermeasures. Based on the blue sub, the only way he can counter is to launch a torpedo and ascend into the sea-ice canopy. This is the case that submarine's relish and he can approach his adversary and eventually localize the target.

"All right," Admiral Henry announced, concluding the briefings. "We're all on the same sheet of music. Where do we go from here? Suggestions?"

"Find out what's so important about the Iranian doctor, for one," suggested Commander Turner. "What's he really up to? What do the Russkies need to make this theory work, and how long will take once they've got it?"

Admiral Henry smiled as he stood up. "Looks like you're on the right track. I'm going to go give a heads up to the boss, just in case this turns into something unexpected. Carry on until I return."

The room snapped to attention as the admiral stepped through the door. He had a nagging feeling that there was more to this than met the eye. For one thing—although he couldn't admit it to the DIA liaison—he'd already known about the agent in Moscow.

Fifteen years ago, in coordination with the CIA and DIA, he had worked out of the U.S. Embassy in Moscow. Of course he knew all about the spy; he'd been the one who recruited her.

SILENT RUNNING

0800 hours Local, 15 November 1990,
Kremlin, Moscow, Russia (USSR)

"HE IS GOING TO DESTROY OUR NATION." Rear Admiral Klos Sloreigh nodded obediently to the speaker, mimicking the other men in the room. Sweaty hands grasped the folder in his lap. He had not anticipated that his working plan to obtain the magnetite would result in this meeting. It was one thing to discuss the plan with his immediate superior. Briefing Vladimir Kryuchkov, the chairman of the KGB, was something else.

"The Soviet Union falls apart around him, yet he does nothing!" Kryuchkov slammed his fist against the table in front of him. "Lithuania thumbs its nose at us and declares its independence. The republics watch to see how Gorbachev responds. Does he send in tanks like Czechoslovakia? Nyet, he allows it to continue!"

"Da, he has lost his way, Comrade Chairman." Another KGB superior voiced his opinion, ensuring it was what the chairman wanted to hear. Political correctness meant survival within the KGB. There was little dissent in that branch of government. Officials who were willing to execute Soviet people had no qualms about silencing their own members.

"We gave him power like Stalin controlled. The world began to fear the Soviet Union again, as did the people. And what does he do with it? Nothing!" Kryuchkov waved his hands in disgust. "The Five Hundred Days Plan. It would have given new resources to the people. At first he agrees to it, and now what? Where once he approved uskoreniye—acceleration—of the centralized economy to compete with the American market system, last month he rejects it. It is madness!"

"He listens too much to Yeltsin, Comrade," spoke another member of the secret group.

58

"Nyet," countered another voice. "Yeltsin is his millstone! We should silence the Russian president. He excites the people against the government with his talk of the new perestroika. It will destroy the Union, my comrades, mark my words. He would allow the republics to walk their own path just to save his Russia, dissolving the Soviet Union!"

Kryuchkov nodded. "This is the work of the American CIA, my friends. While the hand of their army grows in Saudi Arabia, their brain works mischief here. Saddam Hussein in Iraq buys us time. He will keep their forces occupied for several years. I cannot speak more of it now, but there are plans to restore the USSR under one firm hand. The days of Stalin will return. Then we will answer the attacks of the capitalist American government and its insidious Central Intelligence Agency."

Klos Sloreigh blinked. That was the only indication he gave that he realized what was happening. This was a carefully choreographed meeting. The KGB chairman's words were nothing more than a political speech that appealed to emotions.

Knowing it was a speech didn't remove the danger. What the chairman had already said amounted to treason. Anyone in the room who failed to appear as enthusiastic supporters would likely not survive the night.

It didn't matter to him, though. His own opinion was that Gorbachev courted the West too much, giving off an air of weakness. The Soviet Union was a superpower, not a beggar looking for handouts. Glasnost and perestroika were doomed to fail, and he knew it. Only strength would save the Union. The rebellion in Lithuania should be answered with tanks, not talk. After the entire Lithuanian government was liquidated, the other republics would understand. Their obedience was not negotiable.

"We have a new member today," Chairman Kryuchkov said, pulling Klos from his private thoughts. "He holds the answer to our last discussion. Comrades, listen closely to Admiral Klos Sloreigh. He will tell us how the Soviet Navy will take the advantage from the Americans. Admiral Sloreigh, begin."

Klos was surprised by the abrupt introduction. He had expected the rallying speech to continue for another half-hour. The fact that the chairman ended it meant that the only one in the room whose loyalty was suspect was his.

He stood and began handing copies of his brief to the 12 KGB officers in the room. "Thank you, Comrade Chairman. I have been tasked with discussing a new technique to make our submarines silent. There are risks, of which I will detail at length. Please interrupt if you have questions."

Klos stepped to the right side of the only desk in the office. He wasn't ignorant of the game of politics and power. Standing on the right shoulder of the KGB chairman was a calculated risk. It might prove to be the only thing guaranteeing his survival.

When the chairman did not object, Klos knew his first ploy had worked. He began speaking confidently, knowing that he had the attention of everyone in the room. Kryuchkov's silence was consent that the KGB chairman supported Sloreigh's proposal.

"In war," he began, "a submarine attacks from beneath the ocean surface. The nuclear submarine can afford to operate because they can stay under water for many months at a time. In essence, the nuclear submarine can actually produce oxygen that maintains their ability to live underwater.

"Energy is obtained from the nuclear power plant and steam generator. Uranium provides fuel to split atoms, releasing great amounts of energy. From the generator, the reactor pipes carry water that is kept at 320 degrees Celsius. This liquid is returned to the generator. It produces steam which spins large turbines, producing power to run the ship."

The abrupt sound of an uncomfortable cough warned Klos. He had to keep the attention of the KGB officers, yet most of them did not understand how a submarine worked. It was a delicate balance…teaching them the basics without boring them. "It is important to know this. Generating power at 12 knots creates noise. This noise is broadcasting through the water, making it easier for the underwater listening devices to pick up our nuclear submarines. The purpose of this brief is how to modify our conventional and nuclear submarines using a magnetohydrodynamic power generator to lower the decibel noise of the reactor. Our most brilliant Soviet scientists have developed this method. It requires a mineral called magnetite."

He quickly ran over the specificity of crystalline form, hardness and color of magnetite. Then he explained the physics, explaining that the ferrimagnet becomes para-magnetic when heated above 578° Celsius. He referred his audience to several diagrams in their briefing packets that showed the poles of magnetite and its similarity with electricity when it reacts to a coil of copper wire.

Klos could tell that the men hadn't grasped the importance of magnetite yet. He explained how magnetism played a vital part in the interaction of a flowing ionized fluid like water. Then he introduced Shazi's theory regarding the magnetohydrodynamic power generator and "silent running" venturi attachment that would quiet the submarine's revolving propellers. Then the rear admiral paused to see if he had their attention.

"Remarkable," muttered one KGB director as he flipped through the briefing pages.

"Da," spoke another, "this will place us ahead of the Americans. Our plan—"

"Isn't ready to be discussed today," interrupted Chairman Kryuchkov.

The meaning was subtle, but it wasn't lost on Klos. The chairman had just put the admiral's loyalty in question. He weighed his options, and then decided that it was best to wait for the next question. Attempting to swear his loyalty to the group would be taken as a lie. He didn't know what the group was about or what the "plan" was; to take a stand now would be foolhardy. The chairman would decide if he was worth including in the group. Until then, he would show discretion without false promises.

A man in the back row broke the silence. "Da, brilliant research. So the Navy has begun modifying our fleet, yes?"

"No." Klos smiled in an attempt to remove the frown off the man's face. This game was difficult; he was subordinate to every man here. They were all KGB directors or higher and none of them were accustomed to hearing that single word. "No, Comrade. We have a difficulty."

The officer's frown deepened. "And that difficulty would be what, admiral?"

That wasn't a good sign. It reminded the group that Klos was a Navy officer, and not true KGB. The verbal distinction meant that he might not survive this meeting after all. "We need magnetite, tovarisch."

"We have it here," argued the director.

"The field here in Moscow is unacceptable because it appears as a contact metamorphous product. This makes the ore content very small and contaminated with limestone and the leptites. The quality and grade required is insufficient." Klos shrugged apologetically and smiled again. "There is a field in northern Sweden as well. It has a beautiful ore body where volcanism injected the magnetite into the rocks. This would require laborious work digging the substance from the various feldspar rock that contains this mineral. The only choice left is Canada."

Klos shifted his gaze from the antagonistic director and turned his attention to the other men in the room. "Actually, the only choice is Canada. The quality of ore we require is very specific, and is found in only one place in the world: Labrador, or more specifically the island of Newfoundland, in Canada."

He stopped the briefing momentarily to hand out another set of briefing pages. "Labrador is to the northwest of the island of New-foundland. Labrador has about four or five sites. Two-thirds of the population of this province live in Wabash and Labrador City. The iron ore is located along the western edge of Labrador. It is esti-mated that there are more than 11 billion short tons."

Klos knew that he would likely lose some of his audience with the next portion of his briefing, but it was important. They had to understand all of the risks of his proposal. If the plan failed then he didn't want to be the scapegoat. He recited the information from memory.

Newfoundland is Canada's province thrusting from the Eastern portion of North America continent into the bleak North Atlantic Ocean. Position gives it strategic importance in transportation and in communications between America and Europe. The Strait of Belle Isle separates the island of Newfoundland to the south from the mainland Labrador, which constitute approximately three-quarters of provinces total area. These people incidentally refused to become Canadians until 1949. The Grand Banks, associated with the continental shelf off the coast, has offered extensive fishing in this geographic area. Clearly, this has lead to the most critical factor in establishing the history and character of this province.

Labrador is an immense peninsula in the northeastern part of Canada, between the Atlantic Ocean and Hudson Bay. Quebec, the western part, leaves the eastern coast that forms part of Newfound-land. Thus Labrador is really part of Newfoundland that is drained by the rivers flowing to the Atlantic Ocean.

Labrador is the furthest east of any North American island and is separated by the Strait of Belle Isle, which sets aside the island of Newfoundland. Labrador is a land of long, hard, arduous winters, and the interior brackets snow from September to June. The Labrador Current brushes the coast, but the harsh environment has abundant resources, including fish and plentiful iron ore. Most of the inhabitants rely on the supplies from Canada, but all food comes from game meat and fish. Rich deposits of iron make Labrador a vital contributor of the most important product.

The rough plateau is packed full of ancient rocks which cut rapid rivers draining to the ocean. Churchill River is the largest contributor of hydroelectric energy. Labrador has a terrific timber crop, black spruce, balsam fir and beautiful birch. Wild animals include the caribou, bear, minks and just about any fur bearing animals. Atlantic salmon, cod, herring, seals and trout are caught in coast waters. Ducks and geese are favorite birds, which inhabit Labrador each year. Temperatures fall below freezing almost every month of the year. Temperatures fall from -40F to -80F degrees in the summer. The northern coast has a severe winter, but so does the interior. In summer, arctic drifting ice chills the coast, while the interior remains warn. The coast is beset with storms especially during August and throughout the winter months. The storms are called gales.

The cities of Labrador are Labrador City, Happy Valley,Goose Bay and Wabush. Two-thirds of the population live in the mining towns of Wabush and Labrador. Goose Bay grew up as an army Base which was established in 1939. During World War II, the U.S. Army joined hands with Great Britain to prevent the German troops from using these coastal waters as a base. Eventually, the Air Force took over after the war and had a compliment of fighters and bombers located at this base.

The potential has yet been determined of the Churchill River as it was made into a hydroelectric plant. This facility is currently producing five and a half million kilowatts of electric power. It can substantially generate considerably more power if necessary. Most of the power is sold to Quebec at a low price and also to the American state of New York. Labrador has five highways and three airports. During the summer, the Canadian government maintains a steamer and mobilizes motorboat coastal service.

Newfoundland is a roughly triangular island with two large peninsulas hooking into the sea from the northwest and southeast corners. Part of the Appalachian geological province, the land runs from south to northeast. The land in the west of the island rises to a height of 2,600 feet to form a plateau that slopes to the northeast. The plateau region is gently undulating and marked with thousands of lakes and ponds. This provides numerous bays and offshore islands along the coast.

The climate here consists of weather that is 60 degrees in the summer and below zero degrees during the winter. Mid-Atlantic storms moving across Canada and up the Atlantic seaboard have a pronounced effect on the Newfoundland weather. Northeast and east winds, in advance of each storm, blow across the cold Labrador. This keeps summers cool and delays the coming of spring. Northwest winds carry cool arctic air that forces temperatures lower than normal. To the south of the island, the cool air of the Labrador current mixes with the warm air of the Gulf Stream which frequently creates dense fog, common over the Grand Banks.

Much of the land is covered by forests. The popular balsam fir and black spruce are predominate. The conifers are mixed with birches and a wide variety of hardwood shrubs. The best stands of hardwoods are in the mountain areas, which are well drained and lead to the areas where the trees are stunted. In some low-lying areas, bogs are up to 30 feet in depth. Moose, black bears, caribou, seals, birds-ducks, geese, falcon, osprey and bald eagle populate here.

The Avalon Peninsula is the most densely populated part of the island. The city of St. John's is the largest city, with Harbour Grace, Carbonar and Placentia pulling up the rear. Most of these are located on a safe harbor and have evolved haphazardly without any city planning. The houses are generally two-story construction with brightly painted windows to view their fishing boats. The houses are sheltered by small gardens and meadows. The homes are adjacent to the waterfront facilities, such as the stores, wharves and the fish drying platforms called "flakes." The abundance of homes and other facilities confuse tourists when they are looking for a street, square or a block. Only after 1950 was the "planned community" considered.

Argentia is 95 percent British origin consisting of English, Irish, Scottish and Welch. Native Indian and Eskimo people are few and far between. The people trace their origins to four Western communities of Devon, Dorset, Somerset and Cornwall. Incidentally, Roman Catholic is the predominate religion.

The economy is rich in minerals, forest and in marine resources. Historically, fishing has been strong ever since the colony was developed. Cod was the standby, but the fishing has virtually gone to industrial catch that takes the majority of the fisherman's time. Technical innovation has changed the fishing habitat. The salted, dried codfish prepared by the local fishermen was prepared by the many small family-run facilities. Large trawlers in offshore waters take the majority of today's catch. Additionally, the Canadian government extended its rights to 200 miles off the Newfoundland coast. In pursuit of minerals, the western Labrador's copper, lead and zinc have lead Newfoundlanders to travel back and forth between the island and the mainland.

Labrador's position, midway on the shipping lanes between America and Europe, is critical in planning the province's future. Attempts are being made to develop industries that require inexpensive electrical power and ease of open-ocean shipping.

The military use of Argentia continues as it maintains its 1940 lease with Great Britain that expires in 1999. In 1941, the Atlantic Charter was signed by both the United States and Britain aboard ships offshore. Argentia is located on the southwestern Newfoundland coast on Placentia Bay. It was quite busy during World War II, but the number of military elements has dropped since the VAW—Air Warning Squadrons—were disestablished. There are four or five P-3C planes detached here at the U.S. Naval Air Station in Argentia. This base contains numerous facilities. One of the innocent-looking buildings houses the main station for the US SOSUS net.

Clearly, the most valuable component of supporting the P-3Cs is a new operational Tactical Support Center in Argentia. This is a mini-Tactical Support Center, which was created by taking a variation of the CP-901 computer system and utilizing half of the computerized system. The tapes of the mission P-3 flights are taken to the minicomputer system for analysis. There has been limited activity there recently, but the U.S. still monitors all their submarine probes and Bear overflights from this location.

P3C deployments have maintained the flexible ocean coverage as well as the Ocean System Surveillance Center, which is located here in Argentia. The commanding officer of the Naval Facility heads the center and he has about 90 people, who carry out administrative, operational and maintenance responsibilities. The system has watch officers that coordinate the reading of Lofar grams that represents bearing of sound or noise in the water. Naval Facility Argentia has numerous cables that go out past the shallow water to the continental shelf. When they reach the continental slope, the hydrophones are positioned below the "fall off point" where they can hear sounds way out in the actual ocean. Many crews often debrief at their facility to get the exact signatures of ships. This can add another hour to the mission after landing and securing the aircraft.

There is quite a bit going on at the Naval Station Argentia. There are currently 7,000 U.S. Navy and Marine personnel at the base. The air side of this facility has two active runaways. The ground control radar is tops in the field. It is cold and quite breezy, but then too, it is below minimum standards of flight due to fog, snow and, of course, blowing snow. The radar allows the Navy aircraft to take off and land safely even in this harsh environment.

In addition to the P-3C complement of four aircraft, the Coast Guard has two or three C-130s and there are five station aircraft, which provide helicopter and station aircraft. They are used to carry supplies for the base every week. The strangest thing that might be seen is the MST ship that brings tons of logistic supplies to the base.

The Marines guard the base with sentries located at several entry points along the seven-foot wire barrier around the land area with triple-strand concertina wire on top. Incidentally, the naval facility is enclosed with a wire barrier with a gate of similar construction. To enter the base, each man or woman must have an identification pass containing the picture of the person and security classification.

Outside the base has grown a town called Placentia. The town was established to provide apartments for military personnel. The town supplies almost all of the military's housing needs except those that are provided by the base. The other necessary facilities are gas stations, grocery stores and the local liquor store. Bars and other businesses catering to male needs—prostitutes—added to the local economy. The local populace grew as industry moved near the American base and the traditional family fishing fleets increased.

"Thank you for the detailed background brief, Comrade Sloreigh," said Chairman Kryuchkov after the 43-minute brief. "You have been most informative."

He turned to the other members of the secret group. "I trust that you understand what this means, gentlemen."

"Da," replied the frowning director. "We cannot buy this material directly from the Canadians without the Americans wondering why we—or our third-party purchasing agent—want it. The material we need to rebuild the Empire can only be found on our enemy's doorstep."

"Union," corrected the KGB chairman. "Be cautious with your words, Sergei. Not all have sworn loyalty here."

"Pardon," replied the man. "I will take care of the error, if you wish."

"No, that is not necessary, tovarisch. I have heard good things of our comrade and wish to keep him with us awhile longer."

Klos Sloreigh released a slow breath of relief at the chairman's reply. For a moment, his life had been dangling by a thread. It both surprised and reassured him that the leader of the KGB had intervened in what was certainly a thinly veiled request to kill him.

"Yet you are correct, the mineral we need is in Canada," continued the chairman. "Comrade Sloreigh, how much of this magnetite do our brilliant scientists suggest we need?"

Although necessary to question the hated admiral, Klos had already asked the question of Vice Admiral Lawrence Latvia. He gave the same answer to the secret group. "Fifty tons, Comrade chairman. We will need 50 tons per attack submarine. Perhaps more for our missile submarines."

"Fifty tons." The brow of the frowning director, Sergei, furrowed even more. "It is impossible."

"Nyet," countered Klos, aware that he would only irritate his potential executioner even more. "My staff has prepared a plan to obtain the magnetite, 50 tons at a time."

Sergei's look promised dire consequences. "Explain."

"Our excellent Navy has—"

"No money or will to maintain the fleet," interrupted Sergei.

"—finished its modification to one of our Delta IV submarines," continued Klos. "It has completed trials off Korea last month. Using it, we can infiltrate Spetznaz onto any coast in the world. The diver excursion module is capable of holding 50 tons of raw mineral, if necessary."

"And how would you get it there, admiral?" scoffed the KGB director. "One shovelful at a time?"

"Sergei." The tone from Chairman Kryuchkov was not subtle. It promised painful retribution if his subordinate did not stop needling the thin admiral. "Let Klos continue without interruption."

"Yes, Comrade chairman," the man replied obediently. He understood how the game of power was played. For now at least, the chairman had chosen to protect the insolent Navy officer. Like the Russian winds, there was guarantee that the protection wouldn't change direction quickly. He could wait.

"No, Comrade," explained Klos. "We have several draft operations plans that cover many contingencies. The primary plan is to infiltrate Spetznaz into Argentia using a Bear aircraft that 'strays' into Canadian airspace. We have done it before and are assured of its success."

"Very good," stated another director. "You will have Spetznaz in Canada. Now what?"

"The Spetznaz will rendezvous with KGB agents who have ordered the ore and had it delivered to the base airport. The Spetznaz will take control of the three aircraft and fly them to Russia."

Kryuchkov shook his head. "That does not make sense, admiral. We have agents who can pilot the aircraft. Using Spetznaz risks revealing KGB and Navy involvement. It would be simpler to have our friends in Egypt just buy the material."

"I apologize, chairman. I have not explained well. If you would, please allow me to detail the difficulties."

Klos waited for the KGB head official to nod, then continued. "The American naval base has the only runway capable of handling cargo aircraft. The pilots must appear to be American naval officers or else the planes will never be allowed to leave. The Spetznaz are necessary because they have learned their adversary's military system. They are fluent in American English, they are trained as pilots, and they can disguise themselves as American Navy personnel."

"What about the SOSUS facility?" asked Sergei. "Disabling it at this time would be beneficial to our plans."

The room fell silent as the chairman and other directors faced the outspoken member of the group. Kryuchkov glared at the man, then surprisingly barked out in laughter. "Ah, Sergei, you are determined. Klos has heard enough from you to be a threat now. I have no choice but to trust him, or kill him."

Sloreigh could feel the weight of every eye on him. Seconds ticked by in silence as his fate waited for the chairman to speak. He stood at attention, preparing himself to hear the sentence with every ounce of honor in him. Let it never be said that he faced death and was afraid.

"I will trust him, for now." Kryuchkov's words were a stay of execution. "What we plan here will move like the cleansing north wind through Mother Russia, Klos. You have heard too much not to be part of it. Will you remain silent?"

The response was automatic and heartfelt. "Yes, Comrade chairman. You have my word of honor."

"Very good. Arrange with my assistant for a meeting next month. I will tell you everything then. But for now, include the destruction of the SOSUS facility in your planning. I trust that you can find a suitable reason for it?"

"Yes, Comrade." His mind grasped for anything that would justify attacking the SOSUS site. "Our backup plan is to use the Delta IV SSGN. We would need to disable the facility in order for the submarine to surface and transfer the ore. Otherwise the Americans would hear it when it neared the continental shelf."

"Very good. Comrades, do you have any other questions?"

Sergei spoke. "You know me, Vladimir. I trust no one, especially not the Navy. Before we approve this plan, I would like confirmation that this magnetite will do as the scientists promise."

Kryuchkov nodded. "That is a wise suggestion, Sergei. Move some of our agents to Argentia. Have them obtain a sample of this ore and submit it through our friends like Libya or Egypt to Comrade Sloreigh. If it proves acceptable then we will meet again to discuss the next phase."

The KGB director nodded in agreement. "It will be done, Comrade chairman. I know just the man for this task. Ironic, when one thinks about it."

Vladimir Kryuchkov shook his head, puzzled. "What is that, Comrade?"

"To obtain the mineral needed to destroy American power, we will use an American turncoat named after one of their presidents."

Klos wasn't certain he understood, but he laughed with the others. As the meeting broke up, he wondered what he had gotten involved in.

JOHN ADAMS HILTON

1345 hours Local, 7 December 1990,
Bangor, Maine (U.S.)

"EXCUSE ME, SIR. WOULD YOU PLEASE PUT your seat up and store the folding tray? We will be taking off shortly."

John Adams Hilton used his boyish charm on the slender flight attendant, but she was having none of it. Reluctantly, he complied with her instructions. The young shorthaired brunette thanked him and turned away. John smiled in appreciation as he watched her sashay down the aisle.

The flight from Bangor would be short, but he was determined to enjoy it. This was the first time he had ever left the United States. Granted, it was only a brief hop into Canada, but that didn't matter to him. His controller had assured him years ago that working for the KGB would let him see the world. He was glad that the promise was coming true.

The money wasn't bad. He considered it a retainer, really. The KGB deposited a monthly sum into a savings account held in his mother's name. Surprisingly, the FBI background check required for his top-secret security clearance had never discovered the account. It was probably because the account was out in the open instead of carefully disguised beneath multiple layers of subterfuge. John had come to the conclusion that the spy agencies had played the game for too long. They looked for what was hidden beneath the surface and were too quick to dismiss the obvious.

His mother used the account, of course. It didn't matter to him. In a twisted sort of logic, he felt that it was right for her to take advantage of the constant income. After all, if it hadn't been for her, then he wouldn't be working for the KGB.

He was thrown toward the seat in front of him as the plane lurched forward. Engines revved on the wing to his right, building up power. A sudden acceleration pushed him back against his chair and held him there as the plane clawed for the sky.

The stewardess returned shortly after that to ask if he wanted a drink. He took a moment, confident that she would understand the unspoken question, to run his eyes down her slender body. That was the first test. Next, he placed his right hand on her knee, just below the hem of her short skirt. Still no objection, so he slid a finger up the inside of her leg. Based on her warm smile, it was obvious what she wanted.

Women's reaction to his ruggedly handsome good looks failed to surprise him anymore. His broad shoulders and natural charisma let him approach the game of sex as a predator. Dating was for other men, not him. Life was too short. If the girls didn't want what he had to offer, that was their problem.

The flight attendant stepped closer to him and leaned down. His hand accidentally slipped further up her leg and his fingertips touched soft satin. A G-string, how novel. This one was going to be a wild ride.

She whispered seductively in his ear, "Back bathroom. Fifteen minutes?"

He nodded, smiling as he gave his drink order for the benefit of the other ignorant passengers around him. "Bacardi and Coke, please."

The woman jotted it down, winked and turned to the next first-class passenger across the aisle. John flipped open his newspaper and ignored her. There was nothing else to say, at least for the next 15 minutes. Then he would meet her in the bathroom, demonstrate why males were the dominant sex and both would leave having satisfied their animal desires.

That's all sex was to him; gratification from an animal mating ritual, nothing more. What women wanted afterwards was irrelevant to him. That was the only lesson and inheritance he had ever received from his father.

Mark Hilton, his father, was the senior captain on the Clarksville High School football team in 1963. The town of Clarksville, Virginia was predominately a small farming burg on the edge of the Virginia-North Carolina line. Its primary industry was tobacco farming. The second business in town is the lucrative furniture business, started back in the 1870s. Haleveton's Furniture was the largest furniture manufacturer in southern Virginia.

Mark, he was a mean young lad, six feet tall, 185 pounds and a star at every game in which he participated. He treated the girls properly—or at least that was how his son would've labeled it—by pleasuring any girl who asked. There was a brief interruption in this attitude, beginning on Halloween evening and the school's homecoming game. That was when Mark Hilton impregnated Ruby.

It wasn't his fault that the stupid girl was in love with him. She was just another tail, but her lie that that she was on the pill almost ruined the boy's future. Add the fact that her father was the local sheriff and there was only one conclusion. They were married. Nine months later, Ruby gave birth to John Adams Hilton.

John Adams was an eight-pound, two-ounce baby boy. Of course, Mark didn't know until he got home at 7:30 that night. He had been working at the local lumber plant all day, trying to earn money to support the leech who called herself his wife. Things had turned very sour in his life by this point. Instead of going to college as he'd planned, he was saddled with a wife and brat. It was more than a real man could stand, so he did the only thing he knew how to restore his pride.

He left his newborn son and Ruby and headed to the local bar. There he found a willing, yet older, redhead to satisfy his needs. He climbed out of the back seat of her car afterwards and went back into the bar. Two hours later, he was heading home with a brunette.

This continued for several months as Ruby recovered from the childbirth. When she was ready, he added servicing her to his schedule. It wasn't that he considered himself a bad man. Rather, he considered himself a real man. This time he wasn't foolish enough to trust her, though. He wore condoms every time he touched her. Getting trapped once was bad enough; he didn't need any more mouths eating away his paycheck.

John Adams spent time with his father. It didn't matter if it was fishing or at the bar, the young boy soon picked up his father's attitude. Of course, John never considered Ruby as a woman; she was his mother, after all, and so was excluded from the definition of "women." This allowed the boy to accept his father's perception without compromising the love for his mother.

The submerged anger in Mark finally exploded when John Adams turned 10. The man was arrested for drunk driving. A policeman came to the door, interrupting John's birthday party and said Mark could be picked up at the police station. Ruby and John Adams arrived to find Mark totally bombed. Smeared lipstick marred his collar, and his shirt reeked of cheap perfume. Ruby loyally paid his fine for drunk driving and helped him home.

When they arrived at the house, Ruby confronted Mark about his malicious cheating behavior. She called him a worthless whore-mongering drunk and told him to get some help.

John Adams watched, too terrified to move, as his father slammed his mother against the wall. There were punches and kicks until finally she fell to the floor and stopped moving. His father looked at him with murder in his eyes, and then shook his head. "Worthless punk, you're not worth it. Never will be, hear me? You'll never be worth nothing!"

With that, Mark Hilton grabbed the car keys and stormed from the house. He left skid marks in the driveway as he drove off into the night. Young John Adams Hilton threw himself on the unconscious body of his mother. The neighbors heard his heartbreaking wails and called the police.

Several months later, a judge at the Clarksville Municipal Courthouse granted the divorce. Mark had disappeared, even though Ruby had pressed no charges against him. It was 1973, and spouse abuse was still considered the "embarrassing family problem." The court system rarely involved itself with it unless the spouse pressed charges. Ruby was just glad that the man who had ruined her college future and life was gone.

She needed to get away from Clarksville and find a new job. An uncle and his wife lived in Colonial Heights, Virginia; she wrote him and told him of her predicament. The next week, she heard from her uncle. He told her she had a job if she wanted it.

Philip Morris was hiring workers. Uncle Phil knew the hiring director there and had arranged an interview. It was a formality; the job was hers. Ruby and John Adams stayed with her uncle that night and then headed back to Clarksville.

That's when they discovered that the only home John Adams had ever known had been destroyed. Her father—still the sheriff—was waiting beside the ashes for his daughter's return. This time he refused to let it pass. They both knew who had set the fire. Unlike domestic violence, arson was something the sheriff could act on without the victim pressing charges. He obtained a warrant for Mark Hilton's arrest. Two days later, the man was in custody. A jury found him guilty of felony arson and sentenced him to 15 years in prison. The sentencing hearing was the last time that John Adams ever saw his father. Six months into serving his term, Mark was killed after a shower rape turned sour.

The job at Phillip Morris provided Ruby and John Adams with security and stability. After six years of working there, Ruby accepted the proposal of Pete Fletcher. The man had been a chief petty officer on the battleship USS Missouri; on retiring from the Navy at the age of 38, he found a management position at the tobacco giant's headquarters.

Even John Adams liked Pete; they shared a love for baseball. About six months later, Ruby and Pete were married in Colonial Heights Methodist Church. Many friends from work came to see them tie the knot, including Pete's parents and even Ruby's mother. The couple had done some shopping for a home and finally selected a modern three-bedroom house.

John Adams was 16. He discovered that his father had been correct about women; they came to him willingly and left wanting more than he wanted to offer. There was only one thing on his mind during this period: He wanted to excel at baseball. He maintained a .350 batting average. Even college scouts were looking at the varsity-letter sophomore.

Baseball occupied his summers, leaving him time to devote toward schoolwork in the off-season. By the end of his senior year, he held a 3.2 grade point average. His score on the Standardized Aptitude Test was 1,200 points. Colleges wanted him and offered significant scholarship packages. After many trips and tours, he finally decided the University of Virginia was for him. He left high school in the top 5 percent of his class. During his last season, the high school baseball team won state honors.

Ruby and Pete drove John Adams to the university in Charlottesville early in September. He checked in at Dabney Hall and met his fellow students. John had chosen engineering as his field of study. School was a bit of a snap from his prospective. He loved calculus, engineering, drafting and other aspects—the choice of girls—found at the college. He considered joining a fraternity but wondered at their values. It seemed like the frat guys needed to get their conquests drunk before bedding them; it seemed a waste of alcohol to John Adams.

The first year in mechanical engineering, he took basic math, English, chemistry and elective courses to round out his curriculum. John Adams liked football and attended all the home games. He and four of his friends discovered Virginia Gentleman was the bourbon of choice. Along with most of his fellow students, he and his friends drank at football games. Occasionally they were invited to fraternity parties where alcohol flowed freely. John was approached several times about joining a fraternity, but decided against it.

He met several girls, but they all seemed focused on getting serious. He took a girl he'd known from high school to the big football weekend in Charlottesville. Bedding her ended up a mistake, as she began pushing him for a "serious relationship" afterwards. Two months later, after he got tired of her constant pleading for a commitment, she announced that she was pregnant.

That was her last mistake. John threw a hundred dollars for an abortion at her and said it was the only money she'd ever see from him. He stormed out of her apartment and never saw her again. According to one of his friends, she must've had a miscarriage on that very day. She spent the night in the guy's bed and, after six months with her, he still hadn't seen any indication of pregnancy.

John Adams took two vows after that. The first was to never sleep with a woman without protection. The second was to never trust a woman again. They were too unpredictable and dangerous.

Baseball continued to be John's real passion. He started his college baseball career as backup for the shortstop, and then took over the position halfway into the season. He finished the season with a batting average of .302 and won a letter. He retained his scholarship with a 3.1 average his first year and was invited to play on a league in Petersburg. The league consisted of players from Fort Lee, the nearby army base. At the final game of the season, the commanding officer from Fort Lee presented him with the Most Valuable Player trophy.

The next two years went by quickly. John made his way through differential equations, vector analysis, statistics and dynamics and a host of other subjects requiring many late nights studying. Finally, in 1985, John began his fourth and final year. Among his challenging final courses were hydraulics —commonly called fluid mechanics—and thermodynamics. He also began thinking of the job market. Several interviews were arranged, but two were most appealing: Newport News Shipbuilding and the Navy base at Norfolk, Virginia. After consulting with his mother and stepfather, he chose the Newport News Shipbuilding and was scheduled to report immediately after graduation.

During February of his final year at the university, he started practicing for his final season of baseball. The team went south to play several games. The schedule included Florida State and Miami with their last game at South Carolina University.

The pitcher for South Carolina was excellent and the game was very close. In the top of the seventh inning, the Virginia team started off with a walk and then got a single that sent the runners to third and first base. Luckily, John Adams took a walk and suddenly the bases were loaded. The next batter hit a high foul ball to the right of third base for an out. The next batter hit a sharp grounder to shortstop. John took the opportunity and ran to second base, sliding the last few feet. The second baseman got the baseball from the shortstop and collided with John at second base. It didn't matter that he was safe; John was out of the game with a broken leg.

John had a tough time getting around the campus, but managed. Two months after his injury, the cast came off and he began to receive physical therapy. The therapy consisted of exercises followed by whirlpool treatments each day. He still had to use crutches and wear a brace to support his weak calf muscles. By graduation, he was able to walk normally. The Newport News Shipbuilding Company waited for him. John Adams Hilton accepted the job offer and headed to the coastal city.

The Newport News Shipbuilding Company was the premier shipbuilding company in the United States, with nearly 15,000 employees. It was the leader in design and construction of nuclear powered carriers and submarines for the U.S. Navy. Although a producer of other commercial ships worldwide, their Navy contracts keynoted the progress of this little known shipbuilding establishment. Its 550-acre facility included two miles of waterfront along the James River and space for at least eight dry docks with four outfitting piers. This didn't include machine and test shops, apprentice and welding shops and the foundry complex.

John Hilton met the vice president, who thought he was a baseball star. Mr. Green assigned him to the nuclear carrier community and introduced him to his manager, Mr. Skeleton. After John filled out the myriad of paperwork to get a background check, the Federal Bureau of Investigation took the form and interviewed the five or so people he had recommended. After signing an agreement, pictures were taken, fingerprints were made and then John Adams had a classified "top secret" security clearance.

The first thing that was done was to acquaint him with the nuclear power plant. The company sent him to the power plant facility in Idaho where all the Navy people orient themselves with nuclear energy. John was amazed at the structure and how each system performed within the complex.

After three months of testing, moving from different positions around the lab and finally understanding the apparatus, he returned to Newport News. His supervisor assigned him to the advanced ship design team.

Many Navy ships were in a state of flux as they replaced old technology with the latest equipment. Each carrier required the installation of a new sensor system. The newest carrier was already slotted for a systems upgrade with a new variation of the catapult. John Adams wondered whether the civilian contractors had included rapid system obsolescence in their plans or if the technology was simply growing faster than the ability to install it. After he tossed aside his Atari game system for the latest video game, he knew the answer. The fields of computer technology and electronics had simply hit the next evolutionary level.

John Adams reported to the advanced design section of the plant. He showed the guard his plastic identification card and waited. The guard went to the Rolodex and pulled out another card, then assigned the badge number to him.

"You have to wear this at all times where security can see it," explained the guard as John Adams signed for it.

"Got it," he replied, placing the thin metal chain around his neck. The card dangled in the center of his chest.

The guard smiled and pressed a button, releasing the electronic lock on the door. John walked into the secure area, uncertain what was expected of him. He stepped down the long hall until he came to a bulletproof glass window. Behind it sat a secretary who glanced at his badge before greeting him. He introduced himself and was directed to continue down the hall to the third office on the left. There he had to insert the card into a slot. He felt like a fool, bending over to run the card through the electronic reader.

The office was comfortably furnished, yet there was nobody there. John Adams saw his nameplate on a desk and walked over to examine it. A note waited on his desk from his co-worker, Richard. The scribbled note said that Richard was in a meeting for the next two hours and suggested that John Adams should peruse the diagrams on the chart table next to his desk.

The massive table bore a stack of drawings and diagrams designated CVN John F. Kennedy. John Adams flipped through the pages, pausing to look at the power plant for the boat. On page three of the drawings was a sketch of the power plant showing different positions in the bottom of the carrier's afterdeck. He surmised that the vessel was to undergo reevaluation to see if improvements could be made. John studied the connections of all power sources including the steam system that drives turbine, converting mechanical energy into electricity.

Richard Palermo walked in at 11:45 with a mass of charts and welcomed John to his office. He had been to a briefing that had dragged on. John introduced himself and gave his background, including the course at Idaho. After the normal introductions and chitchat, they got down to work.

The reason for the charts on the table soon became apparent. The Navy was unhappy with the way the reactor was placed. They wanted more room for another sensitive device. Richard brought him up to speed on what had already been completed with the research. Then the two men devised a plan and schedule to share the workload.

At the end of the day, Richard showed John Adams the room's safe. He demonstrated how to open it, and then gave John the combination. The charts and carrier documents went into the safe as the senior man explained the security measures. Everything had to be locked up when they left the office including scrap paper, which had to be stored in its own paper bag. "Be secure," said Richard as he locked up the secret container.

The two individuals worked separately over the next few days. Each factor had to be considered. John Adams worked on the fluid mechanics of the system. He had to plan out factors pertaining to the speed of the carrier underway, its ability to sustain velocity, maintaining the coolant compounds to ensure good heat-transfer properties; all the while keeping low neutron-absorbing qualities for safety.

At the end of the week, John and Richard held a symposium for the Navy officials to present their conclusions. Richard began the proceeding by stating emphatically that the power plant couldn't be moved. He proceeded to point out that the measurements were taken in regard to the high-pressure steam and its resulting effect on thermal energy heating water. In conclusion, he was against moving the reactor.

John was flattened by the conclusion. It wasn't what they had discussed at all. What was going on? They had agreed that there really wasn't an issue to move the reactor. What had changed?

As he approached the podium, John Adams felt like he'd been left to dangle in the wind. His entire presentation was based on proving that the Navy could get what it wanted. If he gave it now, either he or Richard Palermo was going to look like an idiot. He glanced at his partner, who simply nodded encouragement.

He painfully began his portion of the briefing, uncertain how to proceed. Richard finally stood up and apologized for him, explaining that John Adams was a brilliant new employee and this was his first briefing. Then he looked directly at John Adams and said, "Don't worry about it, John. Just give your conclusion."

Hilton nodded, relieved that his new partner wouldn't feel betrayed by the conflicting briefings. He gave his presentation, jumping through slides showing sketches and equations. A chart showed the present position of the structure. Then he showed test results of the inputs and outputs of each avenue of production. The by-products involved energy in which billions of nuclei may fission within a small fraction of a second. The thermodynamics put the exact same picture with a different perspective. Finally, John launched into an explanation using advanced mathematics to show that where the Navy desired the nuclear system was perfectly feasible.

The representative from the Pentagon, a Navy commander, beamed at John Hilton. He asked several fluid/hydraulics questions; John immediately went to the overhead projector and scribbled the answering equations. The commander nodded in agreement, satisfied. He requested a hardcopy of the presentation so that he could brief the Secretary of the Navy on the modifications. Then the briefing ended.

Richard Palermo gave a cryptic response when John Adams asked him about the conflicting presentation. "I'm just tired of the game, that's all. Now they'll have a new wonder child to play with. Just not me, not anymore."

The corporate response to Richard's embarrassing and erroneous speech was immediate. He cleaned out his desk that afternoon. Three weeks later, John Adams caught the man's name in a newspaper article. The brilliant scientist, well known for his 17 years developing nuclear reactors for the Department of Defense, had died in an automobile accident.

Newport News Shipbuilding had found a sparkling diamond in John Adams Hilton. He distinguished himself with several major distinctions over a five-week period. The projects resulted in modifications to Navy contracts that meant more funding for the company. Then the bonuses for his work started coming in.

He had quite a time in the Newport News area. He met a girl who he became acquainted with at the bar. They went out for a while but she wanted to get married and he wanted to play around some more. After hours, he signed up for a baseball club. He made shortstop and played quite well for the team. Even though he played with a semi-brace on his right leg, he batted .304 for the season.

Over the next few months, he developed friendships with numerous people at Newport News Shipbuilding. He learned that he could call them at any time for consultations about their area of expertise. One encounter that he had was with Rich Lansing, who came by John's office and introduced himself.

Rich was assigned to the nuclear submarine advanced facility, which is another building on the premises. He asked whether John had heard anything new in college about mediums with low neutron absorption properties. They discussed theoretical solutions for awhile. Then Rich asked if Hilton had ever been to Brandon's, a local bar. It didn't take long before the two bachelors had settled on an appointment at the bar to "sample the local female cuisine."

They met on Friday after work for a beer. Rich had received his bachelor's degree at Virginia Tech and was specializing in structural stress, which was a topic of discussion. Rich spent some time discussing this, however he was most anxious to hear about John's work. After his attempts to remind Rich about discussing classified information in public were brushed aside, John Adams began to discuss his current project. He managed to answer the coworker's questions without giving any specifics of his work. Rich understood and ordered two more drafts. The conversation entered into the neutral topic of sports, then women. Both managed to find a companion before closing time and each went their own way.

The following Wednesday morning, the phone rang in John's office. It was Rich wanting to know if he was available for lunch. Hilton accepted, agreeing to meet with his coworker at 12:15. The weather was nice so they walked until they found a vendor selling hot dogs. Rich had been working on a stress problem concerning nuclear submarine noise. He was worried that the incident could get him fired if the matter was not appropriately repaired. John laughed and said that hydraulic stress, increasing pressure with increasing depth, or whatever the core problem was couldn't be solved in 20 minutes. Both agreed that each would review the problem and then get together to discuss it after hours. Hilton reminded the man that there was only one place they could talk openly about classified subjects. Rich agreed, asking John to meet him at his office at five.

After waiting at the guard desk, Rich came out of the corridor and gave John a smile. He apologized for being five minutes late. John signed in on the master log and went with his friend to the office. The room was spacious and had several tables with diagrams spread helter-skelter about the mess. Rich explained the drawings and annotations for the nuclear power plant and its adjacent primary pump. The chart was the latest design for the next boat.

They spent several hours defining the problem. Then Rich apologized and said that he had to leave; a young lady was waiting on him and he didn't want to lose her. He suggested that John Adams take the chart home to review. Nobody else worked in the office, Rich was the security officer for the room and it would be okay to take it.

That night after supper, John studied the chart. He worked into the early morning hours, scribbling notes and formulas on paper. When dawn finally rose, he had come to a definite conclusion: God only knew what made a U.S. submarine quiet, but the device Rich was concerned about would make no difference whatsoever.

The next morning, Rich called John about the problem. He didn't believe the results and asked to meet that afternoon to discuss it. The aircraft carrier reactor project had encountered another problem, this time with the heating system. John suggested they meet again after hours, this time at his office.

Rich arrived at four o'clock. John walked out to escort him past the door guard. They came into his office where he cautiously closed the door. John opened the discussion by saying that the noise prevention was preposterous. Rich demanded to see the specific data. Hilton showed the mathematics and notes he had worked on all night and then reworked his flow patterns involving sound propagation. Finally, he addressed decreased depth as the pressure increased on the outer walls of the submarine.

His new friend was impressed. "Well, I guess you provided the answer to a very important problem."

In payment for solving his problem, Rich took John Adams out on the town that Friday night. They started the night's festivities at a party where they picked up two girls, then headed off to a local all-night restaurant for breakfast. The night ended at Rich's apartment. Soon the carpet was turned back, the sofas moved and the stereo turned on to provide dancing music. After an hour of dim lighting and heavy foreplay, the two couples slowly drifted toward separate bedrooms.

The next morning, John awoke to the wind blowing a gale from the northeast. The girl from the previous night, Anne, was naked beside him so he covered her with a blanket. He staggered from the bed in search of something for his hangover. He didn't know why, but he could not remember whether he'd had sex with her.

The sound of breakfast cooking came from the kitchen. Rich was the chef with his date setting the table. Suddenly his girl walked past him in the hallway to go help the others. The breakfast was superb. They started with mimosas—champagne and orange juice—followed by eggs Benedict and Bloody Marys.

The girls then started washing the dishes as John and Rich sat at the table. The two women spoke softly in the background in a foreign language. John wasn't sure, but he thought it was Russian.

"John, we have to talk," Rich said from across the table.

"About what?"

"It seems that you've been selling secrets to the Soviets."

Hilton stared incredulously at the man sitting casually in front of him. "You're joking, right?"

Rich flipped a manila envelope on the table. With disbelieving eyes, the young John Adams Hilton read through the contents. They were photocopies of his notes on the submarine noise problem.

"I can't believe this." Hilton threw the envelope back at the man. "So you made copies of my notes, big deal. Doesn't mean I've sold out anything."

"But it does, my friend. You'd better listen to this." Rich pressed the play button on a small recorder. The room was filled with John's voice as he arrogantly detailed his conclusion about the submarine noise. It was a duplicate of the earlier conversation in his office, with one exception. Instead of Rich's voice, a deep male voice with a thick Russian accent asked all of the questions.

"You've sold away America's latest technology, John. Well, that isn't quite true, is it?" Rich flipped another envelope across the table. Its contents spilled on the smooth wooden surface. At a glance, there was at least $10,000 there. "Now it's true."

Hilton stared at the money in disbelief. When he raised his head a few minutes later, it was red with anger. "You set me up, you stupid son of a—"

The distinctive sound of a metal slide chambering a bullet came from behind him. John froze as he felt the barrel of an automatic pistol press against the back of his head.

"Let's not do anything hasty, my friend," said Rich. He leaned back in his chair and looked out the sliding glass door onto his balcony. The winter gale threw sheets of snow outside. There was just enough ice in the mix to make it sound like sand as it pelted the glass.

A clock ticked monotonously in the hallway. Several minutes passed before Rich spoke again. "Every person has their price, tovarisch. Yours was difficult to find, believe me. You don't care about women; you use them like whores and never go back to the same one once you've had her. Money doesn't motivate you, nor does power. We know these things about you. You see, people talk when they're shown an FBI badge."

John refused to say anything. The pistol barrel against his head hadn't moved, either. He wasn't sure if that was a good or bad thing.

"No, comrade, your price is someone very close to you. Natalya, would you bring the television and tape in here please?"

The girl he had known as Anne walked past him and into the living room. She returned with the portable television on a cart. The smile she gave him was as warm and inviting as when she'd turned it on him the previous night. It was all an act to her. From the warmth growing below his belt, John had to admit that she was very good at delivering her non-verbal seductive lines. She pushed a tape into the VCR, turned on the television and then hit the play button.

The screen showed a middle-aged woman bound to a chair. In front of her sat a man, also bound to a chair. John recognized Rich's voice in the background offering one last chance. "Will you assist us or not?"

"Never, you communist pig! I'll see you in hell first!" replied the man in the chair.

A sharp report exploded from the television speaker. John watched, horrified, as the front of the woman's head sprayed blood and brains across the room. "No, fool, that's not the way this works," the videotaped Rich was saying. "You see, first you see your mother in hell. Of course, that means one thing, doesn't it?"

Another gunshot sounded and the man in the chair jerked backwards. A thick rivulet of blood ran from the round hole in his forehead. Rich concluded his monologue by saying, "That means you'll have to join her there, doesn't it?"

Natalya clicked the power button on the television. The image disappeared, leaving John Adams Hilton to consider the blatant message. There truly was only one person in the world that he cared about, and that was his mother. Whether the incident on the tape was real or fake didn't matter...the threat was very obvious. If he didn't cooperate then his mom would pay the price first.

John Adams was a very logical and practical person. He slowly turned his head to look past the barrel of the pistol at the woman standing behind him. Then he smiled, looked back at Rich and leaned forward. "Eight grand a month."

It was Rich's turn to look puzzled. "What?"

"You're going to set up a retirement fund for my mother, Rich." John Adams began stuffing the cash back into the envelope. When he finished, he extended it toward his coworker. "She's going to win a prize or something, and the payoff is going to be eight grand a month for the rest of her life. You can do that, can't you?"

"Yes, but—"

"No buts." He tossed the envelope on the table in front of Rich. "You've seen the quality of my work, and you know that I'm going places at Newport News Shipbuilding. Since you've made my mother part of this deal, then you'll take care of her. In return, I will get you whatever you need on the latest American nuclear innovations."

"I will see what I can do," Rich began.

"Do it or shoot me now, comrade." John Adams raised his eyes toward Natalya. "While you're thinking about it, I'm going to be screwing your assistant. Come tell me what you've decided."

On the airplane flying from Bangor, Maine toward Canada, an older John Adams Hilton smiled at the memory. The past four years had been very good to him. His mother was ecstatic about winning a contest that she didn't even remember entering. He didn't care that she spent the money frivolously. It made her happy, and that's all he ever wanted. One day it would end—most likely in a scene similar to the videotape he had watched at Rich's apartment—but until then she was able to live her life without any worries.

As for Natalya, he tired of her company after three months. It didn't matter, though. Rich always found him a new companion whenever the old one became stale. All told, it was a good life.

He stood up and stepped into the aisle of the airplane. It was time to meet the young brunette for a quickie in the bathroom. Perhaps it was a sign of his paranoia, but he treated all women as if they were Natalya or one of her Soviet sisters. It was safer that way. No strings attached, and it gave Rich no new emotional attachment to threaten.

The latest assignment had him confused, though. Rich had informed him that he would be transferred as the head of engineering for the Argentia Naval Air Station in Newfoundland. Once there, a local KGB agent would provide his instructions.

It just seemed odd that the KGB was willing to take its most prized source from the US Navy's primary contractor and send him to Newfoundland. Whatever the mission was, it must be very important. He couldn't wait to find out what it was all about.

He tapped on the bathroom door. A sultry female voice answered, telling him to come in. With one hand unfastening his belt, he opened the door and stepped into her waiting arms.

WHISKEY CLASS

VICE ADMIRAL LAWRENCE LATVIA GAZED FROM HIS hotel window at the snow-laden city of Murmansk. It had been 48 years since he had first seen the city. It was alive now, bustling with shipping and industry.

In 1943, Murmansk had been a city under constant attack. The German Luftwaffe raided daily from their airfield only 35 miles away. There was little warning during the raids. The German planes evaded the primitive Russian radar by flying on the deck. They would pop up over the hills surrounding Murmansk and begin their bombing and strafing runs.

American and British cargo ships were the primary targets, along with the railway lines. The vessels carried materiel and supplies from the United States and Great Britain, part of a steady stream of assistance given by the American President Roosevelt and British Prime Minister Churchill. Without the aid, which began in August 1941, the Russian military and people would have been lost.

It typically took 10 days from Iceland to Murmansk. It was a nightmarish voyage. Over 21 percent of the cargo sent through the arctic waters was lost. The vessels had to survive aerial attacks from German planes based in Norway and Finland. Nazi warships plied the waters, hunting for the lucrative targets. U-boats sailed beneath the waters, typically only giving away its presence when the first torpedo exploded.

In addition, the merchantmen had to fight the bitter arctic weather. They sailed in a perpetual twilight, lit by a sun that never rose above the horizon. Gales, snow and ice raged from September to May with winds over 80 miles an hour.

The city itself had few anti-aircraft guns, but the Navy escort ships did. After surviving the nightmarish trek through arctic waters, the gunners were only too happy to aid the citizens of Murmansk by splashing a few Luftwaffe planes. Loud cheers would rise from the docks as the Russian citizens praised their American and British defenders.

The people of Murmansk showed their appreciation in many ways. Their hospitality was open as the citizens shared what meager food they had with the Allied sailors. Clubs were opened near the docks. They served the traditional Russian vodka, but the seamen didn't care. The Yanks were especially appreciative of the beautiful Murmansk women who joined them dancing at the bar.

Admiral Latvia grasped the icy railing of the balcony and smiled. It was a bittersweet smile full of joyous memories and tragic loss. He owed much to the Americans. With their warships, they had protected the most precious thing in his life.

He had met Tosarina in this very hotel. It was in September 1943. The NKVD officer who took him from his battalion passed him through the NKVD network. All the secret police were closemouthed about who had summoned him. Their answer was typically, "A mutual friend."

It had been Tosarina. The timing proved miraculous; Lawrence later discovered that his entire battalion had been killed in the second battle to defend Stalingrad. Tosarina presented Lawrence's letters on submarine design to the Navy admiral in charge of her division. The officer was impressed with the brilliant analysis and demanded that the Army officer be transferred to him immediately.

There is always rivalry between branches. The Russian Army commander refused to grant the Navy's request; he felt that Lawrence would better serve Mother Russia on the battlefield. "Men are dying, Comrade," he declared to the Navy admiral. "This man is one we need. He fights!"

The German U-boats were demonstrating a new method of warfare against the Allied convoys heading toward Murmansk. The Russian Navy knew the Nazi boats were the best in the world. In contrast, the Russian submarines were useless. During the initial Baltic campaign, they had performed poorly against their Finnish and German counterparts. The Navy needed a new submarine, yet none within the newly formed Bureau of Ship Design Submarines could think past the current system.

The division director needed someone new, a man able to think outside of the box. He needed Lawrence Latvia. Transferring the soldier between the two military services was impossible. That was when Tosarina provided a solution.

The NKVD operated in every region of Russia. They maintained political discipline within the military and the people. If a NKVD officer accused a soldier of treason, there was no trial. The man was simply taken out and shot. Even the highest-ranking military officer dared not refuse the order of an NKVD agent for fear of his own life.

Tosarina submitted the request through her region director, who approved it. The political officer looked at the three-page document with its explanation for the transfer, then at Tosarina. With a laugh, he tossed the pages into the trash. He spoke like the teacher he had once been when he said, "Remember this: We are NKVD. We do not ever explain ourselves. The skills of Junior Lieutenant Latvia are needed elsewhere. That is sufficient. Anyone who questions this will be eliminated."

That decision resulted in the reunion between Lawrence and his love. She met him only hours after his arrival in Murmansk. He was overjoyed to see her, and very surprised to see the young boy at her side.

"And who is this little one?" he asked, kneeling in front of the child. Lawrence feared the worst. The war had been long. For all she knew, he had been killed in the first battles. He would not hold it against her if she had found comfort with another.

"Lawrence," the boy responded. He looked up at his mother, confused.

Tosarina smiled proudly. "Little Lawrence, this is your father. He has come home to us from the war."

The child looked at the older man in amazement. "You have killed many Germans, yes?"

"Many," laughed Lawrence as he swept the child into his arms.

They talked of many things, including the childbirth. Tosarina told him that a month after Lawrence left, she knew she was pregnant. At first the regional NKVD director refused to accept her for training. That changed after the Germans invaded. The older woman knew that this young girl would be very protective of her son, and training her to protect Mother Russia would be easier. The director's faith was well rewarded. Of all the trainees in that class, Tosarina's performance stood above the rest. The young woman was rewarded with the dangerous position working with the secret Navy design bureau. Monitoring political correctness among the intelligentsia was always difficult. Sometimes brilliant minds spoke in ignorant words that would require executing anyone else. Tosarina was proud of the fact that she could educate them. She had only needed to kill two of them so far. Afterwards she had calmly washed her hands while listening to advice from her superior on how to hold the weapon to prevent back-splatter of blood.

The day of the reunion had been wonderful. Lawrence left the hotel and carried his things to his new home; the apartment that Tosarina rated because of her position. He helped prepare the dinner of goulash. Rations were limited so it wasn't much. The highlight of the dinner was the meat for the goulash; the tiny chunks were surrounded by assorted vegetables and sprinkled with paprika and other spices. Little Lawrence sliced the loaf of bread and then the family sat down for its first meal.

After dinner they went to meet Tosarina's supervisor. The older woman was very practical, suggesting that the couple should take a week from work in order to get married. Friends and coworkers joined them the next day for the wedding. The NKVD Director showed compassion—or perhaps it was a reward for Tosarina's service—by giving them directions to a nearby lake cottage for the honeymoon. The older woman even volunteered to care for little Lawrence.

He and his bride headed for the lake cottage. The lake and surrounding trees were crusted with ice. The log cabin was homey, but it needed a good hot fire in the fireplace. The cabin was furnished and cabinets held dishes, pots and pans. The toilet was a wooden shed outhouse.

Lawrence rented fishing poles, fully expecting that they would have to catch their dinner. They walked around the lake and talked with fishermen on the ice. The brass NKVD pin on Tosarina's coat label helped them gain fish at a reasonable price for their dinner. It was reasonable in that Lawrence refused to take their catch for free; he paid the fishermen. That night, after a dinner of boiling potatoes and lobster-like fish, the young couple opened a jar of caviar—another wedding gift—and toasted with vodka and crackers. Warm lovemaking topped their evening.

After a week of fishing, eating and loving, it was time to return to Murmansk. It was the only vacation the couple took during the war. Lawrence was immediately immersed in the theoretical details for designing the next generation of submarine. One of his fellow workers made the mistake of thinking Tosarina would be more tolerant of political indiscretions. That time she didn't need to wipe her hands afterwards.

The war ended on May 7, 1945. Lawrence received leave to visit his mother in Leningrad. His mother called to him and quickly he recognized another figure standing beside her. Alexei came before him as a brother, an outstanding tank officer who had baffled the opponents' tanks, which saw the bitter end of the German-Stalinistic battle. Lawrence grabbed his brother's body and cried because he had known of Red Motherland they or he represented. His uniform told of his heroism that spread over four years. Now came the question: What now? Do you favor the military because there is not other ways to succeed? Alexei did not know how to respond to the question. He, without any reason, began to cry of his horrors of World War II. Lawrence responded by the cheers of the people who have professed that our men were caring for the blood of the Soviet society. Surely this meant a lot to all that worshipped and made acclaim to the Motherland. In essence, what had the forces of the Red Army proclaimed during the last five years. It was not due to Alexei or Lawrence, but to the effort of the generals on down to each man who fought and yet declares that their victory was won, not sacrificed with their blood that they had spilled.

He learned that his other brothers, Ilya and Marshal, had died in battle during the Moscow siege. His sisters had escaped Leningrad and were now happily married. Obliska told him that the Germans had murdered his father. Alexei and Lawrence mourned the destruction of their family.

That night, Lawrence lay awake and thought about his problems during the war. He wanted to travel and to gain elevated exuberance such that rank would come at an accelerating timescale. With his leave almost over, Lawrence made plans to go to Moscow and enter the military academy. He informed Tosarina of his decision when he returned to Murmansk, and she approved. Her duties kept her watching over the submarine design bureau. Although they would be parted for a long time, they both knew that it would be different for them. There was no war anymore. Lawrence could come home on every school break and vacation.

The train left Murmansk with both Tosarina and his son crying. He felt bad about this, but it was the right thing to do. He arrived in the terminal where most of the ruins had been moved and the thought of blooming flowers graced the air. The bus, which met the many participants, drove to the military building that a guard facility was located. Lawrence had a duffel bag, which he eventually hoisted over his left shoulder. The guard inspected his credentials, and directed him to the officers' quarters. He checked in, found his room and it had gotten dark, therefore it was time to eat.

In order to achieve high rank you need an opportunity to enable a college degree while academically seeking to embellish on this vociferous occasion. The training of officers was carried out by the higher military colleges. This was an excellent soldier in front of the man questioning him. Lawrence confessed he entered the army a tad early, but was advanced through fighting and was an officer. The officer recommended a two-year course, which would make him a college grad. He left the office with a feeling of respect, but he faced the two-year period with great pride.

The next day the whole division (250 students) stood at attention and the lieutenant general and the commandant walked out and faced the audience. At first, the speaker welcomed the officers, which earnestly were trying to assess the qualities of the speaker. Then he dealt with the war-college at hand. The war has had an iniquitous effect on the school. Many classroom books had been destroyed, sections of the chemistry and physics departments were analyzed as annihilated, he voiced. Essentially, the construction crews were repairing the facility, which can be done in five to six months. The commandant apologized to all, but the content of each course would be according to the success of the class—not to lesser individuals. Lawrence was without a doubt eager to start his myriad of subjects. At last, he offered them a chance to excel, and he walked off the stage.

The next morning began with an early start. The first class was listed as math. The teacher was a civilian who made his introduction. He announced that he had three textbooks, however he had loads of notebooks to annotate. And of course, he had a voluminous blackboard, which made everyone happy in his classroom. Then he started with plane geometry with the cosines and tangents. Lawrence laughed when he saw the question arise only in the middle of the period. It was coming back and 15 minutes before the class was to end, the math instruction handed out a short quiz. Lawrence aced the test and he was ready for more.

At the end of the day the 24 students were exhausted. Every class they attended had a pop quiz at the end of the session. Lawrence was excited about this attitude of the teachers. Despite the lack of textbooks and the like, he thought this was top drawer.

The 24 students were continually surprised. The next day the plane geometry professor had them periodically take to the blackboard to prove their hypotheses. Every class had its superior treatment, or staying away from rudimentary treatment. These necessary homework requirements were to review systems contained in notebook fashion. Many papers, no doubt, were assigned and expected to be completed the next day. This made a chore out of a military course, but one that made people perform at their best.

Little by little, upgrading the chemistry/physics departments up to snuff was just about finished. Most of the classes were in dire need of multipurpose labs. Meanwhile, Tosarina and little Lawrence were brought to Moscow to be with his father. Lawrence met them and kissed them both. They were staying in a subsidized apartment building on the eighth floor. Living in this apartment consisted of four rooms: A living room, kitchen, a bath with a washer and two bedrooms. Obviously, the bedroom for the son was small. Just think what it would be for the parents if the baby was born in five months. Predominantly, the households of Russia were in serious condition. The military ranks a far better house, but rubles are the money.

In wartime, the system for tempering the Soviet Union, the countries, which they have taken over and the entire united armed force is stripped of its totalitarian decorative superstructure. In peacetime the blending of operations/administrative forces are blended with one another. This may seem a bit confusing, but we can figure out the minus/pluses to see what happens when the switch goes to the peacetime category. Despite this, one must restore and not disestablish old worn out embellishments. Lawrence has now put himself on the clothesline. In order for him to achieve high rank, he must perform to a senior executive position. He has accelerated among the best and with two months remaining in his class, he is the class' cum laude. His instructors are proud of him and it looks like only a half year more will award him a college degree. The intervening months between June-August will be devoted to training and tactical maneuvers.

During this time, in her normal business-like manner, Tosarina informed Lawrence by mail that they were going to have another baby. They made plans for the delivery and her father went to get his mother did not take any time at all. A month later, the baby arrived. Lawrence received word from Murmansk about the unexpected birth. A bright, loud scream came as the baby girl let out her first cry. Tosarina felt the child had been delivered. The midwife deliverer said that she only took 48 minutes to deliver. Patssi was the baby's name and she weighed almost eight pounds. Little Lawrence was beside himself, running this way and everywhere in the apartment.

The fall semester of the war college scenario was just another semester. Lawrence, upon being introduced from his second assignments, was asked what he wanted to do next. Without regard to the fatherland, he asked what should I choose. Apparently his supervisor wanted to know what was wrong with the professional offices. "Whether I come into this world as a Red Army man with war experience, I would rather like to try submarine work." The Board of Inquiry studied this. His final verdict was to transfer to the undersea elite.

At the end of December 1946, he had attained the coveted university-military college degree. Masterfully, he accomplished this semester as cum laude and spoke for his class. In his words: "We are graduates of mathematics, chemistry, physics and are ready to achieve a newer beginning of the Soviet Union through rebuilding and modernizing our armed forces." His wife and two children plus his mother were in the auditorium to witness his degree. The menu for Lawrence has been modified with his stand to go into the submarine Navy. The school of instruction for submarines was located near the military academy. Incidentally, the professor of the military academy pinned on the rank of senior lieutenant. His wife, no doubt, was very proud of his new accomplishment.

The lay of the land at the submarine school was bleak. The powers-to-be raised money, but only 55 percent were devoted to undersea warfare. By dividing, powers of 10 to negative 12, and fantastic substitution on munitions, there was only three submarines designed to be built. The initial new class—the one Lawrence had helped design when he worked with the Bureau of Ship Design Submarines—was the Whiskey Class submarine. This was the first sub that was Soviet design for a medium-range vessel. Naturally, the older World War II boats were figments of imagination compared with the Whiskey. Each design drawings produced numerous new deck-plate such as a new ECM (electronic counter measures), a new search radar and the ship armament. This class of ship evolved from the German prospective, which the Russians gained by studying gas performance of gear.

His first day at the school was spent orienting himself to where the classes meet and the various pools where he would practice with submarine escape devices. After all the small things were complete, Lawrence entered the class the next day. His schedule went like this: He got four hours of lectures in the morning with labs, swimming skills and similar escape maneuvers. The morning session began with a movie explaining the base parameters of a sub. The final thing that the film professed is to know beforehand what you are telling the submersible to do. The basic population unit is diesel-burning engine, which correlates to a snorkel when the engine can be operated while the ship is submerged. When the submarine dives, it goes on battery. This forces the ship to rely on numerous large batteries, which must power the submarine. The crew must limit the use of a series of batteries. Actually, there was some system when the battery limit is 24 hours. The major difference of the operational part of the submarine is the action that takes place there. The periscope is there, the navigator takes up shop, the vessel is driven from this advantageous point and the executive officer assists the other arrangements such as sonar and radar contacts. Last but not least is the armament officer giving his recommendation if this was a real war. Intertwining with this lecture were the afternoon experiments, which the class undertook. They proceeded to another gym and heard from an instructor who was going to prepare to escape from a submarine some 50 feet down below the surface of the water. The students were ready.

The formulation of the Soviet Navy was a long and drawn out process. Then spots were processed for positioning conventional submarines. Budgeters fought religiously over rubles concerning new ships, new subs and whatever. Along these lines, in 1952, the entire mass of mediators met in Leningrad at the Arctic/Antarctic Research Institute (AARI). Discussions involved exploration under the ice with the submarine getting the spotlight for this investigation. Altercation and then modification led to many hours of discussion. Finally, a solution was hammered out and voted on in the affirmative. Three senior members of the AARI then carried the plan to Moscow. This plan was to identify the structure of the ice, develop tactics should an intruder detect the submarine and what tactics would be developed, and, if the case was deliberate, determine the shooting of torpedoes if this was an actual experience. The Moscow admirals were in favor of this plan, only if the AARI scientists were onboard the conventional submarines. All in all, the plan was modified, in that the bi-functional program was approved to cement both programs.

In Murmansk, the news was rewarding as Admiral Koschak called his staff into conference. The admiral weighed this opportunity as a vanguard into the unknown. He directed his staff to begin this ice operation. Basically, the ice practically humbled this port, except during the days of summer. Oceanography capitalizes the fine art of data that the scientists have gathered. This, plus one week of planning, let a commander with a speech dedicating a ship, a planning course and two AARI personnel to collect this data. After two hours of questioning, Admiral Koschak approved the first engagement of the plan.

Even though the Foxtrot and other submarines were on the drafting board, the Whiskey conventional submarine was chosen. A plan of attack was set forth selecting the sub route and described the ice edge it would live under. Case in point, let's not stay underwater because they have to snorkel at least once every 24 hours. The submarine was inspected and found to be shipshape. Finally, after midnight, the ship left Murmansk and proceeded to Svalbard. The ice was spotty with bergs quite large going northwest. All around the island there was ice with patchy ice crystals. The skipper was Lieutenant Colonel Zoloxki and he ran a tight ship. The two personnel were onboard taking wind and water samples. They proceeded west on the surface until they hit the coast of West Spitsbergen. Just west of this island was the wide-open sea of Greenland. North of this point the sea was covered with ice. The navigator and the operations officer met with the skipper before plotting a course under the ice. The captain was certain that the procedures were followed to a "T."

At 1500, the skipper turned the submarine toward the ice, at which time the order to dive was given. About 1,000 yards from the ice, the Whiskey submerged. The boat was going down to 100 feet. With the skipper at the periscope, he saw a fantastic sight. The sub was about 500 yards from going under the ice. The pattern of ice underwater was a sight to see. The underside was crammed with great chasms, clarifying them, especially since they bounced back the sonar's rays giving the distance in range and bearing. In fact, the sonar had many echoes. The captain kept on going heading magnetic north for five miles and then a loud noise was heard in the boat. The captain stopped the boat and went 360 degrees around the periscope and found that a segment of ice called a stalactite rubbed the top of the submarine sail. "That's enough for today," he remarked and gave a new course of 180 to get out of the ice.

Captain Zoloxki maneuvered his submarine for about 20 miles collecting data and measuring the depth of the Greenland Sea. Another interesting sight was a green/brownish algae under the ice. What small life or a form of oyster is found in this muck? By and large, this vessel picked up a merchant and noticed by periscope that the submarine was undetected. This was used several times in the investigation of the ice.

The investigation was turned into a brief by the skipper who went before Admiral Koschak. He cited the numerous events that the submarine experienced. The measurements by the AARI representatives were outlined on a chart, giving the admiral proper time to analyze the data. The captain told of the top of the submarine scraping in a low-lying pillar that undoubtedly caused a probable mess in your pants. The highlight of the trip was the target of merchant ships did not know he was there. Admiral Koschak was amazed with brief. He congratulated the captain and he was decorated for his actions.

This initiated numerous submarine intrusions under the ice, which built up a mass of data. The area covered by the conventional boats was generally between Greenland and the West Spitsbergen Island. Eventually all ice work was abated as the winter winds set in. Analyzing the abundant data was started during the winter. This, plus new avenues of ice study, including tracks under the structure, was developed and the impending plans for the spring were set.

Soviet sailors were aware of this assignment, but were leery of the unknown. The basic assignment of this exploration was the area known as the Fram Basin. This area was above Greenland to the east of the North Pole. No one knew the depth, sounding or any means of measuring the depth of the Arctic Ocean. The first candidate left Murmansk in mid-April with a case and a half of paperwork giving the skipper a hand full. The submarine sailed to Spitsbergen and conducted escape drills and other emergency drills. After every man recognized his part, The captain set sail towards the entry point. Naturally, he had ice observers on board and they were ready to go under the ice. Soon the submarine was approaching the ice edge. The ice was severed into great blocks as the cold mass was thawing and would eventually break even further. "Dive, dive, dive," said the captain. By looking through the periscope, the ice in fact was breaking up and there were pools where the submarine could surface and reconnoiter the area. After five hours taking measurements, the sub surfaced in a pool of water. The wind was cold but many of the oceanographic people made climatologic measurements including depth penetrations. Many of those working depth soundings were amazed at the preponderance of some form of plant life exhibited when they recounted their travels.

There were polar bears looking for food with their cubs trailing behind them. The mother bear was searching for ring seals that had built a covering over an ice opening. The seal would then sleep for several hours keeping in close contact with the scent of the polar bears searching for food. Many of these critters eat quantum amounts of food and blubber for a family of three. A white stealthy fox follows the band of white bears hoping for a cleanup of the seal dinner.

Arctic cod is prevalent in areas of the Lancaster Sounds. Cod attracts other animals including the fleet of ice whales, commonly known as the beluga vintage. This white sturgeon appears in the vicinity of Lancaster Sound in June, which is quite a sight to see. Beluga whales are white and lack a dorsal fin, but hearing these animals make a sound ful of whistles that create melodies ending in a crescendo.

Oftentimes the Russian sub sees these fish when they come to the surface. The seals are too busy also with the preponderance of algae, fish and other wildlife was available in the confines of the Arctic. Eskimos travel to these fissures or commonly carved avenues of the ice opening and perhaps closing due to the push/compressing of the Arctic. Seals are the way of life and they are there to provide for their kills of this beast. Each participant of the clan will gather his store of seal meat.

The last of the sea animals is the walrus, a large gregarious marine mammal. His favorite morsel was the bivalve mollusks. Each walrus weighs over 2,000 pounds with his ranging two-foot tusks. Believe it or not, he feeds on clams that are in beds at 200 feet. He is related to the seals, but has more motivation to seek new ways of catching the enemy.

By September the conventional submarine was tied up in Murmansk. The captain sent the crew on leave while the necessary lab material was being off-loaded to the Arctic/Antarctic Research

Institute. Captain Kamchatca was supposed to report to Admiral Koschak tomorrow about his trip. Also, he was to prepare him for the highlights of the trip and would guess when this report would be briefed before him. Admiral Koschak was desirous to greet him the next day. Nonetheless, he queried the captain about the particulars of the venture. The precise way the captain addressed the admiral, his confidence was assured. Also, the submarine did notice many marine and sea-life that would be included in this report. In essence, the information would be presented in three weeks. Koschak was instilled, confident and impressed. He thanked Kamchatca and made a data for his post-deployment brief. As he left the admiral's quarters he felt relieved and paused for a cigarette. He knew his men and the AARI would present him the brief two weeks from now, with one week polishing job.

Finally, the AARI representatives completed their sections of speech that contained four parts. The collection analysis, the sub navigation, pre-flight including charts and the captain's viewpoint. The collection was indeed fascinating, but so were the other factors that blended in with the overall conclusions. Captain Kamchatca was elated when he absorbed all the data that was presented. He asked very few questions and wanted to know where are the pitfalls? "None!" said the participants.

Three weeks from the conversation between the admiral and the captain, the admiral walked in for the brief with everyone standing at attention. "At ease," the admiral said. Captain Kamchatca began by introducing his speakers and then gave an objective view of the submarine's trip to the Fram Basin and returning to Murmansk. The captain said they penetrated the Fram Basin, but there was more to be done farther north. The first speaker was the navigation officer who outlined the track, showing the star and sun shots that were highly accurate. Several radio lines of bearing were effective, however, not all radio bearings are useful the farther north you transit. As a wrap-up, the navigation officer was precise considering the cold. The admiral was pleased.

Front and center was a strapping young fellow from the science division. He started by showing a diagram that depicted the chart running from south to north. He described each point that fixed on the initial map. Each point was discussed giving the surface temperature, which was generally 5 degrees Celsius. The depth of all the points was unknown and that was the first statement he made. In other words, we need longer measuring devices.

The clarity of the water made a difference in all endeavors of testing. The unity of temperature meant a great detection of a freighter at a long distance. Incidentally, this was forecasted by one AARI representative, which caught the attention of the admiral. Finally, the topic was wildlife, fish and other aquatics. This led to specific animals that suddenly appear in the Arctic. The hodgepodge of critters really amazed the admiral, who laughed about the polar bear with two cubs. Finally, he closed with the concern that the Arctic is moving its ice in a random fashion. In other words, the ice seems to go in a roundabout way, drifting to the northeast.

The admiral was flabbergasted by the reality of this analysis. He professed that the new frontier was truly in the dome that the Arctic now covers. He was equally impressed with the detection capability and wondered why they could not determine the depth in the adjacent areas. He asked several questions which were answered immediately. The captain spent five minutes explaining some of the idiosyncrasies which cause the skipper some problems when making headway. Finally, Admiral Koschak stood up and said this was, without a doubt, the best brief he had received. He thanked the briefer and told the captain he would see him after his staff has reviewed the data.

A week later, the admiral woke up and he had on his mind a submarine being chased under the ice cap. What are the parameters of being able, or even stealthy at tracking a submersible target? Sharing was not a winner, as he scratched his face multiple times. He approached his office and greeted the petty officer who had coffee waiting. Over the intercom he wanted a staff meeting set up within an hour. The staff meeting represented all of the admiral's interests with all interested looking to the boss to speak. He announced the under ice problem that he had been dealing with for the past week. Case in point, where is the report on the second ice adventure? The colonel in charge of the reconstruction admitted that the final draft of the ice adventure is due by Friday next week.

"Let's make the draft due this Friday," the senior man said. "I would like to go to Moscow to present this report and to use this scenario as a major task in next year's ice exercise. Tell me, colonel, what techniques would you use to deny detection under the ice," he said suspiciously. The man, who was decorated as a commanding officer of a Whiskey submarine, was dumbfounded. He just sat there, turning red and was embarrassed. The admiral got up and said he wanted an answer to the question, to wit, he stormed out of the conference room. The chief of staff or second-in-command was fuming. He ordered that the draft be delivered to him by noon this coming Friday. The operations officer objected and was antagonistic about the matter. COS answered and said that the report would be on his desk at the appropriate time.

By 1200 hours the report including the pertinent enclosures were delivered to the chief of staff. The report was detailed and was practically correct. Several changes were annotated which showed the rush to make the deadline. At 1400 hours, the COS went to see the admiral. The report said what the commander of the submarine said it would. The narrative was excellent, but the ramifications permeated it and caused much fury in Moscow.

Admiral Koschak and his aide went to Moscow to present the brief. It was cold with snow coming down in the amount of many inches. Several dignitaries attended the brief from Arctic Research Institute plus several analysts that were there to refute the recommendations of this formal study. Prominent among the other members was the admirals that were senior to Koschak, yet represented the Soviet military monument. The brief was presented by Captain Kamchatca who dealt with questions that blasted away at his posture and was building to a crescendo! Finally, he broke ground and said that he will take no interruptions until after the brief. Admiral Koschak concurred with the captain and all was quiet after that brief pause.

The necessary things to discuss were not being verbalized. Two main items were the noise of the ships, i.e., submarines, the actual depth of the Arctic mass and finally how submarines defend themselves. The melting point of any brief lies in the validity of personnel attending the meeting. One such gentleman was speaking in the AARI branch when he offered the following solution:

The KGB had come into information pertaining to the noise of ships. The amplitude of sound relates to the range or how far away the creator is from the sound.

The length of the measuring data should give an accurate measurement of the depth.

A medal should be given to the captain and all of his crew.

The meeting bought all of the topics and were agreed upon. The conference was called to a close.

On the first of February, the admiral's staff received a task message. The third ice exercise was laid out in intricate detail. All of the criticism about the last exercise was absent, as the tasks they underscored would be run accordingly. Unbeknownst to the submarine carrying out the ice experimentation, a trailer was being dispatched. The newest Foxtrot Class would act out the role that the admiral thought was an excellent tactic. Also, the ice investigation would provide with the basic knowledge of sound from the engines with specific horsepower settings.

The third expedition left Murmansk the end of April. Captain Latvia was aboard and they were anxious to get underway. The journey was supposed to take them to the furthest point in the Fram Basin. Captain Latvia was eager and an optimist. At one point, about half-way through the Fram Basin, he was advised that sonar had a contact. The contact was snorkeling and was identifiable by the noise it creates. "All stop," said the captain. The target submarine was below the surface of the water near an ice formation. The Foxtrot snorkeled past the ship as if it had not detected it. The mission was stopped as the Whiskey played cat and mouse. The trailer played about three or four hours and then the Foxtrot pulled the plug. At five miles, the Whiskey boat could barely hear the propellers. At the end of 10 hours, the Foxtrot turned 180 degrees and began backtracking to pick up the Whiskey. Once again the boat stopped in the water to let the Foxtrot pass them. The captain waited until they were two miles away and then came up to the surface. He contacted the Foxtrot and told him he was dead in the water. The captain then got on the VHF and wondered where it was. The captain of the Whiskey signed off.

The success of the third submarine in the ice brought outstanding results, as noted by Admiral Koschak. The experiment in the ice was soon alternated to the nuclear proponent. Eventually, the Arctic Ocean was surveyed or analyzed which was expanded in certain operations. The western side of the Arctic Basin was explored used the Chukchi Sea and various inlets of Wangel Island.

At the submarine facility, there were candidates who Lawrence had run into during the last war. The opening speaker introduced the subject at hand. His opening remarks were exhilarating when he spoke of a vessel that can operate completely submerged in the water. A warship, which was designed to be independent underwater, is built for military purposes. Additionally, the development of submarines was based on the late-19th century inventors in Europe and in North America, which led to major navies placing top priority in the first decade of the 20th century. Both in World War I and II the submarines were used with great preciseness and effectiveness. Up-front, the most important deterrent was the use of radar by the British aircrews, which allowed them to attack the submersibles on the surface with bombs. Additionally, the convoy technique was useful by grouping merchant ships that were patrolled by surface ships, which were fitted with sonar and antisubmarine weapons or mainly depth charges.

Throughout both World Wars, the submarine operated on the surface, submerged in the final stage of attack or when trying to evade detection. High surface speed was a characteristic and essential in this type of naval warfare. Therefore, the body or the hull was designed for minimum surface resistance. With the patrol aircraft catching on to radar detection of the sub, the crews stayed below the surface of the water. Eventually, the snorkel was invented before World War II ended. A breathing tube extended above the water's surface allowing the submarine to get air to ventilate its diesel engines without being on the surface. With improved radar, a snorkeling sub may be detected and suffer a dismal view.

Lawrence had heard something about radar and its effectiveness in finding submarines. He participated in the afternoon with respect to modify the color and creating a disclosure problem. The rationale is valid, but the sub must come up with a different bag of tricks or tactics to even this predicament.

The next subject was classification, or what classification is, basically the resultant primary mission is that attack submarines are fast, long-range boats and can fire torpedoes. They also carry underwater sonar receivers and transmitters (sonar) that are used to detect enemy submarines. They may be armed with a surprise mixture of torpedoes, mines or some types of decoys.

The hull and associated fixtures of the system were next to be studied by the class. Most submarines have a pressure hull and a nonpressure hull. The pressure hull is the water-tight, pressure-proof enclosure where the equipment is located and where the officers and enlisted live. A non-pressure hull of lighter substance forms the main ballast tanks. Above the superstructure is where the bridge is enclosed which includes the periscope, mast supports and finally the conning tower.

The pressure hull is the strong apparatus that resists sea pressure once the vessel is submerged. The instructors spend quite a bit of time illustrating the cone shape or nearly circular cross section, which is built for the best strength with the least weight of structure. Some boats have this technique with watertight compartments that become the spaces for equipment and the crew.

That afternoon, the lab sessions capitalize on the hull and the pressure hull. They worked out on their slide rules what the pressure and assorted components would be in order to calculate the pressure when a sub is submerged at its deepest depth. Another problem with the diesel sub is the main ballast tanks. The fuel tanks are built in-between the pressure and non-pressure hull. Fuel tanks must be kept full of fuel and water, or if you use fuel, water is pumped in to maintain this internal pressure, thereby reducing the sub from collapsing when it's submerged. The main ballast tanks carry most of the water and these tanks have large flood holes at the bottom and vent holes at the top. Very simply, the air escapes and water comes into the tanks while the sub dives. Likewise, the sub surfaced by closing its vents, blowing into the tanks and this action forces water out the flood holes to keep the superstructure awash.

In turning to the equipment of the submersible, much of the useable equipment is associated with the personnel onboard. This includes the power plant, radio, sonar and the operations station. The discussion of the main tube involves the stuffing box at the top of the hull or the highest part of the ship. Periscope depth, defined, as the depth at which the submarine has the upper window of a raised periscope extends above the surface of water. This causes a bit of controversy among the class, but Lawrence straightened out the participants.

Prisms may be used to define the range of what you are seeing and it can compare through other parameters. The upper prism may be tilted when the ship is rolling or pitching to observe, for example, enemy aircraft. Auxiliary devices may be used for various magnifications. Also, a telemeter scale is used to assist the periscope viewer assess the range of the target and are azimuth circle which he quickly obtained a bearing to the target. Eyesight is the only true virtue of the sub and the device services all the needs of a true submarine officer.

Navigation depends on the submariner like a sore thumb. There are no external sources such as stars or the sun. The submarine has a complicated system which figures in the roll of gyroscopes, flux value compasses and all values of pitch and roll that equal the best navigation system that is going into the Whiskey. The class will want to ask many questions. They wanted to know what the primary source of navigation is today. What causes the sub to roll and what about deep dives, or sudden rises to the surface? A complete problem is not solved but here are many professors who are at work, as we speak, trying to resolve this issue.

Fire controls of any sub is crucial in the hunt for victories. Diesel submarines receive data from an analog computer that takes the target information from sonar, radar or from the periscope. This determines the target course, speed and course. The importance of the precise date is that the sub may change course, go deep or whatever. This information is timely and necessary to be updated prior to a reasonable attack.

With the fully pledged class crammed full of knowledge, the class went for three weeks of hands-on gear. Lawrence, by his supervisor grades, became the class representative. The group arrived at the factory, where the initial steel hulls were being put together for the new Whiskey class submarines. The first segment was the hull and arrangement of the sub. The students were worked over until they had to design a new hull for the future. Lawrence had five other students and they designed a hull which they professed was for the first nuclear boat. Many mathematical formulas were left out of other drawings that they manufactured. Most import thing was it lead to many ideas of the future which would be thought over, tested and realized on the nuclear boats of the future.

Finally, the graduation date was set and all of the class was going to Murmansk to design and learn how to run a submarine. Lawrence was excited as he drove his family northward. They talked of going into the Arctic, but nothing would survive the cold and inclement weather. The base accommodations are fairly nice with room enough for a third child, which the wife was overjoyed to hear.

For the next six months he was extremely busy. For two months he rode WWII boats where gave him the lay of the land. He tried navigation and realized how slow he was moving. Fire control, ordnance and periscope work quickly advanced his seamanship with respect to handling a submarine. They took many trips out and many trips back with a new idea. For a month, they were preparing a document describing their assessment of their recent trip in the submarine. Lawrence, without a doubt, turned in the best report to date. As a result of this, he became part of the engineering design force. Behind the production door was the KGB representative. He checked his credentials and gave him a badge with directions to his immediate supervisor. The present plans had run aground with the present plans calling for just over 73 meters. The basic hull had been laid out and the submerged parameters did not work out as planned. Lt. Latvia was given this problem. The diagram was before him as he looked at each parameter. He added, subtracted and still came up with the basic design. As he quickly turned the pages, he noticed that the ship had guns both forward and aft of the conning tower. If, for example, the Whiskey V had only one gun forward it would make the designated length. Lawrence wrote up the incident and had the secretary type it up for him. By 1600, he carried the typewritten piece to his boss. With all mathematics correct, his analytical analysis was correct. Immediately this new product was adopted and Lawrence was congratulated.

Whiskey's demeanor achieved numerous results as the hull took form. The steel gloss in the night had apparently the cutting edge of the steel sail was predominate as the boat took shape. The length of the Whiskey was in fact 240 feet with a beam of 27 feet. This needle-nose creature was the epitome of what the engineers call "the finest hour in construction." The next step is stuffing the interior with things like a diesel-electric engine and the unknown assortment of electronics, that make up a conventional warship. Let us not forget the arrangement in the weapons room. There are six torpedo tubes (four bow and two in the stern) where it represents a total of 18 self-propelled underwater projectiles. In addition, the underwater experts have planned that the sub could be used for mining, which it is considered it capable of planting upwards of 40 mines. Back to the horsepower for a minute, there are two propeller shafts which are driven by diesels rated at 4,000 hp and when called on for electric power, the batteries put off

2,500 horsepower which equates to a maximum speed of 15 knots underway. In essence, it is an excellent product that has been evolved from German engines plus Soviet ingenuity.

Lawrence had found himself testing the new model by going out to sea. He was assigned as a navigator and he carried numerous charts. Above him were the captain, the executive officer and the operations officers. In the conference room aboard the boat, they met with the plant engineer and he went over the week's worth of tests. The charts were unrolled and the civilian began his brief. They proceeded to the west where they were supposed to commence shakedown. The drills, emerging escape drills and all other situations were explained in detail. The next portion of the test was for the ship to rendezvous with a target ship. Here the sub will unleash its armor. All torpedoes were dummies and would not explode. The mines would have to wait for a second test run. Of course, the engines and power supply will be tested both above and under water; case in point—the snorkel system. When the questions were answered, the civilian left after a handshake.

After four o'clock in the morning, the captain of the ship barked orders and the forward deck hands let loose the ropes and tie downs. Then the aft freed the submarine and the engine came to two knots as the boat eased out into the water. About 10 minutes later, a tugboat would meet them and show them the way down the fjord to the open sea. Lawrence was down at his station monitoring his particular compass. At last, the open water had arrived and the captain transmitted that he was free to go. The tug flashed his response and turned back to the base. The captain turned the sail watch over to the watch officer, as the submarine headed to the wave-ridden, but not too choppy, seas.

"Dive, dive, dive," the captain ordered. Every sailor onboard jumped and assumed his primary task. Once underway, the list of leaks amounted to five or so spurts which were quickly fixed by the ship technicians the navigation equipment was doing fine, but the Dead Recovering Tracer died just minutes after the sub dove. The next problem was the sextant being utilized when the sub was at the surface. Lawrence did not like this technique. What if the surface was not the right place for shooting the sun or star? This was to get a dumb shit for the piece of gear. Why don't we somehow take these shots through the periscope?

The next maneuvers were the series of emergencies, which the boat must endure. Lawrence was officer of the boat and he knew the procedure back and forth. The captain watched him perform and later commented that he would receive the rank of operation officer if he had anything to do with it. The next test of the system was to join up with the tugboat when he would fire dummy weapons. The boat had put in several targets, which the sub was supposed to hit, coordinate and get away—the word of today. The dummy torpedoes apparently did well hitting the target. The total number of hits equaled all but one that went ballistic about half-way to the target. The boat captain said it was the sharpest shooting he has seen since World War II.

When the sub returned, the ship's crew underwent debriefing. The subject was different leaks repaired on board the ship, the navigational problems and finally the crew's overall success with the Whiskey Class. The foreman was overwhelmed and congratulated his crew of 60 men.

After three years of testing the boat was commissioned and she went to sea for a month. She sailed around the coast of Norway and positioned herself between Iceland and Norway. It was summer and they saw several whales, which Russian trawlers would soon to be there to harpoon them. This was the first post-war Soviet submarine for a medium-range submarine. Incidentally, two future models of the Whiskey will be connected to oceanographic and fishing research. After a month they were very happy with the boats, looking for new subs that they could play with.

YANKEE CLASS

A MEETING WAS SET UP THIS WEEKEND in July, which will give the master planners a chance at selling their plan. This cottage was on a lake isolated by woods. Lawrence was vivid that his foremost plan was to split up the avenues of officers arriving at this log cabin. Some hiked and some entered the cabin by boat—from all sides except Admiral Lativa. He and two friends (guards) came a day early. Lawrence and these two gentlemen went fishing and caught enough fish for a supper. The next morning the guards protected the house as eight men broke out of the woods or from the lake. The admiral welcomed them and asked them to join him for breakfast. They settled in on hot bread, sugar rolls, sausage and a hot cup of Russian coffee.

The first brief was given according to the mission statement given by the higher-ups. The speaker began with the task of getting magnetite from Labrador to Moscow, which they did on time. He left out many specifics, such as, relaying this need through back door sources. Invariably, a KGB agent who was in different clothes, spread the word that Moscow needed two pounds of this substance by the first of July. This challenge was passed to Newfoundland to get this sample, which he picked up and sent it by mail, which was received in Russia seven days before the deadline. Incidentally, through channels, we had the sample behind closed doors where testing of this mineral is ongoing.

The admiral congratulated him and asked what steps have been made to counter this shipment. The commander said that his son had filed a missing package of mail. "Excellent," the admiral said. The second speaker stepped up and had a chart before the rest of the men. He pointed out Moscow and then he pointed out the iron ore outside of Labrador City, Labrador. His first proclamation was that this was a bloodcurdling episode. The first option was to launch the Spetznaz force behind the Naval Station Argentia base and enter the base with the 50 pounds of magnetite. But, of course, the spies now in the vicinity of Argentia will provide several trucks so that the team may be vectored on base and transfer this mineral to a waiting ship or perhaps a submarine. Now, we will discuss the parameters of this maneuver:

1. Our undercover man in Labrador City must go through expeditious means, to move 50 pounds to an airplane and fly this to St. John's, Newfoundland. A Navy truck will meet him there and transfer the magnetite for delivery to the Navy facility. The obligation ends when he turns over the shipment on the trucks to the base outside at the rendezvous point.

2. The Spetznaz group will then mount the truck dressed in U.S. Navy fatigues and take the northern gate by stealth techniques. Their boat will be given to them at a later date.

The next plan is shaky at best, but we are undecided on whether we should fly a plane over to pick them up and the iron ore. Our second guess, although not completely thought out, is to send a submarine to pick them up from a boat approximately 100 miles at sea.

At this point, the briefer sat down and gasped at the silence they endured. Finally, Lawrence stood up and reviewed the bidding. He saw the advantages and disadvantages of this scheme. He wanted to know if the charts of the Argentia base were held, by whom, and who takes care of this. Second, what is happening in the Arctic Ocean with respect to our submarines? The second member of the group of three assigned to planning this theory answered his question as best he could. He understood that there was a map and they had custody of one. "We will make copies and have them sent to you. I am not sure what is going on under the ice. Several submarines, at least four, are undergoing tests with exercise torpedoes. I will endeavor to retain this information by next week."

Communications was a very touchy subject as noted by the briefer, Asadollah Shazi. Controls, which the Soviet had placed on this transmission, had shut down this vital system. They had devised a quick effort, which would solidify their efforts. Morse code systems will be the answer. A quick series of simple, one, one, one figures meant, for example, the mission was achieved. Another group may mean the contact has failed to meet the required goals. The Morse code should be sent on a specific frequency. This was agreed upon. The secret community had made its offering by sending a piece of igneous matter, which may reverse the underworld travelers. A hunt is planned for the force which yet, Admiral Latvia had brought on the forces which could make it happen. Inside his safe were the list and file of every Red Star agent that cleverly worked for him. He reviewed the names and finally one name filled the bill. His job was in the warfare section of the Moscow strategic force. He called this individual and told him that he must see him about the impact warfare had on the eastern front. A time was set at 5:30. Lawrence met him and announced that he would listen to a brief that offered support for warfare. Immediately the tape recorder came on and Lawrence showed him a piece of paper. He received a high sign from his associate, and he followed Lawrence out the back door. They climbed three flights of steps and out of the door was the top of the building.

After looking around the area, Lawrence pressed his concern about the secret service group parachuting from a plane. Who was the contact point? Admiral Koschak was the overall seer in the mess. What, how can that be? Don't worry, the admiral does and believes in your courage and tenacity. He is retired and works in between these two areas. Well, I am impressed! Tell him that we must have the elite group of 20 individuals and they must be top-notch in everything from killing with the hands and powering a boat to meet the submarine. They checked out several other items and the admiral said we had better go back to my office before the tape expires.

Over the past years, Sasha was mired down with desk projects. He suddenly lost interest in his work when his wife developed breast cancer. She died of this horrific disease and caused a stumbling block on his road to success. A caller by the name of retired Admiral Koschak paid him a visit. He expressed great sympathy for his wife and wondered how he was handling things with this factor in the past.

Sasha told the truth about things and he was not, according to other sources, to be a contender in the coming Olympics. Mary (his wife) was his revitalizer, companion and mother of three children; he missed her dearly. The admiral quoted many newspaper articles that stated he and only this individual, above all, had achieved the final goal. Yes, he was aware of these things, but never more. The adversary then spoke of things that had happened over the past 10 years. Blunders after miscalling had led the Soviet military to a default dilemma. Time after time the feelings had hurt numerous men of service and the admiral was one who supported the listing of Soviet carelessness. "Would you help us?" said Koschak. Sasha thought for several minutes and shook his colleague's hand.

They walked outside and went to a park about three blocks away. The recreation area was tidy and they sat down overlooking the waterfall. Out of Koschak's pockets came the chart, which depicted N.S. Argentia, Newfoundland. Twenty special agents were to fly a night mission in a Russian Bear aircraft and parachute over Argentia where they would land on an area four miles from the Naval Station. At this point they would be picked up by U.S. Navy trucks with rights primary stars, magnetite, ready to go on base to a boat which was scheduled to meet a Russian submarine. The Spetznaz would wear U.S. Navy enlisted clothes and the contact that he had would assist him on base. "You will carry your standard weaponry, and once you get on the Naval Station you head for the water. Here is a map of the base. This is where you will go to meet the vessel ready to move out and meet the submarine some five hours out to sea."

Sasha reviewed the mission and had several questions to ask. The main stumbling blocks were details of who to meet before entering the base and over three troops gathered at the gate. The admiral appreciated the concern, but at all cost, get the piece of magnetite aboard the submarine.

Asadollah Shazi was in his office when he heard the phone ring. The vice admiral informed him of a major flaw in Iran's paper. Word from the higher echelon did not like the letter and therefore the subject had been dropped. Shazi was horrified at this juncture. He asked if he could talk about the details of the letter. Frankly the need for representation was not in good taste. "Thank you for your understanding," the admiral exclaimed.

One month from the last meeting, the confidant met at a secret location. The brass, including the vice admiral, Admiral Alexei Latvia and the co-leader, were present. The proposed sequence of action was passed out to the distinguished numbers. The briefer was Lawrence who had received all necessary hard problems of this strike. This material was set in three stages, the initial parachute drop, the movement of the material and the joining of the submarine. The admiral, with his fellow workers laid down the flight number for the Spetznaz group and parachute to land in a field just outside the naval station. They would be met by trucks and would dress as U.S. Navy enlisted. "Once through the main gate entrance of Argentia Naval Station, you will proceed to the water front, whereby you will man a cutter boat. Then go out one hundred miles to meet the submarine."

The second priority of this scheme was to take a modified nuclear submarine on a trip to the Arctic. This, of course, is now an old revived nuclear submarine, but it is a new version of a SSGN Class.

The Echo II had been reconverted by closing up the eight short-range missiles from the outside and making it a survivable stealth platform that was designed for shallow water support. The deck had been made into a modified special forces carrier and dispensed special forces that are capable of going ashore in a combat readiness surprise encounter or if need be it could place Spetznaz forces as need be. It had torpedoes, could lay mines in defensive tasks, and was equipped with an assortment of other short-range weapons that had not been able to judge their accuracy. The commanding officer was one of them and the departure was August 15, 1991.

The details of each episode of this surprise evolution was worked and worked by this group. The coordination of flight plans of the Russian Bear aircraft was somewhat of a sticky situation. The aircraft must fly at altitude to reach this attended drop zone. The flight over the North Pole made sense, but the flight would have to fly over/near Argentia on the way to Cuba, its final destination. Another bug-a-boo was the communication tie-up within the multiple phase of the engagement. Strategically a ground station had been set up to send the affixed Morse code messages. The only time you must send any information is when you had done what you are told to do.

Now that the entire secret mission has been reviewed, he advised that all of us are creating a discovery that will exalt a new magna vehicle that will lower nuclear submarine noise. May the words of your mouth be silent! From behind the door's top-secret group, the magna has been worked to its designated temperature. They are engineering a design, which will funnel this substance into the steam, from which the nuclear propellers get its power. The facts of this investigation are so covered up that the briefing schedule for this project is nonexistent. Operation Poppy was the code name for the project and will be used to tie in the communications system of symbols.

Back in 1946, Alexei was disturbed about the Army tank command. Just before the war broke out, he was awarded a T-34 tank and a crew that accompanied this armor. He did a difficult job keeping out of harm's way. He was granted many acts of heroism, including the precedence of honor with many acts of valor awarded. And yet, when the war was over, Alexei was pleased but not satisfied with his success.

He talked things over with his older brother, Lawrence, and realized that he had a difficult view of the mechanics of war. Instead he went to the east coast of Russia and still participated in the Army. Finally, he went to his commanding officer and requested to be transferred to the submarine force. Such a brilliant officer, the commander listened to him and his request was granted to the submersible force. Like Lawrence, he learned about submarines, the remains of World War II boats, the Whiskey Class, the Foxtrot Class and then into the Echo I nuclear boat.

The first Echo sub he took out, he was commanding officer of the vessel. He deployed off the coast of the western United States. He was tracked by the SOSUS system during periods of his deployment, which led to VP coverage during this period of time. Many lessons were learned as the nuclear power plant was reduced to three or four knots, thereby, causing a reduction of detection to one to three miles.

Admiral Alexei Latvia (promoted again) was ordered back to the west coast where he was being groomed for the Yankee Class ballistic missile submarines. He checked in to Murmansk when he attended school. He married late in life and had a young wife named Natalia who had a three-year-old son. He studied hard and sailed twice, ironing out the hard spots of the ship. It was early in 1967 when he got the word to take a Yankee Class to sea for 60 days. He and his wife were surprised that he was going on the ship's first patrol. The major feature of this ballistic missile boat was the power contained on board. The vertical launching tubes were arranged in two rows of eight SS-N-6s that had a range of about 1,500 nautical miles that placed many major cities on the east coast of the United States in jeopardy. Additionally, the MRV warhead had been tested and if the word is go, the missile threat becomes active and airborne.

The cold had hit the southern fleet base at Gadzhievo. The calendar said it was the first week of September but here at the head of a twisting fjord the Arctic Circle exposed men who knew that winter had already arrived.

The fjord's rocky hills were covered with snow. Flurries fell from a sky the color of wet cement and it accumulated on the concrete docks, the rust painted loading cranes and the gravel roads and on the black decks of nuclear submarines.

"Engines astern, slow," said Captain Alexei Latvia, commanding officer of the ballistic submarine. His order was acknowledged by Vladmirov, the new executive officer, stationed in the central command post below the sub's open bridge. Finally, the Yankee's twin screws began to turn.

A young captain of 42, he was a handsome man with a fringe of dark hair that contrasted with brilliant blue eyes. His bushy black mustache and bald head gave him the look of a pirate but up here on the exposed bridge atop the con tower, what American submariners call the sail, he was just a pair of frosted lashes peering out from beneath a fur of his head. Amazingly, each breath that passed through five layers of wool and oilskin was enough to lodge directly in his ribs. Close to the spray screen for shelter against the wind the K-300's flag snapped.

Launched in 1966 at the nuclear submarine yard in Severodvinsk, she was a newer example of the Navaga known as a Yankee in the northern fleet. Nearly 400 feet long, her twin VM-4 reactors provided light, heat, water and fresh air to her 119-man crew. Amazingly she could make 30 knots submerged, but Latvia would be satisfied with 20. "Right full rudder." The screws turned the black icy water to froth and the stern began to slip away from her berth. The lookouts to either side of him on the open bridge were completely exposed, their unhappy faces red with cold, wet with snow, melted snow and their shoulders dusted in a huge white flakes. "Rudder amidships," the captain ordered. The warship shuddered as her screws beat water already coated with a thin skim of ice crystals. Leaving port was no easy matter. The boat looked and handled like a wallowing log and the channel leading to the open sea was treacherous. The 10,000-ton sub backed away from her berth, her bow giving the attending tugs a place to push.

The RSM-25 missiles were her reason for being as well as her most dangerous weakness. American submarines carried missiles filled with solid propellant. Russian rockets were fueled with nitrogen tetrosid and hydrozine: two volatile liquids stored under tremendous pressure.

Those missile hatches were a Navaga's weakest point, even more than her two strong nuclear reactors. Weld all those hatches shut and the submarine would be noticeably safer. But the mission was to carry her 16 missiles and their 30 warheads to the various shores of the enemy and that was precisely what the skipper was going to do.

His wife, Natalia, would be there, silent, holding both children. The youngest, barely four months old, hardly knew him. It was his fourth six-month cruise: it added up to a full year away from her, mostly under the sea; a year away from the light, the sun, the sky and the air. It was amazing when you thought about it, which he found himself doing more often these days. It was good Natalia had so many friends. "Engines all stop." Steam generated by the VM-4 nuclear reactors was diverted away from the turbines, her big bronze screws slowed, then splashed to a stop. The tugs moved in eagerly. A thump, a thudding jar and the K-300 began to turn under their push until her bow faced north. The fjord swung into view. Ahead was the first channel buoy. Two chuffs of black diesel smoke and the tugs backed away, taking position to either flank. Off in the distance the open ocean, the barren sea was the color of slate.

"Helm," he said. "Engines ahead, slow," said Star Commander Vladmirov.

The screws began to churn, sluggishly at first, then faster. The beat of the bronze blades against the sea became a continuous, consistent rumble. The steel hull vibrated with life, thought the skipper. Soon the fourth channel buoy loomed ahead. "Right rudder, helm. Make your course 358." The tug skipper quickly released his latch against the icy wind. Done. The tugs pulled away and allowed the submarine to go her way alone. All of the con tower, the orange-vested surface detail made their way to the hatch and disappeared, leaving only the captain and the two lookouts remaining topside. They could see natural light. They would not see natural light nor breathe clean air for another 60 days. The fifth buoy and the sixth buoy were passed, leaving a sheet of frigid water flowed completely over the bow. Conning tower sliced it cleanly and neatly in two. Who else in all of the Soviet Union was as free as the captain of a nuclear submarine? Who else lived and worked so far from the eyes and ears of the state?

"All ahead two-thirds," he said into the intercom. "Clear the bridge, lookouts below." He took another deep breath. "Prepare to dive." The blue and white flag with its predominant red star came down. The spray screen was carefully stored. Latvia checked back to be sure the weather deck was empty, the lookouts below, the open bridge set for the dive. Only then did he go to the main trunk hatch, stepped down to the ladder and grasped the chain attached to the heavy cover.

The U.S. Sturgeon class submarine stationed at the Barracks Sea Station. The sonar operator listened to the noisy boomer churn overhead. Her twin five-bladed screws made a lot of racket. The American intelligence boat was sitting on the shallow sandy bottom, absolutely silent, on station off the fjord leading to the Soviet base. Her job was to keep tabs on all Soviet submarine traffic coming and going, to record coastal radars and above all to remain undetected. He fed the print into a digital analyzer and in a few seconds knew all he needed to know about the newest SSBN steaming by overhead.

Alexei went to his cabin with the radio officer immediately behind him. He went inside his room and went to the safe. After turning the combination several times, he opened the locking device. Then the remote keys were made ready in each. The captain inserted his key followed by the lieutenant radioman. Once the two keys were inserted the inner safe opened and revealed a folded piece of paper. Alexei sat down and read the piece of paper. His assistant key holder was dismissed by the captain. He read each line and yet he understood exactly what the superiors wanted from this mission. Quickly he grabbed the telephone and wanted the executive officer to come to his cabin. He poured himself some coffee and sat down to once again reread the mission assigned. Five minutes later, the star commander knocked on his door and entered. "Here, read this," the captain snapped.

Alexei had been a dedicated, top drawer military officer throughout his military career. His peers bestowed privileges, which he gratefully accepted. On the other hand, he could not carry out the fail-safe mission, which he had just read. After 20-plus years, a stumbling block had disfigured his mental and calculated mind. He must do what must and shall be done to protect the Russian philosophy by placing the Yankee inside the missile range coverage.

The exec sat down and began reading the instructions for the mission. He was quite concerned as he looked up, but he continued to read the final part of the brief. Well, this mission was written by a nuclear submarine writer that has the gumption of an asshole! The routes were not good, and for that matter, the depth during transit was not explored, the listening devices that were booming out were a threat in range and the sense of surprise was not on that piece of paper.

The captain and now the exec were of the same grain. Pencil in hand, he wrote out the precise depth based on the temperature, depth and below the depth to prevent convergence zone detection. What if the enemy was to employ a trailer? He quickly wrote down those tactics, which would eliminate that blundering shadow behind him. This was agreeable to the exec and so this was enough to brief the crew. Let's get one for the skipper.

As soon as the captain had read the modified brief over the loudspeaker, the crew was peaked. The officer crew disbanded and went to lunch in the officer wardroom. As soon as the meal was served, they dug in. Captain Latvia began by announcing that they are aboard the first nuclear ballistic missile submarine, the Yankee. "All of the tests that we have endured had sent us to the leader of the pack. Unfortunately, this was left out in our mission. This verbose undertaking was totally wrong and will not be followed on this mission." He precipitated a blow up that was covered and even the youngest ensign understood. He defined what he wanted, needed and if he caught one officer computing errorless data, will be escorted to the brig. "Are there any questions about the brief?" If the operations officer was concerned over some info on future courses into the North Atlantic. The commanding officer predicted that the vessel will reach the turn point in 10 hours. "The route will be given to you in five hours. I will need the assistance of the navigator."

After sending the alert message, the USS Sturgeon began following the suspected Yankee. The alert sonar operator was extremely adroit and had each beat count tabulated and entered in his log. The commanding officer stopped by and asked the operator what were his primary characteristics. Numerous properties keep jumping out and the submarine must be new with its many drawing points. The CO thanked the petty officer and told him to report any dangerous activity. The next thing that occurred was the communications officer to show the commanding officer a top-secret message that came in. The two were walking together to the operations room.

Back on board the Yankee Class, the navigator and the skipper had worked out a course down through the Faeroes Island down past the Grand Bank that lies to the east of Labrador. This course was not traveled very much but at the same time, maybe sonar could not detect them. Finally it was about time to alter course for the Faeroes Islands. After altering course, the speed was steady at 11 knots.

At Naval Station Keflavik, the oceanographic unit had picked up the contact. The contact showed signs of a Yankee two months ago, but the submarine was going on patrol. The grams were mapped with characteristic blade rates and numerous high frequencies in the upper spectrum. Then the message lines hummed with vigor as numerous frequencies were reported. So now is the time to wait and it could be a new setting for a new or modified patrol area.

Captain Latvia was on the bridge when the submarine was heading southward. He asked the navigator what was the depth and by the submarines bathythermograph which measures water temperature as a function of depth. In retrospect, the systems were still in agreement because it showed the water to be a degree within 800 feet, the time was about five to the hour. The captain knew what was going to happen. At seven o'clock, the captain grabbed the loudspeaker and announced, "Crazy Ivan, Crazy Ivan." The alarm was sounded and the sonar once asleep was now reaching for a trailer. Frequently, the captain had implemented this tactic on the Echo I, which provided a nuclear submarine to "see" (hear) straight ahead on either side. Installed behind the bow sonar are baffles that prevent any noise from the rear, i.e. a trailing hostile submersible. This maneuver was known as clearing the baffles—changing course so that the sub can look behind by positive listening or sending out a burst of sonar. The submarine either turns right or left placing each inch with coverage trying to nail the unwanted follower to complete the cycle. It takes about five minutes to take numerous sweeps and resume base course.

At the 360-degree turns, the sonar man shouted into the microphone. The helmsman moved the power lever to monitor and the U.S. ship was only three miles behind the Yankee. The entire crew could almost hear the Soviet boat sweeping but they could not detect the ship behind them. After 10 minutes or so, the Yankee assumed base course. The captain ordered initial speed and wandered over to the plot. A series of functions plagued the skipper. This track will certainly get to the Atlantic waters, but this is different from others to date. He looked down range and saw the Faeroes Islands. "As a matter of fact this looks like the track we are following." Immediately he drafted a message stating that the Yankee's course will pass by the island on its eastern side. This might be a problem for the submarine detectors as the island will distort or block their view. Additional information was included as well as current environmental data.

Alexei was writing up a report when he received a message. He was asked if any planes were on him, any hostile sub and what was his current position? He was overjoyed when he saw the request for the position. At any rate he complied using the old instructions of the initial mission outlay. He pulled two more Crazy Ivans to no avail. He decided to take a nap for three hours and then go to the operations before they hit Faeroe Island.

The captain of the U.S. trailer submarine was extremely interested in this boat. This must have been the first time the Yankee had sailed through the Gap and into the waters of the North Atlantic. Apparently she has ventured to periscope depth to copy communications and assumed course at 250 feet. As far as his Russian tactics about these rapid look-backs, he had not detected him. Another situation report was due on him, so the skipper marked his position and relayed that the Soviet boat was headed for the Faeroes Gap and will report when this has taken place.

The scene was the operations area and there the navigator and the captain were plotting beyond the islands into the South Atlantic, Faeroes Island is a volcanic outcrop, which has an area of 525 square miles. It has a population of 45,000 people who obviously are mainly fisherman. The captain wanted to pass 10 miles east of the island. This would disguise his being there and the water profile would substantiate his seeking cover below the seasonal thermocline. Once this dilemma was solved, Alexei patted the navigator on the shoulder and went looking for the exec. He found him chewing out a weapons officer, he acknowledged his presence, and followed him to his cabin. "Close the door," the captain ordered. With the hatch closed and the exec seated, the captain started opening the orders for the mission. "We have been in boats for a long time and I felt that we are among the leaders of what might happen, we can share our experience with pride and give our all to Russian supremacy. This was not the case. This smells of dung heap!" The piece of paper which he now unfolded and put on the desk so his exec could see wanted him to follow the course southwest like all Russian boats did. That did nothing, they had no case if there was a U.S. nuclear sub behind them, but what is the take of the mission? The star commander reacted and stated that he as well as the skipper was through a loop. He mentioned that the ballistic missile boat had a mission, which certain targets had to be in range at all times. Maybe this was cause for a pause in the superstructure in the future. After a short discussion, they were in complete compliance of the mission and the changes were forthcoming.

The watch said 10 minutes to go as the navigator put on a new chart. The Yankee was examining the new reading of water velocities.

He decided among his self that there was a new thermocline just south of Faeroes. The clock stopped and the captain ordered periscope depth. This caused the submarine to start rising upward. Finally the shallow depth was searched and the captain eyed the island. She was there inundated with fishing boats tied as it was just about sunset. A sudden 360 sweep of the periscope and he gave the order to go down to 275 feet.

Commander in Chief of the Navy Atlantic fleet was in due need of knowing more about these new 16 missile carriers. He was briefed by a Navy intelligence officer, which included the pickup by the U.S. Sturgeon class detection, and apparently nearing Faeroes Island. The admiral thanked him and wanted him to keep him abreast of the situation. Additionally, he asked the intelligence officer about the missile standoff and what are the options for such targets.

They charted a course based on the captain's approval. The course heads southwest over the Rockhall Rise and then it intercepts the Mid-Atlantic Ridge. Captain Latvia's plan was to traverse the ridge on the eastern side giving more predictability in movement toward the country of the United States. He found what he was looking for a layer of 180 feet fit his tee and soon the Yankee was at 200 feet.

Meanwhile, back in Keflavik, Iceland, the Sound Surveillance Systems has lost contact as she passed Faeroes Island. She appeared again south of that island. The Yankee was maneuvering because the contact appeared to be under a layer trying to keep quiet or lose SOSUS contact. This was reported back to Ocean Systems Atlantic, the master of all reported contacts, either conventional or nuclear on the east coast.

The static settled down on board the nuclear Red sub. The particular mathematics, the course evolution and the elements had seeped in to reach a national consciousness. Captain Latvia went back to his cabin and fell into a hectic sleep. The majority of the crew slept, while every four hours a new man replaced the former candidate. At four o' clock they tried the 360 degree evolution which caused a major panic when the enlisted men awoke with these bodies 45 degrees in the swinging hammocks.

As usual, the U.S. submarines were aware of their techniques. The first thing that you do is pull back to loiter and wait for him to complete the evolution. The times of this tactical maneuver appear to fall at the hour. The last and the initial 360-degree occur at this time.

The captain was now considering a turnover with another submarine. The turnover point is at 52-00 north and 020-00 west. This is a fairly consistent turnover point, at which times the USS Sturgeon heads north and goes back to pick up another contact. The communication chief had no advance word, but he had been told that this was the first Yankee to perform a deployment. About three hours later The captain broke off of the Yankee to perform its turnover. He went to the appointed place and time and soon he raised his relief.

The new tracker was talking on the secure phone about the Yankee. His course, speed and peculiar activities were noted. The captain of the USS Greenling was satisfied with the briefing and said, "Roger out."

The Russian ballistic carrier has received all checks as usual. The nuclear power plant was performing beyond expectation. A review of the chart showed that the position is 50N, 27W and with a course of 175 true. The recent result of the sonar was no contacts ahead or else where. The captain was once again worried about U.S. shadowing. He and the navigator consulted again to verify that the chart is correct. They measured the distance from the future position the landfall of the missiles they carried; the course that they had plotted was 200 miles east of Bermuda. The captain recognized that the coming hour we would find out if there were a trailer behind us. He talked with his operations officer and said there will be modifications to this 360-degree drill. He went over to the sonar operator and bent down to tell him how to monitor for a trailer. The sonar man agreed and the captain went to the bridge.

Finally, it was time for the latest and greatest adventures. They began the Crazy Ivan on the hour and came to a four-knot crawl turning to the right, completing the 360-degree turns. The captain was sweating but just as they turned the sonar man came up and gave contact to a nuclear submarine. "Dive to 1,000 feet, and steady on course 330," said the captain. He then announced that quietness is imperative. The U.S. nuclear submarine had left his pants open and the closed secret of his system, which made the submarine the laughing stock of the Cold War. Finally, the plans to the proverbial fire drill led the SSN to a monitor role. The sonar man produced a fix, which the captain liked.

The navigator plotted the fix and the captain had the ship to turn to 270 at four knots. After 15 minutes of no contact, the sub increased speed to eight knots while steady at 270. The captain initiated a 360 and no contact was gained. The navigator was standing by as the star commander moved up and the ship centered on 220 true. The captain looked at this position and asked the star commander what if we transitioned down the western side of the mid-Atlantic ridge and went to the Altair Seamount to seek escapement from the hunter. Everyone nodded in agreement, and so it was. The captain of the Greenling was never in a foul mood, but this instance he had the whole crew wondering where the Yankee went. The sonar man was asleep, the helmsman was driving right along and he was the culprit for the Soviet government detecting a United States nuclear submarine. He had to take full responsibility. Furthermore, where is the son of a bitch? Number one, the true course was known, as well as the speed before the incident occurred. The tape was replayed and he attempted to start a 360 turn and then he reduced power. That reduction caused detection because of a sleeping sonar man. Second, the Greenling went motionless which took two or three minutes. The red nose bastard escaped! Third, the incident was reported and the message back to the skipper's hand burned with fire! Fourth, we have got to find him! The help of the operations officer, he and the navigator wondered which side of the ridge he is. The first inclination is to keep traveling down the eastern side, but we didn't see him opt for the western side. But, the western side spoils the limitation of his missiles. The ranges shown are complete variations of scenarios. End result, follow the eastern side of the slope and hope for the best.

The undersea community has seen many objects beneath and exploring its dark depths. Captain Alexei Latvia was exuberant over the spooking of a U.S. Navy submarine. All the talk aboard his vessel was of this achievement. Two attempts to try to intercept him again failed, but you never can tell. The seamount was dead ahead, about an hour away. The navigator approached the skipper and wanted to know how to handle this matter. The captain wanted to pass the treacherous undersea topography and go around the system, catching the victim from behind. Now that the plot was set, the star commander wanted to see the captain. The captain was informed of a suspected impostor onboard. The specifics indicated that he was a KGB man in disguise, and that his actions were strictly limited to taking notes on a pad, which could be nothing at all. "Keep a strict watch on him and, if this gets out of hand, bring him to me. That's in chains, too," the captain ordered. Fifty minutes later the skipper was at the navigator's station. When the submarine was at the beam of the seamount, the timing was of essence. Once the turn was given, the sub turned to the left. Speed was reduced to three or four knots as the ship turned to the north. Nothing at all was reported from the sonar station. The captain gave instructions for course changes and the course was set to head east to the mid-Atlantic Ridge and proceed with an eye on the missile ranges, with orders not to exceed—or pass—them.

Naval Station Keflavic had lost long-range contact, Argentina Naval Facility gained a five-minute contact, and that had been the frustration of the first missile carrier. The U.S. attack boat assigned to the trailer still didn't have contact. The commander in chief of the Atlantic fleet now was the query of the Pentagon. Norfolk, for the purposes of this single ballistic fortress, had called on immediate recall of its men and women second-guessing on where, what or who that submersible was. Meeting at Ocean Systems Analysis, numerous men from the submarine community, and other men with patrol background, listened to the brief. The leader of the brief showed the track of the Yankee until she was lost. The exact point of being lost was east of the Mid-Atlantic Ridge. The next sound surveillance contact was from Argentia, which had contact for only five minutes. This was validated by comparisons with previous sound information. This brought a flurry of questions, which ranged from everything imaginable. "Attention," the lieutenant's command announced. The commanmder in chief walked in and sat down in the front row. He asked the following questions:

"What track do you suspect he is making?"

"We believe the Yankee has joined up to the west of the ridge."

"Based on the speed of the target, do you have another trailer notified, or are there more attack boats that will be dispersed to get back on this critter?"

"Admiral, I am Admiral Miles." The CINC turned around and recognized him.

Admiral Miles related that he had broken off two submarines, one off the shore of North Carolina and the other transitioning back from Rota, Spain to sail the proposed position of 40N and 050°

West. "They have the backup information on the Yankee's last position. By the time the two submarines arrive, surely we will know which submarine gets the bait."

The CINC responded, "I want VP coverage immediately! Take the last fix and send the patrol ahead of the Yankee and let's begin laying sonobuoy barriers. Finally, I would like you to plot the east coast areas with references to the missiles carried by the Yankee at sea."

The CINC rose, and everyone stood at attention as he exited the conference room.

The status of events was right behind the admiral's move. Thirty minutes later, a P-3B (VP-8) was airborne out of Bermuda. The only holdup was plotting barriers well ahead of the intended or likely position. Once the tactical commander got, obtained and ascertained the sonobuoy information and position, the plane launched. Plans were set to make all available airplanes operational ready. The next airplane would take off in six hours.

By the time the two submarines were near the underground point, they shut down their acceleration and steamed the area at 16 knots. They traveled together and then they broke off, expanding the search by 15 miles. Even this did not help. The navigator got out a chart and measured the killing range of cities in his virtual path. He and the captain examined his demonstration. The skipper recognized how impressive it looked. With great restraint, the navigator re-plotted the course and began following it.

Once on-station, the P-3 crew began loading sonobuoys with the Tactical Coordinator ("TACCO") directing each sonobuoy drop. The buoys were SSQ-41s and they were set at 300 feet for three hours of operation. The sonobuoy life was separated by the recorder. The eight buoys were allotted to print for 10 minutes, and then another eight buoys were allotted to the AQA-5 (sonic recorder). This was, in fact, a tedious way of doing business! Every hour the Jezebel operator would relax, get up and have another cup of coffee. After three hours on-station, we moved up 25 miles and started over again. Once the sonobuoys were in place, we started again with this buoy chain. Not too many ships out in this part of the world. The first hour passed uneventfully, and the sonic operator went to the head. Twenty minutes later, he thought he saw something. "Oh well, I think I'll have another sip of coffee."

The TACCO was tapped on the shoulder, because the operator thought he had contact. Under anticipation of help, he described the contact suddenly appearing. The officer peppered the operator with questions. "Is that oral contact? What direction is the target moving?"

The operator responded, "No, the target is hanging out, but we had better go and check the buoy."

"Set condition two for localization," directed the PPC (Patrol Plane Commander), Maypole 14 was the buoy in contact, 75 miles to the east.

The tactical coordinator was with the navigator drumming up a contact report. Meanwhile, the relief aircraft was about 100 nautical miles from the on-station area, and held sonobuoy 14. The PPCs agreed they had made contact, however, the relief aircraft suggested that the contact might be a convergence zone contact. The oncoming PPC agreed that he may solve the convergence zone first, and the relief was completed. This contact had detected the sound of a submarine that had caused the sound to bend about 30 miles in moderate waters.

The message was received from the VP-8 aircraft that had contact. The first aircraft said it was in valid contact and turned it over to the second aircraft on-station. The commander in chief broadcast this contact intelligence to the boat dispatched to the Yankee. The contact was about 60 miles north of where the U.S. submarine was positioned. The captain looked at this contact and read the message again. He borrowed a compass from the navigator and plotted a 30-mile circle about the buoy. There is where the target is, due north of the buoy. So, therefore, they were only 30 miles from him. The captain noticed that the bastard was west of the ridge. Ten minutes later, he sent a top-secret message that he would search out the target and, in essence, he would be the trail boss. Commander Submarine Force copied the signal and agreed with the solution.

"Captain, just in case the whole ball of wax explodes, COMSUBLANT sent a signal for the submarine returning from Rota to report to Norfolk as planned! Acknowledge."

Yankee's sanctuary was a place of refuge and protection. Its plight has been of rebuttal and enraged anger for the commanding officer being trailed almost half of the way from Murmansk. How ludicrous, brainless and irrational this escapade had been to him, the exec and to his entire crew. With the help of his executive officer, they went bit by bit, piece by fragment, and with each new idea of both men, the two were fallacious with this mission. The hate mechanism was overpowering, and the result was half of this deployment was a total debacle. So the two submariners plotted and changed the remainder of the flight. They proceeded into the South Atlantic near the island of Bermuda. Next swinging to the west, well within the missile range of onboard weapons, the exec suggested that we become more elusive in our reactions. "For example, look for vessels headed for the States that will provide cover while they are tauntingly closing in undetected near to the shore. Then, of course, what will occur with the trailer? We will work that out when it occurs," replied the captain.

Through mindless hours of searching, the U.S. attack crew finally intercepted their elusive Yankee. The feeling was one that no one knows who knows can define. The sonarman was again in control and don't make him drop the ball. The captain went on the loudspeaker to announce the event. This time he wanted all men to be quiet and to pass slowly in the event of a rapid maneuver by the Yankee. The exec and the navigator were completely aware of the situation. The head boat was at 270 feet making 10 knots and the trailer was steady at 400 feet. The message went out with the contact report and both underwater advocates are boring their way into the south Atlantic.

The join-up of both boats brought a sigh of relief to the Ocean Systems Atlantic. They reoriented the arrays and began looking with renewed vigor. In half an hour, they regained contact on one line. Incidentally the second P-3 that had contact passed to him tried to convert the contact to a direct path. In doing this, the P-3 lost an engine and had returned to base. Making calculations on the plotting board showed that this was, without a doubt, a convergence contact and fits in with the position offered by the U.S. sub. The third plane finally got out of Bermuda and was four hours late covering the search area. The brass, meanwhile, was preparing a brief for the Pentagon and the Joint Chiefs of Staff. This word came to Norfolk by red phones indicating the security of this urgent matter. Underwater sources were making a revolving course, little do we know, but he transit tells a story of uncertainly and modification. When to stop this record of navigation is undecided, but they take off from Norfolk at 0700 the next day. A complete gram analysis is drummed up and loaded for display.

At 0400, an urgent message is received from the second follower. The Yankee has altered course to 300 degrees true. This coincided with the last of sonic data. In essence, what in the hell was going on? Was this theory something new and to coincide that this is something new or delusive? Analysts were scratching their heads in amazement. Yankee, you are unlike the rest!

At 300 feet, the Yankee was headed toward the east coast of the United States. The captain commanded that this submersible come up to periscope depth. A few minutes later, he spotted a shipping liner that was sailing 295 for a course. The sonarman was advised and the captain wanted to know if we could use this ship as a decoy to hide beneath. In three minutes, the sonar reported that the ship was making 18 knots. The executive officer nodded his head and the captain went down to 300 feet and he directed the helmsman to follow that surface vessel. Finally, the sub was almost under the ship, but he settled down about 500 yards astern of the liner. Of course, they had picked up speed but who could tell if this ship was headed right for New York City? He hoped that the concealment would last from 300 miles and then he would do a turn 180° true.

Sonar was on the loudspeaker saying that the Yankee had gone up to periscope depth to send a message or something. The U.S. captain showed up on the bridge and attempted to resolve the situation. The sonarman reported another contact that was making the same course as we were. The silence was once again broken when the sonarman reported an increase to 18 knots. In addition, the Yankee had apparently hidden beneath the liner. He was hoping his propulsion would go unnoticed! For the next 20 hours at 18 knots represented almost 400 miles closer to New York carefully hidden by the ship's mountainous props. The Russian skipper must be laughing, for this was the perfect strategy.

Washington and the Pentagon were jumping left and right, followed by arguments and standoffs. The present alternative to the action was counteract; the ASW Carrier and the Destroyer Force against this resurgence. Another point the Department of Defense and the Central Intelligence Agency have was there was no definitive position of this intruder. The Navy intelligence said that the trailer was just behind the Yankee boat. Besides, he was under the liner that would dock at New York City. Finally, the following data was decided:

Launch a Hunter Killer ASW Carrier and forces to detect and track the Yankee.

Report when the ASW forces have set sail.

Coordinate SOSUS fixing and report as soon as possible.

With Captain Latvia at the bridge, he commanded that they stop. Action was demanding and the ship began to slow down. The liner continued on by itself, not knowing it had lost a partner. "Come port to 180 at four knots," commanded the captain. The navigator had the instructions for over three hours and he flipped a chart, which was correct. The captain had some vibrations from the presence of listening devices below Virginia Beach, which is south of Norfolk, Virginia.

"Captain, he is slowing down," the sonarman exclaimed. "All stop," the captain said. Why would he do that? The skipper was patiently waiting for him to restart, but to no avail. What about the liner? Jesus Christ! Once again, he asked the sonarman about the missile carrier. He reiterated the surface liner, and the only thing that he has was 10 minutes ago on the Yankee. After questioning him, the skipper threw down the mike. It was now 15 going on 16 minutes since they had contact. The communications officer was notified and he was to send the last contact report. What else can he do?

Boris, or whatever the Yankee maiden name of this vessel is called, had an inconvenient voyage. Hatteras had a devil of a time with this aircraft giant, but neither ASW Carrier (S-2, SP-2H or P-3) could eventually contain and track her. Through trickery and cunning, this missile carrier ran over all obstacles. After steaming 18 knots and shutting down to four knots caused a frenzy up and down the east coast. Yes, he got the President's attention, which the Chief of the Navy, the Joint Chiefs and Department of Defense spin different parallelograms about how to quell this bodacious submarine. The result of the voyage was headed back to Murmansk. It headed east and joined up on the ridge headed northeast bound.

The super submersible came back to the waters that protected the wives and children. The Yankee had performed its mission without difficulty. Tugs were readied and they maneuvered the ship until it touched the slip. Captain Alexei Latvia standing on the main portion of the sail was blown about by the winds. It wasn't the wind but the efforts of now and ice that traversed the air. It was early December and Natalia, his wife, was there, standing with their two children. Finally, the bow and stern were tied up sufficiently. The chief of the boat asked permission to leave this ship. The men were excited and they piled off the ship to their loved one's arms. The admiral was there to congratulate him on a successful voyage. The captain returned his greeting with a handshake. Admiral Biron reported that a review of their traverse would be held at two o'clock tomorrow. The captain agreed and the admiral went to his car and motored away. Captain Latvia spoke with the operations officer and wanted him, plus the navigation officer, to meet at 1100 hours aboard the ship. Of course, he told the exec, and of course he would be there.

The KGB or the State Security Committee did have a spy or undercover agent aboard. His duties were to take notes if proper procedures were not followed, plus variations of course, etc. He showed up at the headquarters, which received a manila folder, which was marked "urgent." Ordinarily this was the proper procedure but they were waiting for him. The guard escorted him to the room where he would be questioned, or perhaps interrogated. After four hours of questioning, the second-class officer was dismissed. Tomorrow will be a day which neither rats desire.

On board the Yankee at 1100, the captain led the discussion about the mission. He admitted outright that there was a KGB representative on the ship. Now what can be done about this? The exec said we should start with the reading of the orders. Then take each instant and expand on it and give the course of action that must be taken. Both the operations and the navigator spoke up acknowledging the positive points of the way The captain devised the only commonsense approach to the problem. The four-man group set up an alphabet listing which we followed to the letter "S."

At 1400 hours, Admiral Latvia and his party entered the court of inquiry where they were seated in front of many distinguished delegates. First and foremost the KGB, the admirals of the submarine force and the judge, which came from the Russian Navy, were to be seated. "All rise," said the administrator. In walked the delegation of distinction, with faces devoid of insolent behavior. When seated, the announcer called the others to be seated. The judge raised his eyes and began reading the deposition placing the Yankee under control of Captain Latvia has created a repertory of kaleidoscopic events, which have created oblivious behavior with his submarine crew. Accordingly, the judge read the charges. Occasionally the admonition against him was a big adrenaline shot focused on his anal pore. When the time came for his side to respond, he complied.

At the outset the captain led off by saying that the mission was written for an earlier class of submarine, namely an Echo II. Second, his course into the North Atlantic went down the mid-Atlantic Ridge that led to the interception of a U.S. nuclear submarine.

"Captain, did you record this information?" the judge inquired. Most assuredly, and where driven by adversary tactics, we lost trail for the remainder of the mission. In need of a break, the court called recess, which lasted for 30 minutes.

Devious and senile tactics followed the exponents who put the sailors on the stand. The tally of retribution was staggering and the detail of this petty officer caused the captain to become unglued. Finally, the judge broke up the meeting and asked that the captain and crew be excused. Yankee class representatives were escorted out of the courtroom into a separate room. Men of a submarine were unstable in such a room. When men have survived such an ordeal, why in All Mighty Hands had such power been given to the other way of society?

At the termination of the court proceedings, the judge found the captain guilty of belligerent misuse, pugnacious wrongdoing and employing/deploying the important missile carrier to the reaches of the United States coastline.

A DAY ON THE FARM

WHEN MOST PEOPLE THINK OF RUSSIA, THEY conjure up an image of a huge cold country with lovely villages scattered amid deep forests across open steppe and bleak tundra. There is no denying the dimensions of this spectacular country, but in reality it is an urban country. Moscow is the center and is the largest medium with 8.5 million inhabitants. This beyond control leads us to a fantastic achievement and terrible failure.

Almost every adult, male and female had a job, holidays, lots of activities and leisure time. Children are lavished with affection. They are jealously protected and (indoctrinated) in a massive school system. The state regulates every aspect of life, yet cracks down on demoniac behavior—even including a counterculture. Russia's sweep of Germany at the end of World War II led to a new era. The red flag of communism rose in Europe with the takeover of East Germany.

In 1958 a well-decorated Soviet Army master sergeant—the equivalent of an American sergeant major—retired after 25 years of service and headed home. Belorussia was the land where his mom and dad had once lived. His parents had not survived the holocaust of WW II, the Great Patriotic War. Dimitri Ivanov was a distinctive, proud and collective retired enlisted man. He was not married and wanted a farm to earn a living. He remembered as the train carried him home, he had three other brothers and sisters besides him which he had not seen or heard from for years. He noticed the farmland that was approaching was being attended by two individuals, which were too few for the fields. According to his watch, he had about two more hours until he reached his home site.

Finally the train rounded a bend and he was home. He got off at a small community which was overburdened with small shops ranging from hardware to grocery stores and finally with numerous clothing shops. There are several oddities such as bars, barbershops and mainly seed and fertilizer stores. Dimitri found his bearings so he rented a horse and buggy, which he rode out to his father's abode. He rode for three miles and then sighted an oak tree that encompassed a small hut that adjoined a field that consisted of potatoes. He stopped abruptly and noticed a pile of rubble that was the hut of his fathers.

After viewing and seeing the signs of the past 30 years, he was dismayed. He returned to town and checked in with the government agent. He showed the paperwork that proved he was discharged from the Army and showed his Communist party affiliation. After seeing these credentials, the official shook his hand and asked what he could do for him. He identified he had a father who farmed the parcel that had been his father's land.

The government agent went over to the filing cabinet and looked under Ivanov. Yes, he said, the Ivanov family was killed and their farm destroyed when the Germans passed through here. Dimitri said very little, but finally he said that he wanted that plot to take over.

Overjoyed, the agent told him that there were several farmlands that he could occupy. He asked if the resigned Army man would fill out a form, which he did. After signing it, he was awarded three portions of farmland equaling about 100 acres (2.47 hectare equals one acre).

The plans were worked out and he was given the foreman's name to contact with all of his authorization for owning his 100 acres. Since this was August, he wanted to know how the flats or houses were. The agent responded with they are building more huts with an estimate of September or the 15th of October as the latest date they would be available. Noticing the time, Dimitri left the government's office and went to a hotel. After renting a bed for the night, he went to a restaurant where he had soup, cabbage and potatoes for dinner.

Early in the next morning he went back to his coordinator for his farming plot. He arbitrated with him, and he realized what he needed. Two hours later he was helping the other farmers get their crops in. Dimitri was tired at the end of the day. The next day, one farmer plowed up the potatoes and he plus another lad bagged the potatoes. His corn awaited the next day where he cut the corn and harvested it for the young cows. He also had fresh tomatoes and other ingredients that made the soups that were famous in that part of the world.

By the time it was September, the winds from the northwest had arrived. Fresh droplets of rain and cold winds caused the flowers to fall and quickly told everyone that it is autumn. That night he had gone into town to get some clothes for the winter. In the store he met a new store worker. She seems alert and helpful, but Dimitri was impressed with her willingness to help him. Sofia was her name; he liked her smiles and he loved to hear her laugh and the way she somehow understood him. Dimitri made a date with her next week for dinner. He unfolded his life, recounting his childhood through World War II and his time with the army. Sofia related the same about her child experiences, which led her to a degree in art. They were in love with each other. He was 42 and she was 23, which wasn't unheard of for relationships.

In December they got married at the church in town. Her mother and father made the wedding and the pastor made it happen as the two kissed. The newly married couple sped into the night, although it was snowing, but they only know that they had done the precise thing in their own life.

When they arrived at their hut, the abode looked handsome. The door swung open, and the groom marched in carrying the bride. He kissed her passionately and took off her coat.

Then he showed her around with the beds on one side and the living room/dining room/kitchen around a fireplace, which was providing the heat for the entire house. He quickly went outside and took the reins off the two horses. Dimitri put the horses in stalls, with plenty of hay and water. The wagon was pulled inside the barn and he took her bags inside. The husband poured each of them a glass of vodka, which they toasted to the sanity of life everlasting. The second toast brought undo pains of love and wanting until they climaxed together amid joyous pleasure. On into the night their gradation for pleasure ended as they came out of the bed for some soup and hot bread.

The winter of 1958 was a snowbound, ice-covered scenario with fierce winds. Sofia made numerous curtains, made deerskin rugs and made numerous plants, which provided green leaf salads plus raisins' that her husband saved. March of 1959 clearly brought the first signs of spring. Late that night when the two got in bed, she told Dimitri that she was pregnant. He was so happy for her, and she was really 100 percent sure. By the end of the week he took her to the doctor and confirmed that she was with child. The physician prescribed additional medication so that she should see him in about three months. Once they returned home, it was the husband's turn to get started on the farmland. Soon he had the horses turning over the soil and then he went to the manager to see how he intends to plant the necessary fields. Hay, potatoes and the old standby, corn, round out the farm acreage. Needless to say, the wife would take care of the chickens, the cows, possibly a pig or two and the tomatoes/greenery. Most important is the bread, which is the mainstay of this family.

Hot and muggy, the end of May produced young plants coming up and the rains were giving each crop equal opportunity of reaching their growth. His wife was developing an extended roundness about her waist. Dimitri had gotten pinewood and made a small cradle for the baby. It took him awhile before he mounted the undercarriage, which gave the bed proper rocking phenomena. Sofia made the necessary bed sheets and lo and behold, the nursery was almost complete. That was done so now let's make a table to wash him or her, dress the infant or make something to change the baby. Even her mother had many items to manufacture, re-invent or make new gadgets for the new arrival.

In August she went to the doctor to see how she was doing. Things were going great as she was healthy as a bear. The doctor said that she would have to wait until the first of December before the baby would make a show. Numerous pills were dispensed and the next appointment, if necessary, would be in November.

Gathering in the harvest along with several farmers is still a turmoil of confusion. Starting with the potatoes, the farmers fight about this and that, which leads to controversy and alcoholism. Finally, though thick and thin, all of the crops were squared away before the first signs of winter approaching. Bargaining this year brought several trades and swaps that Dimitri effected. He got several bales of hay for his four animals, he sold his two pigs and got half of the pigs' meat, sausage and bacon and a cow that was to provide milk for the child and family.

November is upon us, and Sofia is way-overburdened with child. Traveling to the doctor's office is a task, especially when it is cold with the wind gusting to 45 miles per hour. Concerned, the doctor once again said that the child could come at any time. He advised that she should have someone with her; her mother would assist her. Essentially all things were discussed and a plan was made to handle the particulars. The trip home was painful and arduous, but they made it, as he helped sweet Sofia into the house. He went the next day to get her mother, as he left someone with his wife. They celebrated Thanksgiving and they had fun cooking popcorn over the fire in the fireplace. Suddenly it happened; the baby started to move and immediately it broke her water. Her mother took over and he was to make hot water. The labor period was long, and then finally after 14 hours, the vagina was ready to pass the infant to life. With one final push the path that granted life to a baby boy was realized. He screamed and he was at her side. She smiled when he handed her the boy wrapped in bands of cloth and laid him in her arms. Radiant she was and smiled as she realized this was worth waiting for.

Sasha was the name his parents had agreed on and his mom really adored the baby. Breast-feeding the child, he looked just like his dad; he smiled and laughed like him too. It was extremely cold this winter and Dimitri had difficulty keeping all the farm animals comfortable. Abruptly the weather turned warm and everyone knew spring was on the way. Sofia liked to play with her Sasha. In fact, it brought life's greatest pleasure playing with him. She used to rock him on her knee, cuddling, cooing and singing nursery rhymes. She nursed him until he was six months old and transferred him to milk and pablum. He started grinding his gums and soon baby teeth appeared. Soon his mother would say, "I want 10 more like him." A mother that loves and offers protection is one that can never void his needs and she never deprives one of the necessities of life.

Two years later the government agent that Dimitri works for recommended that the party official transfer to Kiev and act as a coordinator for the collective farming bureau. He decided and his wife agreed and soon, they sold or traded all of their belongings and moved to Kiev. They were booked into a 12-story apartment block of flats in the city. Through a bit of hook and crookery, both joined the government as she was accepted as an art teacher in Kiev High School. In summary, Dimitri gets 300 rubles a month, while his wife earns 160 rubles a month. The monthly grocery bill equates to 230 rubles due to subsidized staples such as bread, milk and sugar.

Ivanov's flat had two rooms for living and sleeping, a bathroom and a separate cubicle for the toilet. One room displays a prominent view of books and a black-and-white television set. One addition to the bathroom was the installation of a washing machine. Clothes are hung out to dry on the balcony. All three of us moved into the flat, inter alia, the boxes, furniture and suitcases included. Sasha was really excited and he was walking beside his dad. He liked the apartment and played with his toys and a new airplane that magically appeared on the living room floor. When all of the putting away was accomplished, supper was served. Sasha was bathed, and finally put to bed. They sat down and with their shoes off watched TV. Happy they were and truly blessed to be selected to move to Kiev. Indulging a traditional penchant for hard drink, Dimitri went and got two glasses of vodka. They toasted each other and downed the liquid. Point of note, the average adult drinks 14 liters of vodka annually, more hard liquor than is consumed in any other country. Both husband and wife hardly drank 14 liters, but that really fits the bill of a drunkard!

Well-established in Kiev, they sent their boy to daycare and went to work. With certainty and assuredness, Sofia announced she was going to have another baby. Dimitri was dumbfounded as he heard the news. He loved his wife, but now he realized that she was the one for him. They hugged and, of course, their son butted in. Six months later, Sasha was three years old, pampered and spoiled. Soviet children are almost never punished or scolded at home. Yet they grow up to be a disciplined young man. They are indoctrinated to conform, to subjugate individual desires to the aims of the political organizations, which they are suitable. Among the many factions that are available are the Children of October (7-9 years) and Young Pioneers (10-15 years). Children are rated from one to 10; with 10 being the highest commendation while one is the lowest of the worst reprimand.

The first lesson in conformity starts as early as three years old, in other words, when a child enters nursery school. Nearly half of all Soviet children do. Each year in school the structures intensify. At seven the child starts elementary school. The girls dress in black or brown socks and the boys in blue jackets with shoulder suspenders. From 0830 to 1430 six days a week they learn basic courses, with heavy concentration on math and science. Interestingly enough, right hand writing is instituted to provide the art of penmanship. In school the children become a leak that means they are formed in a juvenile (each members standing depends on the standing of the link).

Sasha progressed through the seventh year. Progress is related to his rapid knowledge of learning and equating to his own ability to understand. This student's ability to learn is an amazing feat. He felt impolite as far as being among the students but sensed that he was in competition with members of his class. He told his mom and dad that he felt this rivalry between his fellow classmates. Wanting to excel, he must do this to fulfill his destiny. The abundance of activities including swimming, soccer and whatever the game of winning, Sasha was a champion.

Aboveboard, Sasha was proud of his parents who were joyous to have two other children. Two girls, six and three, were tearing up the apartment and dazzled the eye of the beholder. The older of the two was in the second grade and the latter is about to start school. Dimitri had advanced in his word and had moved to a larger apartment, which always had more space to move in living conditions. Sasha had been engaging in several outdoor activities, such as soccer, football and, for the heck of it, running. Running is his sport, in that he's running the pants off anyone who runs against him.

The eighth grade begins with examinations, which try to point the student down the ivory placards to a ideal which vies innovative technology with society. His examinations yielded an exponentially brilliant student, which is destined to attend a university or exceptionally gifted position. With accruement in scholastics at present, he must excel onward until he must deduce which road he would depart upon.

Algebra, biology, chemistry and running were his favorite topics. Progressing by his knack of picking up mathematics and applying them to other subjects. As he went from one year to another the studies got harder, but not Sasha, he welcomed them. In the 11th grade he finished algebra 1 and 2, and plane geometry, he embarked on calculus and chemistry not to mention Russian and English. Track offered a new goal, and that was the mile. He ran the mile for the first time and as always, he was the top of the draw.

By the time he was 19, this student had set a record in his schooling. Totally qualified in everything he was ready to serve his two years in the active military. Professors of the school desired him to go on to the university, but the active military took preside. Sasha had reached the highest of honors in a graduating class. His mom and dad were right beside him with each sister holding his hands. After receiving his diploma, he got his orders to Army boot camp.

At some juncture a short time ago, before Stalin, in Lenin's day, the wise decision was taken that the state apparatus should be manned accordingly. Comrades of proven worth were responsible or experienced to the common cause. In order that the state should not be infiltrated by alien elements at some stage in the future, it was decided that successors to this group should be prepared and that it was essential that these young people were educated. Educational means were therefore set up to prepare the future ruling class, and these were filled with children of the comrades, who were dedicated to the revolutionary cause. The individuals were very pleased with this initiative and have never since contemplated any deviation from the course approved by Russia.

As an illustration, the Minister of Foreign Affairs of the USSR is, of course, a person of proven power. It follows that his son must be dedicated to the people's right; this underlines that he can be a diplomat and further move, checking out his credentials, can enter diplomat service. He, too, is a trusted person, dedicated to the national cause and this means that the road to success is open for the shining star.

The comrades of proven worth got together and agreed among themselves that, since their children were already dedicated to their Motherland and were prepared to defend its interests throughout their lives, there was not need to enter the service. Accordingly, when the sons reach 17 years old they are not required to register for military service. Instead, they enter the Institute of International Relations. After qualifying there, they go off for two years spending their lives defending the interests of the Motherland vis-à-vis the front line in the battle against capitalism. Case in point, this is how the children allude being ferried around in dirty railway cars, are not abashed by sergeants, and do not have their teeth pulled out, and why their girlfriends have to wait for them for three years to come home.

Lest the absurd idea should enter anyone's head that the sons of the comrades are not defending socialism, they are given awards for their service from time to time. Many sons that are responsible spent years defending the cause in many foreign countries. He, for example, was given a decoration, which exuded his glory in the highest.

Now what happens if your father is not among those of the highest powers at the helm of the workers' and peasants' state? Money speaks. For example, a few thousand rubles can make you unfit for military service and your name would be removed from the register. What if your sire doesn't have a propensity to unleash these rubles to spare? With out a doubt, one could cut your finger off with a knife. Or, you could place a small piece of foil so the X-rays reveal tuberculosis and that's the end of the Army. Basically, you could go to prison, or you can go to boot camp in that dirty railway car.

Sasha Ivanov and the column of recruits finally reached the division to where it was going. The hushed, rather frightened youths leave the train at a station surrounded by barbed wire. With there heads quickly shaven, driven through a cold bath, their filthy rags are burned, they are issued crumpled greatcoats, tunics and trousers that don't fit and small squeaky boots and belts. With the first grading process completed, the student does not know what is happening. Political reliability or his father's record of participation in all meeting (Communist mass meetings) mean nothing to his height, physical or mental development. These factors are predicated in the analysis of who is category 0, 1-10, and so forth by allocating him a number.

Socialists make the lying claim that it is possible to create a classless society. In fact, if a number of people are thrown together, it is certain that a leading group, or perhaps several groups would emerge. This had nothing to do with race, religion or political beliefs. It will always happen. If a group of survivors were to reach an uninhabited island after a shipwreck, after they had been there only a week, a leader would have already emerged. Realistically, in German concentration camps, no matter who is imprisoned together, they would stratify in societies with class differentiation.

Shorthaired recruits nervously entered the enormous barracks room where between 200 to 500 men live. The sergeants split the soldiers up and at first everything goes without chance. There was the bunk, the bedside locker where the washing kit was kept, four manuals, brushes and the storage space for the handbook of scientific communism.

But at night the barracks come alive. All in all, the newest men realized they were part of four groups. One group left after six months, the second after a year, a third class waited for 18 months and the last segment would stay two years. Definitions enter the establishment are many, for example; high castes guard privileges jealously, and the lower castes respond to seniors as their elders or betters. The lowers must be there 18 months before they can serve as superiors of the "scum," the lowest of the recruit.

The night after the new group arrived was a terrible one. The naked recruits were flogged with belts and ridden bareback by their seniors, who used them to fight mock cavalry battles. Individuals in the new group were often driven to sleep in lavatories after their beds were fouled by their elders, etc. Commanders knew who's on first, and obviously, they did not interfere in the undertaking.

The lowest class had no rights in this place. They, the scum, cleaned the shoes, made the beds of their seniors, cleaned their weapons, relinquished their meat and sugar and sometimes gave them bread. Soldiers who were about to be released give the new recruits new uniforms. The commander of a platoon was quite content with this situation as they invariably ordered the sergeants to get some done. The sergeants gave this job to the senior soldiers who hand over the job to the scum.

Meanwhile Dimitri Ivanov had not heard a word from his son. Granted, about six months ago he and his wife said goodbye to their son who promised he would write faithfully. Being a resident of Kiev, Russia and a decorated World War II master sergeant, he made some calls to Moscow to ascertain the problems that affected his son. Initial calls to Moscow took the necessary essentials, name, age and the rank of the individual. He received a call from Moscow that stated that he was assigned to boot camp and was scheduled to be trained as an enlisted man. Dimitri blew up! He was fuming and disruptive because his son was in the top 5 percent of all graduates and was promised to be trained as an officer. He wanted a complete investigation, including the KGB, as to why, what and who diverted this individual's life in a torrent of hell!

Two days later a letter arrived in Kiev. Sasha Ivanov was to be pulled out of boot camp and sent to officer training. His standing would be critiqued and he would be assessed as to attitude and excellence of worth.

Sasha Dimitri was found cleaning the lavatories when the sergeant told him that the commanding officer of the boot camp wanted to see him. Sasha changed his working uniform, washed his hands and face and brushed off his shoes. The sergeant opened the door and presented him to the administrative sergeant who then knocked on the commander's door and went inside to inform him of Dimitri's arrival. With a nod of his head, Sasha and the sergeant went inside. Both were standing erect when the commander looked up. Out came his hand to shake Sasha's and asked them to sit down.

He talked into the voice box and 30 seconds later there was a cup of coffee for each of them. Now that the acknowledgments were through, the CO had the floor. Six months ago he was one of several hundred recruits that arrived at this facility. Lower than dog shit, he was the first to undergo this heinous act of abomination. "You were known as scum," said the commanding officer, "but why did you put up with that?"

Sasha explained that each time he complained or asked about something, a sergeant thrashed him. Plus he got extra duty because of his insubordination on the way he was treated. He spoke freely when the commander wanted to hear from him. Sasha told of four letters that he gave to the sergeants, which he believed were destroyed.

A few minutes went by while the commander thought and suddenly announced that he was sorry that there had been an error in the assignment desk. "This mistake was unfounded, and Sasha Dimitri you will depart this facility by 1600 hours as there is a seat on the train. You will take leave until the 24th of November where you will report to Second Chief Directive of General Staff of Training Facility to begin officer training."

Quickly he stood up, followed by Dimitri and the sergeant when the commander shook hands with him. He gave the file to the noncommissioned officer. The next stop was to get his orders, leave pass and lastly, he had to pack his clothes that had suffered six months of abuse.

The conductor stopped by Sasha, awakened him and told him that they would be in Kiev in 20 minutes. He got up from his sleep and went to the men's room to wake up. Water was thrown into his face and a comb would satisfy his slept-in hair. Back in his seat he watched the glow of light of the metropolis. It was good to be in Kiev and he wonders how mom, dad and the children have changed. He lit up a cigarette, something he shouldn't do, but the boot camp community supported it. At last the train slowed down and the train station came into view. They came to a stop and the conductor wished him luck. Sasha was basically a soldier without the basic tools except of ostracism.

Finally he walked out of the train and he heard voices. He looks up and he saw his two sisters running to him with his mom and dad in the distance. They must be 12 and nine years old. They hugged and kissed Sasha until their parents arrived.

"Mom," Sasha cried. His mother was crying as she held him so tightly.

"I am so sorry you got sent to that dissident camp," said mom. Father was looking well but he wanted to comfort his son and welcome his son home for such a short time.

After the children were in bed, Sasha gave his parents a bit by bit blow of his military experience; lets call it debauchery that he went through for six months. Most of the story was covered over by his attempt to clear the air from this escape from the devil. Explicitly, he told of the "lower class" and how he rebounded from the filth and vermin to maintain sanity in life. He wrote at least four times and his pleas of hunger and anger were translated into a blending of help. The non-commissioned officer, who took his letters to be mailed, should be shot with no questions asked. His dad had the platform and told how he played a part in uncovering this buzzard happening. He was agonized by the actions of the Soviet Army, inter alia, the KGB for permitting such an action to transpire. Dad was crying and so was mom as he hugged them and they went to bed looking forward to the next day where they could enjoy each other in anticipation of another holocaust.

The next morning Sasha awoke with the two daughters Gala and Jan smiling, to tell him they loved him and to come to breakfast. The table was set and he had on his former clothes, not military attire. Breakfast was a dream; eggs, sausage, bread and good hot coffee. Mom remarked the he had lost weight. Twenty pounds was a terrible loss of weight, so his mother fixed him another piece of bread with special blueberries on the toast.

It was Friday and he had seven more days before he had to report to the Army. They spent the day shopping with the family, because dad had to work Friday. It was chilly in November so they hit the road. They went to the grocery first and then they went looking for clothes. Mom asked him to help her pick out some additional sweaters/pants for the girls. They found cute sweaters and bought two combinations for them. Dad needed a winter shirt so Sasha picked out a wool plaid variety and having some money with him, he bought a shirt and a crew-neck sweater. The ride home was refreshing since it was on a bus. At home the girls went outside and played while Sasha put on running shoes.

At three o'clock in the afternoon the sun had just set. Running is life. Everything in his body responded with his movement; heart pounding in accordance with the calibrated motion of his legs. Sasha had been running at a slow pace, but now the calibration was more profound and Sasha advanced up to near maximum strength.

After running for about 50 minutes, Sasha slowed down less than a mile away from his house. Suddenly Sasha saw another runner from the left. She was a good jogger and Sasha hastened to come along side of her.

"Hi," he said. She looked startled, but smiled when she saw him. She slowly came to a halt and so did Sasha. Mary was her name and she was quite nice. They talked for 15 minutes where she was going to the University in Kiev. She was staying in an apartment with an aunt while she went to school. They talked about school, where he grew up and what they were planning to do. They said goodbye and they hoped they could meet again.

The weekend was fabulous as his parents took all of them to see the ballerina dancers, the symphony orchestra and finally they went to church. Dad continually talked about the military and the problems that his son had been though.

Sunday afternoon Sasha went running. He saw Mary again so he joined her as she talked verbosely about her parents, her brothers and sisters, and everything about her life. After jogging for seven miles they sat down and talked some more. She had exams on Tuesday and early Wednesday morning. Would she be available for dinner to meet his family? Yes she would, which pleased him. They parted with a hug, but damn, Sasha wanted a kiss instead of a hug!

Wednesday morning Sasha proceeded to the train station to buy a ticket to Kuybyshev where he was to report to the 2nd Chief Directorate of General Staff. The tickets were to leave the station at four o'clock on Thursday afternoon. Through various connections and train changes, Sasha arrived at nine o'clock on Friday the 24th of November.

The whole family was excited when Sasha asked if his friend could have supper with his family on Wednesday night. His sisters wanted to know all about her, including the essential details. At five o'clock Sasha walked a block and went upstairs to her aunt's apartment. Mary opened the door. She had a pretty dress on, which drew many compliments from Sasha. Meeting her in running gear told a different version of her; she was beautiful. Each one of his family met Mary, and they all liked her. The girls took her to their bedroom and showed her their dolls and talked. Dad poured him vodka and said, "This is the first drink I offer you. Salute."

Down went the drink it burned, but tasted good. When Mary returned with the girls, a small plate of caviar was served with condiments to enhance the flavor of food. Dinner was served with a touch of wine and meat. Mary thoroughly enjoyed the meal and particularly the talk with his mother and father. Before they knew it, it was time for the girls to go bed. His date helped them change their clothes while Sasha straightened up the kitchen.

About 2130 the evening was showing its wear; Mary was yawning. Sasha stood up and said she must get back to her apartment because she had classes the next day. Mom and dad said goodnight and how much they had enjoyed meeting her. They left the house and started walking to the apartment. It had turned cold and his arm fitted around her body, and she liked it. Sasha didn't believe she realized it, but he was falling in love with her.

They get to her apartment and she told him she had a great time with everyone, including him. She opened up to him and gave a sign, as he kissed her again and nibbled her right ear. Mary told him that she would miss him and please write if it's all right to do so. Sasha told her that he would write the address as soon as he arrived at the next facility. One more kiss, and he thought they were in love with each other.

Dimitri, Sofia and the kids carried him to the train station Thursday afternoon. Sofia packed a lunch for him including a slice of pie. He had his uniform on but he promised that someday soon he would be an officer. The train arrived and Sasha kissed the young girls, his mom and lastly his dad. His dad didn't say much but he knew his son could factor out the good and the horrid experiences of training. Dad and the rest of the family watched the train disappear on the way to Kuybyshev.

The Spetznaz is the name of the Soviet Special Forces controlled by the Main Intelligence Directorate (GRU). The mission quite simply stated that the forces are to neutralize the military and political-economic systems through surprise, shock and preemption by deployment. Starting in the enemy's rear, he is easy to resist, reduce his forces and it is easier for the main forces to carry out his mission. In war this Spetznaz are tasked with killing (by passive means), identifying the nuclear facilities and other designated targets for other Soviet airpower and mobilization of command systems which inevitably would cause massive communications loss and, finally, dilatory disrupting of the enemy's power system.

The organization of this special force is responsible for Spetznaz and is called GRU. This apparatus is known as the Second Chief Directorate of the General Staff. The Second Department of Staff exercises this all-arms in five groups. This problem, of course, is how much total firepower do you need to do this job? In essence, the outbreak of war demands an organization of men that are tested to be superior and demand that they get the first crack over other outfits.

At nine o'clock in the morning the train pulled into the station in Kuybyshev, where it had snowed last night. Sasha got off the train and quite frankly did not know where to go. He did see a sign mentioning the Army base so he meandered over to this area whereby a sergeant asked if he needed a ride to the base. "Yes sir," replied the young lad, and followed him to the pickup truck. He asked to see his orders that he read, and he said a new class would start Monday. That was a comfortable feeling, as they departed the area.

They traveled out of town for about 10 miles and they saw the sign. The entire area is closed-end by a barb-wired fence with a guard checking each vehicle. Sasha showed his identification card and they were cleared to the administrative area. He checked in at the desk and the master sergeant said to wait for a minute.

The door opened and a Lieutenant Kliestoly met him and escorted him into his office. The Lieutenant closed the door and offered Sasha a seat. He reviewed his orders and confirmed that there would be not more false assignments with these orders. Sasha's training would begin on Monday, November 27, but first he had to get an up chit from the doctor, review what type of work he desired to do in the army and they would assign him that task.

At the hospital he pissed in a bottle, a medical corpsman took his blood pressure, eyes, ears and throat and he stood partially covered waiting for the doctor. Finally he showed up and was quite surprised/ pleased with what he had in front of him. He listened to his heart and felt his ribs, and you guessed it, the one finger job proved nada. "You are all set," said the doctor, "and thank you for waiting." The next stop was the quarters where Sasha would be billeted.

The barracks were located near an open area where the men exercised. His escort followed him into the living area. The bunks were on either side of the establishment. There were people there already which caused them to look up and acknowledge his presence. He checked in at the barracks and was assigned a bunk. Signing for his bed sheets and a pillow, he received a note to report to the physiological department that afternoon. Sasha made his bunk and the adjutant presented him with the uniforms that were made for work or stress. He reported that all recruits would wear the same uniform.

Sasha and others that joined him enjoyed lunchtime. The candidates for next week's class came from all over Russia. Most of the group they qualified beyond belief and were eager to end the wait. At least the mess hall started closing so the joyous group departed. Sasha found a way to his next stop, the physiological ward.

Upon reporting, the corporal found his record and proceeded to contact a medical doctor. He led Sasha to a room and said he would return shortly. After the doctor arrived, he went over the indications of his record. High scholastic attitude and marks, overall general athlete and a fine example of leadership. Without a doubt, he was a candidate for officer, but what then? Sasha replied that he had a difficult time in boot camp. "Pray tell, what happened?" queried the doctor Patiently Sasha told of the camp and set forth the dislikes of the superiors who kept this man in the doldrums of dejection.

After Sasha said his final word, the doctor walked over and patted him on the back. He advised him that he must not lose hope, and he would recognize some of the methodical processes in the four months of training. He shook his hand and wished him luck.

Over the weekend he had time to meet some of the guys who were going through the training with him. None of the men had been through such agony as Sasha. They had better be ready or something begins to unravel about this resemblance of men versus scum. He also had time to write to his girl, Mary. He told her of his train trip and he missed her. On Monday, he wrote, he started training that would last for four or five months. Graduation would mean he would become an officer although he had not chosen a field of endeavor. Finally, he told her how much he loved her and told her to keep in contact with his parents.

"Reveille, Reveille, Reveille. All hands will hit the deck," the loudspeaker announced. November 27, 1968, the class started with 80 people. Practice makes perfect accordingly, each trainee goes through the same cycle four times. This takes about five months, but this leaves a month to get reorganized before the next class. In this first month the recruits go through a basic course of physical awareness. Maintenance work must be done in the repair and overhaul of weapons, plus a great amount of indoctrination at the barracks, general cleanup areas and at the firing range. All subjects are introduced according to the training schedule, keeping in mind how the trainee is progressing. A soldier who is just starting out would do, for example, 30 push-ups and after six months he would reach 40. The standards increase as he stays in active duty. These standards of mobility apply as one increases in every activity, such as shooting, running, driving military vehicles, driving in a tank and developing a resistance to CW materials.

The second month of training involves the improvement of individual skills. In some cases, these already exist since the first group had been there before and the initial recruits gain quickly on the older man bound for the rank of officer. From the second month the weapon training is defined as "whole sections." At the same time, members of these sections learn how to replace one another and how to stand for their commanders. They practice sub-machine gunners firing grenade launchers, machine-guns, and then learn to drive/service armored personnel carriers and different rocket teams are taught to diversify their strengths to become highly proficient Russian army officers.

The inroads of the third month are devoted to perfecting the unit and exponentially increasing platoon unity. Exercises are run lasting for several days, which dwell on field firing, river crossing, negotiation of obstacles and anti-gas and anti-radiation treatment of personnel. Exercises such as these, they differentiate because they let the recruits carry out the responsibility as platoons. Then come field firing and other practical exercises lasting for two weeks each, first at company, then at regiment and finally at separate level. Finally, the last two-week period was taken up with large-scale maneuver, involving armies, fronts or even complete strategic directions.

After this an inspection of all formations that make up the Soviet Army is carried out. Checks are carried out on individual soldiers, sergeants, for example. Thereby, the cycle of instruction is completed. A month is set aside to repair and to allow refurbishing of equipment and the necessary training facilities used. Now the beginning of a new training cycle would start up as the new men report to this facility.

After the physical training session is accomplished, the men fell in for a march to breakfast. With full stomachs, they marched by the barracks for cleanup and inspection. After the series of bunks passed inspection, all of the 80 strong men received new clothing, replacement sergeant fatigues and a brisk winter coat with gloves. At eight o'clock in the morning there is a regimental parade or simply a march. This was the testing of the men to see which could hack it or not. Snow was falling and several lads had their left feet tied up, so the drill instructors had them doing push-ups. For the remainder of the period, this is really a review to find out what the candidates know or how they react to changing situations. They are told what to memorize so that they can vie on to officer quality. During the session, the questions range to the minister of defense can lead to prison sentences. If the review, the period ends early, the remainder is devoted to drill. Immediately after this, the students start a series of lectures, hands-on equipment, which follows for three periods.

Time spent in these subjects depends on all men who are climbing up the ladder of success. At the end of the day, 10 cadets dropped on request "DO." In a short while, it gets interesting because Russia is losing more officers.

The wind and the snow was winning as Sasha and his company came in from the blustery weather. Recently, the physical therapy was held in a old gym, which did not have any heat. Needless to say, the movement brought tons of pleasure from the guys. Four weeks have transpired and it was the 18th of December. After the barracks inspection, the sergeant's met with us to announce the Christmas plans. The major, who walked in unannounced, said the they would take a Christmas holiday beginning on Friday the 22nd of December through the 31st of December. All candidates were expected to go on leave and plans would be posted about railroad schedules. The troops were ecstatic and the phones were going to be busy tonight! Sasha made a quick call to his dad and told him he would be home on Saturday. He said hello to his mom and told her to remind Mary that he was coming home.

The number of hours spent on each subject varies, depending on the arm of service in which the soldiers are serving. However, the general work plan is the same, in that a review period, drill and then six hours on the subjects listed above would solve the necessary training schedule. Ninety-five percent of all work is done outdoors rather than in the classrooms. Most outside work is done in tank training areas or in tank depots. All periods, especially often strenuous activity, are very extricating. Insurmountable, the tactical training may involve six hours of digging trenches in the middle of a cold, frozen winter. A high-speed crossing of rivers, ravines and a rapid erection of camouflage—and everything is done at the double! Instruction in tactical training is usually without equipment. Programmatically, the dedicated tank crew is told that they are attacking the enemy on the edge of the woods. The tank crew carries out the mission and returns to hear what the observer had to say about their tactics. Once the system of instruction is supplanted, the crew can learn the viable tank scraggily quite easy.

Weapon training involves the study of weapons and of combat equipment. The sergeant conducting the lecture describes the elements of a gun and assemble/breakdown an assault weapon. He then treats the weapon as his own and strips it. Again he breaks the weapon down, and each time he must break down the system in 15 seconds. Then there is the tank, it carries 40 shells which weigh 21 and 32 kilograms according to type. Incidentally, all shells are loaded from their containers through the hatch and into the tank's ammunition store. You've got 23 minutes to do this, on your mark, go! This technique is practiced again and again.

Any process from changing tank's tracks or its engine running in a rubber protective clothing during CW training, is always learned by when practiced so often that it becomes automatic. The final bidding: Make sure you do it right.

Exceptional physical strain is put upon the Soviet soldiers. During the first days in training, a young recruit loses weight. Despite the recopying food, he begins to put it back on, not as fat, but as muscle. He begins to walk differently, with his shoulders back, a twinkle appears in his eyes, and by God, he acquires self-confidence! These gentlemen are becoming a specimen of a real fighting authority.

The camp, barracks and all facilities were evacuated except a straggling few that guarded the spacious Army complex over the holidays. Sasha rode the truck back to the town of Kuybyshev where he and others got off at the train station. It was 1245 when they arrived, but the next train to Kiev was at three o'clock this afternoon. Outside it was freezing cold with a blizzard spreading snow everywhere. Total inches of snow this morning was 40 inches, plus the wind was at its highest peak. Sasha suddenly realized that he had gifts to buy but you cannot find presentable gifts at the train facility. The only use of this station was to keep warm and to keep wood on the fire. Word from the paper, which was yesterday's, was poorly written and then he purchased a cup of hot chocolate, which tasted good. Finally, he heard the train that he was supposed to take. Eleven men and he boarded the train and they headed west. He was excited but he still about 15 hours before the locomotive reached Kiev.

His shift in balance woke him up as the engine rounded the bend and the lights of Kiev were looming in the background. The weather here was -10 C. and bitter to the hands. With a Soviet Army winter coat with sergeant stripes, he walked to the station with a new piss cutter fore and aft cap with the Soviet emblem. He entered the station and looked for his family. It was eight o'clock in the morning and he searched all over the place and then, he wondered if he took a taxi to his father's apartment. Outside, he noticed a car that was approaching the area. The horn sounded and Sasha realized it was his dad. They embraced and his dad jumped back and took a good look at him. "You look good, son," he said. Dimitri wanted to know about everything, so his son said the training was going excellent, and as a matter of fact, he was class leader in physical training. All in all, this was a good, quality training had prevailed and he felt he would make an excellent officer.

They pulled up in front of their home. Dad got his baggage and Sasha was first at the door. Mom, Gala and Jan met him with hugs and kisses. Mom escorted him to the table that was set for breakfast. Sasha took off his winter coat, and began talking to the girls about what they wanted from Saint Nicholas. With keen amazement, they went on about dolls and numerous assorted items. Dad told the girls to wash their hands and Sasha was right behind them.

What a classic breakfast mom had dreamed up. Orange juice was served, followed by hot oatmeal, poached eggs and bread. It's not only good, but his stomach devoured these condiments that embellished the flavors throughout his body including the mulberry jelly. Next on the schedule was what they are going to do today. Mom mentioned Mary, who had gone home to visit her family. She said, however, that they would talk more of her later as she was to return to Kiev the 26th of December. The first priority was to make myself a list and to use some of his rubles for Saint Nicolas gifts. Mom could supply the needs of the girls, whereas, she could help him purchase Mary's gift. So, it looks like they should go to the mall to get presents.

They got to the stores about 11 o'clock. The group split up to do some shopping. They bought various things but first and foremost, they got the girls a bracelet. Mom indicated that Mary needed a sweater so she and Sasha picked one out. Suddenly, it was one o'clock and they had agreed with the family to all meet in the center of the mall. Gala saw us first and they were playing devil's advocate about our St. Nicholas gifts. Lunch was brief, and they were back shopping with different partners. Sasha asked dad what he planned to give mom. He did not know, but he listed several ideas. Unfortunately, he had not given her a birthday present earlier in the month. Immediately they were in the women clothing section whereby dad took out the dimensions of his wife. Number one, she needed a coat for outdoor wear. A lady helped us and she showed several nice long length wool wraps. One of those that she was wild about was the one with matching pullover head cover. The coats were 100-percent wool with buttons to fully cover one from head to toe. This caught his dad's eye, and when he asked him about it, he said let's get it. Well, the Ivanov clan did well shopping and the packages began to mount when they reached home.

After supper they concentrated on the tree. This tree had been bought several days ago and placed in a stand with a bowl at the bottom of the trunk. Sasha saw that the tree was without nutrition, or it was in need of water. He found a bucket in the kitchen and filled it halfway and poured the water on the spruce tree. Next, the bag containing the ornaments were broken into strings of lights, balls, an angel which sits at the top of the tree and other things like making popcorn to make a string that encircles the tree several revolutions. They started at seven in the evening and finally gave up the ghost at five minutes of nine. The girls were tired, and so was he. They all said goodnight and he quickly followed the girls to bed.

The night before the exciting visit was upon them all. He got up and relieved himself and then heard mom and dad fixing breakfast. He hugged them and accepted a hot cup of coffee, which made the heart burn! Gala and Jan were awake and soon they, in their bathrobes, came running in to announce that today is the eve of St. Nicolas. A change in scenery, they had hot cakes, which soaked in warm syrup; boy were they good! His dad lent him part of the newspaper, and he enjoyed catching up on the local news. After six hot cakes, he had his fill. He then proceeded to clean up the mess and washed, dried and put away the dishes.

As he looked out the window, the snow and drifts were approaching eight feet high. The wind, however, was really blowing to new heights. Yes, the weather is getting worse, but that's what winter is for. It is time for the children sans the parents to wrap their gifts. Mom inspired him to embellish the gifts, which made the presents more revealing. His dad managed to ransom him, and the two of them prepared the gifts for the girls, as well as mom. After Sasha was through, he started wrapping Mary's gifts. He had a special box and the gift paper was just as nice. The last thing he did to the present was to ravel about three yards of gold ribbon and tie it in a three-inch loop. He then maneuvered it and came up with a beautiful gold rose. He was proud of that masterpiece and he thought of Mary as he put the gift under the tree.

The remainder of the day went by quickly, when mom was busy in the kitchen stuffing the turkey, making pies and doing all those good things that foster the holidays. He asked if he could help, but she said no. Finally, he put on his jogging clothes and went running. The weather was clear, but the cool was penetrating. After 10 minutes of running, he was warm and the wind in your face, it was refreshing. There were not too many runners out, but this made the day as Sasha ran 14 miles before the coldest of the wind started to freeze his face. Incidentally, it was -5 degrees outside!

It was St. Nicholas Day and the girls were up before dawn marveling at the gifts the Saint had brought. Dolls, dollhouses and many clothes tallied the youngsters' bounty. Sasha was no mistake as he wallowed in clothes, especially the warm flannels, and dark 100-percent wool sweaters. Mom was surprised at her coat, which was the greatest gift of the whole family. Dad was surprised, but he was thrilled beyond belief. The girls played and played some more. The dinner was delicious and even all were setback, stuffed and didn't want another bite. A day for thanks and a day that all of the children were home to be with mom and dad.

The next day the whereabouts of the presents under the tree were decimated; the only presents remaining were for Mary. The children knew exactly where their odds and ends were. These are heavily disguised by numerous pillows and chairs. He was up early, as he had to go get Mary. The train was due at 10 o'clock and he was going to leave early. They had breakfast and he left his dad's house at 9:15. Yes, he knew how to drive, but it was quite a struggle getting to/from the train station, as there were several accidents and rough driving. He parked about a block away and he entered the rail area. He checked the arrival area and the locomotive was on time. He waited for about 15 minutes and the loudspeaker announced the arrival. There she was. Sasha sighted her a hundred yards away as she was in a light blue coat with a fur piece on her head. Quickly she saw him and they ran to each other. He grabbed her, looked her over and then kissed her. A compelling, convincing kiss turned into a volition of will. They separated and Sasha said, "Mary, I love you and someday I want to marry you." Then Mary said, "Sasha you may have me, life, soul and body!" They again touched their lips as Sasha kissed her lips, her eyes and then her left ear that Mary wanted. Finally they got all of the bags and quickly walked the block holding each other's gloves.

Sasha listened to the story spun about the beginning of the vacation till the day the Saint came. She got many presents that she wore the new coat and the new fur coat. Sasha told the story of coming home, going shopping and the children opening presents. Soon they reached home; the two girls were waiting for her.

Mom and dad greeted her and made some lunch for her. The best thing was the soup, filled with deer, vegetables and garlic fixing. Next Mary pulled out presents, which she gave to Gala and Jan. They ripped into the presents and were overjoyed to find a puzzle and a small Russian doll. Both bugged Mary and gave her a peck on the cheek. Mom received the next present, and it turned out to be a box of chocolate candies. Next it was his turn, but he wanted her to open it first. She opened the gift and was excited; it was a sweater that fit and looked good on her. Now it was his turn, the box yielded a blue turtleneck sweater with a Nike letter on the sleeve, with a pair of running gloves. Sasha, though he had tears in his eyes, caressed her and said thanks a million.

Being bundled up, they walked to her apartment later that afternoon. Mary had one bag, and Sasha had two big luggage bags. The apartment was vacant, but look out for the crowd coming back for school at the New Year. Mary unlocked the door and damn, it was frigid inside. Mary turned up the heat and started unpacking her luggage. After almost an hour went by sorting, hanging and putting underwear or assorted items in the assigned drawers. Mary and Sasha continued our conversation as they made it back to his house. Dad had mixed some drinks with assorted hors d'oeuvres. The dinner was fantastic and Mary went along with the girls to get their baths.

They watched television and soon it was 9:30 in the evening. Mary started yawning, so Sasha said it was time to put Mary to bed. She kissed dad and mom also she hugged them. Back at the apartment Mary thanked him for being so observant. She promised Sasha that she got up at five in the morning. He kissed her and she longed for him to spend the night. She missed him, like no one had ever missed him in eternity in ages. Sasha mentioned he loves her, the way she was shining in life and the way she carries herself. One last kiss and Mary must retire to the heavens, being uninterrupted slumber.

The next day the children went to the market with their mom. Dad was working, so Mary and Sasha went jogging. They ran for 40 minutes and then stopped for a cup of java. They conversed over the Army, school, what to do when Mary finished school and everything under the sun. That afternoon they went to the museum downtown and literally walked through the oblivious artwork concentrating on their courtship. All from the group went out to dinner. The girls have something like pizza and the grownups had a broiled sea bass dinner with all the trimmings.

That night Sasha took Mary home early and they had a reason; they wanted to make love to each other. Mary unlocked the front door and as soon as the door was closed, they kissed. Mary was all over him, and she began to take off his turtleneck sweater. They loved each other for an hour. Finally, at 11 o'clock Sasha said time out. Mary astutely accepted his call and they embraced as he went home. When he got home all was quiet. He got into bed knowing that Mary was the dream that could make him happy and proud. One day she would be his bride.

The next two days were filled with love, secret talks and new avenues of discovery within the stems of the two human bodies. They ran together, fixed food for the Ivanov family, and they, the parents, knew what was happening. The last night together was spent in the apartment, toasting the vodka, which they sealed their true devotion to love, which would hold their promise until Sasha returned as an officer.

The train was about to leave in 30 minutes. Sasha was telling Mary not to worry; they would be together again. Dimitri, Sofia, Gala and Jan were there, consoling and wishing Sasha was going for a day to be an officer in the Red Army. Finally, it was time. Sasha kissed all of his family and then he whispered in Mary's ear that she was engaged to him; don't let go!

The train sped into the night with the typical sound of the wheels passing over the tracks. Sasha did not hear this sound or vibration as thinking of Mary transfixed him. No one in his right mind should be this way, but he must snap out of the doldrums or a state of stagnation so her can go on meeting the goals that lie before him.

Sasha was asleep as he pulled into the Army base near Kuybyshev. With his bags assembled, he walked to an Army truck, which was picking up the men that were returning to base. After loading the bags, the men went inside the station to warm themselves by the fire. It was at least -15 degrees with the wind gusting to 25 miles an hour. Finally, they mounted the truck and headed toward the Army facility.

The barracks, which they were assigned, were colder than a witch's ass. They started a fire in both wood-stoves, which apparently the walls began to feel cool, rather than outrageously cold. Many of his friends returned and they were sporting stories left and right. Sasha told them of Mary and immediately they climbed all over his intent to make her his wife when he became an officer. The schedule was posted and since it was Saturday, the next day was off and then the work/slave detail started on Monday. Sasha spent the next day writing to his parents and to the love of his life.

Monday morning was the day of all days. The name of the proverbial game is physical training. Each man anguished as each lateral copulation extended over the straining of bilateral brawn. By lunchtime the spurs, or sore spots, were all worked out. The lads were a tad hungry. The afternoon was a tactics lecture, which the Russians instilled in these troops. Each technique was drilled over and over, while admittedly, several men fell asleep. The drill sergeant rapped their desk and made them stand for the rest of the lecture.

Things expanded to a rapid proportion as the battalion went to higher ground to develop the arts of skiing. Sasha had no experience in the motion of habituate, but jumped in and fell into the snow. He stood up again and tried it again. The next time he was skiing better than anyone. The battalion went full pack, including all gear on the backs increasing the weight factor. They skied down the hill and stopped when the instructor reached a large clearing area. At this point, he ordered that the troops make camp and designated five men to go hunt for food. How were the men going to spent the night here? No tent, no cover, why not make branches to cover oneself. Sasha and his room mates decided that Sasha would go hunt food while the others would break evergreen branches and use them to sleep on to protect them from the snow while covering them from the severe cold. Sasha reported to the sergeant and he plus four went off into the woods to hunt for food. They decided to hunt for deer, fox or anything that looked good. Two of the lads passed a small creek where they saw signs of beaver and set up traps for them. About 10 minutes later several caribous feeding in a thicket were sighted. They got two eight-point racks of deer which they guesstimated about 190 pounds. They started back to the campsite and they reached the smell of fires burning just before sunset. Incidentally, the stream boys had some luck, so it was a feast of Russian quality!

Early the next morning, the sergeant called everybody out of bed and coffee was provided. Rolls and coffee were okay, but all learned the lesson. Each element of the battalion was criticized, rewarded or flunked the preparation of the cover over the men. The next lesson was how to fight and protect yourself in that horrendous cold. Down the hill the skiers went. They followed the instructor for about a mile. They stopped and circled the man as he began to speak. He told the men what to do and what to expect when the troops are at the edge of the battlefield. What should they do? Sasha suggested that they should dig in. Excellent observation, and they began to move the snow and form pockets where the men crouched down with carbines looking for the enemy.

Survival training is by far the most secretive, sinister and the most intriguing part of the four-month training period. Within two weeks of completing this course, the group entered new lectures and training. Basically, each student made a backpack, Devoid of any mechanism of protection Sasha was separated into groups of four or five. The snow was evaporating and they walked or hunted whatever came along. They camped near a stream, which yielded fish, which enabled each to have a bit of food. Rain woke up the candidates and they forged their way as they went another 20 kilometers. At this site they constructed a drop cover that gave the men protection from the rain. Preparation for the final day was quite revealing. Being a prisoner or an escapee was something, but this was a prisoner of war trying to escape his aggressor.

Several KGB representatives briefed the audience. Case in point, the candidates were to escape and to evade the KGB while trying to get to point Bravo. Maps were handed out and Sasha plus three looked at the map. Open country faced them over woods and a creek dividing both sides of the terrain. They decided that they would cross the creek and head up through the woods. The five-minute period was up, so they headed out. After three minutes they heard noise; they hit the ground. Struggling, running, and men were knocked over and captured. Across the creek was where this was happening. They stayed pinned to the ground for a minute and they started again. Birds flew again, but they were very cautious, including disguising their bodies.

As they came to cross a road, Sasha approached the road tracks, but through hand signs, he told them there was a truck coming. Yes, the truck was looking for you. All clear, the infamous force crossed the road. Thirty minutes later they found point Bravo. It was the center of the concentration camp. Forthright and into the camp, they were giving open hands to the conniving attrition of the KGB.

Drill week maintained the last week as letters, phone calls and finally the results came through. Mom and dad were coming but Mary could not make it. Finally, the day came and the battalion marched in with the band leading the way. Dimitri was proud of his son, particularity of the accomplishments that were produced in the program. Sasha stood proudly as the regimental commander placed on his uniform the bars of junior lieutenant. He saluted and marched down the steps to fall in with the others. At the reception he hugged his parents and both were proud that he was an officer.

That night the Ivanovs were staying in a downtown hotel and Sasha had dinner with them. After the dinner was finished, Sasha thought that now was a good time to talk. He explained that he was asked what field of service did he desire? The officer said he was a good candidate for Special Forces. His adaptability was right down the alley of espionage. Spetznaz was and is a top-flight outfit, which deserved the best in every soldier. The second Department of the Staff here in Kuybyshev had a Spetznaz training facility here. Mom and dad listened, but was this what they wanted the son to do? Fifteen minutes later they understood and hugged their son.

Before the Ivanov's climbed about the train the next morning, mom gave Sasha a packet of letters from Mary. As the train left for Kiev, he opened the first letter and cried faintly; he wished she had been there.

Sasha Ivanov had survived the short intensive course, whereby the leaders are singled out as military training is rapidly accomplished with an excellent byproduct. Once this man wore the bars of junior lieutenant he set about earning them. At the Army camp Kuybyshev this training begins, that of a Special Purpose Force (Spetznaz). The group of officers was, of course, brand new. The first thing is physical training, with special emphasis on breaking the habit of having a gun for security. Pressure points, for example is where a blood vessel runs near the bone and may be compressed by the application of pressure. In and of itself, it is a force that can overtake the opponent or kill him if the action of the force is against an opposing constrain. Precisely, there are many ways to down an object by using this device.

The next topic is the discussion of reconnaissance, which is an exploratory military overview of enemy territory. One may counter-reconnoiter as simply covering the same mission. Each officer is drilled, using planned laboratory techniques, which cause him to ask questions about the knowledge he would retain. Finally, Sasha and his teammates would form groups of eight to 10 men and they would penetrate an area, which they would discreetly dress as normal or old people. Collection of every small and imperceptible object must be grasped and reported. The collection must be viewed by all convened and the final analysis is presented to the instructor.

The second environment is the intelligence field. This is capitalized by presenting lectures and showing movies, which is death instinct related views. To pass the course for the particular segment of shrewdness, the students were assigned to a particular airplane or a design that they had to take a picture which they extracted the measurements for the object.

Sasha was assigned to take a picture of the latest design of the Georige attack fighter. This aircraft was under construction at a town 55 miles away. They met and tried each idea on the other. Finally their plans were set. Through stealth and cunning, the team, which consisted of eight people, stole a van and headed to the facility. They stopped short of the gate, which had only one person at the gate. The man who was to be the gatekeeper had everything on but the stripes and coordinated guard equipment. All of the team got out and one person snuck up behind the sergeant. One gent moved the branches of a tree and the guard came to this edge of this spotlight and said, "Who goes there?" The lad saw his way clear and turned his neck from right to left, automatically killing the watchman. Immediately the guard was dragged into the bush, while the other six marched across the road.

The designated "guard" retrieved and put on the gatekeeper's shirt and revolver, plus the Kalashnikov automatic rifle. He announced his readiness, and the other seven got into a pickup truck. Sasha took a map, which was taken out of a library. The truck was about half a mile from the factory, which consisted of four hangars. The final hangar was supposed to have the latest readiness aircraft. The guard force was still in existence. The two men jumped out and, while the truck waited for the two that had marched right up to the guard shack. They were to relieve them, but one of the men turned leery and the two were blown away by gunfire. Soon the new guards waved them ahead and when they had passed through, Sasha had five minutes to take pictures of the new fighter.

The driver stopped in front of the hangar and four men left the truck. The men went inside the hangar and saw two maintenance men moving a forward hydraulic pump. The four men split, and Sasha leading the man with him said "Hi," and the two men said hello. Sasha then ordered the two men away from the aircraft. The two men moved over to the side, but he reached for a gun. Sasha side-kicked him as the second mechanic remained motionless. Sasha took four or five pictures and there was a noise at the end of the hangar. Sasha was ready to leave, and the two returned to the idling truck. One minute was left and here comes the other two running. They jumped into the truck and were being chased by one or two guards. The watchman jumped aboard and the last pickup was the outside guard, or the main base.

As they got to him his phone was ringing and the base was on alert. The truck was evacuated and was set on fire with a small grenade. By the time the men reached the last gate, Sasha started the truck and they were gone. The night was dark but the lights were not lit. Five miles down the road another vehicle was headed to the base. Sasha made a decision to pull over. He told his troops to hang tight. As the lights got closer, it was an ambulance with the precautions light burning. Sasha saw the wagon pass and then Sasha motored this vehicle until within a mile of Kuybyshev. They abandoned the truck and made it back to the Army base.

The next day the photos were developed and the measurements were worked up. One of the members of this team had commercial pilot experience, which was a great help in reconstructing the aircraft's dimensions. The brief was held only Friday. The base commander attended the brief. Sasha was elected to give the brief. He quietly stated the problems with only eight individuals assigned. He then went through each assignment, including the guards and finally he took the pictures while three of the team kept the guard from apprehending him. The base commander was disturbed, so he asked many anarchical questions. Sasha solved this rabid or furious individual by countering his attack to the base commander. Eventually the leader finished the brief with a full-blown picture of the Georige attack fighter. He showed various angles and he was now open for questions. The only hard but good point of this fallacy was the men that were wiped out or wounded in this guile and trickery. The final remark was that they had performed a superior job. They received a 95 but were warned on the use of self-conservation in the case of killing an individual.

In sight of course completion, to illustrate how much realism and complete fabrication this task entails, the objective was to be dropped by parachute to destroy other opposition's command and communications building. Sasha Ivanov was involved in planning the episode, which occurred in the woods of Belorussia some 400 kilometers from our base. The objective was to annihilate this strategic position, even if it required using all of their men. Primarily the base was a bitch to get into. The plans or a map showed that there were two railroad bridges and there were numerous sections that new surprise attacks such as this stronghold could get to the base. Numerous specialized motorized infantry guarded the targets. Finally, they realized that it was water and that caused concern for all candidates.

The rules of engagement pronounced that 24 hours was to prepare for planning, and the mission was underway. After each man was outfitted with special explosives, including devices and for one-person radio equipment. Personal firepower consisted of machine guns, which did not expose flashes. All men were given dry rations for three days. Sasha voted with the other seven and they gave up two days of rations in order to take more ammunition. The last item to be considered was the skis, which were to be dropped with a small radio in a protective handle. This device sent out a homing signal in his earphones when he used the conductor. In reality, Sasha and this group picked up the maps and charts that they worked out to minute detail.

The night of the operation was black and snow was falling. Before midnight they leaped out of an aircraft and 13 minutes later they had assembled, with their demon white disguise. By two o'clock in the morning they had covered the 18 kilometers to the target. The guards, five in all, were easily taken care of. The barracks were booby-trapped in the doors and windows with various quantities of explosives. This would really mystify the 20 or so men inside without undue pain. The last explosion they heard was the communications building. A total of many mines were set off as the eight men were really moving away from the base. At noon they were camouflaged in the woods, getting some sleep, concealed among the ground leaves.

The gang continued to march at night and sleep under cover during the day. They stole provisions until they were spotted from the air and soon they were surrounded by ground troops. Sasha decided to seize an armored car to affect our escape. He kept looking for a command vehicle, which only carries other men. When one such vehicle appeared, a man who had stolen clothes from a peasant stopped the command vehicle. The car was turned over to this sabotage group who headed home to their base. Looking like forest bandits, they passed this test, which could be in preparation for their role against the missions of the West.

Sasha was assigned to a Spetznaz brigade in the western part of Russia. Mary would be his wife and he would marry her when he took a month of hard-earned leave. He climbed off the train in Moscow and immediately ran into her arms. She kissed him everywhere on each side of his face. He gave her a bouquet of roses, which caused tears to fall from her joyous eyes. They met her parents, who were impressed by his sharp and immaculate uniform. The next day they went to buy a wedding ring. Mary could not believe it, but the diamond actually sparkled. They were married the next Sunday with his sisters present and his mother and father. The wedding was stupendous as the crowd of people was awesome and monstrous after the girls ran after the bouquet was thrown into the air.

They settled down in quarters outside the base where Sasha was assigned. The base was the first assignment he had been placed. His first task was away from the platoon way of doing things. He was tasked to study various aspects of warfare, thereby improving or disappearing this tactic, also primarily in the field of athletics, was the running ability of this man. Sasha wore out all of his competing runners. This made him proud to compete and Russia was prime to permit him to run in the coming Olympics. The coach was provided and soon the proponent was advancing in stamina and endurance. Spetznaz looked for recruits with the best physical ability. The number of top athletes recruited by this avenue had been extremely successful. This program had initiated an opportunity to visit new areas, which they may have to be in times of war. The most interesting thing is that these promotional programs centralize most of the women athletes.

A year later, the Russian delegation to the Olympics was staggering. About one-third of the delegation was of that trait. Russia won hands down the majority of the running and track events. Mary went with the majority of others and cheered her heart out. She wanted to tell Sasha that she had become with child. Russia was third when the final tally was rung up.

Sasha Ivanov's successful career had been due to a faultless climb up the chain of command. His mentor or accelerated movers, have hastened their progress, but Sasha had left them in the dust. Wearing the apparel of special operations meant nothing to him as he, deep down inside, knows that he is destined for a major accomplishment or in the Olympics. Yes, it had been quite a time since he finished the basic Spetznaz course. He remembered that course. The Main Intelligence Directorate (GNU) was responsible for the type and in-depth training that he and his comrades finished.

The second division of the staff drove all elements of the brigade, which consisted of intelligence, reconnaissance, information processing including radio interception, and all phases of spying. To be at top shape, Sasha ran and worked the hardest, especially at running. The mechanics of killing the enemy started without a weapon. Each course in this segment was a deal with demonstration, practice and then the students were put to field to herd a group of killers and they could practice all of their techniques.

The practice sessions would last until every last man proved his worth. The next segment went to the water to experience this type of water-based supporting units. The students were led out to swim and learned many different ways to survive in the water. Next, they have three days of instruction on the parachute. They went over the rudiments of landing with a parachute on. Finally, they all boarded a twin-engine plane and jumped out over water. The class did excellent and then in the classroom they learned about even more gear, which would lower them below the surface of the water with snorkel gear or using an oxygen mask. The use of oxygen and a powered device, they would parachute two or more miles from the assent to the target. Skis and masks were for the young-at-heart. Each man took to the hills and was a master skier in a few days.

The final group of personnel was used, such as, the intelligence agents, and of course, the sabotage units. Intelligence people are recruited however; they are not involved with classified materials. Mature persons, they enter restricted areas and the GNU provides them money if they can locate a house near a very important target. These agents live near vital electrical facilities and in time of war they are to take out these paces of opportunity. By and large, these agents have no connection with the USSR and form "sleeping" networks that may be brought to attack in time of war.

The final years of being a soldier led to the conflict of Afghanistan. This had the Soviet Union in a hard place, because of the rebel forces at hand. The Soviet brass in Moscow battered about the way to stop surprise attacks on the Russian Army. A vast mountainous area, the lackadaisical was the generals laughed at this unpretentious task and the rebels continued to blast the Red Army. Back in Moscow, a general was to expose a new deterrent in the game of warfare. The Spetznaz element was alerted and he gave the information as to how, when and where the attack would be made.

The generals listened and they acknowledged them, which made a commitment to take care of business.

The crux of the mass was the way the counteractive team did their work. The map force rolled out the charts of the mountainous force around the capitol where the president's palace was located. They were in a hazardous zone, which made every person apprehensive about planning an airdrop of this elite force. After a brief plan was construed, this was presented to the intelligence set, which promoted many questions. Once these were answered, the plan was approved. Now who would make it work? Admiral Anviolaski was approached and asked who was in charge of the elite force. He told the intelligence man that he and his staff would be at the brief at 1400 hours tomorrow.

Senior lieutenant Sasha Ivanov, accompanied by two junior officers, met the briefing officers the next day. This set about the brief but was asked questions about everything except the real mission. Sasha stood up and asked a few questions. He clarified the brief and insisted that they employ procedures that were successful in 1968. In essence, the overthrow of the capital of Afghanistan was ready to be executed. Sasha shook hands with the briefers. Sasha and his two coordinators drove off and headed back to the nearest Spetznaz camp. He was in charge of 120 men, which were well drilled in every manner of secrecy. Back in their briefing room they looked at the plans again. They assessed the entire operation from nose to nose. There were many changes to this plan. The group would land outside the city, preferably at night. The elite force would camp out until the regular force signals attack. Sasha and his force began to march into the city and surround the city with a 360-degree circle of men. In combat, every Special Forces soldier had a standard range of weapons. An AK-47 rifle was with each soldier. He had 300 rounds of high velocity firepower plus six grenades. The radioman also carried a special encryption and burst transmission modes. The force does not carry heavy armor, but they may seize tanks or other vehicles to play the part of the enemy. This alternative weaponry gives a lot of leeway and gives his advantage in warfare techniques.

At precisely 72 hours later, they were on three aircraft flying towards their designated areas. The mountains in the area caused the Soviet force to fly quite a bit higher than usual. Finally the light showed green which meant "preparatory for drop." The men stood, checked each other for chutes and other gear. The red light came on and they hit the silk within 30 seconds. The cold wind hit Sasha in the face. He looked around him as the moon established distance and bearing. The landing was uneventful as they took off all of the parachute attachments. They buried these items and were ready to silently proceed to the capital. The sound of the radio was the keynote of the next setting. All was set; the signal was given that meant the special purpose forces advance. The clock on Sasha's wrist read three o'clock in the morning and the force complied. They were the only force capable of moving and they kept up the pace. At the next intersection there were three soldiers guarding this particular crossing. The three were eliminated and the battle group entered to within a half of a mile from the entrance of the Capitol.

Fierce firing was reported to the commander and he told the sergeant to gang up on this concentration. He waved the rest of the ventures, on to the center of town. Suddenly the group was about to be surrounded by rebels. Sasha saw one jump in front of him. Sasha thrust him with his AK-47, whereby he rushed the rebel and twisted he neck to the right until he heard a crack. The rebel fell among the dead. Sasha reached the gate to the president's enclosure and the Spetznaz forces were climbing the steps to capture him.

The containment was awful shaky as it took two days for the Russians to begin moving forces. The fight for the leader of this nation caused an outrage among the Russian generals. This and other episodes caused two key factors that were finalized in the last 50 years. Russia had taken from the U.S. the nuclear monopoly thus giving Russia a total global reach where it can multiply power projection if necessary. When Sasha and his Special Forces returned to Russia they were received in a big parade. They received medals and Sasha was given the Legion of Honor, decorated with two silver stars, plus the increase in rank to captain.

WHISPER ON THE WIND

1350 hours Local, 21 February 1991,
Washington, D.C. (U.S.)

ADMIRAL JOE HENRY READ THE COMMUNIQUÉ FOR the fifth time. He didn't understand the Moscow agent's sudden desire to talk. It was very concerning. Normally she was very discrete. The sudden burst of almost continuous information from Moscow was unprecedented in her 15 years of espionage. Something serious was happening in Russia, he could sense it.

The other admirals refused to consider his warnings. They were too busy with the air war against Iraq that had kicked off in January. Like prized horses in a race, their blinders couldn't let them see what other nation-competitors were doing. Their focus was decimating the Iraqi army that had invaded Kuwait. Nothing else mattered to them.

Joe could sense his agent's desperation in the latest report. The KGB had authorized a Spetznaz strike against Argentia. It was foolhardy. What did they hope to gain by it? The USSR was on its final legs, barely managing to scrape together enough rubles to put a boat a month to sea. Any fool could see that the totalitarian system was on the verge of collapse.

The key seemed to be magnetite. He didn't understand that either. According to the plan sitting in front of him, the Spetznaz team was supposed to hijack 50 tons of the stuff. Then the team would either fly it from the Naval Air Station or transfer it to a submarine.

Wait a minute. He read that section again. It wasn't just any submarine. The Russians intended to use their modified Delta IV for their backup plan. Granted, the excursion module replaced four missile tubes; but that left 12 others. Placing a submarine with nuclear warheads in American coastal waters would be tantamount to a declaration of war.

Except the waters weren't American. They were Canadian. That might make a minor difference. Still, there was little chance that the

165

sub would get close enough to fulfill its mission. SOSUS would detect it in advance and the P-3s could drop enough sonobuoys to shatter the sub captain's eardrums. He'd know that he'd been spotted and would have no choice but to withdraw. If he didn't, he would risk the destruction of his vessel.

Joe Henry was nothing if not precise. He picked up a pen to calculate response time between when the first P-3 located the sub and the next Navy asset could respond with torpedoes to destroy it. That was when he realized the flaw in his thinking.

"Shit," he muttered, drawing a curious look from Captain Bill Blast at the desk outside his office.

"Sir?" Bill asked as he stepped to the doorway. "Did you want something?"

Joe rubbed one hand through his silvered hair. "I'm an idiot, Bill. Mark it down on the calendar, today I finally realized it."

"I don't believe that, sir," Blast replied, grinning. "What's the idiocy of the day, if I may ask?"

"You've read the latest report from Poppy, our agent in Moscow?"

Bill stepped into the room and closed the door behind him. Even in the Pentagon, walls have ears. "Yes sir, I've read it. Doesn't make any sense, though. Why is the KGB willing to take such a gamble for 50 tons of iron ore?"

"Good," the admiral stated. "You've been thinking about it. Pull up a chair and tell me your conclusions. Sometimes more heads are better than one."

The DIA liaison complied, seating himself in one of the two office chairs in front of the admiral's desk. "Why do I have the feeling you're going to tell me something I don't want to hear, sir?"

Joe Henry laced his fingers together and leaned forward in his chair. "Because you have good instincts, Bill. Now tell me, what do you think of Poppy?"

"He's a reliable resource, hasn't given us any bad scoop in 15 years."

"True, for the most part."

"Most part, sir?"

"He's a she."

"What?"

Joe grinned at the shocked look on the captain's face. "Surprised you, didn't I? I met her in Moscow. She approached me to be 'the spokesperson for her husband,' I think she said." He gave the intelligence officer a few minutes to think over the revelation.

Bill leaned back in his chair and rubbed his face. "That puts a new spin on things, doesn't it. And you know who she is?"

The admiral nodded. "I've been wondering when the time would come to pass the baton. Looks like this is as good as any. You'll be in this chair—or one similar to it—shortly. Sure you're up to it?"

Blast nodded slowly, understanding what the senior officer was offering. It was very rare for a recruiter to ever reveal his field agent's identity. Typically it was fatal if the person learning the information mishandled it. "You're scaring me now, sir."

"Good."

"I take it, based on the 'eyes only' information being reported, that her husband is a naval officer."

Joe Henry simply nodded, letting his subordinate come to his own conclusions.

"Since this is research material, that officer would have to be a rear admiral or above, or one of their scientists. You just confirmed he's Navy, so the scientist theory doesn't work."

The admiral nodded again.

"Poppy has been providing material for 15 years. I'd always assumed he was a scientist or other civilian member of the Bureau of Ship Design Submarines. No Navy officer is ever kept in the same position that long. They'd be rotated out for other assignments. You're sure the husband is Navy?"

Joe simply grinned and nodded.

"That narrows the field of candidates. Matter of fact, it narrows it to—." A look of shock and sudden amazement crossed the captain's face. "No, it can't be. He's been there since the beginning!"

"True."

"I don't get it," Bill said, confused. "He's one of their most decorated officers, been around subs since World War II. Why would he suddenly start—"

"You know, Bill, if you keep answering your own questions then I'll go get a cup of coffee," the admiral teased. "Let me know your final conclusion when I return, okay?"

"It's because of her, isn't it? His wife, I mean. There was some conflict with the brother, what's his name—"

"Alexei."

"—and some KGB spook that Alexei had cashiered off his boat."
"Rear Admiral Klos Sloreigh."
"Yeah, that's him." Bill was amazed. It was like stepping 50 years into the past and running into Churchill or Hitler. He knew the names and tons of historical details, but he'd never really saw them as real people. "Sloreigh had it in for the younger brother. Would've killed him, too."

"Except Lawrence interfered," Joe finished for the younger officer. "It isn't wise to get in the way of a KGB officer on the fast-track to the top."

"That's for sure. Sloreigh couldn't touch either Latvia, and so he gave the order to knock off the wife. Admiral Latvia has always been a family man. It was a cold-blooded reminder that the children and grandchildren were vulnerable as well."

"So, what's your conclusion? Why did Admiral Latvia start handing top secret research information to us on what the Soviets were doing?"

Bill shifted sideways in his chair, cradling his chin in his palm as he leaned on the chair arm. "Now there's a puzzler. Latvia could've pulled some strings and made Sloreigh disappear. It would've been politically inconvenient for awhile, but he would've survived it. Why didn't he?"

Joe laughed softly as he watched his subordinate drift away. After a minute passed, he said to the room, "I'm going for that coffee now. Want some?"

The intelligence officer waved off the request. He was lost in thought. The Soviet political system was ruthless. Any sign of weakness was exploited. Rivals had a tendency to disappear, especially if they offended a member of the KGB. The fact that both Latvia's were still alive was testimony to their power within the political system. That power was sufficient to demand Sloreigh's head on a platter. KGB or not, at that point in time he was only a minor player.

Something nagged at the corner of his mind but he couldn't get at it. He let his train of thought flow freely, hoping it would provide an answer. Latvia was raised extremely loyal to family; it came before anything else, including country. He was from Leningrad, which meant he was raised as a member of the party faithful. However, he was also a WW II vet. That meant he held a deep love for country. Family, then country; but not just any country.

Latvia was a Russian. His country was Mother Russia, not the USSR. Bill Blast recalled something about the admiral's early career. He'd been an infantry soldier, then army officer and then—that was it! Lawrence Latvia was transferred to the Navy for submarine research duty at the request of the NKVD. That branch of the Soviet government was later to become infamous by another name; it became the KGB in 1954.

That's when the missing piece fell in place. Latvia's wife had been NKVD and later KGB. Bill had read about her; she was one of the first international espionage agents for the Soviet Union. He remembered discussing her in his criminal psychology classes during DIA training. She was the example of how a loving, nurturing mother could at the same time be a cold-hearted executioner of the State's enemies.

The puzzle shifted and took another direction. Now it wasn't just a case of why Latvia hadn't organized the murderer Sloreigh's demise. The KGB was divided into different directorates. While there was some competition between them, there was also an extreme loyalty to the KGB as a whole.

Whether he knew it or not, Sloreigh had assassinated a fellow KGB agent. Latvia wouldn't need to arrange a hit on the man. His fellow KGB officers would've silenced him for his disloyalty to the organization.

Yet he was still alive. Why? What had prevented her fellow KGB officers and husband from killing the man in the most brutal manner?

Admiral Joe Henry returned to his office and placed a cup of coffee in front of his intelligence officer. "Maybe this will help. There's nothing like a hot cup of java to get the mind working."

Blast retrieved the cup from the desk. "You've thrown me for a loop, sir. Why is Sloreigh still alive?"

"Let me know when you figure it out," teased the admiral. He caught the almost childlike pleading look on his subordinate's face and grinned. "Okay, a hint. What does the term 'proportional response' mean to you?"

"It's used to delineate the theoretical levels of nuclear war. Assuming an accidental launch then we'll retaliate in proportion to the level of destruction we've taken."

"Okay, that's all you get. Now let's get back to the problem at hand. You asked why Admiral Latvia would suddenly begin providing assistance to us after his wife's death." Joe sipped the hot brew. He regretted that he'd grown older; as a young ensign, he could drink his java black. Now his stomach demanded that he add cream and sugar. It was embarrassing, really.

Bill verbally nudged his boss from the distraction. "Why did he?"

Joe sipped again, then placed the cup on the table. "A power struggle rose within the KGB about 16, 17 years ago. The First Directorate, in charge of international espionage, began competing for funding with the Third Directorate who's in charge of military counterintelligence. Actually, that's a misnomer. Third Directorate is responsible for maintaining party loyalty within the Soviet military, including the GRU and Spetz. They're also the protectors of nuclear weapons."

"Right, I knew that," Bill commented, hoping to stave off a lecture. "In this instance, Sloreigh is Third Directorate; a naval officer who transferred to the overlords. I'm sure his fellow Navy officers hated him for that."

"There's an understatement," laughed Joe. "So, you've got Admiral Sloreigh in the Third Directorate. He gives the order to knock off a distinguished member of the First Directora—"

"Hold on," interrupted the intelligence officer. "Tosarina Latvia was First Directorate? Wait, that makes sense. She helped write the book on international espionage and covert operations."

Joe didn't want to bias his subordinate's conclusions so he picked up his coffee again. He slurped the steaming lifer juice and waited.

"They were already fighting over budgets and funding, right?" Bill leaned forward in his chair, excited. "When Sloreigh, from Third Directorate, knocked off the lead agent of First Directorate, there should've been open war. Why didn't it happen?"

"There you go again, Bill," admonished the admiral. "You're close to answering your own question, just can't see the forest for the trees. So let's change the landscape a bit. What's going on in Russia right now?"

"Looks to me like Gorbachev is heading toward a Stalinist response to Lithuania. He's appointed Boris Pugo as Interior Minister to put down the rebellion there. Pugo also had troops take over the television stations in Riga, Latvia recently. Wait a minute, he's also KGB, isn't he?"

"Right. And Gorbachev was—"

It took Bill a moment to see the connection. "He was the protégé of Yuri Andropov, the KGB chief."

"Again, right. Although the link is tenuous, the three of them were mostly aligned with First Directorate. Starting to see a theme running here?"

The younger officer nodded. "We've got a power struggle 15 years ago between two of the KGB's directorates. Sloreigh waxes

Latvia's wife, who then starts handing secrets to the U.S.. They're nothing phenomenal, really, and nothing we couldn't get from other sources. Yet he's kept us in the loop as to what the Russians have been planning when it's still in the design phase."

"I've always considered him as a weathervane, myself. You know what I mean?"

"Yeah, he's showing us the direction that the military wind is blowing in the Kremlin."

"Right. So now, through Poppy, he's showing us something new. What is it?"

Bill considered the question for several moments. "It has to do with the magnetite. I'm not an engineer myself, so it doesn't make any sense to me. But from what you and the others have explained, the magnetite will make the Russian subs almost invisible to our sensors, right?"

"Exactly." Joe's coffee had turned lukewarm. He hated drinking cold coffee. Reluctantly, he chugged the remnants before it could chill further. "If it works, they could modify their entire sub fleet in six months to a year. How do you think the White House will take that news?"

The answer was obvious to the Navy officer. "They'd see it as an escalation. The Russians would have a first-strike capability. They could lay off our shores and decimate most of our bases and missile fields before we could scramble bombers."

Joe nodded. "Why would they, then? What would they have to gain from it?"

Bill threw a fake glare at the admiral. "You're playing with me now, sir. The USSR is on the verge of collapse right now. Several of the republics have increased their rhetoric to break away from Russia, especially the Baltic States. Gorbachev has tried the traditional method of silencing them, yet he isn't Stalin. He's not brutal enough. In all honesty, that tactic is backfiring."

"It does seem a rather half-hearted attempt, doesn't it? And how has the KGB reacted?"

"They want Gorbachev to send in the tanks."

"Why hasn't he?"

"Because of his policy of glasnost. He understands that economic stability for Russia can only come from close ties with the West."

The admiral eyed his empty cup, then sighed. "Okay, Bill. I'll make it easy on you, if only so I can grab another cup of this addictive poison. We've got a schism in the KGB starting 15 years ago or so. Andropov, who sided with First Directorate and more personal freedoms for Russians, briefly rises to power. He's succeeded by his protégé, also a First Directorate supporter. Through Admiral Latvia, we're hearing that the KGB is planning on sending Spetz into Argentia; that's the Third Directorate. They're looking for a mineral that will silence their subs, giving them first-strike survivability. So, what conclusion do you make about all this?"

Captain Bill Blast grew cold as the pieces fell into place. "They're going to kill him, aren't they? Gorbachev, that is. Third Directorate is going to take him out, and then they're going to launch a limited nuclear strike against the US. We'll respond with a proportional response of warheads. After all, we can't declare war on the Soviet Union if some nutcase sub captain gets confused during the coup and launches. So it'll be a limited response. Third Directorate will take the reigns. Then—probably under the guise of a 'state of emergency'—they'll send in the tanks to wipe out all of the breakaway governments. We'll be back to a Stalin era in no time."

The admiral lowered his head. "Thank you, Bill. I was afraid you'd come to the same conclusion."

"Sorry, sir."

"I hate this." Joe slammed his hand against the tabletop. "We're the greatest nation in the world, and you know what? We're being played like pawns in a 15-year-old game of Russian roulette!"

Bill agreed. Hesitantly, he broached the next delicate subject. "They're not going to believe us, are they, sir?"

The admiral's face was expressionless as he looked at his subordinate. "Who's that, Captain Blast?"

"The Joint Chiefs, sir. The President." Bill picked his cup off the floor where it had fallen from the admiral's outburst. "They'll say that we're just making a jealous play for attention because we're not in the middle of the Gulf War. Everyone's heard the rumors, sir. The Cold War is ending and we're just another department that's about to be axed. Nobody is going to believe this at all."

Joe grinned sardonically. "It all depends on how we present it, Bill. I intend to take a page from the Russian playbook; after all, three can play at this game. It's my stars if I'm wrong about this, but it's worth the risk to me. So, here's what I want you to do. Pay a visit to your DIA, CIA and any other '—IA' you know of. Tell them that you're getting traffic out of Moscow about a coup attempt against Gorbachev. Don't provide any specifics; let them activate their own networks. When they have the evidence, then we can go to the Joint Chiefs."

For the first time that day, the DIA intelligence officer laughed. He rose from his chair and headed for the door, then paused to look back at the admiral. "You've been playing with the Russians too long, sir. Now you're thinking like one."

Joe made a dismissing wave with his hand. "Go on, captain. I have some more webs to weave here and you're better off not knowing about them."

"Yes sir." Captain Bill Blast nodded, serious again. He snapped a sharp salute and closed the office door behind him.

Admiral Joe Henry stared at the phone on his desk. Reluctantly, and with a heavy sigh, he placed the receiver against his ear. He dialed the number from memory. The signal passed through the secure Pentagon switchboard and headed out on a secure line. It reached its destination in Little Creek, Virginia.

The line rang only once before a voice spoke. "Special Operations."

Joe was very glad to hear the familiar voice on the other end. "Hello, Patrick. Joe here. Are you recording?"

The voice replied with a brief, "Yes, sir."

"This is Admiral Joseph Allen Henry. For the record, I am authorizing OPLAN Magnet on my authority. This is not a drill. The order is: Stand by to lock and load."

LOCK AND LOAD

1457 hours Local, 21 February 1991,
Little Creek, Virginia (U.S.)

LIEUTENANT COMMANDER PATRICK SPENSER RETURNED THE DUTY phone to its cradle. The last voice he had ever expected to hear was that of Admiral Joe Henry. It didn't bode well for the home team when the Pentagon's chief spook gave an order activating a SEAL team.

Patrick knew the admiral. They'd worked together on a few missions in the past. The admiral would run the operation from the war room in the Pentagon or the U.S. embassy closest to the action, whichever was more convenient. The young lieutenant commander carried a secret that few others even realized.

The silver-haired admiral was a spook. Even more impressive, Joe Henry was an old spook; which was very impressive in an occupation where most field agents either retired to a desk or were retired permanently. His expertise was the Soviet Union. The older officer had joined the team on their last mission into Polyarny, where they had "borrowed" a Spetznaz mini-sub for several weeks. The innocent-looking admiral spoke fluent Russian. Technically, he spoke seven different dialects of Russian. It had helped the SEAL team get past the numerous security guards their way across the secure pier to the mini-sub. Patrick had been scared half to death, yet Joe Henry had carried them through it.

The young Navy officer considered the ramifications of the phone call. His team had just been placed on standby; they could receive no other missions until this one was completed or rescinded. That would make his boys happy. They hated the fact that their counterparts, the other SEAL teams, were busy hunting SCUD missiles in Iraq. The sixteen-man specialized unit had started calling themselves the "hurry up and wait team" instead of their normal motto of "let's go!"

Admiral Henry's authorization said volumes about the mission. It meant that there were only two more steps required to go from standby to active. The admiral had to brief the National Security Advisor, and then the President. Whether the Joint Chiefs knew it or not, the two-star admiral could go over their heads. In this case, he just did.

Patrick stepped out of the office and into the secure operations room. He spun the dial on the safe and pulled out a file labeled "OPLAN Magnet." The contents were a recent fax from the Pentagon, barely a day old. He scanned several pages before pausing on one key word.

Spetznaz. His team was most likely going to face a SPETZNAZ team. That was troubling enough, but the furrow on his brow deepened as he read about their operating arena. Argentia, Newfoundland.

"Hey Tom, get me some coffee, willya?"

Patrick settled into a chair as his second in command, Tom Wechenski, headed for the 30-cup coffee pot. When they weren't on an active mission, SEALs were like their typical Navy counterparts. They drank; and coffee as the beverage of choice kept them out of trouble.

He read the operations plan—OPLAN for short—through several times. Lieutenant Wechenski returned with his coffee. Patrick extended the folder toward his subordinate. "Better read this, Tom. We've just be placed on standby by Alfred Hitchcock."

The nickname had popped up over the years as the team worked with the admiral. The moniker wasn't meant to be insulting or imply that the senior officer was overweight. Rather, it was a characteristic that the admiral and Alfred Hitchcock both shared: They both required an appearance, even if a cameo, in any operation they ran.

"Well, so much for the easy life," commented the lieutenant. "I assume you're going to want mockups built of the key structures, plus ingress and egress rehearsals? Anything else?"

"Yeah, we'd better brush up on our airborne jumps and air assault skills. No telling how we're going in on this one. Coordinate some C-130s and a couple of Blackhawks, willya?"

"Can do, sir. What's our drop-dead time for this op?"

"None given. We could head out in an hour, so you'd better get cracking on the training plan."

"Yessir." The lieutenant headed toward the door, grinning to himself.

"Hey, wait a minute! Isn't that my coffee in your hand, sailor?"

Lieutenant Wechenski glanced down at the Styrofoam cup in his hand. "I'm sorry, sir, but we've got a schedule to keep. No time for coffee!"

"Place the cup on the table, lieutenant, and back away slowly so I can see your hands. I don't want to have to hurt you."

"Yeah," teased the subordinate as he followed the instructions with exaggerated motions. "You and which unit from the Army? Better grab the Rangers. I hear they're pretty good."

Patrick was still shaking his head after the lieutenant left the room. "What's a guy gotta do to get some respect out of here?"

His thoughts returned to the phone call. "Stand by to lock and load," the admiral had said. Not a promising sign, that.

"Lock and load" is a command often used on all U.S. military firing ranges. By the dictionary it means, "Get ready to fire," but this term means more than that; it becomes a conditional response for a Navy SEAL. SEAL is the acronym for Sea, Air, Land team. Taking its name from this unique special force has evolved from its conception back in World War II to present day where it joins today's versions of the quiet professional. Yes, it is hard to measure or advocate a particular code this creature carries in his back pocket. They shun publicity, welcome anonymity, and generally a measure of uniform that displays a measure of a SEAL.

A "respected operator" is regarded as an outstanding warrior that includes 2,200 active duty members. The majority of the SEAL missions only involve 16 men assigned to a platoon which builds up esprit de corps and respect among team members. Infiltration and exfiltration by water. If their working environment is harsh, no SEAL dead or wounded is ever left behind. Secrecy in the countless missions that they undertake must give more than covertness and stamina. All in all, thirty years of the collective critical component in the SEAL's upbringing, describes his will and well being of his challenge to succeed.

Many of the SEALs are direct descendants of the early Naval Combat Demolition Units (NCDUs). The first attempt at this event was in Pearl Harbor when the bombs were disarmed after the attack. The leaders were given the distinguished Navy Cross and were sent back to the United States to set up a course whereby the team set up a new school. Another new command post was set up for training of "amphibious commandos." Eventually, both grades of the two schools were sent to Europe and were not used until the Normandy invasion was planned. In the Pacific, the evolution in Tarawa cemented the formation of the Underwater Demolition Team (UDT). The merging units were formed when units of scouts and raiders participated.

The "frogmen" began transforming during the Korean War. New procedures were altered to permit men from dropping in the ocean (parachuting) and adding a new perspective to their repertoire. Their air constituent was nonetheless as they parachuted behind the Korean lines to set an example. The President of the Unites States honored this group for expanding unconventional warfare and its name had already been chosen—SEAL. Thus, the bases on the east and west coasts have been authorized and the new Naval Special Warfare SEALs had a name, a home and finally a mission expansion.

Vietnam was a thorough testing ground for each service member. The men with "green faces" put the fear of light in the eyes of the enemy. The SEALs quickly revised the use of explosive intensity. Unit fights with quick caliber delights caused the enemy to digress and run in retreat. Their cunning, technique and stealth lead to a mythology that follows them today. They continue to be regarded as the most physically alert, fit and highly capable of combat in service.

The Navy Special Warfare Command is the smallest unit on command at present in the U.S. Special Forces Command. As always, the Army and the Air Force whether three or two star entities lead the way, the Navy has a one star to lead the vigilant forces. The tasks are many; they include direction action, reconnaissance, unconventional warfare, foreign/United States defense, counter proliferation/combating revolutionaries and warfare of any type. There are two basic components of Navy Special Warfare: SEAL teams and Delivery Vehicle Team, which are located on both shores of the U.S. At Coronado, California, there is a special warfare center, while in Little Creek, Virginia, there is the same with a school with the latest new tactics that are under investigation.

Checking in at Little Creek you suddenly realize that you are in the Navy Security Group No. 2. The first thing that you participate in is the commanding officer welcome. He discloses the five and a half days of long and agonizing training. He points out a large bell, which is located outside the meeting. He specifies that any individual who has had enough, ring the bell and he will be processed out. The master chief training petty officer is introduced and the men are off to get the physicals before the early morning of the next day. No attention is paid to whether he is a second class or lieutenant—he is a recruit!

At four o'clock the next morning, mortar rounds began ringing the men's sleeping quarters. Master chief was running through the barracks awakening the men and ordering them outside. This is the beginning of "hell week" as the men are told to subdivide into seven-man teams. Once that is done a subordinate leads the team to a 176-pound boat. They mount that life craft on their shoulders and it stays there for the majority of the day. They walk out into the sea with waves crashing all around them. They march clear over the height of water, which frees the boat from their shoulders. This is not the only thing that each team does. There are many ways in which the raft becomes supported by two or three individuals. Then it's time for calisthenics. Then they run the trainee followed by going across the ground through mud with rapid firing as to simulate skirting through actual ground fire. It is 1900 and dinner is served. The men are exasperated and several proceed to ring the bell. Thirty minutes later, they are back again toting that damn raft. Then after an hour they are put into a classroom. The light is not very bright, but each candidate is given a piece of paper and pencil. The master chief has learned that there is a feeling of animosity among the untested troops. He orders the men to think about their being and write an essay about "What the Navy Offers." The officer in charge leaves and the light power lowers and presto, classical music accompanies the mosquitoes. In five minutes' time, at least half the newcomers were asleep.

The harassment drudged on at an early morning hour. This time the laborious task was held in the barracks. They attacked the men who were asleep and were bent over screaming at these helpless and tired men while they were doing pushups. They were given guns and they continued marching until they reached the allocated area. Then in-group they went under the barbed wire in the rain while the instructors released literally thousands of live bullets while the famished few crawled their way to safety. This adventure in mud was not the case, because the obstacle course was next. This was a rough son-of-a-bitch. The wall was the prolegomenon of all things that impedes progress. In essence, the obstruction was at least 30 feet tall. Its mighty height must be sealed with a rope dangling from the top. Furthermore, this standard barrier is three quarters of the way to completion, whereby it impedes the progress of the rapid breathing individual. That night all members of the grunt class got eight hours of sleep.

Among the more demanding tests of strength tested are the frequent casualty lists that follow. Hell week alleviates the log PT and the inflatable small boat injuries that pile up. Massive stress fractures are recorded and then muscle injury as well as chopping from the ever-present salt-water rubbing and exposure. Then finally, the sleep deprivation coupled with the danger of hypothermia causes the cap to seal the medical tally.

Next comes the swimming. They were placed in a gigantic pool of water which the necessary power facility used the clear water for cooling the operation. The recruits were taught everything about water. In a controlled environment the men were tied around the feet and were also tied around their back. Beneath each man was a diving mask. The basic forte of this maneuver is for the student to learn "drown proofing," the ability to survive underwater without a breathing apparatus. The student launches on a 40-minute episode of bobbing up to breathe above the surface and gradually sink to the bottom. At the end of the 40- minutes they must pick up their diving masks and bring it to the surface with their teeth.

This is only a fragment of a three-part process when complete it means you are qualified. After the devastations of Hell Week are finished and all candidates are swimmers, the next starts with land warfare. This is a gimmick of what trainees go through, but the instructors warrant more for their men. Equal is not good enough, excellence is the paramount of success. Once this is completed, the BUDS graduate, go on to Fort Benning, Georgia, where they learn the fundamentals of parachute training. This entails many dichotomies of training, in other words, two exclusive or contradictory ways of achieving things. Landing can be confusing especially approaching the ground at a high velocity. Case in point, at night, you jump out of the airplane and when you do the parachute blossoms. For the hell of it you are going to meet the ground at a force that is equal to four times the weight of your body. One tends to think, why me Lord, but you approach land and swing on your side, else you remain there with several broken bones in your legs. Following assignment to this training, the personnel come back to finish their training through some fictitious manner. The final segment is either spent on a U.S. submarine at sea on deployment.

This adventure is the most prestigious undertaking, sometimes marked by trickery that this individual should undertake. This highly technical and most secret form of SEAL brings to form an indurate, hardened individual, which is free and devastating. These are the facts of the SEAL, which makes roads over and through the masses of all human beings.

Still, there are areas that cause the SEAL to be at his fullest stature. Snow, for instance, is quite a change from the climate that these youngsters thrive on. Alaska is also a proving ground for climatic changes. The versatility and the strategic plans optimize the SEAL's ability to cope and manage with dexterity the skill of a mongoose. Philosophically, the man lives on skill and adroit. His enemy is a target of concern and the victim will rely on the rapid escape, which he will outclass his motive. The life in the north is unbelievable. The temperatures are sub-zero in all cases and the runner needs more validity than the designated loser. In summary, it's a robust life going through thickets and great depths of frozen ice with fabricated ice.

The masses of individuals have found a place in our cold-water scenario. One unexplained, ingenious mission occurred during the Gulf War which leaves no argument on the impact a few bodies have one of the surprises of an impending engagement. The Egyptian/Israeli War there were guessing that an attack would come from the east and lands on the opposite coast. Fifteen SEALs were in small boats and six men swam ashore at an island where they planted charges. After the nine planted their ordnance, the nine waited in their small boats until the munitions ignited. Horrific, thunderous explosions from the gunfire from ships destined the coming attack, awaiting the U.S. force. The guns of the opponent were trained to the sea and diverted parts of their forces to reinforce seashore defensives. Meanwhile, the allied forces slipped past them and lead a major distraction of the parent forces that they were left with their bottoms hanging out.

With the United States original ballistic missile submarine (SSBN) finally ready to receive the cutting tool, the analysts stopped and thought over the problem one more time. A brilliant idea was conceived which would modify the SSBN to a newer Trident (SSGW) conversion. By providing a challenge of this concept, the nuclear whiz-bangs put together all the ingredients of warfare. The submarine force has been wanting a strike force which could protect with strike missiles (Tomahawk), this platform would have a Joint

Task Force connectivity with accompanying displays, communications and manned at all times. The SSGW will be adapted to the SEAL Delivery System whereby the Dry Dock system is stopped to the system. Apparently, the Special Operations Forces can inhabit the submarine for either clandestine or stealth operations which support our cause.

There has always been a rivalry among special operations units. Each feels that theirs is the best and is ready to defend their team's honor with fists—if it's friendly—or weapons if against an enemy force. The SEALs are America's best, and their counterpart within the community of international armies can only be found with the British SAS or the Soviet Spetz.

Each SEAL is trained to understand their enemy. They are experts on the Soviet Union. Such knowledge is simple survival for a combat team who may one day be tasked with infiltrating the USSR.

The Union of Soviet Socialist Republics covers a massive piece of land, stretching eleven time zones all the way around the continent. Union of Soviet Socialist Republics (USSR) covers approximately 22.4 million square miles, which encompasses half of Europe and one third of Asia. To the north, the Arctic Ocean is met, and to the south there lies the Black Sea.

Karl Marx said that the state is an instrument of oppression. He envisaged that all workers would manage their own factories and the state would "wither away." This powerful state of the Soviet Union has yet to fall away from this system that proves that it has the authorization to rule.

Supported by an immense military machine and a mighty internal security apparatus, the Kremlin instead to seek control of life. In fact underground and black markets make up a "on the left," enormously challenging the official way. Nonetheless, dissident wards and hold demonstrations of evil poke hate towards official policies.

The power behind the Soviet Union is the Communist party. Primarily the party makes the policy decisions and goes government functionaries carry them out to the fullest. In the Army, case-by-case, party officers are charged to each commander to ensure the party gets their way.

Party members reach about 18 million (10 percent of the population) and are from the mass of Soviet society. Membership reveals rapid advancement, political ambitions, following the twists in the party line and devoting times to meetings, administration duties, and paying dues that support functions (3 percent of salary of top officials) .

At their workplaces, 400,000 members belong to the party. From there the Central Committee, made up of 500 members elected every five years. At the top are the Secretariat which is the party's general staff and the Politburo which meets weekly to discuss on the Nation's (Party) decisions. The man, who chaired the Politburo and the Secretariat, the leader of power, is no other than the Soviet leader.

The executive branch is headed by the Council of Ministers. The chairman of the council is the Soviet premier. The Council of Ministers is appointed by the Supreme Soviet based on the decisions of the Presidium. Elections are voted by the citizens of the USSR These elections are free and open. Pokazuka, which means to make a show or make things look different from reality. In essence, the vote must turn out which it invariably will! Inexplicably, the Communist party and the Soviet Union are intertwined, linking the closely guarded control of the armed forces.

To watch over political behavior, the state operates a ministerial level police authority, the Committee for State Security; better known by its initials in Russian KGB (State Security Committee). Seven hundred thousand agents are employed for domestic surveillance by the KGB. One out of 250 adults is investigated by this agency. Full-time agents are bounded by the KGB as informers, but are better known by "stukachi" or as squeakers. Moscow apartment buildings are a prime example; most people take for granted that the old lady who runs the elevator is paid to report on a visit by a stranger. She makes a note of this and calls in the subject that may be of importance to the KGB.

Looking back over the organization of structure than we have been through is more coloring than real. This drawing of the diagrams is nothing more than square boxes, lines, circles and presumably a bunch of dog manure. Then why, pray tell, does it seem complicated to foreign observers? Let's try to explain the trails and tribulations that these drawing has Communist logic, their own brand of judgment.

Re-looking at our diagram, there is great disagreement with who should be high and lower as the case may be. The general secretary or the president causes the big controversy, or who should be on top? In order to simplify our display, let's cross out the President. If war breaks out then the President or the General Secretary will do fine in every respect.

As far as the presidency, cross out the presidium of the Supreme Soviet. In essence they are not involved with either the government or access of the armed forces. The Soviet parliament meets twice a year, four or five days a year and discusses 30 to 40 questions each day. Funny, none of the committees worry or are concerned with the whereabouts of the military.

But the Soviet parliament is nothing but a laughing stock. Case in point, parliament does not meet for many years and nobody knows why. This is one of many why's that is bearing down rank and file, which is done by the consent of the parliament. Why was this grandiose system created? The answer is definitely a victim of camouflage. The only mystery thus far is the name by which the real 'chief' or General Secretary is called. By and large, this was decided aboard as well as at home. After discussion and yelling, the "president" is completely meaningless and this term becomes general secretary, the true ring of power.

The Red Army is into targets, as the Soviet admirals explain. Today's Red Army consists of:

1. The Strategic Rocket Forces,
2. The Land Forces,
3. The Air Defense Forces,
4. The Air Forces, and
5. The Navy.

Each is different; the Strategic Rocket Forces is made up of arms of each force; there are seven Land Forces; Air Defense Force; three separate Air Forces; and there are six elements that comprise the Navy.

At the head of the armed services is a commander in chief. Three of them are the Land Forces, the Air Force and the Navy makes up the improvement and incentive of these forces. The CiC of The Rocket Forces and the Air Defense Forces are responsible for the whole mission that characterizes these missions in action.

The Armed Services consist of arms of service. To begin with, these forces must have Tank Forces.

1.   The Strategic Rocket Force. The Strategic Rocket Forces are the newest and the smallest of the Armed Services that hold the hammer. The Rocket Army consists of 10 divisions. A rocket regiment has a commander, his staff and a technical base. The

principle task of a rocket unit is the technical supply of its regiments. The SRF faces another, but critical problem: hunger for uranium. The Soviet Union has put a great deal of work into producing a thermonuclear warfare by simultaneous explosion of hollow charges. Rather than launch a warhead-less rocket, the thing may be launched to scatter dust in the enemy's eyes.

2.   National Air Defense Force. Air Defense Force (ADF) is the third most important of the fixed services which make up the five components formed by a marshal of the Soviet Union, they outrank the Land Forces which are five times the size headed by a General of the Army. The ADF force is committed by 600,000 men who operate in Fighter Aviation, the Surface-To-Air Missile Forces and the ADF Radar Forces.

3.   The Land Forces. The Land Forces are without a doubt the oldest and diversified of all services. In peacetime they total between 21 and 23 million after mobilization in 10 days. Impressive, let's view their power:

Motor-rife troops,

Tank Troops,

Artillery and Rocket Troops of the Land Forces,

Air Defense Troops of the Land Forces,

Airborne Assault Troops,

Diversionary Troops (SPETZNAZ),

Fortified Troops.

Of all of the forces displayed, we must pay homage to discuss the Diversionary Troops.

Diversionary troops wear the same uniform as the airborne troops. However, they are parachuted to the enemy's rear. Theses Spetznaz forces are from the Land Forces which are used to carry out reconnaissance, to destroy headquarters, to assassinate political or military heads, command and communications centers and nuclear weapons.

Each tank company has a Spetznaz company with a complement of 115 men, which are split up with nine officers and 11 ensigns. This company has a headquarters, three diversionary platoons and a communication division. This agency operates in areas between 100 and 500 kilometers behind the enemy's lines. Depending on the size of area, or type of tasks to be carried out, they might divide to 15 groups groups, a separate unit or three to four specific entities reassembling to one Spetznaz force. Usually the companies are dropped at night the day before an Army begins the advance. These forces work best as any operational elite unit obtains from the advancing sub-units of the army.

Each Front has a Spetznaz brigade, which makes up one of the four battalions. Each of the fronts operates the same as Spetznaz operates in the rear. If necessary, the brigade can muster up to twelve hundred troops against a single target. Interesting, the headquarters is of particular interest made up of specialist, between 70 and 80 of them. The HQ company forms part of Spetznaz, but even not all is involved in the undermining. In peacetime this organization is covered by sports terms in the Military District. Boxing, wrestling, shooting, running, ski jumping or what they practice in the event of future "liberation." The professional sportsmen are really professional killers.

In addition to the diversionary brigades of fronts, there are several Spetznaz Long-Range Reconnaissance Regiments. The commander in chief of each Strategic Direction has one of the regiments, where the best of these is in the Moscow Military District (Combined Olympic Team of the USSR). As an afterthought, the KGB is also training its diversionary specialists under the all-encompassing spy codeword.

The Navy ranks fifth or the last in importance. The Soviet Navy has four fleets: Northern, Pacific, Baltic and the Black Sea. Each fleet has six arms of service;

Submarines,

Naval Aviation,

Surface Ships,

Diversionary Spetznaz Naval sub- units,

Coastal Rocket and Artillery Troops,

Marine Infantry.

The commander in chief of the navy has a purely administrative function in that, the Northern Fleet for operational purposes to the Headquarters of the Supreme Commander (Stavka) and the three other units fleets to the CINC of the Strategic Directions. In addition to this function, he is Stavka's main advisor on the operation use of the Navy. Technically, he has no operational planning function but awaits the act and cunning of the general staff.

Soviet naval strength is based on submarines, which may be by types of propulsion or by what armament the carried. The Soviet submarine force has ground, in fact, they outnumber the surface combatants! Moreover, they seem to increase their displacement and deploy them away from the motherland. In the next few years the surface force will gain a series of nuclear powered missile cruisers. Tremendous effort has been placed on these and many other vessels, which attain a higher-degree of independence.

The presence of Spetz sub-units is a closely guarded secret. By 1950, each fleet had this closely invisible unit onboard that was under the cognizance of the Third Department of the Intelligence Directorate at Naval Headquarters.

A diversionary brigade has several miniature subs under one division that has two or three battalions of frogmen, a parachute and a communications function. This brigade is an entire unit and from coloring they may wear the uniform of the Marine infantry. Variability, these soldiers were something that is common to what every submarine crew wears. Deceptive behavior permits the Spetznaz force to be situated in various bases. In the first place this group could be used against naval installations (nuclear submarine pens), surface ships or from large submarines and a unit of a large trawler would be used to launch a miniature sub. Case in prospective, the trawler can be rigged to launch and recover a mini-submarine.

Spetznaz brigades in the Navy have special tasks, which are designed for watching political and military leaders. These units are technically disguised as naval athletic teams. These members are highly selected and are an elite member of the Olympic Games.

FOXTROT CLASS

FROM THE WHISKEY, A NEW BOAT WAS being prepared and was in trials. They needed a new captain of the vessel named Foxtrot. Captain Alexei Latvia was approached and accepted the challenge. Quickly, he found himself in school learning the three diesels, which drive three separate shafts. Additionally, each has three electric motors, which can propel for upward of 15 hours. They can manage up to 20 knots maximum and 15 knots submerged. Surface cruising is the best selling advantage. Twenty thousand miles represents its total cruising advantage. Her torpedoes are listed at 20, but that leaves out numerous arguments. At first blush, let's go with that. Numerous other assorted weapons have been tested, however, that is still the chance that the Foxtrot will carry this highly subjective weapon.

With the Foxtrot submarine introduced to the Mediterranean Sea, there are usually three or four or more Foxtrots, and occasionally two nuclear submarines. Russia is most proud to send these boats whereby the presence of the Russian Empire is needed when they are making port stops.

After these months of labor, the captain was given a ship. This was recently overhauled with its new shiny deck plates and its snorkel device ready for sailing. The captain met with his crew and told them what to expect. His executive officer was superior and his officers were the cream of the crop. He discussed the ways of completing a task, and he wanted discipline throughout the crew. He asked for questions; no response! The exec took over and briefed the men on Monday when they left port. It takes about 10 to 11 days to make the long body of water to the south.

On Monday at 0600 they made movement and with the help of a tug, they were on their way. Captain Latvia was on the bridge with his enlisted men scurrying about the surface of the ship. Once out of the dock and with clear water the captain gave the ship to the watch officer and he went below to read his orders. He entered his cabin and took the keys and unlocked a wall safe. Once he had the orders in hand, he contacted the exec and had him report to his cabin. Three minutes later the exec knocked and entered the CO's compartment. The captain read: "Once the submarine was heading out, the ship is to sail undetected until nightfall where he will snorkel until an hour before the sun comes up. While snorkeling, keep a close watch on passive listening, especially the electric warfare devices. The radar shall not be used, but must be used to get a fix and shut down as soon as possible. Soon you have turned south, the rules for snorkeling applies after one hour after sunset." The captain continued reading the mission that contained an enclosure that gave all the routes and courses to the navigator. The exec and captain weighed the mission and found out that it was "old hat." After the mission was locked up and the necessary track was taken, the exec and captain proceeded to the operations center. The officer of the deck approached the captain and wanted to submerge. The captain agreed and the horn sounded. Once everything was settled, the CO came on the horn. He explained the route given and the snorkel times. He wanted a visual watch on the periscope every hour. If something was unusual, please report it to me. The captain announced he was going on a tour of the boat and you are in charge, exec!

As stated at the ordnance/armament station, which was amply supplied with torpedoes, the master chief greeted him and offered to show him around. "This is fine," said the skipper. He introduced himself to several petty officers. He asked if they had any questions. From there he went to the propulsion crew. He was greeted and overjoyed that the sailors knew who he was. He shook hands with all and commented on the diesel force, which made a submarine. He told a story about his own recollection learned in the submarine school. He talked about 15 minutes, ranging from mechanics to sex. Finally, he stood up and everyone stood at attention. The skipper stopped and told the chief that he had a hell of a crew!

By the time he reached the bridge, the word was out that they were preparing to snorkel. He just sat down and watched the crew. Starting at 270 feet, the crew began ascending to periscope depth. The watch officer scanned the periscope and reported no contacts to the captain. "Very well, and keep a close eye on the ESM," replied the skipper. The next three nights were very exciting during the snorkeled session. The fumes from this form of operation can be downright sickening.

The U.S. Navy contacts that were picked up really caused a major trauma with the crew. The navigator was plotting, the ESM petty officer was reporting and soon all of the necessary warning was the P-3 APS-80 radar. Apparently the early warning system gained contact when the crew commenced snorkel operations. The P-3 employed a search pattern with sonobuoys thereby picking up the propulsion diameters of this Foxtrot. The airplane used another tactic to narrow the fixing information. This transition is not the best. Above all when the APS-80 is switched on, and if he is coming inbound, dive, dive, dive. This was the case three times and we escaped before the Orion analyzed the scope. Finally we had progressed south of the territory of the Icelandic Sea. Expecting the doldrums were becoming commonplace and the crew began to watch instead of react! South of 40°N, the action picked up again as the U.S. Navy has aircraft at Naval Station Rota, Spain. The Navy likes to patrol the Mediterranean and the Strait of Gibraltar.

The Strait of Gibraltar is a channel supporting the entrance into the Mediterranean Sea from Europe and northwestern Africa. Critically, the crossroads data sheds both strategic and commercial importance. The strait is 36 miles wide on the western end and narrows/tapers to its narrowest point on the eastern end. Deepest in the eastern end, it shallows out at 1,050 feet. Without a doubt, this channel has great oceanographic potential. The surface moves eastward from the Atlantic Ocean reaching a depth of 525 feet. Below this depth, denser, more saline water flows westward to the Atlantic Ocean. Additionally, this is the reason the sill shuts out the coldness of this water, which keeps the Mediterranean relatively warm.

After taking a radar fix, the Foxtrot really lit up the entrance to the strait. The fix was positioned on the western side of Spain about 50 miles northwest of Rota, Spain. The ship descended to a depth of 200 feet and began its approach and passage through Gibraltar. The U.S. nuclear submarines have a base or layover in Rota. These ships, about half, are ballistic missile carriers, which are quiet as a mouse. The other boats are nuclear attack boats that all Soviet boats should be aware. About 15 hours later, Captain Latvia was becoming apprehensive about being down for so long. Finally he checked and it was dark outside. In addition, there was a tanker passing to the west. "Take her to periscope depth," said the captain. The command sounded and the helmsman drove the submarine to snorkel depth.

The skipper raised the periscope and looked 360 degrees. The merchant ship has just passed them and the diesels were put into operation. While the myriad workers were listening and watching, the navigator showed the chart of the western Mediterranean. He remembered the initial rendezvous with the Soviet trawler. This point was supposed to be a group of islands just off the coast of Africa. The exec went down to the CO's cabin and got the mission directive. His memory was good, because he felt that he would be there in four and a half hours. Believe it or not, a half moon came up and was sighted near the island. Immediately, the Morse code was flashing and it was the ship.

The Foxtrot tied up to the vessel, which was dark in color, but boy was it decked out with antennas! Yes, it was a Soviet electronic intelligence [ELINT] ship that keeps track of all U.S. Navy activities in the Mediterranean Sea. The captain accompanied by the exec and operations officer walked up the ladder and was met by a Soviet naval officer. He followed them down two decks where they entered the operation complex. The admiral was waiting and Latvia knew Admiral Zendoc. They shook hands and the others from the boat were introduced. An enlisted brought them coffee and they sat down at a conference table. The admiral began the brief, which consisted of three major areas:

1) Planned operations in the Mediterranean,
2) U.S. sonar and electronic devices,
3) Coordinated operations.

The planned operations began with an unrolling of a screen being projected from behind them. Each course was provided with stops at Cairo, Egypt and at various other anchorages. The word was "caution" when making a stop. If something is jumpy, get out of this port. Captain Latvia was critical, but wanted to know why we are running away without cause. Admiral Zendoc was almost to the fact that U.S. submarine activity has also capitalized on a recent Foxtrot incident.

The work on U.S. has been null and void regarding the recent Soviet sonic activity. This is ever present in the minds of all Russian submarine sailors. The basic targets are the two carriers floating around the Mediterranean. Right now, another slide projector on the extreme right showed a new carrier coming into the Strait. This carrier will relieve the USS Independence. The rest of the ECM is fed to the operations officer, who has control of these petty officers.

The coordinated operation is a vague technique and as soon as these exercises occur, you will be notified. The carrier is this one who broadcasts tactics and evolutions in which the Task Force plays an important part. Practice and remember to shadow each player in the battle group. The admiral asked for questions and several questions were answered by noting the frequencies that the battle force uses. All data must be recorded and submitted when you arrive in the Northern Fleet. The individuals shook hands and went up to the main deck. The watch officer said we had better hurry and submerge because daylight is one hour away. Down the gangplank and onboard the Foxtrot. The chief of the boat was there and said he was ready to sail. The captain agreed and the chief began the task of leaving the sub from its mooring. Ten minutes later, the sub was 1,000 yards ahead of the ELINT trawler and they dove below the clear water.

After settling down at two hundred feet, the officers had a session in their wardroom. The operations clan presided and they discussed the battle plan of courses they have set before us. This offers many alternatives, but the tactics and all were set for the Mediterranean. To deal with the sound coming from the ship, the captain has to take into account the alternatives and the quietness the crew must maintain on the submersible. The best alternative is to be on your toes and be ready for whatever may occur.

The major part of the deployment is the coordinated operations that Captain Latvia encountered. A message was received from the Russian Med Operations that a combined operation of the two carriers was about to begin. The position passed was well inside the Ionian Sea where a mass of U.S. ships was gathered. Also, there were submarines, which made the adventure more advantageous. Watching this event was the first clue of a procedure. The battle group was formed in armada and proceeded to the south. Based on reason and prudence, the captain monitored his position, which was being closed by the battle group. Destroyers who were leading the pack opened up the sonars, scanning for U.S. submarines. Sonars were of good quality and believe it or not, the Foxtrot was detected. The captain ordered the ship to dive to two hundred feet and make a hard right to 90°. Finally, each destroyer had containment as they were three thousand yards and closing. Now down to 200 feet, the captain again altered heading to 180°. He ordered the torpedo crew to send a shell, what better way to put it, out of the forward torpedo hatch. He heard when it was ready and the captain wanted it fired. "Away," said the chief petty officer as we were traveling at eight knots. Five minutes later, the Foxtrot had eluded the sonar's ping. It was pinging on the deceptive submarine. All of the destroyers were apparently around the counterfeit target. At a glance, this camouflaged mess quickly broke out when the device became silent. Periscope pictures allowed members of this crew to laugh at the aftermath.

Heading westward, the time had come to retrace these steps. The time has come to return to the Motherland and to collect the many records and tapes of the voyage. It was the executive officer's turn to man the bridge. He was an excellent candidate to be skipper of a boat. The long trip up the Atlantic was uneventful. The crew learned many lessons, but each deployment left a window of opportunity, leery that he may catch this fragment of intelligence.

TROUBLE IN THE WATERS

THE UNION OF SOVIET REPUBLICS WAS AN uninvited war player in the World War II extravaganza. Russia was trampled on and revitalized itself knocked down when it realized it was the final hour, so hell; let's fight for love and country. North of this land is the Arctic Ocean with many ports, inlets and fjords which father fishing boats, and even fighting vessels. Murmansk is one of the thriving ports on the coast of Russia and it provides untold amounts of shipping during the war. Undoubtedly, this port handled supply chiefly by rail through Persia and by sea to the shores of Murmansk. Imminent need was critical for the western Allies as they keep opening-bottle necks (as in road operations), but it was the convoluted mechanism of domestic industry to military needs was quantitatively decisive for winning. Many sizable Karelian communities are near the St. Petersburg area and in neighboring Finland.

In addition, the Red merchant fleet operates many additional services to other countries, such as the northern sea route, through the waters of the Arctic. Shippers could carry bulky items like minerals and timber for up to 18 weeks a year with the advent of icebreakers, specifically some breakers were run by nuclear reactors. Almost all ports require the use of icebreakers, especially Murmansk, which may be ice-bound for approximately 50 days a year.

A profound handicap was discovered when the USSR had to divide its Navy into four distinctive regions; Arctic Ocean, Black Sea, Baltic Ocean and the Pacific Ocean. With the size of this great country, many internal waterways hold together the key to bond these three European fleet areas, but only for small vessels. Thus, only in the summer are inter-fleets swapped, which involves the NATO dominated straits or vis-à-vis the northern sea route.

In the case of the Northern fleet, its status was the largest and clearly the most important of the four fleets. Many exits that Russia has to the sea have shallow waters, which resist the drought of ships. Namely, the Baltic precludes the surface ships as well as

193

the submarines. Other sites, such as the Black Sea, they exist by being theoretically regulated by the Montrevx Convention of 1936, although the passage of ships was not hindered. Poorly placed in comparison with other NATO countries for open ocean access, Russia is stymied by a combination of distances and unbelievable angles of departing an anchorage. Principal bases, or Soviet Naval ports, are along the Murmansk, fjord Ronstadt and other ports near the Baltic. From 1964 a naval presence was sought in the Mediterranean Sea. Soon a small force was keep alive in the Indian Ocean. In 1975 or thereabouts, the relative strength of all ships at sea was achieved in the Atlantic and the Pacific Oceans.

Starting with 1948, Communism was in the center spotlight. In Moscow the military regime began a plan to solidify the armed forces and to embellish a new force that could overpower and to annihilate those that could not accept the overpowering cause. This plan took effect quite by accident. The Navy, the admirals of course, went back to Murmansk and started planning for the future. All along the open spaces were docks besieged with worn out battleships, defunct cruisers, and deleterious submarines which must be reduced to metal or iron that could be molded that would be augmented to a new fighting instrument. The final blow of this analysis is the plants that must be constructed to reap the fire of force of the new empire.

Russian Soviet Federal Socialist Republic met in Moscow and programmed money for the engineers, tacticians, and design architects to get this plan off the ground. Not noticed by the vanguard of personnel involved in this scheme was the planning of a new submarine, a nuclear vessel. Last but not least, is the KGB contribution to this force. Even in 1948 there are many Americans who dwell in secrets all day long. Their spirit and their well being disavowed most of these individuals to give up the secret of being an American. Nevertheless, the KGB is working and the Reds are developing a lot more than we can admit. And lastly, the Soviet tactics have to be elaborated to include new weapon systems, and a defense against electronic counter measures plays a big part in meshing out the missile system. Soviet tactics are of utmost simplicity or they can be condensed into a single phase—the maximum concentration of forces in the decisive sector. Anyone who thought of shooting or eventually tried to kill the dispersing forces was shot with without further ado. Modern tactics were used by Genghis Khan: Concentrate and you will win!

An unprecedented buildup of the submarine forces are struggling with a tremendous budget with several conventional boats at the forefront. Also the nuclear boat components are getting together with pertinent and development ideas. The first submarine in which to play with was the Whiskey Canvas Bag that was used to develop radar and radar picket devices. With the Whiskey Class the boats moved out and deployed around Norway in to the North Atlantic. This gave the Soviet Navy a chance to develop a sound and stable radar. The first radar was called a Snoop or a derivative of a Snoop Plate radar. This variable radar was good at detecting a long-range target, but was also good at intercepting radar of other ships and airplanes. Along with improvements to radar/ECM, the Russians looked at the torpedoes and thought they had better rethink their employment into the seventies.

Although unnoticed by Murmansk, several countries undertook the development of the atomic bomb. The Soviet Union tested its first fission bomb in 1949. Several countries forged ahead and developed a nuclear fusion bomb. On November 1, 1952 the United States tested the thermonuclear fusion device on an island in the Pacific. Anticipation by the Russians lead to responding by setting off its first device in 1953.

The planned hope of new weapons and systems came to fruition in the mid-1950s. The first submarine was the Foxtrot submarine. Granted there were others, which developed its structure and viability. Foxtrot Class exemplified the nits and grits of the scientists and engineers, which gave to the sailors this thing of beautify. The power plant became the conventional power plant, the Type 37 D diesel. The torpedoes were ready-made and the ship was full of goodies that could supplant the enemy and get the job done. Along with the undersea craft were many others that followed. Some were sent to the Pacific while the mainstay kept coming to Murmansk.

The next significant means of creating and threatening other world powers is the nuclear submarine. The November Class is the first submarine that was launched in the early 1960s. Surprisingly, she withheld all course records and she was faster than a Chinese bullet! The three important submarines were the November, Hotel and the Echo I and II. The warmongers figured that a fast boat was necessary, but another factor was to protect the boats from surface ship pinging and regardless of the unthinkable case of depth charges around the nuclear power.

Murmansk was mounting a new task when the new ship building area was controlled by vast means of security forces enabled identification cards be shown at all times. No one knew what was happening, but the admirals and their staffs were busy and tight-lipped as always. Soon a new complement of ELINT ships came to Murmansk and carved out a substantial part of the pier. ELINT ships were configured with everything imaginable: Satellite communications, talking to underwater submersible objects and collecting samples of tactical communication within the battleground. Yes, she was stationed alongside the carrier and was quite evasive about this important post. This can be said in the Med because there are many incidents of close aboard encounters are recorded. Finally the doors to this super-secret phenomenon are closed. At 11 o'clock at night with cold wintry winds, a new nuclear-powered ballistic missile submarine, the Yankee Class, was moved out of the shipyard and was moved by tugs to the harbor. Shortly thereafter, accompanied by an ELINT, she escaped to the Arctic Sea to conduct some tests. This was a massive machine that could handle the strategic problem with sixteen SS-N-6 SLBMs. It has as additional 18 torpedoes as antisubmarine warfare weapons, and low- frequency sonar. Its steam turbines provide great speed when evading or underwater. In fact, the Soviet SSBNs are significantly faster than their western counterparts.

After several launches, early in the morning the admiral went down to the docks to send off the skipper on the Yankee on his first patrol. The admiral gave him the orders sealed in an envelope. Away the submarine went on the surface with the ELINT in the lead. When it was time to submerge the ship was contacted by radio. Believe it or not, the ship dove and headed though Iceland and Norway into the North Atlantic Ocean. The vessel continued heading southwest during which time many tests were still being done. Instead of normal exercises, the Yankee played spy against the United States. The ocean facilities were having a ball with this target, especially since he kept his speed up to 12 knots. In fact, he (the skipper) made many high-speed runs against numerous parts of the Eastern coast of the United States. And of course, the U.S. Navy had to work its ass off.

The Iceland Tactical Support Center (TSC) at Naval Station Kelflavik was awakened by vacuum cleaners and seaman waxing doorknobs. The center was undergoing a personnel inspection at 1100 hours today. The Tactical Support Center is the main gathering of information, which prepares the Navy antisubmarine forces their bread and butter. This is the place where crews come to receive their brief before they fly the mission to gain contact on a Russian nuclear submarine. The overall coordinator and verification authority is the Naval Facility, which designates a contact and thirsty gives this information to the TSC as soon as the authorities say launch. The ready duty scrambles to determine that this submarine one detected will have numerous missions, which will determine its destiny for the next 60 days.

Three months ago, the Soviet hierarchy called on secure line to Lawrence Latvia. He answered the phone and was delighted to talk to an old colleague. The caller wanted him to take a submarine out to sea. The submarine was a Yankee class that had been picked by the admiral of the Western Force. Admiral Latvia was surprised since he had been in this job for one year. "No sweat," said the caller, "but there are certain qualifications that you undoubtedly fill the bill." He hung up with the agreement that he would attend a meeting at two o'clock today.

The meetings were attended by eight Navy men. Five of the group were submariners of whom were two Yankee commanding officers, and there were representatives of this new submersible. One was an intelligence officer and that left himself and the admiral. The admiral started the meeting by introducing himself and went around the room each addressing his name and current job. He began his discussion by noting the nature of events that the nuclear guided missile carriers had achieved. Numerous events have hurt the Russian image in this situation and must be corrected. Case in point, the Russian submarine skippers are embarrassed with the thought of SOSUS picking them up and following the clandestine movement down to the Bermuda on station area. The lights dimmed and a screen came down from the ceiling. The slide projector came on and showed an Arctic Ocean Projection that had been stolen or was an original offering by the Arctic/Antarctic Reach Institute (AARI) in Moscow. The admiral continued and cited that 30 degrees east longitude we begin to be detected by underwater surveillance. That necessary evil continually harasses us until we reach the North Atlantic waters. We have got to do something and we are trying several plans. The one that is inviting is this plan, which takes the submarine through the Greenland-Iceland gap. By prior intelligence the turn point to enter the Faroe-Iceland Ridge had been calculated whereby the speed is reduced and a turn to the west is finalized. The admiral turned to the intelligence wizard for the next portion of the brief. The specifics of the brief were disclosed by the newest Yankee being two decibels lower than previous Yankee class boat. The briefer showed a course when plotted showed the submarine coming North of Iceland and coming down the Denmark Strait. Then, very quickly, he asked for questions. The submarines were wrapped up in the depth of the water. The water depth is not a problem but the navigation accuracy is a must. The admiral jumped up and said that Admiral Latvia will be in command of the new submarine. The executive officer and his operations officer are here, so let's end this presentation and now it's time to do some talking.

The executive officer and operations officers were men of his caliber. The exec brought a set of documents, which designate the length, size and breadth of the new submarine. Lawrence has never been on a submarine such as this. The operations officer brought him a set of orders, which begin tomorrow afternoon with a train leaving for Murmansk. He had two and a half months before sailing.

Day after day it became closer to starting the cruise. Lawrence had two weeks of training and soon he knew the Yankee boat backwards. His eagerness and mentality impressed the crew and soon he was acknowledged as the commanding officer. The day before the deployment, he turned on the loudspeaker and told all of the preparation of sail was 24 hours away. He spoke with dignity and clarity and led them with a song that was dedicated to them at their commissioning.

The tugs came and moved the submarine from its berth. The wives were waving and it was a cold, blustery day in October. Lawrence waved to his bride as we started moving. The ELINT ships were there, awaiting our call and they moved both forward and astern of us. The exec reported that all men and equipment were stored aboard. The captain acknowledged and the exec took charge of the bridge. The flashing of light meant that the ships would pull off and the Yankee was set to go her own way. The code and blinder system was unique and the ships reversed course and headed back to port. The captain came up on the bridge and acknowledged that we should begin the mission. The exec gave the order and the captain, inter alia, went below as the ship dove under the water.

With things settled down, the captain called the radio communications officer and the exec to his cabin. The captain and radio officer performed their duties and the orders were in the skipper's hands. Lawrence read the subject instructions and gave them to the exec. He read and then he commented on the brief, which showed the track of the Yankee. Additionally, they had stockpiled the charts for this area and with that in mind, they called up the operations officer and navigator to show them the course they were supposed to take.

By the time the submarine was passing the 30-degree parallel, it headed west; the vibrations were turning in the Naval Station Facility. The contact was reported to Norfolk and the tracking began. It was called a Yankee but the boldness of the lines was faint but readable. Also, the TSC, which had a thorough inspection, grouped the watch officers for a ready duty launch. That would take at least 24 hours.

At 0100 hours, the Yankee passed 70-00 N 00-00 W at a course of 220 making 10 knots. The navigator was working on the next point and he was to call the captain three minutes before they reached it. The night watch was on and the pace was over to awaken some of the men. The galley man brought him a cup of java, which he appreciated. The submarine was running quite well, particularly the internal system was tracking properly and each of the plotting boards were without a doubt, top drawer. The navigator did not notice, but the captain was standing directly behind. "What's up?" asked the captain. The young man turned around and was shaken. He reported that all systems were go and we would be at point Bravo in nine minutes. Coffee was selling good as the CO had a cup but that did not concern him. He confided in him by pulling a "Crazy Ivan" prior to slowing down to four knots at point Charlie. He then went over to talk to the watch officer and spent sometime with those gents. Eventually, the navigator said it was three minutes until we turn. Lawrence came over and saw the red circle moving on top and then the navigator said, "Come to 240 true course, speed 10 knots," said the navigator. Time passed by quickly and soon it was time to penetrate the 360 evaluation. At the turn of the hour the alarm sounded and sonar was searching for a trailer. The craft dove down to 700 feet in a right-handed turn. This took at least five minutes with no contact reported. Once back on course, the submarine climbed up 200 feet and crept along at four knots.

Naval Facility Iceland was just about to relieve the watch. The briefer was analyzing all the targets, but one was missing. What happened to 027, the Yankee that the ready duty was to launch at 1200 local time? The commanding officer walked in at this time and wondered the same. This warranted a review of the tapes. They went back to the tapes and found the 027 tape and replayed it. They tape-recorded the submarine, which at four o'clock and then it faded out prior to the target disappeared. The gram readers did not report the lost contact and the watch officer forgot that this target was to be handed off for a possible extended or multiple flights while a submarine is brought over to shadow the target. The captain of the Navfac was totally pissed off. He called a meeting with all the watch officers including the operations officer. "The task at hand is to find out where the bastard is," said the CO. The only provider of the whole mess lies in the water, which listens and reports his beacon as a bearing to the coming target. This device has also the characteristics of giving an anonymous bearing which may have been the issue. Immediately the watch team went back to the detection of 027 and tracked him to the last contact without concluding about what and where he is. Another thing, let's check again with the intelligence force about this contact. Everything sounds questionable about this demon!

It has been wonderful in this slow boat to China, but that's what the skipper wanted, so let's wait it out. The current track has proven an assist whereby we are making six knots with the added push. The next point is estimated at 0100 just after midnight. The exec and the crew had been studying for promotions, in other words, making the next grade. Many of the so-called lower rank are competing within themselves. Whether it is an engineer, a plotter, the enlisted boat petty officer, the battle goes on.

In the middle of the night the commanding officer of the Navfac storms into the facility. He called for the plotter and the watch officer. They met at 2:30 in the morning. The skipper woke up an hour ago and had an idea that this Yankee was still going past Iceland into the North Atlantic. The first thing he asked for was the hydrophone that lost contact. Two minutes later he was looking at a picture of it. The bearing from the submarine was so strong as it was detected at first contact. One hour before lost contact they plotted the bearing. The bearing was steady, but what happened to the submarine? Upon looking at the microphone, the submarine ran over the hydrophone and the bearing reversed, or maybe it did not. Upon further investigation, the sub slowed to about four or five knots, which added to the diversion. So the answer to the missing problem is, how long did the sub, after cutting back his power, remained at four knots on a bearing headed south? The watch officer illuminated when he thought how much time the delay of sound between the hydrophone and the Navfac grams. "I believe we have stumbled on the right track," said the watch officer. He went to the chalkboard and drew the bearings and at the time she slowed down to four knots that edge built in a fair confidence that the submarine went west! The plotter threw north of Iceland on the drawing board. The commanding officer and the others put the bearings and the distance on the chart. Now, if the submarine was going four knots to get out of the sound surveillance network, will he traverse north of Iceland at four knots? "No," said the others.

The man with silver oak leaves agreed with the group and laid out a course commensurate with four knots across the north of Iceland. Denmark Sea Strait separates Greenland from Iceland and he likewise, plotted a straight line ending of line southwest of Iceland. After much consorting, bickering and agreements, the two had their best guess as to what happened to the bloody varmint. It was now five o'clock when the message was ready for review. The commanding officer signed the message and it went operational immediate to Ocean Systems Atlantic. Regretfully, they approved two flights to take off at 1400 hours.

At 1300, the squadron duty officer answered the phone. He called the ready duty number and told them to get down there ASAP; they were launching. The SDO called the squadron skipper and advised him that the ready duty was launching and we are briefing at the TSC. Eight minutes later they were met by the tactical coordinator/navigator. Quickly, they opened their locks and with backup they suddenly disappeared. The crew was briefed on this incident this morning. They were to lay two barriers with the first barrier the furthest from the contact and the second 30 miles closer to the target. Upon receipt of this sensitive information, the tactical coordinator ran down the steps and out the hangar door to a windy walk to the auxiliary powered P-3C aircraft. He walked up the ladder and then the door was closed. The number two engine started breathing life as it turned into one hundred percent power. "Set condition five," said the plane commander. The tactical coordinator put on his parachute, gloves and hardhat, making a tour about the aircraft. The plane has all engines turning on the taxiway and the TACCO announced condition five was set, meaning everyone was in their seats, visors down and ready for take off. At 1355, the P-3C Orion took off and heading west to intercept the unsuspecting target.

At 66-30 North 30-00 West, the Yankee resumed 180 degrees and increased speed to 10 knots. It was also time to copy the fleet broadcast, so the skipper took the boat up to periscope depth to copy necessary traffic. The communications officer reported the traffic was copied and the sub went back to 200 feet. The main concern was what depth they should be at. The water, which they were in, was affected by East Greenland Current, which was colder than the depth of 200 feet. The skipper thought there was a layer at 50 or 70 feet. He elected to remain at 200 feet. He was interested in the Irminger Current, which they would use running into coming from the east before the Regganes Ridge which runs across their path.

At the ASA-70, the tactical coordinator's multipurpose display, he had just put symbols on the display representing an eight-buoy pattern spaced 10 miles between the intended buoys. At which time the plane turns and proceeded to drop eight buoys set for three hours at 300 feet, starting at 62 North and 30 West. The next barrier would be at 6230 North and at 30 West. As an additional safeguard, he dropped a bathometer buoy that verifies that the water was isothermal to 80 feet and then the water is warmer down to 1,000 feet. The noise in the water was not too bad but the sound of a distant trawler kept everyone alert. After three hours, no contact, so the aircraft moved further north and put in two more barriers. The navigator interrupted the tactical coordinator when he copied an hourly message. The message informed the aircraft that an additional plane was relieving them on station.

The TSC and Navfac are joining bonds in the futile search. They have tried to guess what the boat, or if there is a boat, plowing south through the Denmark Sea Strait. They have got another flight through consultation by secure telephone. The commanding officer is betting his career today, but just one more sortie. Analysis has just received the ready duty flight tapes and they are reviewing them. No contact, said the chief petty officer, and the crew were dismissed.

After spending the three hours monitoring the first barrier, the buoys began to lose life and gently end at the bottom of the sea. The plane moves northward and again lays eight buoys. Five and a half hours the AW2 operator sites something on his grams. He places this sonobuoy on his 'Bearing Frequency Only,' which compares a 50-hertz spike with what the lofargram is printing. The line of 51 hertz is very suspicious and the operator will wait an additional three minutes for the signal to print out. The operator reported five minutes later that he had the contact on 50 hertz with up Doppler. The tactical coordinator looked at this and reported to the cockpit, which departed station. Halfway back to Keflavik, the plane communicated with the TSC that they had partial contact, convergence zone or what's on the last barrier. They will be at the TSC in 35 minutes. The replay was ready as the two AWs ran all the way to the analysis section after the plane touched the runway. Yes, it was contact and the sub contact was about 50 miles even further north of the barrier. Soon after much enthusiasm, commander in chief authorized four more flights on this target.

Tremendous success was accomplished by these vivid and vicarious tactics, which cleared the forecast conditions to a worthwhile experience. The first flight gained contact right away and employed Difar sonobuoys, which fixed the contact. Flight number two picks up the contact and had an easy time fixing the target. The third sortie had a bear of a time with the Irminger Current. This current was distributing warm water with numerous pockets intermingled with the cold water, which created a Bermuda current effect. Submarine range was reduced to two to three miles. The last flight settled down to mini-barrier tracking and marking the closest point of approach on sonobuoy as a fixing technique.

Sixty-five days later as Admiral Latvia entered the pier the admiral and the wives were there. All tied up the admiral came aboard and vibrantly congratulated Lawrence on a successful voyage. He added that the reduced noise of the boat really helped. In reality, the lofar/difar detection of the Yankee was unknown to the crew, 18 hours later they were in trail by a nuclear attack boat, and had at least 50 percent coverage of long-range detection by the underwater system.

UNDERCOVER AGENT

NEWFOUNDLAND WAS IN ITS PRIME TIME WITH the advent of fall. The colors were excessively beautiful as the technique of multitudinous color crossed the island. Naval Station Argentia was in an exciting place with freighters, coal ships and numerous passersby that carried needs for the station. For example, freighters were used for avionic structures that were too big to be moved by air. From the air the naval station offered a detachment of patrol planes that keep our surveillance up to speed, but also the intelligence force that was evolving beneath the surface of the ocean. With station aircraft the airfield is quite busy with the Coast Guard C-130s who tour the upper reaches to detect icebergs that may become prevalent to many surface ships. Additionally, the station sends one or two four-engine aircraft to Quonset Point for medical and food supplies. In fact, the helicopters (three) were used to provide a search and rescue vehicle while one of the aircraft encountered a difficulty.

Naval Station Argentia was commanded by Captain John Blanes. Captain Blanes was passed over for admiral, but he was selected as commanding officer of this facility. His wife and young son came to Argentia with him as both of his daughters are in college. Well-liked by his men and women on base, he was understandable, but a demanding man. His wife was supportive to all women concerned. She was active in the hospital as a volunteer and was vibrant in all supportive women's programs.

John Hilton arrived via airplane and it shut down right in front of the operations building. The commanding officer was present to meet him and immediately the CO's car stopped and the captain got out of the car to meet him. At the bottom of the ladder they shook hands and John followed the skipper to his car. Just before the car took off, John gave the CDO his baggage to look after and the gear would go to the bachelor officers quarters. Captain Blanes was most cooperative and asked if he was bringing his wife. "No, of course not. I am not married, but I'm looking," said John. The captain laughs and about that time they were at the administrative building. We went behind closed doors with a cup of coffee and chatted. John gave a brief resume of his work with the Navy. He worked with planning and incorporating nuclear carriers at Newport News and also had worked on nuclear submarines. Captain Blanes then challenged him to bring up to excellence his support team. Unequivocally, the measure of support versus the result is reducing the flow of items by unaccountable loss of goods. This must be stopped, said the captain. He acknowledged that he was brought up to this facility to be head of engineering, but also to be in charge of shipments and in essence, all of the supply movements throughout the base. When the caffeine was gone, they stood up and the captain said he must be going to another staff meeting. John then proceeded to the car where he was further transferred to the Hilton bachelor quarters. He was given a nice two-room suite on the seventh floor with a nice view of the airstrip and the base.

After moving in and breaking down the various suitcases, he took the elevator down where he was taken to his office. A matronly woman was at the secretary's desk and stood to properly introduce herself. John was impressed with her unscrupulous behavior and her name was Marie. She then showed him his office, which was grandiose in size with a head on the right side. The door at the back of the office lead to a small conference room with a table that could seat 12 representatives. Incidentally, there was coffee available and John took a cup. He listened for an hour as his secretary went over the files and showed him the worrisome files, which had created heartburn. The remainder of the afternoon was spent reviewing the files and making a brief list, which the secretary will work up tomorrow. He wrapped around a cup of coffee and read/studied the problems that were facing him.

At 8:30 in the morning, he had a department meeting. John had the commissary officer, the navy exchange officer, the air operations officer and finally there were 11 officers/civilian department heads who were present. John, who introduced himself, gave a short presentation about his background and present job. Each person was polite and right to the point. Then the secretary gave out the agenda, which was passed around so that each member had a copy. The first item on the list was the elimination of the boat that carries supplies, namely, spruce lumber when the base is doing reconstruction. This part of the program went by quickly. John, being his first adventure in the staff meeting, said little, but his pencil was working! Fifty minutes later, he saw that the particular business meeting was done. Then he thanked the members, and wanted each of them to report tomorrow afternoon at 1600 hours when each division would show him their office spaces. Without further ado, the staff meeting was over. By 1130 hours, Marie had a draft of the staff meeting. It was comprehensive and conservative. John then wrote on the draft. In reality, he wanted all members to brief him on the financial status of the budget, and needs for the remainder of the fiscal year. This surprise meeting was next week instead of a meeting next month. Marie tiptoed in to lay down the draft of the meeting, which was in for signature. John looked up and he looked at it and signed it. "Good job, Marie," he said. Ten minutes later there was a phone call from the CO; Captain Blanes had wanted him over for dinner. John accepted.

At the end of the day, the staff members called in the dates for "show and tell." John thought they were funny sounding appointments. The supply area was sort of stretched out in the long rows of buildings, which contained everything from soup to nuts. Many of the employees arrived from the United States. The other employees are from Newfoundland. They have a funny, unusual French accent which is the predominate language. The foremen are specialized in specific categories. For example, for proper assistance it has a carpentry division, plumbing force, engine/aircraft support and other mechanics that handle the complex runways.

The first weekend was a drag because household goods notified John that his shipment was here. The house that he had been given was relatively moderate with three bedrooms. Public works house manager told him that the furniture could be moved into the house on Monday. Good, he thought. At the last minute before Marie left, he told her about moving into the house. She wrote that in on his calendar.

On Saturday morning he drank a cup of coffee while placing his furniture in the house on building blocks. He was picky about where to place the dining room or how to position the kitchen. His driver, who works from Monday though Friday, had off on the weekend. John went out for a drive. He rode out to the Marine guard at the beginning of the base and noticed the high seven-foot chain link fence that surrounds the base. He made a note of it. He then rode down the bottom of the hill towards the water. He turned left and moved up near another chain link fence. He noticed a guard positioned there which was a Navy sentry. He wondered what this was about, but with making note of its place, however, there was a building enclosed in the barbed wire. Yes, there is a sign that reveals that this is the "Navy Oceanographic Unit," or something like that. With that noted on his inkpad, he did a 180-degree turn heading back towards the intersection. He stopped at the Navy exchange and did some buying for the new house. He bought necessary items such as soap, toilet paper, etc. which one must have. The commissary store was right there so he purchased many canned goods, green food plus tomatoes to be stored in his refrigerator for two days. Finally, he visited the meat section noticing that lobster tails were on sale not to mention native salmon. He visited his list and paid the cashier for the food. Next was the liquor store. Now haven't you guessed why I have privileges on the Navy base? I got a card with my picture on it, which is the key to success. The liquor store was a madhouse! The store stocked cans of soda, mix, beer and all kinds of liquor. The prices were still unbelievable so John bought more than usual being he has to entertain people since he is one of the station's highest paid employees. For $50 he made out like a bandit; hauling a cart of booze, mix and a case of Cokes and Sprite.

At the Hilton, John used the trunk of his car to store most of the things he had bought. He took with him the greenery and the meat to be stored in the freezer.

By the time he had put away everything, he looked outside through the window and saw that the wind had picked up and rain was beginning to fall. Most of the signs of fall were gone and the water has distinct patches of ice along the banks. Finally, he sat down on his sofa and turned to his briefcase. He opened it and there were two full folders jammed with work coming up next week. Time for coffee and as he washed the pot he thought of the man that was supposed to get in touch with him. He was sorry that this whole crisis came to a head. Maybe, well, we will wait and see. With the coffee and three bright Technicolor pencils, John got through the folders. Each one was commented on and Marie was to make up a list which he will question the staff member that submitted it. Next on his list was the Navy Argentia newspaper. The Officers' Club had a fantastic meal tonight offering two fresh lobsters, clams and baked potato for a special price of $5. That fills the bill for me. As a matter of fact, he had a candy bar for lunch, which his stomach pains were beginning to signal hunger. He took a shower and dressed semi-quasi with a blue sport coat, tie and khaki pants with a top off of a pair of new Bass Weggins.

The Officers' Club was packed at six o'clock. In part, the rain continued as a low sweep by Newfoundland headed to the northeast. John stepped easily into the bar. The bar was full of people. The commanding officer, the operations officer and many of the colleagues were having a very good time. The other end of the bar was a configuration of ladies. Some were nurses, but yet there were women Navy officers. John chose the middle and he tried a scotch and water from the bartender. The drinks were superb and the bartender put a sliced piece of lemon on the glass. One of the girls who saw the light and was sipping on a third gin and tonic, came over and toasted him. "Cheers," she said. John introduced himself and her name was Nancy. She was here with a contingency of officers from the Naval facility. One of the women officers was going back to the States on Monday were she will be reassigned to Norfolk. She had been here for almost two years and she worked as watch coordinator at the facility. John countered by stating that he was the new supply director and he was only a week old. Once again glasses were raised and John finished his drink. The bartender immediately refilled their glasses and the file of girls came to see what kind of trouble Nancy was getting into. John could not remember the five names that were thrown at him. He figured that the one who was leaving Argentia was the homely one. "Well, John, I see you are having a good time," said the captain. John turned around and shook the CO's hand. John related he came into the bar to have a drink and now look what he's into!

The lobster meal, with bibs draping down into their laps, was a real feast. John was combined into the party, which by the way, he thought it was appropriate and correct! The wine was flowing and the hospitality was phenomenal. Nancy and Linda sat on either side of him and John was besieged with conversation about his schooling, his engineering background and his duties at Newport News shipyard. Wine and then coffee; John was starting to feel the buzz within his body. After finishing the check, everyone went back to the bar for after-dinner drinks. Nancy continues to pinpoint John and it must have been the booze, but Nancy moved closer to him and finally grabbed his hand.

At 11 o'clock, the party broke up and Nancy saw John look at his watch. He helped the girls put on the rain gear for the long hike up the steep hill to the BOQ. The wind was gusting to 30 knots with rain coming down in drenches. Outside the Officers' Club in driving rain, they started the long climb up the hillside. Nancy was right beside John and suddenly a strong wind blew causing them to face down while John reached out and pulled Nancy by his side. They finally got up the slope and into the doorway. What a hell of a way to get drunk and with the walk back up the hill, you are stone sober. With the girls ready for bed, they said good night. Nancy wondered if they could have a drink in the second floor bar. "Lead the way," he said. They took the elevator to the second floor and Nancy found the bar. The bar was crowded with 20 or more people. The bartender was fixing drinks for some participants in flight suits. He had a beer and Nancy wanted one more gin and tonic. He found a table and they sat down. The trip up from the club had John's pants drenched, also the same for his date. They raised their glasses and took a sip as John felt her hand coming over to hold his. "Should we go upstairs and change clothes?" she said. He agreed and in five minutes time, they left the bar and headed for the elevator. As they waited, Nancy looked up at John and then kissed him. An instant later the elevator arrived. They stepped in and John asked what floor. "Your floor," she responded. At the seventh floor, they got out and walked to John's room. He found the keys in his pocket and opened the door. He turned on a lamp on the desk and Nancy came to him. Her mouth was unbelievable. John was starting to feel the warmth of his loins, and Nancy was starting to feel relaxed. Off came her sweater and then she began to undress him. Nancy was a cute gal, but I took off her blouse and out jumped two ample breasts with erect nipples. John kissed and caressed her bosom until he felt his pants hit the floor. He maneuvered and in 10 seconds her pants did the same. John removed her panties and dropped to kiss her external parts of her vulva. She moaned and they moved to the bed.

At eight o'clock the next morning, John woke up. His partner was still asleep, but boy what a time they had. John got up and went to the bathroom. In the other room that he shared, he put on some coffee. He noticed some orange juice in the refrigerator of which he had a glass. After 10 minutes, he poured the coffee and checked to see if Nancy was awake. "Good morning," she said. John took her some coffee. She kissed him lightly and told him what an immense lover he was.

Monday was full of excitement as many representatives were questioning the policy of the new supply officer. The pundant was alive and the policymaker was aware of their actions. Marie was constantly on the phone; however, she had little authority over and to persuade him of his deceitful action. John was aware of this but let bygones be dammed. We, the commanding officers, must know deep down inside the feelings of corporate oneness face failure.

The next day, Marie came into the office that John had drafted a new instruction concerning care and survivability of the parts, supplies and all matters pertaining to Naval Station Argentia. Marie started by laying a paper in front of John. John, I am Marie, a special agent whom you are with us. Upon reading this, he was suspicious of her. She then laid on the paper a document of the KGB and her photo immediately below. John was satisfied, and he shook her hand. She took his hand and silenced the two. She went over to the radio and turned it on. She told him of his actions this last week. He was unaware in his travels about the base. The episode Saturday night was a godsend in many ways. How was Nancy? The camera, which was hidden two miles away, was focused on John's room. John sat up when he heard this. How was he supposed to react? Marie explained that his movements were in high order, but had done this for sacrifice the attitude, which the KGB installed in you. John agreed, but has the agency had something for him to spy? Marie said that the movement of resources had not tasked him with anything necessary to complete. She did mention the gate, which John seemed interested in on Saturday. "By the way, John, what can you tell me about Marine gate requiring security?" John recited the Marine sentry was guarding a gate that had an apprehensible entry/exit case, but never before tried on this base. Marie acknowledged this fact and she recognized this was a serious matter for the record.

On Wednesday, the group met again in a board meeting of the supply officer. All of the subordinate members had completed their assignments. First, the Navy exchange representative gave his current story with respect to the budget. The presentation was good and on course. The most glaring fact was the Air Operations budget. The participant put the majority of funds to snow removal, but the addition of ground control radar was a problem. Asked of this new deficit, the Air Operations presenter did not know why. After 50 minutes of review, John had noted five major areas that were, shall we say, going to hell and back.

Captain Blades listened to John, which somehow invited his attention. He listed the five deficits on the table and said this was a refusal to take notice of last week's meeting. The obvious meaning was further action, which the captain was thankful that John had uncovered.

It was now Wednesday night and John was in his new house on the base. He had set aside two hours to fix his furniture or whatever, that he decided to unpack the silverware. He got started, but was interrupted by the phone. It was Nancy who apologized for not calling. "Well, it was alright," he said. Nancy spent the next three days on watch and she was off until the weekend. John explained that the board took a hit and he reported to the CO the discrepancies he found. Nancy changed the subject, by saying that she really missed him. He missed her too and wondered is she could come to see his new house. John apologized but he had to get his silverware out of the box. However, it's eight o'clock and do you have a car? Fifteen minutes later a knock was heard on the door. He opened the door and Nancy rushed into his arms. "I missed you so much," said she, as she kissed him without closing the door.

The next week the cold winds were blowing from the West. The supply officer was making his tour through the spaces and asking many questions. The next and last of the facilities was the Naval facility. His car arrived at the gate, which he recognized. The Navy guard looked in the window and then waved the car through. At the entrance of the building there was the Navy duty officer, a lieutenant junior grade. John followed him inside and then wrote his name on the log. Lieutenant commander Stone, the CO, met him and went with him to a small briefing room. With coffee poured, the CO began his brief. Secret information followed which brought John to a new awareness. He had been working on the same problem of reducing sound so that the sonar system could not detect them. The Soviets, on the other digit, could get intercepted by these arrays and they could not stop this detection. The lecture indicated some offshore detection systems, which were out of date. If only I had the slides to give to Marie!

Despite the cat and mouse game of tricking the task of supply was quickly shaping up Naval Station Argentia. John Hilton had many options, but he kept his loyalty in this respect, to end useless waste and the CO decorated John with a 10-percent increase in pay. His worth was well apparent, but his obligation to the other side was just beginning. Nancy's relationship with him has grown in leaps and bounds. He thought of marriage, but then again, he desired to wait and see what Nancy wanted. During Memorial Day, they took off to St. John's. They toured the area and saw many of the fishing villages that had tremendous tides. They found numerous shops that they browsed through many items. They had dinner at a nice restaurant and went to a movie. It was tremendous to sleep with Nancy and she announced that she had six more months left in the Navy.

Marie was working in the office at eight o'clock in the morning when John walked in. She looked up with concern and that meant she had something up her sleeve. John poured his coffee and went into his office. The calendar for the week was spread out on the top of his desk. Captain Blanes was first on the agenda with consulting department heads. That afternoon he had three appointments with other representatives. He signed out three letters and Marie stepped inside and closed the door. She told him that the last appointment was with an "agent." John wanted to know what this was all about. Marie devised the reason for such an advanced meeting. It was 10 of nine, so John excused himself and was off to the CO's meeting.

Like clockwork, the morning shifted into the afternoon. At three o'clock, a Mr. Zack was introduced to John Hilton. Marie sat in the corner and John showed his identity and Mr. Zack did likewise. The KGB has sent me to find you to brief you and to let you know the urgency that accompanies this mission. He pulls out of his pocket a letter that has to do with the iron ore mine in Labrador City, Labrador. Russia has prominent interest in magnetite. This word has been passed to three people, you are the third, and this mineral or substance must be in Russian hands within 18 days. The only way we can do this is for you to drive to St. Johns and meet this agent. John broke in and questioned why this substance was needed. I do not know why this rock is supernatural. Immediately, they got into discussing the different angles of involvement. Finally, John wanted the specifics of meeting the agent. Mr. Zack gave him the hotel and he would be in the bar at five o'clock. He suggested that you wear a brown sport coat and a red shirt. The final question was, how much would be passed to John? About two pounds of the mineral would be sufficient.

Being July, the wind was blowing when he left driving his car to St. John's. The road was a complete bare but had potholes all over the place. Moose, both bull and otherwise, were out hunting food and berries were running rampant on both sides of the road. Nancy was working the 72-hour shift. He told her he had business to attend to. He finally got there and found the hotel. He parked the car and checked into the hotel. He waited in his room until five minutes before the hour. Now let's see, he had a brown coat and a red shirt on.

The bar was not crowded when he stepped inside. The bartender was respectable and poured John a scotch and water. He noticed that the television set had the New York Yankees on and they were winning by three runs. Ten minutes had gone by and the bar was filling up. Eventually, he had two drinks and his stomach was beginning to feel the hunger pains. Damn, he wondered, where in the hell is the contact man? Five minutes later a man came and sat down just to the right of John. He ordered a beer and entered into conversation with John. He asked John what he did for a living. John stated that he works in Naval Station Argentia. Do you know Mike Douglas? Well, I am not sure, but can you tell me what kind of work he does? "It doesn't matter," he said. They entered other topics of conversation and finally agreed to eat dinner together. Ned was his name, either true or fictional, but he agreed to come by John's room to give him the two pounds of mineral ore.

The box which the magnetite was contained in settled nicely in the back seat of his car as he drove back to Argentia. Once at home he looked at the package. He opened up his desk and retrieved the address in Russia where it should be sent. John wrapped and addressed the package and wondered how it was going to make it by the U.S. Postal Service. On Monday, the C-118 airplane leaves at 1400 or two o'clock Argentia time full of mail and those persons on leave. So their package should clear the post office on the base and then take a flight to Quonset Point where it should wind up in Russia.

PATRIOTIC TREASON

0930 hours Local, 10 March 1991,
Dacha outside Moscow, Russia (USSR)

REAR ADMIRAL KLOS SLOREIGH STOOD AT ATTENTION before a small group of eight men. They were all familiar to him. He had already met and gained the confidence of Vladimir Kryuchkov, the chairman of the KGB. Beside the man sat Gennady Yanayev, the Soviet vice president and Gorbachev's right-hand man. Next followed Defense Minister Dmitri Yazov, Prime Minister Valentin Pavlov, Oleg Baklanov of the Soviet Defense Council, Vasily Starodubstev of the Soviet Parliament, President of State Enterprises Alexander Tizyakov and Gorbachev's chief of staff, Valery Boldin.

Klos was terrified. There was only one reason a group of powerful Socialists like this would gather in secret. He dared not speak a word without permission; showing initiative in front of this council would be a demonstration that he didn't know how to keep his mouth shut.

The men had gathered to discuss a coup. Even though Mikhail Gorbachev was responsible for placing most of them in their positions of power, it was obvious that they were going to betray him.

"Admiral Sloreigh," barked Kryuchkov.

"Sir!" the admiral replied at a roar as if he was once again a plebe at the military academy.

"You wear the emblem of the Komitet Gosudarstvennoi Bezopasnosti, the KGB. Do you know its meaning, comrade?"

"Yes, Comrade chairman!" Klos began reciting the history of the bright crest that he wore on his lapel. "It is the shchit i mech, the Sword and Shield. The Shield is for defense of the Revolution and the Soviet Union against threats, both internal and external. The Sword is the strength of the KGB to hunt down and destroy all threats facing the people."

"You say all threats, Comrade admiral," spoke Gennady Yanayev. "Threats such as whom?"

"The capitalist Americans and their CIA warmongers are threats, Vice President Yanayev. Those who incite violence and revolution in the republics." Klos revised his opinion about his chances to walk out of the secluded dacha alive. These men expected something from him, a definite stand for or against their cause. If they truly served the Soviet president then his next words would condemn him of treason. However, if he failed to say them and the men stood for revolution, then he would be guilty of a different treason. He determined to take the side of patriotic treason. Holding himself rigid, he spoke. "And, if I may suggest to this renowned group: The greatest threat to the Soviet Union is its president, Mikhail Sergeyevich Gorbachev."

The room was deathly silent. Klos waited for one of the men to speak. They waited for him to continue condemning or saving himself.

"Comrades, Gorbachev has lost his way. The people turn against him. Even Edward Shevardnaze has spoken of the changing times. Either the president must lead, or another must take his place who is strong enough to control the country."

"You speak treason to some, Admiral Sloreigh," stated Valery Boldin.

Klos waited for the man to say more. After a hundred heartbeats, he broke the silence in the room. "I speak the truth, Comrade Boldin. The Soviet Union has been weakened by weak leaders. It is time for a revolution of the people to restore our nation."

"Very well," Oleg Baklanov said to his companions. "He is loyal enough for our purposes. Explain to him his task. I will wait for you outside, as I have little stomach for this part of the plan."

"Yes, go, Oleg." Kryuchkov waved the man from the room.

"You have need of me, Comrades? How may I serve?" Klos was relieved that he had gambled correctly. The stakes were higher than he imagined.

"You are KGB, Klos, and you are a naval admiral. We have need of both." Kryuchkov motioned for him to sit. "We have examined your plan to obtain magnetite from the Canadians. It is the hand of providence or fate, giving us exactly what we need during this time. We approve of it. There will, however, be a modification in your instructions."

"My instructions?"

"Don't repeat my statements as a question, admiral," warned the KGB chairman. "These are pressure-filled times, and my temper is short. Be warned."

"Yes, Comrade chairman."

"We have need of a Navy officer aboard the Delta IV submarine that your plan requires. This man must also have the ability to authenticate launch codes for the missiles, should that be necessary. I assume you know such a man?"

Klos nodded. "Yes, Chairman Kryuchkov. I am such a man, should you need me."

"Yes, we considered you."

The fire popped in the fireplace of the country home. Sloreigh jumped at the gun-like report. He was greatly relieved to realize that it was only a burning log. The chairman's words hadn't been the code to silence Klos permanently.

"I stand ready, comrades."

Kryuchkov nodded. "Very well. It is critical to this matter that you take command of the submarine. Once at sea, you are to act on nobody else's orders except the ones we have given you beforehand. There will be two transmissions during your voyage, no more. You will use any means necessary, including armed force, to remain undetected by any western vessel or aircraft."

"Any means, chairman?"

"That's twice, admiral. Do not make me warn you again, or the consequences could be irrevocable."

Klos determined that he would censor his tongue to prevent any sentence from passing it that ended with a question mark. "My apologies, chairman."

"Noted. To answer your question, yes. You will use any and all means to remain undetected. The submarine will operate at a state of war. Do you understand now?"

"Yes, Comrade chairman."

"We have amended your plan, comrade. Agents in Argentia will disable the SOSUS facility there. Once you receive confirmation of that, you are to move the submarine to the appointed bay and take on the magnetite we require."

"Disabling the SOSUS center is not critical to the operation—"

"At least you did not phrase that as a repetition. That is good, you learn quickly." Kryuchkov stepped toward the fireplace and began stirring the coals with the nearby iron. "You are correct, it is not critical to the operation you originally planned. It is, however, critical to ours."

The admiral considered the benefits of destroying the SOSUS installation. There was only one conclusion that he could make based on the information he had already learned. He realized that his life was no longer in danger. The group needed him. There were few men with both qualifications to meet this mission's requirements.

"You intend to launch nuclear warheads against the United States of America." He said the words as a statement of a fact, not supposition.

The KGB chairman used the hook to shift the logs in the fireplace. Sparks flew as he took his time responding to the admiral's statement. "Yes," he said finally. "There will be an operation, the details of which do not matter to you. On its completion, you will be sent the codes required to launch all missiles on your vessel. The destinations will be programmed before you leave dock. Suffice it to say that the targets are minor cities; populations of a million or less."

"So you do not intend a massive first strike. This is what, a test of the American's response? Or is it—" Klos closed his mouth as he understood. Hesitantly, he voiced his conclusion. "You pull the tiger's tail with this mission, Comrade chairman. There is no guarantee that the American President will not retaliate with his full arsenal."

"The Americans and their Western allies are occupied in Kuwait and Iraq at the moment. They have pulled their European corps south to fight in the desert. So long as our military forces do not mass on our western borders, the Americans will believe this to be an accident that occurred during a time of chaos. Nothing more."

"And what of my submarine? We will be hunted with every pack the Americans have."

"Let me be honest, Comrade admiral. I do not. We do not care whether you return safely or not. There will be many other things occupying our attention. Destroying the SOSUS station will buy you some time and afford you a chance to escape into the depths of the Atlantic. After you have fulfilled your mission, your survival is solely in your hands. Do you understand this?"

"Yes, Comrade chairman. My submarine and I are expendable to the cause of Mother Russia. That is as it should be. We live to serve."

"As do we all, Klos. Now come, let us wake the cooks and have lunch. I am starved!"

Klos stood his ground. "There is one request I would make, Comrade Kryuchkov."

The KGB chairman turned to face the impertinent naval officer. "Make it then, and be quick."

"I have a condition. That upon news I have launched the missiles, the KGB will immediately arrest Rear Admiral Alexei and Vice Admiral Lawrence Latvia. Should I not return within a month, they will be executed in Red Square as traitors."

"And if you return?"

"Then I wish the honor of shooting them myself."

The head of the KGB recognized madness when he saw it. The look of a maniac danced behind Klos Sloreigh's eyes. "Very well, it is agreed. The admirals will die."

Kryuchkov waved the man toward the kitchen. He didn't understand the cause of the murderous rage in the Navy officer, and he honestly didn't care. The madness, though, he would have to take care of that. It was never wise to leave a wild animal in the same kennel when you wanted to domesticate the other dogs. There was only one solution to the problem. Three admirals would be put down on the same day. It was the only way to be sure.

JEALOUSLY IN THE RANKS

MOSCOW WAS A BIG CITY FULL OF born-again people with a zeal of multitudinous human beings. The metropolis was dedicated to the art of communism no matter what it stood for. Way behind the monstrous mall was where Rear Admiral Latvia worked, he came here as the senior rear admiral who was to work in the Naval Plans and Requirements section. He was allotted a small staff that consisted of an aide, a secretary and two runners who assist in driving or whatever the need might be. He walked into his office and it was reasonably modest. His aide removed his outer coat and then began to make notes about what the admiral wanted and needed. Unequivocally, he did not like leaving the submarine force. The number one admiral told him to take this job that gives him a close look at what the Navy is proposing for the future. Bell's phone was ringing and the secretary answered it. She took the call and announced that it was for the admiral, who then talked for about 30 seconds. He asked his aide the location of the so-called "Red Room." The admiral then turned and blurted out what she must do. In a flash, he and his aide were gone to a brief.

The Red Room was a briefing room where decisions to buy—or no—were made on things/weapons and naval systems that had been tested. Numerous people were there, and interestingly enough, there was Alexei, his brother. They embraced and they had not laid eyes on each other for 10 years. They were talking and then the announcement to take their chairs. In essence, this was a brief of the latest sonar, which was to be mounted in the Yankee Class submarine. The brief told the audience the background of a sound device, which would send out and detect a target by reflection. The sonar is presented and depicted on the Yankee as a superior system. They utilized this system on a Soviet conventional submarine, which validates the ranges and targets it detects. This was a monstrosity of a brief. Of 20 people who heard the brief, not one said a word. Admiral Lawrence Latvia stood up and read the riot act. He concentrated on three questions: What are the ranges of the U.S. submarines—nuclear or conventional? How can we tell whether we have a valid echo or not when we are working in the Arctic Ocean? And lastly, where are the listening devices that power this exotic listening apparatus? Many eyes were looking at this flag officer that has come out of the woods with concrete questions. The briefer was replaced with a specialist who talked about testing with ships and occasional subs. The only answer that they could dig up was in the Arctic where a long range is detected. The admiral stood up and was infuriated because the sonar system would have many echoes and which one was the target? Quietness prevailed. He could not wait for the last question to be answered. He asked if the diagram of the sub could be shown. Ultimately, Lawrence took off his coat and walked up to the briefing platform.

His eloquent discourse and the way he used persuasive thinking made the audience feel a sense of stupidity. After clarifying that his calculus was correct, he proved that the listening antenna had not been placed in the proper position. Quite by chance, he asked his older brother to verify his mathematics. Alexei came up to the blackboard and said that the mathematics were, in fact, correct. The chalk was at work and the inserted new arrays covered the boat. Alexei certified that the additional sounding devices have to counter the strong noise about 30° to 44° on the starboard side of the nose of the ship. Alexis then admitted that he had been selected as the first skipper of the Yankee class. Lawrence hugged him and was extremely proud of him. A hand extended from the audience and refused this analysis. This old snotty professor was barking up the wrong tree. He tore up Latvia's equations and applied a physical property and phenomenon technique, which got stuck in the where-with-all section. Admiral Latvia solved this by remaking the wrong mistake that had saddled Russia since 1946. Clearly, and with his hand focused to shake the admiral's hand, he hugged him because he had solved a lot more than his fulfillment in life. On the path of glory once more, the brief ended at 1800 hours. It was decided that the new class of nuclear submarine would go back once again to adopt a new antenna arrangement plus expand the lessons learned under the ice and what this means when they encountered this phenomenon at sea.

Admiral Latvia was a man who led the plans of the secret bombsite. His brilliance in physics and his highly improbable mathematical forte made many candidates fall from the podium. Many admirals and generals were amazed at his actions, but the requirements were not sufficient so they have to be rewritten. In a matter of a year the requirements were unfolded, including a brief outline of how the designers should proceed, and all the mechanics are fulfilled. Wondrous gains have been made during this upheaval. The maker of submersibles was making a killing with many new variations of submarine technology.

Remnants of the past several years ago keep haunting Lawrence. From the moment Lawrence heard about the Yankee dilatation, he immediately called Alexei. His wife said that he was at the office getting ready for a desk job at Moscow. Lawrence tried to reach him at the base and a staff sergeant answered the phone. "He just left for home, sir," he exclaimed. He went for his car and met Alexia at home. They hugged each other and then Alexia got a bottle of vodka for them to sample. Arm in arm they went to the den and closed the door. Lawrence was tapped on the shoulder and turned around with Alexia signaling him to be silent. He went to check out the lights for bugging, and everywhere to no avail. They sat down and the story began of Alexei as he told of the factors that influenced his refusal not to follow orders. The account of the end of Admiral Alexei Latvia's career in the Soviet Navy was remarkably similar to many professional officers own demise. After a dangerous and successful 60-day reconnaissance cruise off the American coast that included the penetration of New York harbor, his brother was summarily relieved of command. Alexei's immediate protest was an investigation of "alleged irregularities" in the way he had been commanding the boat. He soon sensed that his downfall had been secretly engineered by a malicious and conniving political KGB agent whose superiors followed his every deed. The admiral ordered him to Moscow where he was to man a desk.

Yankee boat 001 had orders that would make a good dog wonder. There was no magic, no guidance regarding trailers and action concerning theirs and finally the missiles should follow standoff distances from the eastern coastline of the United States. His executive officer argued wholeheartedly with him, as he was the frontrunner off the U.S.A. Lawrence recognizes that certain quandary which forces the captain to modify the priority of the mission. Lawrence then considered a KGB agent aboard the boat. Alexei admitted that they had an enlisted man spying on their boat.

Alexei, after a long swallow of vodka, admitted that the vile KGB agent had introduced a series of violations from the moment the vessel left port. The accuser jumped right on the affairs of the CO who put a brand on this and he was resigned to a desk job.

This moment of shock dazed Lawrence and after a helping of colorless liquid he asked him if he had problems over his tour of active duty. A rather blunt, no, but then there were accounts of actions that Alexei did not understand. There were several problems that he encountered during his training on the East Coast. Many indications were copied during his submarine evolution and then again in the training of the Echo II nuclear submarine. Lawrence asked him if he could remember the specifics of the altercation. He remembers his operations officer invalidating his specific commands during the Pacific deployment of the Echo II. Lawrence wanted to know what was the problem. The operations officer denied the route near the west coast and when he found this out he came to a verbal contract with him. After demoralizing him, he told him that he was to report to his bunk and the assistant operations officer continued the mission. "Was the operations officer recommended for command?" asked Lawrence. With a profound statement, he said no; without a doubt a mischievous trick has been done to a miscreant who has come back to haunt Alexei Latvia. "Do you now the whereabouts of this officer?" Well I imagine he was destined for a ground job, but you know he took out an Echo II as commanding officer! Lawrence could not believe that!

A plan of action was devised by the two brothers. First and foremost, he would be found in the administrative records in Moscow. Second, the subject would be found and what this individual is doing. And thirdly, we will meet again in Moscow where our paths will cross again. "Where all you going?" asked Alexei. "I am to report to the vice admiral in charge of productions and increasing effectiveness. I will get in touch with you by the end of next week." They both hugged and each left with a plan that will alleviate the fink!

Moscow was the center of all military planning and produces new weapons that must be received. One man had been selected to represent the government Navy representative: Admiral Lawrence Latvia. Dignitaries and a crowd of his personal friends saw the fleet admiral put his stars on both shoulders. His job was to evaluate the design and weigh its task to replace or energize a new device that will emanate a more effective way of doing operational planning and evaluation. Admiral Latvia was in charge of the Operation Test and Evaluation that paved the way to a more proficient, step-by-step approach, turning this new method into a gain of effectiveness. Commensurate with rank, a staff and an administrative driver, Lawrence met in the fourth wing, which necessitated the new research/development cadre. The admiral met with his staff and asked each individual to stand and give a brief statement about himself. Halfway through the introductions, he realized he had the mathematical, physics and skill or common sense to perform his mission. He applauded his staff when he told them of his acknowledgement of their expertise. The next agenda item is who has the schedule of coming events? A former executive officer of Lawrence's Foxtrot stood up and handed out the schedule of events. These were to start at 1000 hours tomorrow. A list of new weapons to new ships paraded this list with many interesting derivative statements. At the close of this session, the admiral paid his respects first to all who attended, but he wanted a watchful eye to recognize where the faults lie and ideas to correct them.

It was the next morning and there had been numerous changes to the personnel roster. A new aide was the big change while several other administrative staff, namely secretaries, were added. After finishing a second cup of coffee, the admiral finished the messages board and was ready for the first morning brief. At 10 o'clock the admiral walked in and was preceded by the flag lieutenant. The first speaker was from the laboratory near Murmansk where the submarine force was based. Apparently the sonar equipment was tuned to a new sound receiver, but that did not ring a bell. Abruptly, the admiral was full of questions. He wanted to know how the signal varies from the more sophisticated sonar. Then he became aggrieved because he had not proved anything. Two attendants brought out a huge drawing board and the admiral picked up a piece of chalk. He then proceeded to amaze the lecturer and with a demonstration he proved that the old system was cutting the mustard. "Now," he asked, "what's wrong with the system we have?" Again, the lecturer went over the same system before Admiral Latvia broke in. Finally, the new sonar did not get anywhere and they retired red-faced, because that did not prove mathematically on the blackboard.

At two o'clock in the afternoon the admiral plus five of the operations staff filled his conference room. Beforehand, he requested the basic instructions pertaining to how a brief should be prepared. Now taking this instruction at face value, what was the true purpose of this brief? Three hours later the gang had re-written the document and a message went out over the wire warning all participants that this will be the brief as specified in the instruction.

The Operation Test and Evaluation was the talk of the town. Overnight, many irate systems were bilged in the coming years and were worthwhile systems into the maze of criteria and could be fixed units of the active Navy. Admirals called Lawrence and were appreciative of his staff's work. Many men would win command of ships and submarines due to their valiant efforts working for the admiral.

Friday was the secretary's day to shine. She brought in and arranged a pretty bouquet of flowers. Right behind her was the admiral. He commented on the beautiful arrangement. The flavorful rich coffee was waiting for him. He opened the calendar that had Alexia's name on it. He rang the intercom and in walked the aide with a notepad. His first assignment was to locate Admiral Latvia and the second was to find Lieutenant Commander Klos Sloreigh. We need to know what, when, where and how long he was CO of an East Coast submarine. And I need this information by noon. The aide excused himself and was out of the room in a flash. By 10:30, he had received four officers who had dropped by and paid him a courtesy call. By 11:30, he was getting hungry. A slight knock on the door and Lawrence said enter. The aide appeared and said he had the information that he had requested. The data was in a folder which the aid had broken into three phases: (1) background; (2) military life; and (3) commanding officer and present status. He asked the aide to take a seat while the admiral checked the details. His background appeared to be in accordance with all conceived, the military background looked all right, but the fitness reports had been thermographed and the admiral homed in where he was: operations officer on Alexia's Echo II. The fitness report showed he was immaculate, astute and received the highest grades and was recommended for command! There at the bottom of the page was his brother's signature! The last segment showed that he was CO of a submarine and was selected as an admiral working for the KGB. How interesting!

At two o'clock in the afternoon Lawrence called his brother. Briefly, he called welcoming him to Moscow. He wondered if he could buy him a drink. It's all set. I was to meet him outside of the workspace at five o'clock, then to the bar.

At five o'clock sharp, the admirals met again and talked over the dress of the last week and a half. Shortly they pulled in front of the bar that happened to be in the nice part of town. Lawrence told the driver that's it for today. He saluted and was off back to the staff headquarters. Lawrence got a table out of way next to the wall. They spoke directly and when Alexia got to the fitness report he became unglued! Repeatedly the thing that he disallowed is this piece of paper. He opened his briefcase and produced the original. This was one document that we will cherish! Suspension never fails as he finally found a notch to fill in the KGB!

Vodka was the favorite and both downed the glass. Lawrence then gave his brother a copy of the file; he would also keep an additional copy. With all these answers coming to light, they wondered how to determine what he does for the super secret unit. At any rate, the two officers got up and paid their bill and said good night. Two weeks later his wife and children joined him in Moscow. He began to drink and yet you could see it in one eye that his goal was not superior, but neglect throughout the military engine.

His wife talked and tried to control his fading spirit, which had lead to counts of bigotry and remission. Even Lawrence came by the office and chased the administrator out. They talked about his career and how he was dragging it to a drunken state. Alexia broke into tears and sobbed incessantly. He then quietly blew his noise and motioned to Lawrence to follow him. The black door led to a hallway and then up the stairs to a small ceiling. Upon opening the door, he went outside in the cool air. Out in the cold air he told Lawrence that he was followed every morning and every night going home. The KGB was the culprit with two gentlemen in the car following his whereabouts. The whole espionage effort had been in effect for about seven months. Additionally, a listening device was used to double-check this out and this data would cement our data that made sense. This and other matters made sense, however, the devil's eye was among the beholders. The Latvias put their heads together and came up with a plan. Both Alexia and he were of the same size and body. This contrived plan was to foil the perverted and trick them to follow the wrong man. That evening was the first test of this procedure. At 1730 the first admiral came out of the building. He had gone into the car and sped out. The first was Lawrence who moved on to the plaza. He asked the driver if someone was following. "Yes sir," he said. "Good," replied the admiral. The driver took him to a downtown bar. Lawrence got out and proceeded up the stairs and into the bar. He turned and hid behind the stairs leading to the second floor. Two minutes later, two heavy-set KGB agents came inside to the bar. Lawrence watched them and they looked high and low for Alexis.

Alexis was home by now, so Lawrence took off his coat and into the bar he progressed. The KGB men were really busy wondering what happened. Lawrence had vodka straight up and downed the drink opposite the mysterious two who were puzzled at the disappearance of Alexis. About 10 seconds later a large blast followed by a fire woke up the crowd at the bar. The establishment continued drinking and then a policeman entered the area and began calling out the names of the two men. The men acknowledged themselves, but when the enforcer told them of their car blowing up, they ran outside to see the burning wreck!

CUTTING THE CABLE

IN JULY THE FLAVOR OF SUMMER IS at its peak in Argentia. Nearly all of the birds and scenic flowers are in bloom because it's their last chance to show their finery. Just like the greenery, the asphalt machine is bringing the road to a new look, as the drivers were overjoyed with this undertaking. Everywhere, Mr. John Hilton is turning into a self-doer with much to be accomplished. The CO of the base is about to have a hissy with the satisfaction that his base is turning around. The hangar, which was called the Miami Hangar, was built to hangar the four reciprocating engines of the Willy Victor aircraft, which provided the radar barrier between Argentia and Iceland. This hangar was stripped of rust, paint and given a new coat of silver painted by a spraying machine. In addition, the warehouses were administered to with many receiving new or unkempt roofs.

At the Officer's Club, Nancy and John were having dinner with lobster as the special. They talked about the weather and Nancy wanted to talk about their plans for marriage. John listened, as she wanted to know how he felt about announcing their engagement. There was a lot of talking and John agreed it was to happen. Suddenly, the steward announced that he had a telephone call. John excused himself and went to the phone. Marie was on the phone and she wished to see him right away. John wanted to know if everything is all right, but she said it was imperative that we should meet at his house in 15 minutes. He walked back to the table and informed Nancy that the phone call requested him to meet a supervisor in 15 minutes. He told her to stay at the club and he would not take 30 minutes.

The car pulled in to his house and there was a car parked in front of the sidewalk. John cut off his vehicle and got out of the car. Marie was in the driver's seat and she monitored him to get in her car. They were traveling out of the base and came to a driveway to the right some two miles from the base. This road was rough with many branches brushing beside the passing automobile. Five hundred yards or so, they encountered a log cabin on the lake. They got out of the car and went inside the cabin.

Mr. Zack welcomed them and introduced Mr. Dick Bennett to them. He noticed that Marie was a bit uncomfortable, but he offered her to look at Dick's credentials. Now that the views and nationalities are known, we will continue the brief.

A map of Naval Station Argentia was on the table indicating the precise location of all installations. Of particular interest was the Oceanographic Research Station, Naval Facility Argentia; the security cover for a U.S. Navy SOSUS station conducting around the clock undersea surveillance tracking deployed Soviet submarines. This is the site we are targeting to destroy. Our plan is to knock out the cable system that connects the hydrophone arrays deployed on the sea bottom hundreds of miles out to sea and shore terminus building; Terminal Equipment Building (T-Bldg). The specific mission of the people and electronic sonar set displays in this building is to analyze and report the acoustic signatures generated by Soviet submarines located hundreds of miles away and pinpoint their position for monitoring and prosecution by U.S. Navy ASW forces if required. Based on our experiences, we came to realize that the other boards used on the nets from our fishing trawlers could be dragged across the SOSUS cables inflicting severe enough damage to render them inoperative for long periods of time. However, when the seabed is comprised of sand or silt the cable is buried or settles into the bottom protecting them from any trawler activity disrupting their operation. Such is the situation here in Argentia so the trawler scenario can be disregarded. The best solution is to destroy the T-Bldg and its one of a kind high technology sonar set equipment which will be impossible to replace for a long time. The communication circuits will also be rendered useless. We are fortunate that the Americans believe their cover story provides the necessary security so they never "hardened" the building or the cable entry point to the building.

The room was silent and John asked a couple of questions. Mr. Bennett responded to those inquiries. He was a Navy ETN3 and was part of the oceanographic work team. He worked the night shift and handled the spaces in and around the cable termination box. He would, depending on the need for disruption of the cable, hand carry explosives to extinguish the cable. Marie brought up another question. How do we play in this act?

Mr. Zach agreed with this important point. He said that this project was based upon certain precise acts, especially to eliminate any miscalculations on our own parts. The gentlemen that first spoke to your has been undercover for the last two years. He is trusted and well respected within the confines to the tight-knit SOSUS community. In fact, he will be advanced to petty officer second class, ETN2 next month. He is a professional and earned the highest grades and categories on his last performance evaluation.

In summary, you know the plan, which we will be under next month. With all agreed with this objective, John still did not know how the magnetite was to get to Russia, why was it necessary to destroy the cable, and who was going to head this super secret group? Well, it's got to get better!

The map was picked up and a small map was given to Mr. Bennett, which he safely put in his wallet. The log cabin was destined for fire as kerosene was splashed over the walls and in the kitchen. As we left, Marie and I saw Mr. Zach light the walls and in thirty seconds it was ablaze.

By the time I got back to the Officer's Club, Nancy had caught a ride back to the BOQ. I stopped there, looked at the clock, and it was 11 o'clock. I went up to the second deck bar and she was not there. Oh well, I think the night is over and we will make amends tomorrow.

WORD OF TROUBLE

Captain Blanes was preparing a speech in his office when the secretary came in to interrupt him. He had an urgent message that would come in on the red phone. "What in blue blazes is going on?" he asked. The red phone rang and the secretary left his office. Upon answering the phone he listened to the Pentagon Admiral Sharp that has placed him into Defense Condition Two that he must be prepared to maintain this base in view of hostile action. The captain acknowledged and wanted to know more of this warning. Admiral Sharp detailed what little the intelligence had plus the sudden call from Russia on the hot phone to the president. Further information will be provided in the Mini Tactical Support Center. With this information, he hung up the receiver.

His aide came in and the captain relayed all of the vital statistics. After consulting with him and a review of the appropriate instructions, the aide began calling all departments and the Marine Detachment, which will meet in the Mini Tactical Support Center. The captain proceeded to the Tactical Center.

Marie was busy typing when the phone rang. "No, he is not here at present. May I take a message?" she replied. She gave him the number of the substitute man that was in charge of John Hilton's job. I wonder what that was all about. Finally she put her records in the safe and noticed the door closing. "Good afternoon," said the man. The man was dressed in a sport coat and identified himself as Mr. Black. Marie shook hands with him and he wanted to see John Hilton. "Mr. Hilton was in Saint John's today, but he will be back tomorrow," she said. Mr. Black reached in the coat pocket and showed the identification as a Soviet spy. Marie opened her purse and showed her papers. "You are a fake," he said. "What do you mean?" she said. He showed her the fake papers that had been faxed which left tiny lines in the lower right side. Mr. Flack had such papers. "Now, where is Mr. Hilton?" he said. Marie did not know what to do, but she opened her desk drawer to get the gun. But the Soviet overcame her and shoved the drawer closed. In his other hand was Smith and Wesson equipped with a silencing device that placed two rounds into her heart.

Based on the availability of in-house forces, Argentia pretty much had a toehold on securing the base for whatever tricks or acts of sabotage it was expected to endure. The problem that they face is how the foreign agents will meet with the Delta class submarine? There are three boats currently tied up, but the boats are under specific orders to take goods back to ports in Canada. The only way to solve this immediate reaction is to call the Navy Special Warfare Command in Little Creek, Virginia. At 1800 Zulu time, a C-130 will ship Argentia 20 SEALs that will parachute out in the harbor. Each man will be equipped with a UHF transceiver that will give each man contact with the commanding officer at Naval Station Argentia.

NEEDLE IN A HAYSTACK

THE AIRCRAFT WITH THE TAIL SIGN LN was doing some bouncing on the cold September afternoon. Fall was well underway near the Arctic Circle. Inside the hangar, Lt. Bill Henderson was through with the schedule and making corrections before he took it to be signed by the detachment officer. Lieutenant Commander Dan Otter was in his office, so Bill stuck his head in to get the schedule signed. The officer in command (OIC) grasped the paper and asked if the schedule for the Lajes trip had been planned. The schedules officer indicated that crew three was planned and the Operational Task (green) was being typed. At present, they had one flight in Lajes, one on ready-duty and one flight doing crashing and dashing which was essential for the patrol plane commander check.

VP-45 had been in Argentia, Newfoundland for about five weeks. They were firmly established in the aristocratic 12-story Bachelor Officer Quarters (BOQ). The BOQ formerly housed everyone when the barrier squadrons were assigned here, but once the radar net was established, the squadrons were returned to the United States and were disestablished. Each officer was assigned a suite of two rooms. All personnel on the base were housed in this building, known as the Argentia Hilton. The complex had a movie theater, bowling alley, bar and library plus many other amenities. A squadron and its band of officers frequently visited the bar and then let the wind blow them down the hill to the Officer's Club.

Bill Henderson had just put on his lieutenant bars and had three more months in VP-45. Lt. Henderson did quite well as a tactical coordinator. He had been in this position for a year and had terrific luck in finding snorkels in the Mediterranean. To date, he had 10 or 11 Forward Looking Infrared snorkels at the TACCO station and had four hours of submarine contact (Echo II) in the Ionian Sea. Submarine exercises were successful and the lieutenant was designated Alfa status about three months back from deployment.

The next week, a review of the message board revealed that a flight supporting the Oceanographic Arctic Support was scheduled for the end of the week. The initial message was readdressed to VP-45 and soon the signal would come tasking this detachment. The detachment officer wanted to see the scheduling officer. Bill, dressed in his flight suit, saw LCDR Otter about the readdressed message. He asked who was available and Bill said, "Your crew." The OIC laughed and said, "I will get my navigator and TACCO up to the nav office." The flight, although it is a standard mission, will fly to Sonderstrom that is at the end of the run of a narrow inlet that follows steep cliffs or steep slopes. The tower must be contacted before entering the fjord and conditions must be VFR. The landing field is something else as it has a mountain at the end of the runway. The base was opened at the end of World War II.

After the message was put on hold in the operations file, the normal flight launched, putting the Mini-TSC on alert to monitor the flight's progress. The Oceanographic Station was busy vectoring flights, trying to get ships updated, and, if a submarine came into the picture, be prepared to fly one five zero true until the message is plotted and the crew is ready to prosecute the target. It had been two weeks since the crew had gone after a Yankee Class submarine. The Central Intelligence Agency and several Pentagon officials had advocated closure of Naval Facility Argentia was obvious. The military experts noted the Soviet submarines were rapidly becoming too quiet to track. But, of course, our submarines are also quieter and getting more stealthy.

LCDR Otter's crew was scheduled to take off on Wednesday morning. All preparations for navigating in the upper Northern climates were reviewed. Finally, LCDR Otter and crew seven were airborne at 0730. The plane flew at high altitude until the navigator announced the letdown point. The crew would not be able to communicate with base while flying at low altitude. Crew seven had as a guest an iceberg tabulator who had taken the tactical coordinator's place. Lt. junior grade Mike Place was the TACCO and had found a chair for himself right beside the counter. The iceberg tabulator had brought along a laptop IBM computer and manipulated a track corresponding to the track laid out on the TACCO's scope. Everything went all right with the flight although there were appreciably more noticeable flat masses of floating sea ice and several large sheets of sea ice located near the Western edge of the ice pack. At 1600 hours, the plane commander/mission commander stopped by Mike's station and said they had to leave station to get into Sonderstrom. Mike said, "Let's go ahead, since I think the observer has everything he needs."

The landing was normal and they parked in front of the tower. A truck was there to meet the crew, load up the bags and take them off to debrief. The purple (record of the flight) was easy and Bill finished it so LCDR Otter could read and release it. The quarters were excellent, with a case of beer and Johnnie Walker doubles inside the refrigerator. The drinking stopped at 1900 hours and then the gang went to get something to eat. Of course, they had the steak that had been part of their replenishment in July.

Beams of sun were climbing above the horizon just about the time the crew was checking out of the rooms. The plane had its APU (Auxiliary Power Unit) running providing heat and amperage for the airplane. The station had a JP-4 truck putting fuel in the four turboprop engines. LCDR Otter gave the initial part of the brief and, turning smartly, the copilot gave the remainder of the preparation. For safety purposes, the TACCO made his rounds of the aircraft checking that each man had a survival suit, Mae West, hardhat and had his seat locked. With Condition Five complete, the four Allison engines went maximum horsepower and cleared the field, heading down the fjord until they reached Davis Strait. The airplane turned right and the ice observer set up a tracker so the Flight Engineer could monitor the ASA-72, the in-flight monitor of the ASA-70. The first hour of surveillance was normal, but a glance northward caused concern for the pilots. The weather showed a cold front heading across Greenland that lowered the visibility with the possibility of reducing it below minimums. The co-pilot called Sonderstrom and reported the updated weather conditions across Greenland. Additionally, the station weather forecast that Sonderstrom would be VFR and then fall to bare minimums. LCDR Otter heard that response and was on the headset to the TACCO. "Let's return," he said. They reversed course and got back to the airfield just in time. The snow was making its presence known, hiding the engine nacelles with white stuff.

The submarine Delta IV slipped out under the cover of darkness on the 15th of August 1991. Missing, of course, were the small boats that mothered her departure. Her captain—Vice Admiral Klos

Sloreigh—was true to the cause of the righteous underworld including the death of Vice Admiral Latvia and the rest of the Latvia clan. By cleaver scrutiny, the admiral had secured the torpedoes, and had armed his sail with two short-range missiles. His total compliment aboard was 80 men who were familiar with the boat. These have been on several trips to try out the new nuclear powered configured power plant, which was installed in the Delta class submarine. Another reason for this replacement power source is the oldness of the Echo nuclear power ensemble and this power system presents about three decibels less noise. By the time the sun started over the eastern mountains, the Delta IV submerged. Klos then got a cup of java and went down to his quarters to review his orders.

After unlocking the multiple safes he reached the coveted orders. He read them briefly and grabbed the phone. He told the officer of the deck that he wanted to see the exec (formerly the submarine's captain) in his room. Five minutes later the exec knocked on his door. Admiral Sloreigh let him send the orders and then he pulled out an abbreviation, which cancels out the final portion of the mission. In other words, on September the 18th, we will pick up the Spetznaz off the coast of Saint John's, Newfoundland.

The untouched version of the mission was to be followed. The course was basically northwest until we reach the 180° west parallel. At this point we will come north and proceed into the Arctic Ocean by way of the Fram Basin. Upon exiting of the Fram Basin, be aware of three submarine contacts: A Victor, a Charlie and a new class called the Alpha, which exceeds 40 knots plus. The highlights of the initial part of this mission are that the Alpha class has exercise torpedoes on board. He will not doubt to fire if he thinks the target has control of the sub. We will stay in the area to escape to our mission in our plan. The exec noticed that his experience under ice taught him to remain close to the ice cap. This maneuver is effective to remain under the ice and detest the intruders. The admiral appreciated that but maybe we will use that tactic when we leave the area.

Upon reaching the portion of 180° longitude, the boat turned north following the meridian. About 12 hours later from his periscope view he saw ice about 10 miles. He knew that sooner or later he would run into ice. As we passed a beam of Svalbard we entered the Fram Basin. We were at 200 feet at six knots and had the sonar looking for targets. I announced to the helmsman to come to 030. The helmsman acknowledged and we traveled for about 30 minutes. "Sonar contact, bearing 010 range 10,000 yards," said the sonar operator.

He added that this was a Victor contact that was making six knots in the water. The speed was reduced to four knots as they tracked the adversary. Admiral Sloreigh wanted to know the course and speed. Suddenly, another contact woke up and it was the Charlie making an attack run on the Victor. Both targets recognized the other's position and both went to maximum power. The Charlie was in the correct position as he launched two dummy torpedoes at the Victor and one shot got him.

The Delta IV stayed clear of this encounter. Then after five minutes Klos wanted to make contact with either submarine. He contacted the communications officer and told him to contact them to inform them that he was on station. The Victor acknowledged and wanted him to close on him at 6,000 yards. He would be the third submarine waiting for an attack by the Alpha. The three submersibles ran in a straight line, one behind the other when the Alpha started up its propeller at 15 knots. He shot two dummies and both hit the first two submarines. Hearing this from the sonar operator, he turned into action. Hard 90 degrees to the right and advanced speed to 15 knots. He ordered a depth change to 70 feet and wanted the navigator to check for stalactites or large bodies of ice below the ice cap.

At 70 feet the periscope found the top of the ice cap with a large segment of ice molded into various shapes. The sonar operator kept track of the invader as he approached their last position. Apparently he had lost contact as the admiral had reduced horsepower to one or two knots. Yes, he was coming straight towards them, but he was searching to try to find him. Klos wanted bearing info and he would pass under them in forty seconds.

Soon cavitations were heard and Klos said, "Give me 10 seconds and I will ping him when he travels under me."

The sonar operator acknowledged and reported him being at 250 feet. "Ping!" To see the Alpha skipper in a state of shock is a thing of unequaled humiliation. At that point both skippers passed information and within an hour the hunt will begin anew.

Delta IV survived three out of four runs but the commanding officer called a quick meeting with the exec and the navigator. The goal of meeting the intersection of Robeson Channel, which was the small entrance to the site, was still at the eighth of

September. The charts were there, but the validity of this passage was not clear as how deep the channel is. According to all sources, the channel is approximately 100 feet, plus or minus 30 feet. We must have 75 feet to clear this entry passage west of Greenland.

On the first of September we were at 400 feet making four knots. It was at this time we set a course to the channel. There was no movement during the first regarding the other submarines. On the fourth day we had to come up to 200 feet because we were entering a shallow zone, which required plotting, and of course recognizing the stalagmite-like pinnacles that came pouring from the bottom of the ocean. Fifty miles before penetration of Robeson the sub came up to periscope depth and it discloses the covered mountains that verified Greenland.

At precisely the prescribed time they started down the narrow channel. The channel was slim with the minimum depth between 85 and 90 feet. Admiral Sloreigh reduced power to three knots and proceeded down the thin-like passage. After six hours of maneuvering, the depth became deeper, down to 1,500 feet. The submarine inhabitants relaxed and obviously, so did the officers. On loudspeaker he briefed the boat that this is perhaps a first in traveling this area. He described the Ellesmere Islands on the right, which eventually gave way to the Northwest Territories, which belonged to Canada. He once again reminded all hands to remain on watch, listening for any unusual sounds meaning aircraft of ship activity.

The next 40 hours went by quite slowly but the United States Air Force base caused concern at Thule, Greenland. All systems are "go" on the Delta IV, but the skipper is invariably looking over the charts of the navigator. A Southwestern Greenland current, which gives them an extra kick, awaits them as they pass abeam Thule. A sonar contact was reported a long distance away. Apparently, it was a vessel coming up to replenish the air base for the long winter ahead.

Admiral Sloreigh went below the operations area and went to his cabin. After he closed the door, he opened his safe. He found a top-secret message, which he opened. Reading the "Operation Poppy" order, he was told to rig up the Morse code antenna and monitor this frequency at 2300 hours Greenwich meantime on the 18th of August. He locked up the safes and went to the radio compartment. He briefed the senior radio operator what to do and the frequency he was supposed to monitor at the specified time. At 2255 hours the sub climbed up and raised the antenna with the frequency set in. In the hour the sound was cluttered by various clatter. Suddenly, the Morse code series of dots and dashes started transmitting. The message was coherent and steady repeating the same number three times and lasted only a minute.

The radioman copied all and gave the message to the admiral. The CO and exec went to the commander's office to break the code. The message broke out in a series action of statements. "Execute, speed at discretion, evasive and meet Spetznaz forces at position 45N-50W at 181200Z." The exec looked at the chart he had lifted and plotted the necessary meeting point where the magnetite and the elite force will come aboard. This was critical that this point be made on time. Many things groped in the skipper's mind. He grabbed the phone and asked that the intelligence officer come down to his cabin.

The intel/operations officer looked at the chart and admitted that listening devices did not cover this area, but he was sure. He wondered if Argentia had coverage northeast of the island if this situation had been fixed by fooling with this long-range detection system. Klos said that we have several undercover agents that are handling the adventurous task. The operations officer and the exec calculated the time to reach this point. The skipper reminded himself that the next broadcast time is 18 hours before the pickup on the times at 1200Z on the 18th. It was early afternoon and the skipper decided to scan the horizon. He looked into the scope and he saw nothing but leftover segments of broken ice. One more scan and he saw an airplane in the distance. He called for the identification chart because the airplane looked like a P-3. The airplane has conducted some sort of rectangular search but it did not drop buoys, which detected submersibles. After a minute he determined it was a P-3C, but he could not determine the emblem on the tail. Back at 200 feet he wondered what caused an airplane to be in this neck of the woods. An hour later the interesting sounds in the sea caused the officer of the deck to call the skipper. He thought something flew over the submarine. He was convinced that something was going on.

Again the skipper called battle stations and the ship became alive. Admiral Sloreigh used the sub to periscope depth. He looked and saw the P-3C dropping buoys that were destined for us.

Onboard the P-3C, the weather observer said he could use another hour farther up the Davis Straits. The P-3C radar operator reported ice about 80 miles north of the position they had reached yesterday. Upon hearing all this discussion, LCDR Otter decided he would proceed with the mission and then turn around and head for home. Approximately two hours later the plane was free of snow and took off in clear and windy conditions. They got to the Davis Strait and the navigator gave the pilot a heading that would put them, eventually, in a climbing rectangular search. An hour later, the ice observer was satisfied with his work. Lt. junior grade Place walked up to the cockpit and relayed completion. He looked out the pilot's window and saw the bleak, white Arctic ice. The plane settled on a southerly course and the sea could be seen though the ice caps and occasional sheets of ice remained. Mike returned to the tactical coordinator's station. He made some notes as he filled in parts of the purple. Suddenly, he remembered he loaded a pressurized chute. He raised the pilot and asked if he would drop the buoy. The pilot responded, "Sure." AW2 Jones was available to monitor the sonobuoy. The ordnance was ready and the TACCO fired the lofar/difar sonobuoy. A minute later, the buoy came up. It was buoy number seven, the crew's calling card. AW2 Jones had a cup of coffee waiting for him and he routinely checked and lit off the Bearing Frequency Indicator. He centered the buoy on the hertz of his choice and listened to the buoy. He heard sounds as if the ice was breaking up. He discounted it since there were no biologic data. The only noise he heard was the wind that was at least 25 miles, gusting to 30 miles an hour. AW2 Jones made an assessment of the maypole seven, then Mike said to monitor it until the sonobuoy died or they were out of VHF range.

Mike cleared his way to the galley to get a cup of coffee. He was chatting with a couple of guys on the crew when AW2 Jones came screaming at Ltjg. Place, "I have contact!"

Mike followed him back to sensor station number one. There, on the BFI, was a signature that was beginning to fill in. The grams simply had one or two lines. The operator could not hear the submarine, but was for sure a bona fide Soviet Nuclear Submarine. Mike ran to his station and informed the PPC of his analysis.

The pilot turned 180 degrees and Lt. jg Place came on the loudspeaker, "Set condition two. We have a Soviet submarine on maypole seven." The ordnance man was right beside the TACCO and presented only 15 buoys. The pilot set the homing beacon for maypole seven and raised the loiter speed to 3,000 horsepower. The plane was now 30 miles away from the sonobuoy and the predicted range was just an educated guess. AW2 Jones believed the sub was a Delta Class, heading south. He believed he had a bow aspect and was still up Doppler.

Lt. jg Place laid a buoy to the left of seven about 10 miles and laid another buoy 10 miles east of sonobuoy seven. The second operator, AW3 Check Delash, reported buoy 11 up and presenting a Difar bearing of 010 true. The third buoy was sonobuoy 15 and AW2 Jones reported it up. With a bearing of 010, the TACCO reported to the pilot to return to buoy seven. The pilot agreed.

The first reading from buoy 15 was up and slight cavitation was reported. A minute later, the bearing on sonobuoy 15 was 330 and cavitation was confirmed. Lt. jg Place queried the navigator to see if a contact report had been sent.

"No," he said and he would get busy on it. The current Difar fixes are 7-030, 15-300 true. The TACCO places a fix on his ASA-70 indicating the sub's location.

"I suggest we mark on top for a possible MAD (Magnetic Anomaly Detection) contact," he said.

The PPC reported, "We have only 15 more minutes until we have to return to Argentia."

LCDR Otter came out of a turn and headed for the fix position, 180 at five miles. The P-3C was down to 400 feet and the pilot announced he was inbound. The TACCO went on the loudspeaker to make the crew ready for a MAD attempt.

AW2 Jones reported moderate cavitations, speed 10 knots and the bearings were updated. "MAD MAN, MAD MAN, MAD MAN!" the radar/MAD operator reported.

PPC got on the loudspeaker and said, "One more MAD and we will depart station." The navigator was having a time trying to get Argentia on his covered radio air typewriter and tried Gander Air Base that required in and out voice communications.

"Down scope," Admiral Klos Sloreigh ordered from beneath the ocean's surface below the American aircraft. He and the exec talked and he waited to see what happened. Passive sonar reported a noise approaching them. It got louder as it passed over them. The admiral and the exec knew for sure that the P-3C had found them with the magnetic anomaly detection equipment.

"Arm the starboard missile," ordered Admiral Sloreigh. Based on their order, the XO agreed. It was a minute and 30 seconds since the P-3C was on top.

One mile from the fix, the sea erupted, followed by a missile flying directly at the American airplane. It hit the P-3C between the number three and number four engines. The fragment and debris of the blast ripped open the co-pilot's window and the punctured right wing burst into flames.

LCDR Otter saw the flash, turned to look at the unconscious flight engineer and at the co-pilot who was dead from the bombardment. He reached for his mike and set Condition Five while the plane was being forced down by the weight of all the fuel onboard. Suddenly, the number three engine exploded, as did tank five. It took only 20 seconds for the flight to end in the sea.

Unknown to Admiral Sloreigh and his crew who put distance between themselves and the wreckage, the American plane was missed almost immediately. In the afternoon about one o'clock Gander Air Force Base contacted Sondestrom to see if he had the Navy P-3C which was overdue. The air controller looked up the file advisory and the P-3C was one hour past due on its airways trip to Argentia.

Sonderstrom acknowledged the fact of the overdue time and started checking the airwaves by calling the P-3C by various networks. Meanwhile, Naval Station Argentia was queried by Gander, which of course, they were waiting anytime for the VP-45 aircraft to come in on Very High Frequency (VHF).

A call from the Argentia tower to the VP-45 duty office caused sheer havoc. The man in charge of the detachment was LCDR Jerry Harris. He just happened to be reading the message boards. Acting as command duty officer, Jerry answered the phone and he would be right over to base operations. We had three aircraft on the ground and one of the airplanes is in a minor check. "Do not let that plane get out of your sight," said the LCDR.

At Air Operations they pulled out a chart and began evaluating the copy of LCDR Otter's flight plan. They plotted the points and at 0800 the second plane departed.

Sonderstrom, at 1200 was to check in to Air Traffic Control at Gander Air Force Base. The point is approximately four hours away from us considering the high winds aloft. Commander Long, the operations officer, walked into the room. He announced that Sonderstrom has launched a T-29 aircraft for three hours before nightfall. The aircraft would look for any signs that may be revealing.

LCDR Harris spoke with the commander and said we will launch the ready duty at 0600 in the morning. The commander agreed with him and he excused himself after he gave him his phone number where he could be reached. From operations he went to the Mini Tactical Support Center. He got on the phone to VP-45 in Jacksonville, Florida. After switching the phone lines, the skipper was on the phone.

Harris reported a plane missing under the command of LCDR Dan Otter. The flight plan called for a flight returning from Sonderstrom completing an Oceanographic Arctic support mission. He then went into the flight dates and they were scheduled to land in Argentia at 1500 hours local time. The first hiccup was not reporting to Gander at noon. Secondly, Sonderstrom launched a T-29 aircraft to search the intended area for three hours or until dusk. Additionally, the CDO suggested that we launch the ready duty at 0600 tomorrow to reach the area. The CO was set back by this news and he agreed with the ready duty launch. "I will plan to arrive at NS Argentia sometime tomorrow afternoon. Do I have your number?"

At 1500 the squadron duty officer placed numerous phone calls to both officers and indicating telling them to report to squadron ASAP (as soon as possible). At 1530 VP-45 Detachment fell into ranks and the CDO came before them.

"Parade rest," he said. With great regret, he delivers, "We have a plane missing or overdue." He described the flight, gave the patrol, plane commander, and said it is up to us to pray for those missing and to get our aircraft in flying order. "I have already spoken to the assistant maintenance officer and we will have all three aircraft up. The ready duty"—and he turned to look at them—"will be airborne at 0600 tomorrow. The message traffic pertaining to this event and the three flights in Sondestrom are on the green message board." Then he asked all of the men and women of this detachment to join him in prayer.

At 1700 the CDO answered the phone in the duty office. Commander Long said the T-29 found a small piece of vertical stabilizer and the number was on its side. 567 was the number and yes, that was once a VP-45 aircraft; that was the last three bureau numbers of that airplane. He had the message ready and he called the CO of the squadron to tell him the sad news.

ASSAULT FROM WITHIN

On the 17th of August, John Hilton approached the Argentia gate and stopped to show the paper work for taking two Navy trucks to pick up some materials at Saint John's, Newfoundland. The orders, not specifically warranted, were signed by the Marine Guard and given a copy to John, who was driving the second truck, and I, roared off through the gates. We had everything checked out; diesel fuel, oil and the necessary maps that the special force might need.

Yesterday Mr. Zack went over once more the specifics, including the route taken, and where to park at the airport in Saint John's. He gave out a place in the hangar where we will spend the night. The airplane from Labrador will arrive at 1200 local time on the 18th.

Another item is the Navy enlisted uniforms, which I got yesterday. These, along with the box, which was to contain the magnetite, were neatly stored in the back of my truck. Mr. Zack also reminded me that a Morse code message reaffirmed that the mission was go-ready on the 18th of August.

At 2330 hours the watch changes at the Oceanographic complex. Now second-class petty officer had been congratulated last week as he checked the numerous discrepancy issues the previous watch had. He walks in to the T-Building and laid his rectangular lunch box down. He did a quick 360-degree turn and opened his lunch box. Out came a stick of C-2 plastic explosive. This was the last of the charges that would take out the cable.

Petty officer Bennett then took the connector cables and wired the plastic sticks together. He grabbed the final piece that was the detonator which was set until 0730 tomorrow morning. He turned on the switch and with all work done he began working on his assigned duties. At precisely midnight, a horrific explosion occurred, leaving the Navy Facility destroyed with a terrific blaze of fire reaching 30 feet in height. Nearly all of the structure except the front end of the building was still standing. The guard was shocked beyond belief. The windows of the sentry house had been blown out and the guard was riddled with broken glass. Bleeding in both chest and arm wounds, he called the fire department.

By UHF transmission the news was devastating and the fire radiated the night. Three fire trucks screamed out of the station headed for the blaze. Captain Blanes was headed to the fire also, but, was this the reason for the alert?

A Russian Bear aircraft took off on a night flight shortly after midnight on the 18th of August, which was noon of the 17th in Newfoundland. This flight was really headed for Cuba. Commander Sasha Ivanov was in the back on the airplane with 20 men headed for Argentia to be parachuted to a drop area approximately six miles from the base. There, we will meet with John Hilton driving a U.S. Navy truck plus another vehicle. Rendezvous will take place on the road that borders the cleared field.

The plane commander filed to a new position that he went operational below 5,000 feet. An hour later he went to 1,000 feet where he headed for the North Pole. Apparently, this play was to hide the destination of this aircraft and his intent was to fly over the Arctic Ocean and filter down the Greenland/Canadian border giving his jump team a good jump over Newfoundland.

On the hour the Spetznaz group hit the silk and began plummeting down from the sky. Commander Ivanov's jump was made and in an effort to find the strip he wore infra-red glasses. He found the strip and his companions followed. A bright fire illuminated the sky about five or six miles from the gathering point. After all the chutes were buried and the men were assembled, they marched to a spot in the road where they should meet. They need the woods to protect themselves.

About 10 minutes later, two trucks were coming down the road. The first used his headlights, which belted out "five, five, five" in Morse code. The commander took his penlight and gave him the return signal. Upon stopping the trucks John Hilton got out of the door. As planned by the commander, he alone went to acknowledge them.

John Hilton introduced himself and introduced his right hand man, but before he realized what was happening the second man's head was caught by two hands from behind and his neck turned to the right breaking the cervix. After that hideous example, John showed them the Navy gear, which they put on.

John Hilton went over the briefing with the commander including the chart that would lead them to the boat. He also showed Sasha the box that held the magnetite. Sasha, speaking Russian, turned to his comrades, which have an automatic rifle, a P6 silencer pistol, six hand grenades and food/medical packs, and gave orders including all that he had discussed with John. He designated Group Alpha to ride with him in the lead truck and Group Bravo to ride in the second vehicle.

The trucks left the area and were on the road to Naval Facility Argentia. John reminded the commander to duck down while he was at the gate. Sasha gave some directions to the second truck.

"What the hell is going on?" said John as they approached the main gate. The gate was closed and there were four armed Marines at the gate. John pulled up to the gate.

One of the Marines opened the gate and John drove two truck lengths and stopped. He climbed out of the truck with a pass that he had received from the Marine guard yesterday. He was asked to show his identification.

Meanwhile, the second truck driver was told to get out of the truck. He got out of the truck and quickly stabbed the guard in the back. Another assailant jumped out of the back of the truck and broke the Marine's neck. Almost at the same time the same killing rate was going on around John Hilton. With a runner closing the gate, the trucks moved on inside the base.

John Hilton went down the road and turned right rather than head down to the main road. The noise and the fire that was blazing a mile and a half away were from the Navy facility. All of the fire trucks are there, but why is the readiness of the base so high?

We passed by the officer's quarters and were headed down the hill past the Officers Club. At last we were headed to the main road. Dead ahead there were four cars. The commander said not to stop.

"Roger," and we got 100 yards from them and John took a rifle slug right square in the forehead. Sasha said a few words into the UHF and finally cut the diesel engines off. He stepped out of the truck and ordered his men to attack the four-vehicle blockade. In a flash the Spetznaz force swept the area and opened up with several hand grenades. Several of the Marines were injured and the co-leader of the assault said to bring the trucks on. They stopped and picked up the men, and turned right for the water.

EYES ON THE TARGET

BEFORE THE SUNLIGHT HIT THE RUNWAYS, THE ready duty took off to confirm or identify any wreckage the airplane left on the surface of the water. Upon further checking, the Coast Guard C-130 who was assigned to Argentia, launched to help the people flying the same area. According to message data, the CO and chief petty officer of Forty Five met and told the tragedy to the wives of both enlisted and officers. Also the casualty assistant officers for each family had been appointed.

At one o'clock, Commander Edwards, the skipper, landed bringing with him parts on order for two of the planes and you could tell he was disturbed. The command duty officer met him coming down the ladder, saluted him and gave him a big hug. He briefed him inside the hangar spaces. All of the preparations had begun with the ready duty conducting each man's personal items. These were to be put in a box and stored in a safe place. A knock on the door yielded the squadron duty officer, which reported that there was a message at the Mini TSC. Finishing their coffee, they rode over to the TSC. The lieutenant met them and signed in the CO. The commanding officer of Argentia was there to meet the skipper and apologized for not meeting his airplane. There was interest in losing a P-3C, but more important, what was a Delta Class submarine moving down the Davis Strait? They moved into the room, which displayed the overview of Newfoundland, Greenland and the area to the east where the listening devices were located. A SURTASS configured Operational Test site was exploring waters to see if the ship handled well in view of the strong winds and ocean waves. The ship detected a Delta Class submarine and got a fix, which is shown here. After satellite sent the information, they lost contact. This morning at the Pentagon brief, it went to the Joint Chiefs and a brief was scheduled for the President later this afternoon. At this point, we will wait to see what will happen.

Commander Edwards was duly apprehensive as he queried how the Delta got there. Lieutenant Commander Bight broke into the conversation. He said that no other contacts have explored this particular way of entering the Baffin Bay. There are top-secret means that tell us that three Soviet submarines conduct exercises under the Arctic. Most of the submarines are fast attack, nuclear intermediate mission attack and the newest class, the Alpha submarine. The position on the 17th Delta is the position at 51 North 50° West. The Labrador Current is a difficult current to combat. The closer the submarine gets into our area the more difficult it becomes to detect it. "Where are the arrays located?" asked the skipper. The arrays are located along the continental shelf approximately 250 miles east of the island Newfoundland. The only way we can obtain contact is before he penetrates a line that is drawn from Newfoundland to the southern coast of Greenland.

As we speak, the message arrives from the planes searching the Davis Strait. Numerous prices of torn, broken fragments of aluminum and pieces of what turns out to be lifejackets were floating on the western side of Greenland. The wind over the past two days has blown the flotsam to the eastern side of the strait. Pictures were taken and the plane is returning.

Finally, Commander Edwards raised the question about where the Delta was during the previous 48 hours. Since the contact was heading 190 at 12 knots the computer displayed the reciprocal bearing 288 miles prior to the SURTASS fix. They placed the contact inside the search area that the airplane searched 48 hours ago. Commander Edwards looked at Captain Barnes and remarked, "There's something amiss here."

As the meeting ended, an additional message which was received for the SURTASS ship that had brief contact and the position was 53N 050W. The ship left station for Norfolk, VA at 1714007.

The newest SURTASS (Surveillance Towed Array System) vessel was making its final Operational Evaluation Period, taking a tour of the northern Atlantic. This vessel had a full complement on board which totaled 28 men. They had left Norfolk on the second of August and had long range detections of the Yankee coming on station which is known as the patrol areas, whereby they could aim their missiles at targets on land or even inland. SURTASS has the ability to transmit the targets by satellite transmission back to Ocean Systems Atlantic for analysis. Each ship, with more watch standers, man the writers and when they display a contact they have the initial say before it is sent by satellite. Having detected several Yankee contacts, the ship moved out of the Gulf Stream to 50 North and 45 West. The main reason for accomplishing this is to see what the effects of additional winds and ocean velocity have on the overall mission.

The captain of the vessel looked over the weather that was forecast and knew that all of the autumn weather was gone. The men withstood the change in the weather. The wind was cold, howling winds, and with sea states to 30 knots, it was a rough time to be had.

With two days remaining on-station, the ship sought maximum movement when towing at three or four knots. The next morning the wind and all its environmental effects calmed down to a mere 15 knots. The men were happy about that, but knew that the rations were almost gone. Suddenly, the towed array was drawing a new contact. Several men were looking behind the gram or computer readout. Upon looking at the grams and determining that the contact is up Doppler, the initial guess is it is a Russian submarine coming down the Davis Straits. Since the OPEVAL team was aboard, they saw the contact and estimated it was a Delta Class coming out of the Arctic Ocean into the North Atlantic. The satellite was energized to alert Ocean Systems Atlantic that they made contact. This transmission left the ship and then the coordinator began filling in the final classification. The contact held by the array was 345 degrees true and its speed was about 12 knots based on its mechanical standardized blade rate. Thirty minutes later a bearing of 342 gave the vessel a fix of 190 at 12 knots. This, too, was shot down south to the facility and immediately, they lost contact.

At 0530 on the 17th, the intelligence crew was putting together the morning brief at the command center in the Pentagon. The brief was set but there is a new possible Delta contact that was detected by the newest surveillance ship with the submarine located in the Davis Strait at 62 N 50W at 170 at 12 knots. Upon review of the many submersible targets, this presents a new deterrent to the philosophy of the cold war. Also new to this discussion was the P3C that had crashed in the Baffin Bay region. The briefs made an appropriate slide showing the crash with comments concerning the plane commander for VP-45.

The brief went down at 0700 and the storms began to vibrate. Many admirals, including Vice Admiral Doughtery, was vitally sure that our warplanes were not up to speed with current technologies.

Based on this and new assessment, it must be ready for the Chief of Naval Operations by noon. The others wanted to know whom, why and does Navy Facility Argentia have contact. In response to this reply, the SOSUS hydrophones reach out into the North Atlantic but do not surveil the Davis Strait. It does touch the line stretched out from Argentia to the southern coast of Greenland. This is an earthshaking and most troubling experience. "Did our satellite photographs reveal this submarine penetrating the Arctic Ocean and into the Baffin Bay?" asked VADM Doughtery. The pictures do not reveal this target transmitting through the massive ice crust. We have guessed, however, that soon the new construction will eventually have long-range missiles based under the Arctic ice.

NORTH WIND

1800 hours Local, 18 August 1991,
Moscow, Russia (USSR)

IN MOSCOW, ADMIRALS STEUSTAL AND LATVIAS HEARD the reports. The Third Directorate had finally made its move. At 1650 on Sunday, Yuri Plekhanov of the KGB and a group of agents had arrested President Mikhail Gorbachev in his Crimean vacation home. Valery Boldin, Gorbachev's own chief of staff, had then declared his loyalty to the new regime and flown from Crimea, destination unknown, with the president's briefcase containing all nuclear launch codes.

The citizens of the Soviet Union didn't even know about the coup yet. Admiral Steustal knew the plan, though. Vice President Gennady Yanayev would appear on television sometime on the 19th to announce that Gorbachev had serious health problems. In the interim until the president regained his health, Yanayev was assuming all powers of the presidency and establishing a State Committee on the state of emergency.

The Third Directorate had already started arresting members of the Soviet parliament. They barely missed catching the Russian president, Boris Yeltsin, who surrounded himself with loyal military guards.

Orders were already being relayed to the military commands. Since they didn't know of Gorbachev's enforced "illness," they accepted the orders as legitimate. Tanks and armored personnel carriers began moving toward the capitals of the Republics and towards Moscow.

The three men listened to the reports of their own agents—not surprisingly, consisting of loyal Navy Spetznaz and retired members of the KGB First Directorate—and then sent out a radio message of their own.

In an unpopulated area of the Urals, a group of Spetznaz received the attack order. They had intercepted the broadcast of a

Morse code transmitter. The approximate position, a 25-mile radius, centered the area to a land of farmers. The secret Spetznaz team found a small cabin that appeared likely for clandestine operations.

The KGB agent in the outhouse heard something that sounded like a radio. Luckily for him, the coded message transmitted by the Spetznaz captain to his men was that he wanted the traitors taken alive. As a result, when the KGB agent stepped out of the wooden building, he received a butt stroke to the head instead of a bullet.

Quietly the Spetznaz team reached the cabin and heard the Morse code. They used explosive charges on the triple-locked door and then burst into the room. Two men, both KGB, sat at the radio. They were sending out signals that could mean disaster to the Soviet Union.

Both men turned around and, seeing that they were outnumbered, put their hands in the air. A Spetz radio specialist went over and investigated the Morse apparatus. He found a code that matched the figures that the admirals in Moscow had given the team. The soldier notified his captain of the find, who reported it back to Moscow on his secure radio.

Back in Moscow, the admirals looked at each other. Their team had been too late. The hidden radio shack had transmitted the launch codes to the Delta IV. There wasn't anything they could do to prevent Rear Admiral Klos Sloreigh for launching 12 nuclear warheads at the United States.

"I am the senior officer here," Admiral Steustal declared with a voice filled with false bravado. "It is my duty to take what information we have already and present it to the Supreme Soviet. Should it be impossible to reach our parliament, I will brief the Russian president on the situation. Perhaps he will be able to rally the people and defend Moscow from these terrorists."

"You are a brave and true friend," Lawrence told the older admiral. "Go then. Alexei and I will take care of our enemy on the Delta IV."

Admiral Steustal wanted to ask, but Lawrence glanced at his watch and made a shooing motion towards the door. "Go, while the streets are still open!"

Lawrence waited until his old comrade had left the secret bunker before turning to his younger brother. "We have to warn the Americans."

Alexei shook his head vehemently. "Telling them now will mean we knew about the strike beforehand! If we fail—if they don't believe us—then they will respond with every nuclear warhead in their arsenal. Lawrence, we dare not risk it!"

Vice Admiral Lawrence Latvia simply smiled. "Don't you think I planned for this, brother? A mutual friend has been keeping the American Pentagon informed of each stage of this madness."

"No." Alexei looked at his brother as if he had gone mad. "You aren't suggesting bringing her in from the cold, are you?"

Anger blazed in the older admiral's eyes. "It has been too long already, Alexei. You know that. She has given her life to Mother Russia once already. Isn't that enough?"

"There is no turning back if you do this, Lawrence."

He nodded, understanding his younger brother's concerns. "The world changes around us as we speak, younger brother. You may believe it will end in nuclear fire, if you wish. I believe in something better. There is no better time to start life anew."

Alexei Latvia took his brother by the shoulders, pulled him close, and then kissed him on each cheek. "You are right. Mother Russia has need of joy and laughter. It has been missing for too long; and especially from yours."

Lawrence could not speak for fear of bursting into tears. Instead, he hugged his brother briefly and then walked from the tiny room.

"God be with you," Alexei whispered behind him. "And to your Poppy as well."

GREEN LIGHT

THE CHIEF OF NAVAL OPERATIONS AND A cast of important dignitaries, including the Joint Chiefs of Staff, were seated, waiting for the President to arrive. The Pentagon briefer, Admiral Sharp, had the most significant data that has broken. The members were called to attention as the President walked in. The admiral started his briefing, while in the background a slide depicted the Arctic Ocean and the area between Greenland and Canada.

"Mr. President, we have received two Morse code signals intercepted by the Central Intelligence Agency. It apparently coincided with the transmission from a Delta class submarine—most likely a response to the first one—that passed through the Arctic Ocean via the Robeson Channel. A SURTASS ship on trials picked up what could be the Delta's location. The submersible has been fixed by the Oceanographic Station at Argentia, Newfoundland showing a track of 185 at 12 knots," said the briefer.

"Stepping back a few days ago, a VP-45 airplane left Naval Station Argentia and went on an ice patrol with a stop at Sonderstrom, Greenland. On the third flight this airplane was overdue and the next day a piece of the aircraft's vertical stabilizer was found floating in the water. We have everyone of our decoders trying to decipher these two messages."

The President wanted to know about the new Delta class and its place in the so-called Yankee box off Bermuda. The CNO explained that the Delta class was not in the war plans but it will during this fiscal year's Anti-Submarine Warfare Appraisal. From the Joint Chiefs view, what was the Delta Class doing coming down west of Greenland? Is this a hole-in-one defensive posture?

Rear Admiral Joseph Allen Henry simply sat in the background, forgotten by the higher-ranking brass in the room. Then the phone rang. An aide picked it up and then—in a confused voice—asked if Alfred Hitchcock was in the room.

One person broke out in laughter. Oddly enough, it was the President of the United States. He created even more confusion when he turned toward the lowly rear admiral and said, "Joe, I think that's for you."

Admiral Henry stepped to the phone and listened to the female voice on the other end. "Thank you, Poppy," he said when she finished speaking. "I'm going to put you on speaker phone. Please repeat that message for the President and the Joint Chiefs."

He pressed the speaker button and stepped back to watch the show.

"Good evening, Mr. President," spoke a rich female voice through the speaker. "I have information but must be brief. You are aware that President Gorbachev has been taken prisoner in Crimea, yes?"

"Yes, we are aware," the senior executive replied. "Our agents on the ground tell me that he is in good health, if limited in his activities. We stand ready to assist in his 'liberation' if you require it."

"Thank you, Mr. President, but that is not necessary at this time. Rather, I have to inform you of a threat to you and your country. There is a Soviet submarine—"

"The Delta IV that you told Admiral Henry about, correct?" he interrupted.

"Yes, that submarine. They have received launch authorization for their weapons."

The other military leaders began muttering, shocked at the news. Admiral Sharp was loud when he asked, "They've been authorized to fire nuclear weapons? At us?"

The female voice responded with a sharp, commanding voice. "I do not know you. Be quiet so that I may talk with the President."

"You heard the lady," the elder statesman ordered, chuckling. "Please, Madame Poppy, continue."

"I simply call to tell you this, and to let you know that loyal members of the Navy are working to restore order here in Moscow. As the ranking officers, they have given their approval—and deeply request—that you find and destroy the Delta."

"Mr. President, you surely aren't taking this at face value, are you?" asked Admiral Sharp. "There's no telling who this person is!"

"I know who she is, admiral," Joe Allen Henry replied in a cold voice. "As does the President. Now please do as Madame Poppy requested and shut the hell up."

"We understand the risk you are taking, dear lady," the President said over the two admirals' voices. "Thank you for thinking of your friends across the ocean. Please reassure the loyal admirals that the sub is as good as sunk."

"They will be please to hear that. Dosvadanya, Mr. President, and thank you."

The line went dead, leaving the room in silence. It was broken first by an executive order. "Admiral Henry, implement OPLAN Magnet immediately."

"Yes, Mr. President," the admiral replied. He immediately dialed a number and spoke into the phone. The signal was relayed through a Pentagon switchboard and a secure satellite transmitter to a radio on an AC-130 Specter gunship flying near Argentia, Newfoundland. Admiral Henry's next words made no sense to the Joint Chiefs or other military staff officers in the room. "Spooky, this is Hitchcock. Magnet is a GO, I repeat, Magnet is a GO."

The radio operator miles away in the aircraft responded in the similar military lingo. "Roger, Hitchcock, we are GO for Magnet. Spooky, out."

The admiral then dialed another number and spoke to the OIC at Naval Station Argentia. Again, he spoke in code. "Northern Watch, this is Hitchcock. By executive order, you are authorized HOT on Crazy Ivan. Confirm."

"Roger, Hitchcock. Northern Watch is HOT on Crazy Ivan. Wilco. Out."

The two phone calls set several things into motion. Aboard the AC-130 Specter gunship orbiting over Argentia, Lieutenant Commander Spenser completed his final radio coordination with Captain Blanes on the ground. The captain gave a brief situation report on activities at the base and gave his recommendation that the infiltrators had made their way toward the docks. LCDR Spenser turned to his team, gave the thumbs up to the pilot who had monitored the transmission, and waited for the plane to line up on the bay.

The plane commander announced, "Five minutes!" and the crew chief opened the tail ramp. An altimeter in the depressurized bay slowly fell until it stabilized at 5,000 feet.

"Hook up!" commanded LCDR Spenser. He clicked his D-ring onto the overhead cable and then ran for the open sky showing beyond the tail ramp. There was a brief tug as his jump line reached its limit, and then a parachute billowed above him.

Jumping from 5,000 feet doesn't take long. At 10 feet above the water, LCDR Spenser released the parachute to free-fall the final distance. The wind rolled his chute about 20 feet away, ensuring he wouldn't get tangled in the lines as he plunged into the frigid water. Then the SEAL officer was lost in darkness as he scissored his legs to stop his descent. His reactions were automatic, the result of years of training. He reached behind him to open the valve of his SCUBA tank and then pulled the mouthpiece to his lips.

He felt more than heard the other members of his team hit the water. With practiced ease, he swam to the surface and waited. Other heads surfaced moments later. He counted heads to verify that everyone had survived the jump, and then signaled toward the vessels tied at the distant pier.

The divers crossed the distance in complete silence. Four climbed over the side of the first ship; several moments later, a SEAL signaled the all clear. Spenser directed the team to move to shore and take up an over watch position to cover the other teams. Then he silent signaled two four-man teams to investigate the other two vessels. Team Three relayed that there was one man aboard their vessel; the other team's ship was empty.

Spenser signaled Lieutenant Wechenski to take teams Three and Four and establish an ambush site to the right of the manned ship. The LCDR then joined the other two teams on the shore to set up the other half of a wishbone ambush.

The first indication that their trap was about to be sprung came from the sound of squealing tires. The Spetz team drove past two burning trucks at the edge of the harbor and then continued at a madcap pace toward the docks. That was when the sole occupant on board the third vessel moved to the stern and flashed a signal three times. A block and tackle crane was swung over the side toward the trucks.

The vehicles stopped at the edge of the docks. Men jumped out of the trucks and attached the ship's crane hook onto the first crate of magnetite. The man on the ship tossed the free end of the block and tackle to the crew on the dock. They began pulling the rope. The magnetite rose out of the truck bed and swung free into the air.

LCDR Spenser spoke into his throat mike. From the night sky came an intense beam of light as the AC-130 circling overhead clicked on its halogen spotlight. "Deictbite Max!" the SEAL officer barked aloud. He repeated the Russian command to "put your hands up!" as he stepped out of the shadows.

Captain Sasha Ivanov pulled the quivering figure of Asadollah Shazi with him into the darkness. The element of surprise belonged to the Americans. Even though he had been told to expect them, he had never noticed the SEAL until the man stepped into the open.

Regrettably, his second in command did exactly what he expected the idiot to do. The battle cry of "Klactb Tbai Pyki Bber!" —Long Live the Revolution—broke the still air. Before Sasha could order him to stand down, the man opened fire with his silenced weapon.

Watching a battle of Special Forces is different than seeing typical combat. For one thing, it is so quiet. The SEAL team responded with a volley of fire from their silenced weapons. Sasha would swear that the sound of the bullets ripping through flesh was louder than the guns.

"Nyet!" he yelled. "Cease resistance, Comrades. This is madness!"

Once blood has been spilled, though, there is no stopping a battle until the last soldier has fallen. The other Spetz returned fire, shooting at shadows. Sometimes they guessed correctly and a cry would break the air. Most of the time, though, the advantage lay with the SEALs who had already established their defensive positions and ambush.

The battle took less than 15 seconds. At the end of it, the Spetz troops lay still on the dock. Two SEALS had been hit, one critically. LCDR Spenser spoke briefly into his throat microphone. The AC-130 relayed his request for an ambulance to Captain Blanes, the base commander.

Then he stepped back into the dim light of the dock and walked toward a pile of boxes. His second in command watched him and was puzzled as he spoke to the darkness. "You must be Zeus and Ali Baba."

A voice chuckled as a uniformed figured stepped from the shadows. "You must be Spooky. I see why, now." Sasha pointed toward the dead soldiers on the pier.

"Yeah, sorry about that. We were expecting you Spetz guys to put up more of a fight."

"Spetz? Them? Ha!" Sasha spat. "They are KGB, not Spetznaz. They act like your American Chicago gangsters, all mouth and no finesse. Attacking a Navy base, what stupidity. My plan would have worked."

Patrick Spenser grinned and offered his hand. "I have no doubt, comrade. None at all."

Sasha smiled in return, grasped the hand and pulled the American to his chest. "I formally request political asylum, tvarisch. You do have vodka in this decaying capitalist society, da?"

"Vodka?" Spenser asked, incredulous. "You've been drinking sludge, buddy. Wait until I introduce you to Kentucky bourbon!"

By this time, Lieutenant Tom Wechenski had moved forward to stand beside an equally confused Arabian man. "What in the hell just happened here?"

"I do not know," replied Asadollah Shazi. "But I also ask for asylum in the United States of America."

Wechenski turned as if just noticing the Iranian.

"But please," Shazi continued, extending his hand, "no hugging or kissing from you, yes?"

LCDR Patrick Spenser controlled his laughter at the two as he spoke into his mike to the gunship overhead. "This is Spooky. Relay to Hitchcock that Zeus and Ali Baba have arrived safely. Let me know when Northern Watch bags Crazy Ivan."

The tiny speaker in his hear crackled as the pilot responded with, "Wilco, Spooky."

Far to the east, a Navy P-3C subchaser was closing in on its target. If it hadn't been for the executive order, the plane would probably still be sitting on the runway at Argentia. It wasn't Commander Edwards' fault; his decision to have all personnel provide security for the aircraft was prudent considering the circumstances.

The status of Naval Facility was bleak. The cables were blown up in the T-Building. The explosion had decimated the complex except the front end of the building. Fifteen personnel were dead.

The CO of VP-45 had a responsibility to protect his aircraft from attack. He dispersed his personnel with the instructions to protect the Miami hanger and the adjacent aircraft outside.

Commander Edwards was livid when he was briefed on the true situation. The emotions changed after the President authorized VP-45 to find and destroy a Soviet submarine. It turned into a nightmare. In all his years flying missions against the Russian subs, dropping a torpedo had only been a daydream. Most of the time, the P-3C Orion aircraft weren't even authorized to carry torpedoes, much less arm and drop one. Now he had received the mission of a lifetime and he'd been caught with his trousers around his ankles.

It was the fastest arming and fueling mission his ground crew ever performed. He had one plane full of sonobuoys. Eventually, four MK-46 torpedoes arrived and were placed in the bomb bay. The plane was prepped and on the runway in record time.

The flight briefing was also the shortest he'd ever given. He methodically gave the mission brief. Then he suffered through the mandatory read-backs. The read-back was designed to prevent pilot error caused by misunderstanding the order.

The only known position was at 1808 Zulu which could place the Russian Delta anywhere from north to south or 000° to 180° time. Several questions were brought up pertaining to hostile submarine's potential location. Commander Edwards suggested that a series of "walking barriers" be placed to the east of the target's last position. The distance to the buoys would be about twelve knots speed of advance for the submarine. Edwards and the plane commander worked out a three-hour semi-circular pattern. They agreed on a six-hour pattern if the first failed to locate the sub.

The P-3C was airborne at 1130Z. Commander Edwards was the Flight Commander. Upon arrival on-station, the sonobuoy pattern was laid out on the APN-70, the tactical coordinator's screen. Sixteen buoys went out. Sensor Station One and Two reported all buoys were up and operational. For two hours the watch continued. Neither operator reported any noise that would announce the presence of the undersea Delta.

Unaware to the aircraft on-station, the new SURTASS ship had been ordered back into the area to try to regain contact. With their upgraded electronics, they made contact beyond the barrier that the airplane had laid.

This message took five minutes to relay to the aircraft. The message gave the fix and a course of 080. Commander Edwards looked at the message and inserted it on his scope. He told the pilot to head for the position. He set up five buoys ahead of the position, about 10 miles farther to the east.

The first buoy was laid further south and the three more dropped as the plane headed north. Sensor Station Two drew a cheer from the crew as he caught the contact on the first buoy. He amplified the contact as up Doppler. Then Sensor Station One called "Contact!" on the second buoy with an up Doppler aspect. The third buoy barely had contact so Commander Edwards erased drop number four and inserted a difar drop near the second buoy drop. Difar was dropped and, based on the contact findings of the acoustic operators, a second insert was made for a second pointing buoy. The result of the skipper's work was that the target was progressing 082 at 12 knots. The plane dropped a third difar on the projected course.

The next procedure was the most difficult and dangerous. The mission commander, CDR Edwards, spoke to the crew. "All right boys, we're to convert to MAD—magnetic anomaly detection—and come around for another MAD run. This procedure, I believe, is what cost Lieutenant Commander Otter's crew their lives. We will not attempt a second MAD; instead, a thousand yards before we should do a second MAD, we will perform a 90° turn to the right. I expect the Russian's one-mile accuracy missile will miss us and then he becomes dead meat!"

The commander paused for a moment. "No pressure here, but we'll only have one shot at this. The submarine below us is a Delta IV carrying 12 nuclear missiles. It has received authorization to launch on the United States. Right now, he knows we're up here. I'm praying that he will expect us to act like every other sub chaser he's encountered in the past. He'll assume that we're only carrying buoys and no live fish. That means he won't be concerned about launching his nukes. He'll want to splash us and then move closer to the U.S. coast. Soon as he hears torpedo screws in the water, though, he's going to reach for that launch button. We can't let him get there. Gentlemen, let's make this shot count."

"Battle Condition One," announced the TACCO. The pilot steadied over 082 true course and the Senior Three operator called out, "MAD, MAD, MAD!" With an intercept point entered, the tactical coordinator knew his exact position. They were 3,000 yards from on top, slowly dropping to two.

Suddenly the TACCO yelled, "Hard to the right! Missile inbound!"

The pilot reacted immediately and followed Commander Edward's orders to turn 90 degrees to the right. P-3C responded slowly.

A second later the missile broke the surface. Even with the preplanned evasive maneuver, the P-3C escaped the missile by a fraction of a second.

"Now we've got 'em. Let's kill that son of a bitch!" Commander Edwards leaned forward in his chair, body tense. "Master arm on!"

A weapons fly to point had been entered into the TACCO's scope. The bomb bay doors were already open in order to provide critical seconds. Station Eight was armed.

"Drop now! MAD MAN and drop the weapon!" Commander Edwards yelled. The difar buoys already in the water would monitor the MK-46 drop.

"The torpedo is running," called the weapons officer. "Target acquired."

A brief second later, Sensor Station One and Two heard the distinctive sound of a torpedo detonating. The pilot reported the giant plume of water that sprayed into the air.

"Anything, sensor?" called Commander Edwards. "Did we get 'em?"

"Aye, skipper," replied Sensor One. "I can hear her. She's breaking up in the water!"

There was a loud roar as the crew cheered. Commander Edwards contacted the SURTASS ship and requested confirmation, then circled the plane over the site for 20 minutes.

Debris floated to the surface. Neither of the Sensor stations or the SURTASS ship registered anything on their monitors after the detonation and breakup of the submarine. The Delta IV was definitely dead in the water.

EPILOGUE

THE WORLD IS NEVER HAPPY WITH THE outcome of this strategic blunder. Had all of the molecules been of the right order, the elite special group would have pulled off the sweetness of virtue. As one former United States Army general once said, "Old soldiers never die, they just fade away."

Prior to this Newfoundland undertaking, Spetznaz operations had led to overwhelming results back in the late 1940s. But the big shortfall was they were the only secret force there. There were no major vanguards that would advance from the main force, whereby special troops will not crush the vanquished. Secondly, getting control of the air was not in the cards. The four engine aircraft called the "Bear" was later shot down by U.S. Navy F-14 aircraft by not landing at a Navy base. Finally, our own special forces led by the U.S. Navy SEALs causes concern which is not overlooked by Soviet elite forces. Ultimately, the Russian super achievers were stymied by the U.S. Navy team.

A new nuclear submarine was indubitably the likely choice to participate in Operation Poppy. Delta IV, as you may know, played in the ice cap with these predecessors. The SSGN is a sign-off of a Echo II which the finished version was armed with two short range missiles and torpedoes. This ship also had space for the Spetznaz, which never arrived. The communication transaction that was a loser from the start, should not be used at all. The odds of any break of action, or otherwise, would work in getting the magnetite to the awaiting submarine.

And know the missing persons of humanity who are still living and why? In Argentia, Newfoundland, Nancy would be married to John Hilton, was found dead in the ruins of the Naval Facility after it suffered a deep-seated blast. Incidentally, Petty Officer ETW2 Bennett set the devise, which he was told that the blast would ignite 30 minutes after he was relieved from duty. Realistically, the agents who were involved in undercover, sleazy, logistic procurement faded into the background.

On the Russian side of the border, Alexei and Lawrence were somehow protected by the smallness of the cadre of people that the mission required. Both were admirals and both retired within a month or two, never to be seen again. The KGB admiral was wasted when his car blew up into a thousand pieces one week after Operation Poppy was withered away.

"The first task, then, is planning for a war is to identify the enemy's center of gravity, and if possible, trace them back to a single one. The second task is to ensure that the forces to be used against that point are concentrated for a main offensive."

Clausewitz, "On War".